June 2021

To KIM .

I don't know how
much if any headway
you made into
the book, but this
fifth book is a
particularly good place
to start in or
pick up again.

all the best.

Peter B.

P.S. I'd love to hear
your 'entitled' response.

The Three Naked Ladies of Cliffport

A Novel in Six Books

Volume III

by

Peter Boffey

The Three Naked Ladies of Cliffport
A Novel in Six Books
Vol. III

Contact author and place orders at: www.peterboffey.com

Library of Congress Control Number: 2021907228

ISBN: 978-1-64719-564-9

Dedicated to the memory of
Robert Orrin Barnhart
San Jose CA, 1915–Santa Cruz CA, 2001

AUTHOR TO READER

Book Five may be read and enjoyed with or without having read Books One–Four.

Starting with Book Five, certain backstories and passages—of perhaps greater technical or procedural detail than every reader may be interested in following—are marked with superscript numbers ([1,2,3...]) indicating that they can be found in a section of NOTES placed after the main body of the text. Although enriching, these abridgments are not essential to following the story, and to read or not to read them is entirely the reader's choice.

The length, scope, and structure of *The Three Naked Ladies of Cliff-port* encourages a recursive approach to reading and re-reading the six books of the novel in part or in whole; lengthier appendages to Chapter 6 *(Verbatim D)* and Chapter 8 *(DD's Dreamlife)* in Book Five can be found under the NOVELS dropdown menu at peterboffey.com .

Foreign language words or phrases whose meanings are not immediately self-evident in the text are footnoted • at the bottom of the pages where they first occur.

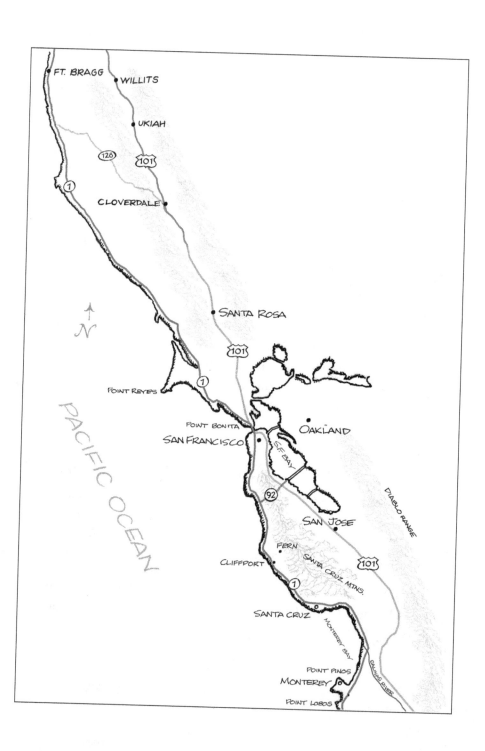

BOOK FIVE

October 1965–December 1975

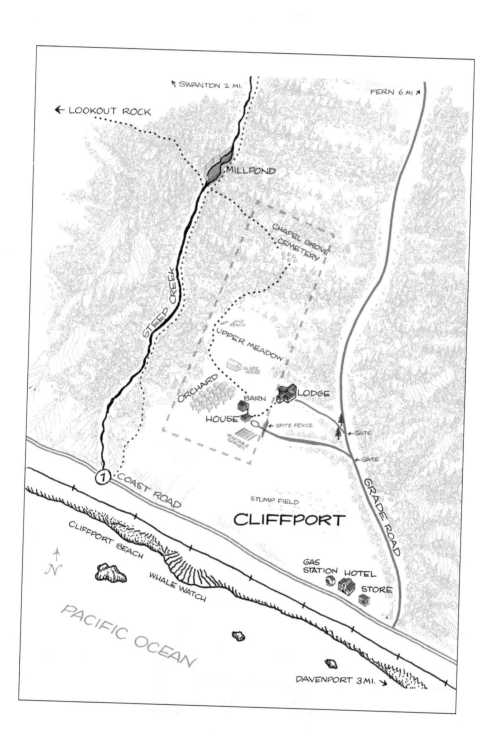

Chapter 1

Jan's Estate

– Hello. Lowrie residence.

– *Mom.*

– Hello, dear.

Silence

  Kaitlin, what is it?

– *She's dead.*

– Who's dead? Jan's dead?

– *Jan's dead.*

– Oh my God.

– *I found her in bed.*

– You're absolutely sure?

– *She looked asleep but I took her pulse. Then I saw her cigarettes.*

– Cigarettes?

– *And a bottle of whiskey.*

– Open?

– *Empty.*

– Oh....

– *And her pills.*

– And what did you just say?

– *Her pills spilled all over the place.*

Silence

– So, she did it. She took her own.

Silence

Where are you right now, Kaitlin?

– *In the apartment.*

– No, I mean where in the apartment?

– *In the kitchen.*

– Don't touch anything. When is the nurse due back?

– *This afternoon.*

– You must call the Police Department right away. You realize that, don't you?

– *I guess.*

– Leave things the way you found them and notify the police. Have you told the superintendent?

– *Mister Luen? Not yet.*

– You haven't moved anything, have you?

– *I opened the windows.*

– I suppose that's okay. Oh, I'm so sorry you had to be the one to find her like that.

– *I found her husband, didn't I?*

– Her husband...? Oh yes ... I forgot about that.

– *So, why not her?*

– Kaitlin, listen to me. Call the police right now then tell Mister Luen. Then call me right back.

– *Okay.*

– Are you all right?

– *I'm okay. I'll call you. Bye.*

Katie cradled the receiver and looked around the kitchenette. The wicker basket of Scottish memorabilia and the banker's box of souvenirs were where she had last stashed them back in the hinged benches of the built-in nook—those she would take home to Cliffport. Fatima could have the dishware in the cupboards above the sink. Turning her eyes away from the hospital bed, Katie passed though the former dining room and stood in the living room. She would dump the foldout sofa bed and armchair but take the items from the display box mounted on the wall: those mementos of Jan's visit to Scotland shouldn't wind up in some Goodwill Store or bric-a-brac shop. Fatima could have whatever other furniture she liked. Katie stepped into Jan's ex-bedroom, where the practical nurse's sparse personal belongings gave the impression that she rarely slept there although Fatima had been present every night—except the last—for two months. On the dresser top, the modest altar to Our Lady of Fatima, a circle of votive candles around the base of a painted porcelain statuette of the Immaculate Heart of Mary: white robe, golden crown, bulbous red heart, pink face, pink hands. Tucked into the mirror's frame, a giant postcard of Our Lady of the Holy Rosary of Fatima with its stamp of authentication from the Chapel of the Apparition in Portugal. Katie opened the freestanding wardrobe closet. Hanging from wire hangers: two long, pleated, gray skirts; four white blouses; a maroon cardigan sweater. At the other end of the rack, dressier specimens of Jan McLoughlin's own design and handiwork leftover from decades as Mary-Helen Belcanto's private couturier; some museum might appreciate receiving those.

Katie returned to the kitchen and dialed the Daly City number taped to the refrigerator; the nurse would have to deal with the morphine. Katie toned down her rendition of the suicide scene, but Fatima gasped as she understood the news. She confirmed that Sunday morning was the last time she had been in the apartment then prayed sotto voce in her native Portuguese. Katie waited for her to finish then told her she would probably be required to give the nurse's phone number to the police but, unless contacted, she ought to stay away another day. Fatima said she had already bought her bus ticket back to the City; Katie insisted that Fatima postpone returning as planned and promised she would pay her back for the ticket and compensate her with full pay for another day off. The nurse's voice trembled: would she lose her job with the agency? Would they take away her license to practice home care, and the permit to store and dispense morphine? Katie reassured her she had done nothing wrong and everything right:

she had been granted thirty-six hours off duty—for the first time in eight weeks—and Katie would take full responsibility for having left Mrs. McLoughlin alone.

Navigating the tools and supplies set aside by the workmen renovating the interior of the building, Katie went downstairs and knocked loudly; Mr. Luen answered his door without enthusiasm, looking like a man who had received all manner of news delivered across that threshold over the years. As usual, tears quaked on the brims of his swollen lower eyelids as if welling up from reservoirs under his eyes, threatening to spill should he dip his face. He was wearing his everyday uniform: suspenders strapped over a plaid flannel shirt, cuffs unbuttoned; Dickey work pants; cloth slippers. He screwed his head about so that his favored ear jutted toward her and waited to hear whatever the familiar figure had to say. Katie raised her voice over the TV and announced that Jan McLoughlin had died in her apartment. He looked toward the ceiling then lowered his eyes without asking how or how long ago. She let him know that unless he wanted to make the call, she was about to phone the police. He shook his head no and again shook his head no when she asked him if he wanted to view the long-term tenant's apartment before any official proceedings. Katie went back upstairs and reported the fatality to the San Francisco Police Department; the dispatcher instructed her to stay put and disturb nothing: the nearest squad car would be arriving within minutes at 999 Zelkova Street.

∗

Beep. *So this's the way your story ends in a stinking world you couldn't stand it anymore. How'd you manage to get your hands on a bottle of booze and snag one last pack of cigarettes? This place does stink. You 'took your own' and didn't even bother to put your teeth in* **Beep** *The slack jaw. The last gaze. The glazed daze. Those little purple crosses one two three they never got to fire at their targets at least you dodged that bullet you old codger you* **Beep** *avoided treatment like the cancer evaded detection. Where's the fourth one's* *somewhere down there in the wattles. Who knows where the cancer was besides your throat? Maybe I should've made you do the radiation as if anybody could've made you do anything* **Beep***. I could pull that plug and shut that machine down for how long before they get here? So here we are again, Jan, just you and me the day after the night you 'took your own' oh for god's sake Mom could at least say 'took her own life.' What, were you fulfilling a pledge to your brother Glenn or something? That's so weird to think about* **Beep***. What about your remains? It'd kill Mom to bury your ashes in Chapel Grove but what remains? Ashes eyeglasses dentures and a rack of clothes. Three framed photographs 'don't touch anything' like now I'm a murder suspect or something* **Beep***. Maybe I'll just spread your ashes over the McLoughlin side of the cemetery without even telling Mom and sing The Castle Song oh Jesus Jan, Janice, Janet, Jeanette or whatever you're calling yourself now you crusty old gal you sparkled for me like the light inside your geode* **Beep***. It's been a long haul but we can relax now at least you can. Always trying to talk then coughing griping about how the nurse refused to go against doctor's order and amp up the dope* **Beep***. God bless that woman I hope she'll say a prayer in Portuguese for me too. Lighting her candle can't hurt either. One last bottle snuggled up against you like a baby 'don't touch anything.' I better call Mom back. Maybe we should've put you in some place against your will oh what am I talking about? It was going to be Nob Hill or Boot Hill for you* **Beep** *weren't going anywhere else. So, you really did it. Leave you alone one night and you dive headfirst into oblivion. You could've burned the building down you crazy old coot how in hell did you manage to get the booze and cigarettes is what I want to know* **Beep** *by phoning someone? Or laying twenty bucks on some workman in the hall to go get you your stuff? Oh you were always a tricky one Fatima found that blue coffee can under your bed with old cigarette butts soaking in it when we found out how you had been sneaking your smokes and peeing in the night without getting up.* **Beep***. When Fatima moved in she found out right away why it smelled like piss in that room even*

5

after she'd give you a bath and change the sheets and air the place out. Maxwell House yum yum, 'good to the last drop.' **Beep**. *Okay Missus McLoughlin with an o not an a so where's the note? 'Please don't hold this against me.' Last Monday you said that or the Monday before maybe that was your suicide note delivered in advance. The last Cliffport McLoughlin lying dead right before my eyes. I wish the cops'd just get here and get over with whatever they do next.* **Beep**. *Whatever you do KT don't break down weeping for the whole world in front of any fucking cops won't care but they'll be interested in that morphine in the fridge. Fatima knows it's all there thank God that's her business not mine.* **Beep**. *'I'm more or less just marking time' you said last week for sure that was last Monday I was sitting right here asking you one last time what you wanted me to do with your ashes. 'O Katie, so many have left that ghost town before me and died and been* **Beep** *buried somewhere else, what difference does it make? The unclaimed remains area in the first cemetery you come across, you can dump my ashes there.' Then laughing, coughing. 'The unclaimed remains area.' I never heard of that before. Then sitting listening to the radio sitting right here with you one last time listening to this damn* **Beep**ing *machine and the radio playing Jo Stafford duets. I wonder what they're featuring on your favorite Monday radio show today oh there they are now okay I'm coming okay okay don't break the fucking door down yet boys I'm coming* **Beep**.

A pair of policemen commandeered the two-bedroom apartment. One placed a radio call; the other summoned Mr. Luen from downstairs and had him and Katie sit down on the broken sofa before questioning them. Three other men from the Coroner's Division arrived then two detectives in civilian clothes from the Bureau of Inspection; lastly, carrying a camera, a man barged in. With an occasional glance through the glass panes of the closed sliding doors, Katie saw the detectives directing the photographer what to shoot before tagging and bagging evidence in the immediate vicinity of the bed. Prepared to handle the body, two coroners stood by. When the detectives emerged from the death room, the older man took over the interrogation as the younger one went about the rest of the apartment, opening closets and drawers. She overheard something about dusting for fingerprints. The senior detective, supervising coroner, and one of the patrolmen held a meeting behind closed two-way doors to the kitchenette and—out of her earshot—used the telephone. The junior detective informed Mr. Luen that he was free to retire to his apartment but should remain on the premises until further notice. The senior detective encouraged Katie to accompany the two uniformed patrolmen back to her own vehicle then follow their car to Bryant Street where someone wanted to speak with her. Katie followed orders, relieved that Fatima had been spared this first brush with officious insensitivity.

———

"May I please have a look at your driver's license?" the young man asked. His nametag read Jason Drew, Student Assistant. He was stationed at the smaller of two stainless steel desks backed by a bank of black, vertical, four-drawer file cabinets. Dressed in khaki pants and a long-sleeved, light-blue denim shirt with a narrow black tie, he struck Katie as more postal clerk than policeman. His short creamed hair was parted to one side and illuminated by the desk lamp's horizontal fluorescent bulb. "Thanks. You can have a seat," he added, indicating an armless office chair; Katie swiveled her jeans up by the belt loops and remained standing, crossing her arms.

Once Jason had the sheets of carbon paper and onionskins aligned in his gray IBM Selectric typewriter, he flipped a lever, hit the carriage return button, and started transferring information from the license.

"Are you booking me or something?"

"Oh no, ma'am," he replied, leaning his face outside the lamp's glare. "I'm just getting down some information. Cliffport? I've never heard of any Cliffport, California. Where's that?"

"Down near Santa Cruz."

"Oh, Santa Cruz, I've been there. You know, you can sit down. I don't know how long before Lieutenant Morrissey will come out," he volunteered, glancing toward a wall with three interior doors of frosted glass. When he returned to his two-fingered typing, he found the middle sheet of onionskin askew and yanked out all the pages, replacing them in triplicate and starting over.

"Can I use that payphone in the hall? I want to make a call."

"Sure, that's what it's for. Need any change?"

"No."

"Go right ahead but ... ma'am...?"

"Yeah?"

"Better not, you know ... walk off anywhere. You know what I mean, don't you?"

Katie smirked. Still within his sightline, she dialed home and explained how she had been led to the Bureau of Inspection by a patrol car as well as tailed by plainclothesmen in an unmarked card following close behind. She reassured her mother that she wasn't under arrest and was well aware of her right to remain silent. Elise Lowrie volunteered to call Gerald Hudson in order to see if he was available—although it was Labor Day—to join her daughter at the police station. Katie said she would attempt to reach Jan's lawyer the moment she felt she was being treated unfairly or threatened in any way; she promised to keep her mother posted on developments and returned to the adjoining room.

"Here you go, Missus Lowrie." Jason passed back her license as she neared his desk. "Shouldn't be too much longer now."

Once she was occupying the freestanding chair, he poised his two hands over the keyboard. "Relation to the deceased?"

"What'd you just say?"

"How would you describe your relation to ... where is it now? Missus Janice McLoughlin. I'm sorry, ma'am, but I have to fill out this form."

Katie crossed one leg over the other, thigh on thigh, and crossed her arms over her chest.

"I'm just a sub for the holiday, you know, I—"

"... I was her only friend in the world."

"Oh, I see...." he responded, lowering his voice and his eyes.

"And I had power of attorney."

"... p-o-w-e-r-o-f-a-t-t-o-r-n-e-y..." he spelled aloud in sync with his hunting and pecking of the keys.

"And in her will she left me everything she had left," Katie added, switching the cross-over of her legs.

The student assistant paused then resumed: "I-n-h-e-r-i-t-o-r ... or should I put down heiress? I really don't know." He tried to catch her eye, but she deliberately kept staring at the bobbing tip of her cowboy boot; he hit the carriage return. "You were the one to discover the body, right? I mean, I'm not putting that down but that's what I heard."

"Yeah?"

"That's all. I heard it from the guy who brought Lieutenant Morrissey the field report just before you got here."

"So?"

"So, that was on the report, is all. He said—"

"... I don't care what you heard or what he said," she interrupted, "or what they wrote down. I know what I said."

"Ahh, Missus Lowrie...?" he said, lighting up a Marlboro and shallowly puffing. "I'm just a student called in to work the holiday swing shift ... get it?"

"How old are you, Jason Drew?"

"Twenty. It's Jay, call me Jay. Almost twenty-one."

"Are you studying to be a cop?"

"Well, not exactly. I mean I don't know yet. I'm study criminology at an academy in San Bruno but I don't know where it will go, exactly."

His cigarette halfway to his lips, he paused, apparently confused by her lack of response.

"Right, that's what I meant," Katie concluded, placing the soles of both boots on the linoleum floor.

J. Drew tapped his cigarette on the rim of a square glass ashtray then left it there. He sat back in his chair and raised one scuffed brown oxford shoe, placing his ankle on the opposite knee. "Ma'am ... ah, Missus Lowrie?"

"Yeah?"

"Can I say something off the record? Yeah, I'm going to. I really wouldn't advise you taking any sort of ... 'attitude' let's just say. With Lieutenant Morrissey I mean. He's one of the big shots in Homicide Detail and he's pretty serious, at least every time I've worked for him he is."

"Is that him up there?" she inquired, raising her eyes to a framed portrait on the wall: a black-and-white photograph of a police officer in full SFPD regalia.

"That's his father, as a matter of fact."

"Oh, his dad. Okay, Jason Drew—"

"Call me Jay, come on," he pled, reclaiming his cigarette.

"So, tell me, Jay. Am I a murder suspect or something? Is that the deal? Is whatshisname going to put the cuffs on me? Or am I already under arrest?"

"Oh jeez, ma'am, you've gotta be kidding. I couldn't put you under arrest if I wanted to. And I don't. You came in here of your own accord—"

"... I did?"

"And you can leave of your accord."

"I can, really?"

"But I really wouldn't recommend it, if I was you."

"Because I'm a suspect, you mean."

"You're an informant, Missus Lowrie."

"An informant? What the hell is that?"

"That's what it's called. Technically speaking, you're the key informant in the case."

"I don't like the sound of that very much, Jay," she stated, shifting her weight on the chair.

"Don't you see?" When he tilted the lamp's angle so they shared an unobstructed view of each other's faces, Katie saw the baby skin and wondered if the youth even had to shave daily to keep his cheeks and chin so smooth. "An elderly lady dies in her bed. The death is discovered by the inheritor or whatever. And there are no other witnesses—"

"... and I called the cops right away."

"So, don't worry about it!" he burst out, slapping the forefingers of his free left hand on the edge of his desk. "The lieutenant only wants to interview you, that's all. Then you can make your statement."

"You mean my confession?"

"No, I don't." He took a short drag. "I didn't say that, you did."

"I didn't commit any crime."

"Nobody said you did. I never said you did."

"Well, everybody acts like it. The cops at the apartment sure acted like it."

"That's their job. They've got to be suspicious in a situation like that. And another thing. Whatever you do when you're done here, don't go back into that building until you get the green light."

"From who?"

"Somebody'll contact you. I don't know who. I'm just saying, I really recommend you don't try to re-enter that apartment. One, you won't get away with it. Two, you'll be in serious violation of the law if you break the seal."

Katie reassessed his countenance. "Where'd you say you're from, Jay?"

"Stockton. I'm studying down here but my family's in Stockton. My people are all on the force."

"Everybody?"

"Yeah, even my big sister." He grinned. "Out in the Delta, in Sacramento, not around here."

"Have you got a girlfriend down here? Is that why you're studying here instead of there?"

He blushed, grinned, and extinguished his cigarette: "I think I still do," he mumbled, reorienting himself to the typewriter. "I hope I still do. But I better finish this up fast. Marital status?"

"Single."

"Children?"

"One."

"Sex of child?"

The student's hands hovered above the keyboard.

"A boy. A boy becoming a young man."

He lowered his head and typed.

"His name?"

"Donald Duncan Lowrie."

"His age?"

"Fourteen."

"Does your son reside with you at ... let's see.... One Grade Road, Cliffport, California?"

"He does. At least for the time being. Who knows?"

J. Drew opened his mouth to question her, but Inspector Morrissey entered the room, acknowledging them with a nod of his head—the hair cut to a short, uniform length—before plopping a manila folder onto an empty desk blotter and ignoring them while he surveyed the interior before sitting down. He wore a navy-blue jacket and brown slacks with cuffs breaking over black lace-up business shoes. His red tie was knotted loosely at the top of his unbuttoned white dress shirt. He reached across some file cabinets, grabbed hold of a turning rod, and adjusted the angle of one set of aluminum window blinds, then he peeled off the top sheet from Jason's papers and left the carbons and onionskins on his assistant's desktop before sitting down in the padded swivel chair behind the larger steel desk.

"You get it all, Jason?" he asked, glancing over the sheet in his hand.

"Yes, sir. I mean, not yet, sir," he answered, wincing a smile. "I didn't get to the last lines at the bottom yet."

"Get those when I'm done here."

"Yes, sir." Jay winked at Katie and relaxed against his chair's back.

The detective set the page aside, interlaced his fingers, and placed his clasped hands on the blotter, leaning slightly forward and lowering his head as if about to say a prayer. Katie thought the buzz cut made the older man's hair resemble a schoolboy's stiff fuzz sprouting straight out on all sides.

"Missus Lowrie, how are you?" the man asked, raising his face and laying his eyes upon hers.

Lieutenant Morrissey had looked about fifty until she saw his eyes, when he looked closer to seventy-five.

"I'm okay."

"Do you know why we asked you here?" he continued, altering the arrangement of his fingers so that the left thumb was now uppermost.

She remarked to herself how closely a five-o'clock shadow followed the shape of his wide lower jaw. "I guess so."

"Then let me get right to the point. I know the officers have already gathered information from you. And young Jason here has started a file. Now I would like to have a brief conversation with you then give you the opportunity to make a statement, just for the record."

Katie realized that the tension in his speech partially derived from his habit of barely opening his mouth so that an exaggerated movement of his lips had to compensate for the broad, clenched jaws.

"Okay."

"Okay," he echoed, releasing his hands, pushing his chair from the desk, and tilting back in order to cross one leg over the other before brushing real or imagined crumbs from the raised pant leg.

"How long will this take?"

"What, your statement?"

"No, this whole thing. How soon before I will be able to get back into the apartment and carry out my duties there?"

"Well, Missus Lowrie," the inspector replied, lowering his foot back to the floor, pulling the chair in toward the desk, interlacing his fingers again, and staring right at her. "That all depends—"

"... on...?"

He altered the order in which his fingers were interwoven: the left thumb was on top again. "If your story checks out—"

"... it'll check out," she interrupted then shut her lips upon noticing the crow's feet to the outside of his narrowed eyes and the pulsing muscles of his jowls. "Sorry...."

"And as soon as the medical examiner makes a final determination...." he resumed. "Say, Jason. Would you go find out if the superintendent of the building showed up yet?"

"Mister Luen?" Katie essayed.

"I know his name, Missus Lowrie."

"What's he coming here for?"

The lieutenant squared off some loose sheets of paper inside the folder on his desk and took a deep breath. "He's not coming here. We have asked Mister Luen to visit the morgue, to identify the body."

"Oh God," she groaned, dropping her chin toward her chest. "Is that really necessary?"

"As a matter of fact, it is."

"What else do you have to do?"

"What else?" The lieutenant closed his mouth and kept his eyes upon his guest while addressing the student. "Jason."

The youth scooted forward from the back of his chair. "Sir?"

"Kindly tell the lady here what's customary in a situation like this."

Katie couldn't tell if the older man was genuinely smiling, but a hint of white teeth appeared between the thin lips in the U-shaped mask affixed to his square skull; he seemed to relish popping a quiz on his holiday assistant.

"Well, the evidence goes to the forensic lab for an identification of fingerprints and ... other things. Then the toxicology report—"

"... do you really need a toxicology report?" Katie blurted out. "It's pretty obvious, isn't it? The lady killed herself. She somehow lined up some booze and cigarettes and swallowed her pills and she had no business doing any of that if she wanted to stay alive."

The inspector inhaled and held his breath, placing both palms on his desk and staring straight at her, apparently debating how to handle his outspoken guest. Instead of speaking, he pushed himself up onto his feet. "Jason, Mister Luen, go!" The young man jumped to his feet and rushed out of the room while his superior went to a second set of window blinds and increased the amount of light coming into the room. For a split second, Katie spotted the fracture lines that spread over the man's entire face: a map of fine, shallow wrinkles like the crinkly finish of the discarded onionskin paper now illuminated in a slice of sunlight crossing Jason Drew's desk. Standing, leaning his weight back against the front of a file cabinet, he spoke: "It's our job to rule out foul play in cases like this. Or don't you realize that?"

"Yeah, I get it."

"Then please let me answer your first question. You asked how long it will take and I was trying to answer you, Missus Lowrie." He sat back down, glancing at his wristwatch then raising his arms—elbows out—studying his subject while cradling the back of his skull in his palms. Katie looked for signs of a shoulder holster strap she thought might be exposed by the loosened jacket front, but all she saw were an assortment of pens clipped to a black vinyl penholder in the inside pocket of his jacket. Jason Drew reentered the room. "Well?" the lieutenant asked, lowering his arms and sitting forward.

"He's there now, sir."

Katie sighed aloud.

"So, as I was about to say—have a seat, Jason—if the medical examiner determines it was suicide, the death certificate will read that way."

"What way?"

"Jason."

"Yes, sir?"

"You've read a number of certificates by now. Tell Missus Lowrie how it might read if ... you know ... give her an example."

"Well, Part 1, line A—that's the part that cites the immediate cause of death—it might read acute barbiturates or whatever and alcohol intoxication."

"And line B...?" the detective prompted him.

"Line B is where they put the cause, like due to the consequence of—"

"... suicide," Katie interjected.

The apprentice looked to his master for help but got none. "Yeah, I've seen that: suicidal."

"Is that all it'll say?"

"Personal particulars about the deceased get filled in by the Funeral Director," J. Drew replied.

"How will some funeral director know anything about Jan McLoughlin?" Katie asked.

"Isn't that the case, sir?" the young man replied, again turning for help.

"Usually," Lieutenant Morrissey concurred, "which leads me to my next question," he added, derailing her counter-investigation. "Besides the individuals already identified in here," he said, tapping his finger on the file, "the superintendent, the lawyer, the nurse.... Is there anyone else we should know about?"

"I don't know. I don't think so."

"So, I gather Mrs. McLoughlin was quite the recluse."

"Toward the end of her life she was. When she became bedridden. It got down to me ... and the nurse," Katie added, leaning forward with her forearms on her thighs. "There's nobody else."

"Missus Mariano?" the inspector asked, glancing at the folder on his desk.

"Fatima. She's been living in the apartment the last couple months." Katie kept her back rounded and her eyes downcast. "Seems like I was the last station on Jan's line...."

"So, might that explain how, as you claim, you would inherit her estate?"

"You know," she shot back, straightening in her seat, "you could contact Mister Hudson, her lawyer, for that personal information you were just talking about." She glanced back and forth between the two of them. "He knows as much or more than I do about her statistics and all."

"I see...." the detective stated vaguely, rising from his chair and working his way back to the first set of window blinds then the second, readjusting the louvers of each in order to admit more of the changing daylight. It seemed to Katie that his voice was carrying from a great distance when he next spoke from a position taken up again between two stacks of metal files, his back turned, his elbows propped on the cabinet tops. "Would you like to make a statement now, Missus Lowrie?"

"Do I have to?"

"No. No, I suppose you don't have to,' he replied, leaving his temporary post and returning to stand by his desk. "I'm sure you know your legal rights."

"Yeah, I guess. Even if I don't watch much TV."

The two men exchanged glances suggesting puzzlement over her declaration.

"So I can go home now if I want to, you mean?"

"Your choice," Lieutenant Morrissey retorted, sitting down and laying his palms on the blotter. "You drove your own vehicle here, to the best of my understanding." He looked over to the other desk; Jason nodded confirmation. "So, you can drive your own vehicle away. It's your call, Missus Lowrie."

"Well, on the way here I sort of had a little police escort."

The inspector didn't respond except to interweave his fingers and begin a rhythmic rearrangement of their positions relative to one another: first the right thumb on top then the left then the right again. In the silence, Jason reached for the pack of cigarettes on his desk but, when his superior shot him a glance, the student retracted his hand and sat still.

"I will say, if you make a statement today, Missus Lowrie, it could save you from having to come back some other afternoon soon. You know, it's not an affidavit. It's not a deposition. Do you see any lawyers in this room? Jason, you're not a big San Francisco D.A. yet, are you?"

Katie saw the young man lower his eyes and blush.

"Take as long as you like," the veteran policeman continued, rising to his feet and stepping to a metal cart on which a boxlike shape was draped by a cloth; when he lifted the cover, Katie saw the reel-to-reel Wollensack GM tape recorder.

"You're not going to try to trip me up with any trick questions, are you?"

He gave his subordinate the signal to ready the machine. "No, no I'm not."

While J. Drew repositioned the cart within easy reach, the detective regained his swivel chair. "Missus Lowrie, I know this isn't easy. But a statement from you now should speed the whole process up quite a bit. Examining the evidence, identifying the fingerprints, interviewing the attorney and whatshername, the nurse—"

"... Fatima Mariano," Katie interjected.

"That's right: Missus Mariano. So, once the medical examiner's office does its thing...."—he paused, apparently gauging the impact of his facetious slang but not detecting any appreciation from the younger pair—"we may be able to wrap this up in no time."

Katie heaved a sigh. "What am I supposed to talk about?"

"Whatever you like. Express yourself...." His smirk displayed more frustration with their indifference to his sense of humor. "Just please try to keep on topic, the topic of today. Try to make it ... Jason, what is it the journalists keep saying these days? Help me out ... no wait!" A hint of white showed between his lips. "Relevant. Make it relevant if you don't mind."

"I've got nothing to hide."

"Then take as long as you need. This young man here doesn't like hearing me say that, do you, Jason? He'll probably end up having to type it all." The student assistance placed his finger on the recorder's green button. "Anytime, Missus McLoughlin," Lieutenant Morrissey mis-spoke.

"It's Lowrie," she snapped. "I'm Katie Lowrie, remember?" She averted her eyes from the man and scowled at the colorless linoleum floor.

"Oh, that's right. It's been a long weekend. Excuse me, would you? Of course, it's Missus Lowrie. Go ahead, Jason," he concluded, watching the feed- and take-up reels start to turn.

"I don't know where to start."

"Start with today," the detective suggested.

"Are you going to ask me questions?"

"Just start, Missus Lowrie. We'll see how it goes." He tilted back in his chair, crossed his legs—ankle on opposite knee—and jutted out his elbows, cupping the back of his head with his palms. "I suggest you start with when you arrived at the apartment."

"I've been coming up from Santa Cruz to spend Mondays with Jan. As soon as I get there, Fatima takes off. Monday's been her only day off in the week. Otherwise she's been there fulltime for about two months. Do I have to say exact dates and all?"

"Don't worry about that. If anything's missing, I'll stop you, or have young Jay here make a note along the way to follow up later. You just go right ahead," he coached her, uncrossing his legs, lowering his arms, and pulling the chair closer to the desk where he resumed his standard pose, hands clasped atop the closed manila folder.

"At first Fatima went to Jan's once a week, then it was every other day except Sundays." Katie paused, noticing the detective was squeezing and releasing and squeezing his hands. "You know how it goes."

"How what goes?"

"Cancer. She got worse and worse. Throat cancer was diagnosed but she was in bad shape overall. So, Fatima moved in. I guess she'd been staying with her sister's big family in some crowded little house in Daly City."

"How did you meet Missus Mariano? In the first place, I mean?"

"Through an agency. They're super expensive but she's been worth every cent we've paid her."

"Every cent who's paid her?"

"I wrote checks to the agency from a special account the lawyer set up. I mean, it was Jan's money, but I signed the checks. But I also gave her cash bonuses from the slush fund on a regular basis. I mean, it was still Jan's money, but I've been free to spend it as I see fit. Mister Hudson and I have been handling all her finances for like half a year."

Katie saw the older man raise his eyebrows toward the student and lift the pointer finger away from the rest of his right hand; Jason glanced at the tape recorder's counter and wrote a note on his pad.

"And how did you first come into contact with this Mister Hudson?"

"He's been her lawyer ever since I met her. I got to know him during a real estate deal with her property. She was our landlady. You knew that, right?"

"What real estate deal was that?"

"When Jan split up her Cliffport property, she ended up giving us the twenty acres with the house on it."

The inspector cleared his throat, which J. Drew took as a sign to note the counter and mark his pad. "Did you say Missus McLoughlin gave you and someone else twenty acres of land in Santa Cruz County?"

"Me and my mom, yeah. A couple years back we carved a new twenty-acre parcel out of her hundred and she sold the remaining eighty. Made out like a bandit on that deal."

"Who made out like a bandit?"

"Jan did. That's the pile of money we've been working down the last few years."

"Well, that was very generous of Missus McLoughlin, wouldn't you say?"

Katie stared back at the man; her nostrils flared as she inhaled and exhaled. "So now you'll want to see the binding agreement that Hudson drew up for us to stay on the lease for one hundred and one years or something stupid like that. By the time we got to signing that it was a joke. My mother and I were there to stay, and Jan knew it."

"Jason."

"Sir?"

"Get the realty office contact information from Missus Lowrie, after we're done here. And the lawyer's."

"Yes, sir."

"Please, Missus Lowrie. Go on."

"That's all. If you don't believe me you can go to the Office of County Records in Santa Cruz. And Hudson has all the documents showing how the twenty-acre deed passes to us … upon her death."

The tape recorder's reels turned in a sustained silence.

"Were you always so … close with your landlady?"

"Like I told Jay, I was her last and only friend in the world. She was like an aunt to me. Not a blood aunt but still. We got pretty close, yeah."

"I see. But in the beginning she was just your landlord. Is that correct?"

"That's right. We didn't even know her until 1965 or maybe it was '64. Yeah, 1964. When her estranged husband died, Jan showed up … out of nowhere … actually, she showed up like a bat out of hell," Katie corrected herself, directing her last words right at the recorder. "At first she wanted to sell the place on us—lock, stock, and barrel. She needed money bad and wanted to turn her property into cash."

"To liquidate it…?" the man suggested.

"Yup, I guess that's the term. At first my mother and Jan fought like cats and dogs, but I learned how to keep the peace. For some reason I always got along with the crazy old coot. Eventually I took to socializing with her, you know, like visiting her here in San Francisco."

"Even before she got sick, do you mean?"

"Yeah, before. Every couple of months then every month then you know how it goes. She just needed more and more help to keep it together."

"Missus Lowrie. Were you ever reimbursed for your services?"

"For services rendered you mean?" Katie smiled to herself. "If you mean, did she ever pay me, no. You don't get it yet. I got a kick out of her. She got a kick out of me. And the Lowries wound up with a house on twenty acres, a place to live, raise my kid, run a small business."

"What kind of business is that?"

"A nursery. A plant nursery. For growing containerized ornamentals if you know what that means."

"I see." The inspector raised his eyebrows and shot Jason a glance. "And the name of the business?"

Jason poised the pencil point above his pad.

"The Redwood Coast Nursery. And my best friend and I have been running a summer music camp there for years. For a while, my mom and I tried to run a daycare center for kids after school, but we had to give that up. My mother's not getting any younger, you know? Anyway.... So, is this really what you want to hear about?"

"Yes, Missus Lowrie. Please, go on."

"What else? I got Jan placed on the waiting list at the Hillside Towers, for a suite there."

"Which is—"

"Condo apartments, in the Lower Nob Hill district, I guess they call it."

Inspector Morrissey cleared his throat; Jason jotted down another note.

"It would definitely have been a step up from 999 Zelkova Street. Literally and figuratively. In the meantime, I got her apartment fixed up. Bought her new furniture, new appliances, had it painted. She had money to burn after selling those eighty acres. And my mom and I were already paying the property taxes and utilities and taking care of the repairs on the old house and the twenty acres. It's funny...."

"What's funny?"

"How I never did get around to replacing that broken-down sofa I used to sleep on when I got stuck there overnight."

"Oh, I see.... And how much did Miss McLoughlin make on that property sale if I may ask?"

Katie furrowed her brow, tilted her head sideways, crossed her arms, and stared back at him, lips sealed.

"About how much?" he added.

"Maybe you better talk to her lawyer or the bank or somebody else about that, you know what I mean?" Without any obvious signal from his superior, Jason Drew made a note. "Tell you the truth, I'm not sure much money will be left after the medical bills get paid and all. And I know what you're thinking."

"Tell me what am I thinking."

Katie uncrossed her arms and shifted her weight on the chair. "You know what you're thinking," she retorted. "I don't have to tell you."

The detective shifted his weight in his chair and crossed his arms. "Jason."

"Sir?"

"Why don't you get us few sodas from the vending machine downstairs? I'll take a Coke. Missus Lowrie?"

"I don't want anything."

"You sure?"

She didn't bother to reply.

"Well, get me a Coke and get yourself something, Jason."

"I have change, sir."

"Pay you back, thanks."

The youth left them alone in the room.

"From the report I looked at, I understood that the nurse oversaw Missus McLoughlin's medication regimen. Is that correct?"

"Yup. I never wanted to have anything to do with any morphine. Too freaky for me."

"Yes, well, Missus Mariano must have a special permit and—"

"... oh god, can I just say something right now?"

"Please, by all means, be my guest."

"Fatima is a living saint. I'm not bull ... kidding you. Actually, she was a Catholic sister in the Philippines when she was young, before she came to the United States. Anyway, when Jan needed constant company, let's say, I just couldn't do it anymore. I was taking care of my kid—especially with him messing up in his first year at high school. And my mom, when her back goes out. Then there's the nursery. You can't turn your back on container-grown plants and expect them to make it on their own. I'm not complaining. I'm just saying Fatima saved my life. Leave her out of this investigation, can't you? She made Jan's life more livable and mine too. When it came time to put Jan in the hospital bed we got it set up in the old dining room—Jan would never agree to being relocated to a nursing home—so Fatima moved into Jan's old bedroom. She set up a little camp there. You know what the first thing she did was?"

"What's so funny?"

"Funny?"

"You just looked like you were about to laugh, Missus Lowrie."

"The first thing she did was sanitize everything. Whenever she wasn't doing something else, you never saw that woman without her blue gloves on, a box of baking soda in one hand and a squirt bottle of vinegar in the other. She scrubbed that place down to the bone. 'You'll scrub all our sins away!' I'd tease her and she'd smile her big old smile. She's just a little thing and I love her to death." Katie paused then looked downward as she spoke, shaking her head. "I sure hope you don't have to drag her in here too."

The detective didn't react. Jason returned with two bottles of Coca-Cola. Lieutenant Morrissey reached into his pants pocket, extracted some coins, and pressed them into the youth's hand. Jason took a furtive glance at the informant and retreated to his seat.

"You don't need to know the blow-by-blow on Jan's declining health, do you?"

"Not today, Missus Lowrie."

"Good. The important thing is, she was the one who decided not to go into any nursing home. I lost that argument every time. So, she just stuck it out to the end at '999.' She could be ornery. Tell you the truth, I can too." Neither the inspector nor the student assistant revealed their reactions. "Maybe that's why I dug her so much."

The detective finished off his bottle of Coke in several chugs and wiped his lips with a folded white handkerchief. "Missus Lowrie," he resumed. "You've said you managed Missus McLoughlin's money—"

"… only under Mister Hudson's supervision."

"Oh, of course."

"Jan used to say to me, Remember, Lady Katie—she'd call me that, just to kid me—whatever you and Hudson spend now is money coming out of what you'll get later."

"So, Missus McLoughlin had told you in no uncertain terms that whatever financial assets were left at the time of her decease, you'd be the beneficiary. Is that correct?"

"Not just the financial stuff. Her whole estate. It's in her will. She had me go back and forth between her and the lawyer to get it all straightened out. There was nobody else."

"And your mother?"

"What about my mother? Jan deeded the property to me but that was fine. The lawyer, Hudson, he thought that was the easiest arrangement at the time. No, nothing to my mom. Those two never got over some pretty deep personal feud."

"I see."

Lieutenant Morrissey lifted two pointer fingers like a pair of pistol barrels held parallel in his hands and aimed them at the tape recorder; J. Drew took note of the counter's number.

"Is there anything else you'd like to say?"

"Tell you the truth, it's sort of a relief. No more endoscopies and biopsies and all those lab tests. Poor Jan was pretty much in pain all over then we took her only pleasures away from her—her whiskey, cigarettes. After the diagnosis we had to. A couple times in there she told me she'd rather be dead. When the medical morphine kicked in she finally got some relief. Fatima was administering that, following the doctor's orders to the letter. Jan definitely got hooked on that stuff, but as long as she was out of pain, that was fine by me."

"You've said you had nothing to do with the morphine. Did I hear that right?"

"That was the nurse's gig. She has the knowhow. She had some permit. Fatima took care of the prescription and that beeping machine that delivers the dosage automatically."

"Missus Lowrie. I'm confused. How do you suppose the deceased gained access to alcohol and tobacco? Prescription pills were on hand,

I imagine, but you said you had denied her the other and she was bedridden. Am I correct?"

"You're right. How did she get a hold of her stuff? That's what I'd like to know. I figure one of the workmen got it for her at the corner liquor store."

The inspector's eyebrows lifted; Jason made a note.

"Didn't your men tell you the inside of the building is being renovated? Tradesmen have been coming and going at 999 Zelkova for like a year. Tearing down the inside walls, changing out plumbing, redoing floors. Every time someone moves out—or dies, is more like it—they move in and redo the unit from top to bottom. In between they leave their stuff in the hallway. Or work in the hallway. They always remind me of vultures waiting for the next tenant to croak. I guess they'll be happy when they find out about Jan. That was another reason I wanted to get her out of there: the noise and the dust. Those guys have the radio blaring every time I arrive. I kept asking them to keep it down but the next Monday, it's as loud as ever."

"Did the superintendent—Mister Luen—did he have a key to the apartment?"

"Sure, he did. They knew each other for years. He did things for her in her place. Tell you the truth, I think they were quite the drinking buddies once upon a time."

"Is it possible that Mister Luen—"

"... no. No, I don't think so. He's too spooked out. Nowadays he just hides in his room. The new building owners will probably be happy when they sweep him out with the old plaster. He's just another bump in the road where developers are concerned."

"So, you don't think it's even remotely conceivable that Mister Luen provided Missus McLoughlin with—"

"... no, I don't, okay? He's been avoiding her apartment for a long time now. I think it was just her way to end it all. An opportunity, not an impulse."

"An opportunity?"

"Yeah, with Fatima gone overnight, Jan could've got one of those guys out in the hall to fetch her stuff for her. No, I don't think the old man would've honored her request even if he had been communicating with her, which he wasn't. I think they kinda said goodbye for good—on good terms—quite a while back."

"Could you tell me what you did immediately after you entered the apartment? You found Missus McLaughlin in bed and...."

"I thought you said you weren't going to be asking me questions."

"I didn't say that."

"I told the policeman who grilled me. I called my mom. I called Fatima 'cuz I didn't want her showing up and going into shock. Then I called ... no, first I told Mister Luen than I called the...."

"... cops," the lieutenant inserted.

"Yup. You know, I hope you guys will let Fatima collect her personal stuff, settle with the morphine man, and go away in peace. I'm not expecting her to pick up the pieces in that place. I'll take care of that, when I can get back in, that is."

The inspector took his customary pose: leaning back, one leg crossed with the ankle on the opposite knee, his interlaced fingers cupping the back of his skull. "Shouldn't be too long. You'll be notified, Missus Mc—Lowrie."

The trio sat in silence. The reels turned. Katie studied the scuffed floor around her boots and wondered if she had blabbed too much. She realized she didn't care what they thought about how she felt or looked or spoke, as long as they let her go and left Fatima alone. Did it sound to them that she was disrespectful of them or of Jan? Behind his thick armored vest of procedural protocol, the veteran lawman concealed whatever he thought or felt. And Jason? Katie glanced at the twenty-year-old aping his mentor—arms lifted, elbows out, hands behind his head—and when she didn't take her gaze away, he lowered his arms and blushed, fixing his eyes upon his pack of cigarettes. Jay looked to Katie as if he could handle certain information, so she stayed turned toward him while she spoke: "Funny how the old lady got her way in the end. She didn't want to go through any treatment. The cancer was spreading into her windpipe and her vocal cords—it got pretty hard to listen to her talk. They already had the targets for their x-ray guns marked off on her throat, but she didn't want any x-rays. Or chemo. Or surgery. No way was she going to some center in Palo Alto to get one-minute doses of cobalt once a day, Monday through Friday for seven weeks. She said she'd rather die first, so she did."

Katie lengthened her legs and crossed them at her ankles.

"Yes, she did," the inspector echoed, clearing his throat and folding his hands.

"Think about it. It was perfect timing for her to make her move. They were ready to start the treatment but that had to be postponed because she was suffering from peritonitis."

"Which is what?" the detective asked. "I'm a policeman, Missus Lowrie, not a physician."

"I think I said it right: per-i-ta-ny-tis. Inflammation of the inner abdominal wall. They were waiting for her to get over that but she checked out first. Game over."

After a pause, Lieutenant Morrissey spoke: "You were saying that Missus Mariano was the only person authorized to administer the morphine."

"Yes, and Jan kept begging her to amp it up, turn it up."

"What about the suicide note?"

"What suicide note?" Kate replied, gripping the outside edges of her chair's seat and drawing in her lower legs. "There was no suicide note I know about."

"There was no note?"

"I just told you. Your men in blue asked me that too, more than once."

"Aren't you a little surprised that Missus McLoughlin left no note?"

"Not really. Why should she? Her twin brother never left one either."

The two men exchanged a glance.

"Missus McLoughlin had a twin brother?"

"Who also took his own, if you want to put it that way."

"Jason."

"Yes, sir!" he shot back, lifting his eyes, noting down the counter, pencil point hovering over his pad.

"Missus Lowrie. Are you saying that the deceased had a twin brother who ... you seem to imply ... committed suicide?"

"Yes."

"And when was this?"

"After World War One."

"Oh, I see...."

"Some people said he had 'brain fever'—whatever that is. Others said he was shell-shocked. His name was Glenn." Turning toward J. Drew, she spelled it out: "G-l-e-double n. Glenn McLoughlin."

All three parties looked back and forth between one another several times, then the older man spoke: "Now, is there anything else you'd like to say?"

"I guess not," Katie said.

"Jason, turn that thing off," Lieutenant Morrissey said, rising to his feet. "I'll ask Jason to go over his notes with you, to fill in some information. Otherwise I think we're done for today."

"For today?"

"Were you planning on going back to Santa Cruz this evening, Missus Lowrie?"

"I was planning on it."

"Well, we hope you won't go too far from home for a while. Jason can go over our exact expectations about keeping yourself available. We need to be able to contact you."

"Right."

"And if you do think of anything else after you leave this office," he added, pulling a business card from a holder on the desk, lodging it between two fingers and extending it toward her, "you can always contact me. I want to thank you for your ... forthrightness, Missus Lowrie."

"Okay..." she muttered, taking hold of the crisp white paper stock and examining the embossed, gold-filled, seven-point star of the badge and the blue ink lettering on the card.

"Our job would be one helluvah lot easier if everyone said what's on their mind instead of clamming up on us."

"Oh, I'm pretty good at talking too much, if that's what you mean. But then I've got nothing to hide. I'm sure some people do, coming in here."

"Oh yes, they do. Some people certainly do. Now I'll leave you in the hands of this able young man." He stepped to the other desk and passed back the sheet of typing paper he had previously detached from the rest. "Finish this one off and get her to sign the release. And, Jason, be sure to get her to sign off on the guidelines on witness availability."

"Yes, sir."

Without looking her in the eyes or shaking her hand, Lieutenant Morrissey picked the manila folder off the larger desk and exited the room via an interior door other than the one by which he had entered.

———

Katie cancelled accounts with the home care agency and utility companies, and notified the Hillside Tower, where property management required legal proof of Mrs. McLoughlin's decease before they would return 50% of the first year's lease paid in advance; as per contract, the initial $200.00 application fee was forfeited. In the last week of September, Gerald Hudson telephoned to inform her that, if she would kindly come to his office and go over the Last Will and Testament with him, she would be free to enter the premises at 999 Zelkova Street and attend to her tasks. Katie never heard back from the SFPD and never inquired about the ultimate disposition of Jan McLoughlin's physical remains; she found she could sing the Castle Song in Chapel Grove without spreading ashes, and she did sing it there, more than once, alone. [1]

She coordinated the timing of her first trip back to San Francisco with Fatima—who had already signed off on the controlled substance so that when the medical supply company sent personnel to reclaim the hospital bed, the pharmaceutical agency retrieved the remaining supply of morphine and the dispensing machine—for the nurse still needed to dismantle her shrine and gather her personal effects into a single suitcase. Yet Katie wouldn't let Fatima leave without also taking possession of whatever dishware, linen, and furniture which she could distribute however she pleased among her extended family. The two women carried cartons of housewares to the curbside, and Katie paid two workmen to load the pickup with the wardrobe closet, coffee table, bedroom dresser, and wooden bed with its headboard and box springs. When they arrived at Fatima Mariano's sister's home in Daly City—one of Malvina Reynolds' many ticky-tacky little boxes—nephews and cousins offloaded the booty while Katie gave Fatima a $50 cash bonus. Fatima blessed her in Portuguese, recited a prayer in Latin, and invited her to eat supper with the family. Katie, exhausted, begged off; Fatima expressed her understanding, and they crushed themselves in each other's arms, weeping goodbye.

Katie proceeded south on Route One. The Ford Fleetside's bed was empty, but the familiar Scottish basket and banker's box were lodged in the passenger side's foot well, and other precious cargo sat on the bench seat beside her: Jan's three framed photographs wrapped in kitchen towels; a colorless, threadbare velour pouch; a sealed shoebox. By the time she reached the coast, where the summer evening fog had socked in Half Moon Bay, Katie turned off the highway and parked at the taqueria on Main Street where the cook always welcomed her as a familiar stranger, if not as a personal acquaintance. The place was closing but his wife served their last customer of the day chips and salsa, ladled out a bowl of chili, told Katie to grab a beverage from the cooler, indicating that she could stay seated and eat her meal while she and her husband cleaned up. Katie scarfed down the first food she had eaten since her 6:00 AM breakfast fourteen hours earlier, drained the bottle of cerveza, and left four dollar bills under the empty bowl. In the 7–11 next door, she bought a cup of coffee to go but, before restarting the Ford, she sat in the parking lot's shrill lighting, staring at the velour pouch knotted with a string tie and the shoebox closed with yellowed cellophane.

In all her visits to '999' Katie had never been permitted to view the contents of the discolored pouch or look inside the shoebox; now they were all hers. She used her pocket knife to cut the knot of the discolored velour bag and slid out a gray, dented, rectangular cookie tin. Inside lay an old-fashioned 11" × 7" album. Black electrical tape had been used to reinforce its brittle binding; its black cover's paper was separating from the brown backing. Traces of inlaid golden paint remained in the recessed word PHOTOGRAPHS, and the interior page borders were frayed and torn. White crayon had been deployed in a legible longhand similar or perhaps identical to the handwriting gracing Jan's older sister's wildflower folio to caption the photos systematically arranged on black background: eight-up to sheets with 2" × 3" prints and two-up for the 6" × 3" size. Katie suspected that Mary McLoughlin may have dutifully volunteered or at some point been charged with assembling these heirloom images beginning with the McLoughlin family's arrival in the New World. The sequence was chronological: The Maritime Provinces followed by pictures from Ontario then British Columbia and finally California. The images brought home to Katie a vanished Cliffport from which Jan had run and into which—half a century prior—her orphaned mother had stepped. She replaced the album in the tray and the tin box in the velour bag, cinched its string tie, and turned on the ignition, glad she knew the rest of the highway home by heart as she re-entered the nocturnal fog. Katie sensed she would find the occasion to go over all these pictures with her mother. [2]

———

She brought her son along on her final trip to the San Francisco apartment and paid a pair of workers on site to drag the sofa, armchair, and mattress down to the sidewalk where she could get them hauled away—or not. Donald coveted Jan's radio, and together they carried the TV set and kidney-shaped vanity table down to the pickup. She had DD heap Jan's footwear and used undergarments into grocery bags and make multiple visits to the contractor's dumpster located where the service elevator gave onto the alleyway out back. Katie decided to give the collection of swizzle sticks to Mr. Luen as a token of gratitude for services rendered to the deceased, as well as a gesture of recognition of the mutual affection between him and his former drinking partner. She used the kitchen's padded stepstool to reach the three pint glasses on the cupboard's top shelf; he could have the stepstool, too, if he liked, or else she would leave it for the tradesmen. Various canes and umbrellas, a pair of wooden crutches, an aluminum walker—these were piled into the back of the Ford, to be dropped off at any Goodwill or St. Vincent de Paul's on their way out of the Tenderloin; she could let them know some furniture was also available for pickup in front of 999 Zelkova Street.

Facing the rack of Jan's vintage clothes, Katie knew her mother would have nothing to do with them, but she couldn't see donating or consigning them to some secondhand boutique. Unable to leave them behind, she sandwiched the clothing between two blankets that she and her son carried downstairs and out the front door, reminding her of transporting a body to a morgue or out of the woods after a rifle accident during hunting season—or a suicide.[3] She weighted the bundle down in the Fleetside's bed and went back for the purse full of costume jewelry and the carton jammed with half-a-hundred different perfume bottles from the half-bath's glass shelves.

"Can I have the key?" her fourteen-year-old asked, fiddling with the radio knobs on the dash.

"Here, but don't you dare turn on that ignition, Donald D."

"Come on, Mom!" he protested as she turned to reenter the building. "Can't we just go?"

"I'll be right back. I've got to let Mister Luen know we're done."

The building manager answered the door as if he had been standing behind it, waiting for her knock. As usual, tears teetered on his lower eyelids, threatening to spill. She gave him the pint glasses with the swizzle sticks and surrendered the door keys. He said nothing then or when she offered him the stepstool, so she leaned it against the wall outside his door. Katie was preparing to reach out and shake the man's hand goodbye when he turned, lifted a cardboard box off a chair, and thrust it into her arms. Inside the open carton, Katie saw a utilitarian folding file holder and a hand-painted black-and-gold lacquered chest that looked as if it might have been a music or jewelry box designed to rest on a stand.

Katie shifted the carton in her arms and listened as he explained that four or five years earlier, clearing out the last sellable antiques from the tenant's basement storage bin, these two items had remained. Mrs. McLoughlin would not have them in her apartment, yet he wasn't to throw or give them away. He said that there was no key to the little chest—at least he had never possessed one—and Mrs. McLoughlin had made him vow never to investigate the contents of the sturdy, gusseted file holder. Not knowing what else to do, he had held onto both objects and assumed that their rightful owner had eventually forgotten their existence. Katie had never known the man to speak so many words in such a short span of time. She thanked him, reclutched the carton, and turned away. Donald begged his mother to let him break open the Chinese box right away and to cut the cord around the file holder with his pocketknife, but she forbade him more than once and drove off, on the lookout for the first-come charity shop.

At the crest of Highway 92, Katie impulsively turned onto Old State Route 5 even though following the ridgeline through the Northern Santa Cruz Mountains would double their travel time. As a reward for his patience, she promised Donald Duncan that they would stop in La Honda for burgers, fries, and shakes. Both mother and son fell into silence as she navigated the truck through a staccato rhythm of shadow-and-light within the tunnel-like corridors of oaks and bays. She turned the headlights on while passing through the perpetual darkness of the solid redwood stands. More than two hours later, dropping back down onto Highway One, the teenager was excited to land upon a strong radio signal broadcasting acid rock from Pacific Grove across

Monterey Bay. For as long as the reception lasted, his mother repeatedly lowered the volume, and he repeatedly turned it back up, bobbing his head.

Scanning the two items on the bench seat between them, Katie rehearsed some rainy winter day ahead when, she knew, she would insist upon absolute privacy in order to deal with these unique hand-me-downs. She realized there was no one with whom she could explore the material with any degree of curiosity approaching her own. Donald was too young to care about what he called "all that old stuff" and, unless her dead rival's relics were directly related to John and Dorothea McLoughlin, Elise Lowrie would never look into this surviving evidence of Jan McLoughlin's life. Despite Jan's moody monologues and disclosures when under the influence of alcohol or morphine, Katie had never been told of the banished, rectangular-shaped Chinese chest or the accordion file. If the woman had been so adamant about sequestering their contents, why had she not directed the building superintendent simply to toss them in the incinerator out back? Or had Jan planned to reopen the files someday? Or had she left them intact so that once she was gone someone else—who turned out to be Katie—could pry open the lacquered chest and cut the string around the files? Would Jan have been capable of forgetting the existence of the files and the refined, diminutive Chinese box—misplacing or discarding its key? Perhaps, Katie thought, she should carry the little chest—no larger than a one pound box of chocolates—up to Chapel Grove and bury it unopened in the McLoughlin's family plot. Yet if she consigned the box to the cemetery soil, Katie might never learn answers to questions she felt she had the right and the desire and the need to know.

Besides confirming that the property deed had been updated and recorded correctly with Santa Cruz County, Katie pondered what else was left to be done so she could finalize the affair. She had yet to hear what Mister Hudson was billing the trust and, after more than five years of loyal, courteous, competent, and trustworthy service to a decidedly difficult client, the man probably deserved to be paid twice

35

over. She wondered if, for his last quarterly invoice, the old fashioned lawyer would present a lump sum figure for half-a-decade's retaining fee or provide more detailed billing; if so, she would probably not even scrutinize the line items and instead let him have his due—no questions asked.

———

Katie was granted exclusive use of the rearmost room to house Jan's things and, that fall, periodically opened the door and peered inside. Her mother and her son—at first between themselves then, tentatively, with Katie—referred to the spare bedroom at the end of the hall as the "Memorial Chamber." Elise trusted that, in Katie's private process of grieving, her once wild child was somehow assuming stewardship of the McLoughlin clan's afterlife on the North Coast and, by extension, Elise's own; to her friend Suzanne, Elise confided that her daughter was engaged in "a spiritual reckoning."

Atop the bed, Katie had set Mary McLoughlin's oversize wildflower folio compressing loose sheets within its wooden covers bound by brass hinges. This homemade heirloom had long rested on the fireplace mantle so that, while sipping morning coffee or fighting off sleep at the end of the day, Katie could peruse its pressed flowers and colored-pencil illustrations while studying Jan's older sister's annotations. As the Redwood Coast Nursery had grown, Katie's appreciation of the enduring charm of this by-product of Mary's home schooling had also grown, and her appetite for the knowledge between those thin boards of madrone—kept to a soft sheen by Katie and Elisabeth Lowrie's handling—was never satiated. Elise had understood when her daughter requested taking the wildflower folio to the Memorial Chamber, and she had also allowed Katie to remove the wooden box with Dorothea McLoughlin's handwritten recipe cards from its normal place of residence above the refrigerator—out of sight but within easy reach.

Katie gradually started drifting back into the rear room, closing the door, sitting at the simple wooden desk, glancing back and forth between Jan's memorabilia and the purple amethyst geode on the windowsill. On a narrow redwood plank attached by redwood brackets, where a row of books had once been shelved against the wall, Jan's three framed photographs were now propped side by side. The full-length portrait of Mary, less than twenty years of age, standing on the house's front porch steps—"all dressed up in Cliffport Town and nowhere to go;" the double portrait of Mills as an awkward adolescent standing straight beside his mother, the boy in his Thetford Academy navy whites and Mary-Helen Belcanto decked out in an elegant linen outfit of Jan's making with accessories to match; the 6" × 8" photograph of Mills set in a 12" × 16" gold-finish wooden frame. Even Katie could be mesmerized by this softly lit, airbrushed head shot of the love of Jan McLoughlin's life: Mills Belcanto, aged twenty, Hollywood handsome, with its signatory's dedication: To Aunt Janet—Semper Fidelis, Mills, 1940—written in florid penmanship above the staggered lines of a fanciful font recessed in the matting board:

These images had passed in and out of Katie's sight for the last five years, first when Jan had displayed them in her bedroom and later, when Jan had been moved into the hospital bed set up in the erstwhile dining room, the three photographs traveling with her.

The wicker basket sat under the bed. Katie was familiar with its mementos of Jan's 1932 trip to Scotland, as well as the commemorative platters, spoons, and ribbons of tartan salvaged from Jan's display box on the apartment wall. She had already been through the banker's box containing miscellaneous trinkets and printed matter from the Pan-Pacific International Expo in 1919, the 1938–9 World's Fair on Treasure Island, and the opening days of the Golden Gate Bridge.

She felt no more need to review the items and articles from a 1938 flight on Pan American Airway's China Clipper seaplane or the tokens and pamphlets from Jan's numerous trips on "the most talked about train in America"—the legendary California Zephyr. So, she initially eased into her new investigation by flipping through the recipe cards, browsing the names and ingredients of the many baked and roasted dishes that her mother had cooked, following one or another of Dorothea McLoughlin's instructions written out in an untutored hand. But what about the shoebox?

Even as Katie had become intimate with Jan's possessions at "999" she had been forbidden to disturb the sealed shoebox. Once off-limits, the box was now hers to explore. Slicing through the toughened tape, she opened the lid and found a wad of postcards Mills had sent to his "Aunt Jeanette." The cards picturing landmarks from the far corners of the world still carried eccentric postmarks and cancelled stamps, and Mills had usually addressed some brief, jokey lines to his substitute mother. A history buff might have been turned on by reconstructing the chronology of the postcards; a novelist, by spinning yarns. But Katie felt she could just as well be killing time at Logos Books & Records on the mall in Santa Cruz or at some gift shop counter at the end of the wharf, empty of tourists on a rainy winter's day; she soon lost interest in the contents and closed the box.

———

When "Aunt" Suzanne and "Uncle" Mike Crogan, the Lowries' long-time family friends, drove down to Cliffport for Thanksgiving, they took away Jan's vanity and mirror as well as an armload of the vintage garments. Suzanne planned to refinish the table and donate the wardrobe to the ladies' fashion show being mounted as part of Cloverdale's Volunteer Rural Fire District's annual fundraiser of which her husband, Mike, was the chief organizer. Three weeks later she reported back that an executive decision had been made not to piece out the collection; a keen-eyed St. Helena boutique owner had bid $350.00 for the entire lot. The presentation of dresses, coats, and wraps continued through the evening but without further bidding, while the women in attendance—except the buyer—wondered aloud if the guest from Napa Valley had not spent far too much.

As January rains arrived, Katie's outdoor work moved to the interior of the largest of her three makeshift hoop houses. There she set up a station where she could hack, slice, and whittle away at piles of bamboo poles—their leaves shriveled, the wood dry—sawn from the grove and brought under the polyethylene to cure. Come true spring she would need tall, thick poles for tenting the open beds of sunflowers with protection from the migrating grosbeaks and the ever-present finches. She would need long, stout lengths of bamboo for staking vines and shrubs as she shifted the plants up from 1- to 3- to 5-gallon-size containers. She would use longer, thinner, more pliable lengths to arc under low row covers shielding the seedling broccoli and tomatoes from cabbage moths. And she could always use pencil-length pegs as markers while tending to hundreds of 2- and 4-inch pots. Plus, the work would go easier if all these bamboo lengths received pointed ends in advance. When she could work on the dirt pile outside, she repotted the ivy geranium mother plants with new soil and, before netting the stock plants against the budworm moth, she covered the used soil—with its pupae pests—in a mound kept composting at a distance. As the rains came down in earnest throughout February, Katie's activities were increasingly confined to her propagation bench. Keeping herself warm enough within the aura of a kerosene heater, she spent long hours perched on her tall stool, attending to baby plant starts and daydreaming to the ceaseless gamelan of precipitation overhead. Below the curved, low-ceilinged plastic, she reconstituted wooden seed flats, disinfected the tables, and spent hours dibbling seeds into her mix of perlite, vermiculite, and horticultural sand. Starting in March, she took daily cuttings of the first sprouts from the dahlia bulbs heeled into shallow trays and wooden lugs.

———

"Thank you for the delicious meal, dear. That was simply the best Mother's Day brunch I've ever had."

"Really?"

"Oh, yes, it really was. And this...." She picked up the rustic frame with the McLoughlin family's Short Cake Crust recipe rendered on watercolor paper in a calligraphic style resembling the original 19th century handwriting. "I so love the way you left it just the way it was written on the card:

> 4 cupfulls sifted flour
> 1 teaspoonfull salt
> 3 teaspoonfulls baking powder
> 1 tablespoonful lard and butter
> Sweet milk.

—roll out soft dough sheets ½ inches thick, bake hot oven—
The only ingredient not listed there is love, but it's clearly included. Thank you so much."

"You're welcome, Mom. You're always such a stickler for correct grammar and spelling, I considered correcting it."

"Oh, heaven's no. Those cards originated with Dorothea's mother even before the 1870's when the first McLoughlins first settled in California. We must never amend those."

"Here's your tea."

Katie helped her mother shift from one of the straight-back chairs into the red armchair pulled closer to the dining table.

"Kaitlin, I get the impression that you slept in the back room last night. Am I right?"

"I did. I conked out on the bed."

"While you were looking at more pictures...?"

Katie put the last dry dish in the cupboard and faced her mother. "You're right, I was. That's about all I ever do lately, isn't it?"

"I didn't mean it derogatorily. You know I support your ... project all the way."

"But?"

"Well, come sit down for a moment."

Her daughter brought a mug of hot coffee to the table and took a seat.

"If I may speak honestly—"

"... that's a laugh," Katie chuckled. "Do you ever speak any other way?"

"I am beginning to worry, no ... to wonder.... I'm beginning to wonder if you aren't over thinking this thing."

"Over thinking...?"

"I was remembering when your father bought me the first electric wheel, how many pieces I ruined by pressing the clay too hard or spinning the wheel too fast. Of course, that was when I was—"

"... young and stupid like I am now?"

"No one ever said you're stupid, Kaitlin Lowrie. Whenever will you get over that?"

"And no one can say I'm young anymore."

"Oh, don't be silly. Thirty-three's young."

"Mom, remember how long you slept up in the attic?" She rolled her eyes toward the ceiling. "You lived up in that rat's nest for a couple of months."

"Was it that long? I forget." Elise wagged her head. "What a time that was!"

"So, what's the big deal if I crash down the hall sometimes? I need to do this at my own pace."

"I know you do, dear."

Mother and daughter both turned to gaze toward Donald Duncan, heard groaning as he switched positions on the couch, his eyes glued upon the TV screen.

"Could you turn that down a notch, DD?" After no response, Katie raised her voice: "I said turn it down, DD!"

"In a minute," he muttered, showing no sign of moving anytime soon.

"You know, Kaitlin, your right eye is beginning to squint again." Katie got up to turn down the TV and returned to her place. "Have you noticed that or not, dear?"

"Yeah, a little, so?"

"Isn't that usually a sign that you're looking too long and too hard—I mean, literally? At those old photographs, this time."

"Probably."

"I know business is dead in the nursery right now, but we'll have a run of false spring days soon and when we do, please go back outside. Leave everything in that room the way it is. Nobody here will disturb any of it. Please, dear, give yourself a break. Call Josie and take the boys for a hike."

"Oh, Mom, you're dreaming. Those guys aren't going on any hikes with their mothers anymore. They don't want to be seen dead with us."

"Oh, that's always so frustrating," Elise said, glancing toward her teenage grandson. "In any case, please try to sleep in your own room. It's only two doors down, for goodness sake. Is the bed in that back room even properly made up?" 4

Chapter 2

A County Agent Makes a Call

The flower display in ghost-town Cliffport caught first-time south-bound travelers by surprise: rounding a bend seven miles below the San Mateo County line, the two-lane highway once known as the Coast Road widened for a thousand feet, where motorists' eyes were drawn toward a curious assemblage of some of the same plants they had been noticing—consciously or not—while driving at 50 and 60-plus MPH down Scenic Highway One. Some of the potted plants were always showing color—with the browns and grays of the old hotel, store, and livery cum service station's dilapidated western fronts as a backdrop—and a sandwich board alerted enthusiasts to their possible availability nearby:

Whenever some native or naturalized plant came into color around Cliffport, Katie dug up a specimen or two and stuck it into soil-filled planters improvised from a rusted wheelbarrow, a bathtub, a tire-testing trough, broken half-wine barrels, broken crockery—any neglected materials lying about—and added them to the display. Depending on the time of year, the informal showcase boasted the hot red pokers of kniphofia, the orange of tree aloes, the gentian blue towers of echium, the lavender sprays of statice, and—in August and September—the naked lady lilies, their enticing pink skirts trumpeting skyward atop snake-like stems. In seaside mist or refracted coastal sunlight, the rugged, unkempt assortment induced some passers-by into slowing down and charmed a few into following the directions on the homemade sign.

But the roadside ensemble that Donald called "Mom's Funkadelic Garden down on Highway One" also took on a life of its own. One Fourth of July, someone strung up red, white, and blue bunting, intact until the winter rains came, and someone else tied a banner of Tibetan prayer flags between two poles. As salt-saturated ocean winds shredded the thin cloth, a pair of plastic flamingoes flew in, made themselves a nest, and hatched a clutch, subsequent broods of smaller pink flamingoes expanding into a full flock. An array of freely donated whirligigs clacked ceaselessly, the wood weathering in place. In early winter, while checking for mail on Route One, Katie found enough money in her PAY HERE box to warrant lugging more fruit down from the persimmon tree, the pineapple guava bush, and Jan's dwarf Meyer lemon, all sold by the piece beneath the battered sheet metal canopy of the defunct Standard station. She gave up on keeping buckets stocked with spring's perishable cut flowers—too high-maintenance—but the self-service vegetable garden surplus sold well on its own. Over the years she never knew how often produce from the bushel baskets and wooden crates—or coins from the mangled metal box—were being pilfered by people operating off the honor system.

Davenport, Swanton, and Fern's longtime residents grew accustomed to spotting Elisabeth Lowrie's daughter tromping across the countryside with a shovel and a bucket, ripping some plant or other from the overgrown stump field or out of the ditches along Grade Road. Some honked hello; others merely laughed or shook their heads while observing their own homegrown primitive yanking wads of horsetail and calla lilies out of the soggy muck where—in wet season—Lower Steep Creek flooded the sea-level patch of brackish water before flowing into the culvert passing under the highway. But when Elise heard that her daughter was harvesting wild plants from the banks, gullies, and bluffs on the ocean side of the Coast Road, she worried aloud: Katie was not simply disregarding Southern Pacific Railroad's NO TRESPASSING signs; she was stealing private property. Katie shrugged, assuring her mother that no one noticed or if they did, cared. Besides, she argued, she never took all of any one stand of the abundant, naturally occurring plants: the tough, self-sustaining colonies continued to thrive, even after making multiple contributions to her nursery inventory. However, when Katie helped herself to plants established in the hillside surrounding the old Mackenzie Lodge across the meadow—clearly outside the Lowrie's property lines—Elise confronted her: she was, her mother said, blatantly trespassing on someone else's land and taking materials that rightfully belonged to whomever the eventual property owners might be; surely, if they knew or found out, the speculators would object to her digging up those plants. Katie again shrugged off her mother's concerns, reassuring her that she always left some mother plants in the ground. Besides, Katie claimed, no one was paying attention. When Katie proposed that her mother produce a line of simple, functional clay planters for sale in the nursery—maybe starting with a run of slab-built pots in plain terra cotta with tap-out drainage holes—some moral reluctance to her daughter's reckless transgression of boundaries kept Elizabeth Lowrie from cooperating, while her back and leg pain provided her a credible excuse and did prohibit her from seriously considering the work.

Since its 1967 purchase of the eighty-acre parcel surrounding the Lowries place on all sides, the Santa Cruz Buyer's Association had made no visible changes. Mother and daughter figured it was simply holding onto the land, paying the taxes while playing a wait-and-see game in the wildly escalating real estate market of California's Central Coast. So, emboldened by her resales of purloined plants, Katie continued to raid the beds of perennial plants naturalized around the collapsed lodge. She dug up Shasta daisies and brown-eyed Susans, dividing the clumps into smaller pieces that she threw into plastic and metal cans obtained from garden centers glad to be rid of the used containers which their customers insisted on returning. She cleaned slugs and snails from barrowloads of heart-shaped bergenia, hole-riddled hostas, false lily of the valley, and chunks of bear's breech, hauling them all back to her dirt pile, where she put them into one- and two-gallon size cans before rowing them out for recovery and regrowth. She asked whatever old-time plant people she met about when best to take cuttings from the stem tops and side shoots of the lodge's giant tree dahlias whose root systems, sheltered against the foundation of the derelict building, endured from decade to decade; she over-wintered those cuttings in containers of moist sand or else dug up root wads whole and divided them in the fall. She took a machete or a bowie knife to the unstoppable bush impatiens, slicing sections of the stems and laying the lengths down in shallow trenches full of rooting medium so that the nodes could sprout both roots and shoots. If Bill McGrath's bamboo species had been easier to extricate, she would have ravaged that expansive plantation too. [1]

Katie practiced a more systematic propagation of her three main cash crops; even with ample stock plants of dwarf dahlias, hardy fuchsias, and ivy geraniums on hand, she could hardly keep up with the spring and summer demand for her healthy, rooted, started plants. She had mastered the art of bringing her tuberous dahlias from cuttings to first bloom in less than six months, and she was rarely able to hold back her baby fuchsias for shifting up into larger-sized cans: when Ida Mackenzie's old bushes burst into color visible from the Coast Road, whatever was rooted in a four-inch pot blew out the door of her fuchsia hoop house or sold off the bed of her truck when she called on the garden centers. Barring a hard frost, her ivy geraniums festooned from prominent stumps on the lower hillside, advertising themselves all the way down to the whale watch turnout on Highway One, and established geraniums were generous with their offerings of semi-hard wood for cutting slips. Katie tried to have her all her hoop houses full—the no-name 4-inch potted plants tagged only by color—before their first blooming cycles began.

*

When the $1,450 refund from the Hillside Tower apartments arrived in March 1970, the Lowrie women purchased Donald some new clothes and footwear, and Katie bought her son an electric Fender guitar and a portable amplifier for his fifteenth birthday, on the condition that he run a grounded electrical cord to the barn and play it out there or she would pull the plug. The dentist enjoined Katie to take him to an orthodontist, who prescribed a retainer; the teen said he would refuse to wear it no matter what. Katie escorted her mother through a series of medical appointments and a battery of exams during which Elise's excruciating sciatica was traced to a prolapsed disc located between the third and fourth lumbar vertebrae and a partially herniated disc between the fourth and fifth. Surgical procedures and costs were discussed. Elisabeth Lowrie, aged 68, was left to contemplate the value of a back operation rated as providing only a fifty-percent chance of relief from chronic pain.

Katie paid Ross Stewart to install a high-line cable zigzagging above the stump field where—when not chained to a stake—Bamboo Billy the Goat could range, keeping the volunteer bushes chomped down and trees trimmed up. The fire hazard of freely growing grasses necessitated high weed mowing every spring, a job Katie usually hired out to someone in the Avila family workforce, while foisting upon her son the task of trimming the perimeter of the house and garden with a regular lawn mower. When the vet made a long overdue visit to trim the goat's hoofs, administer shots to the laying hens, and examine the two sheepdogs conforming to the line of the McLoughlin's former Aussies—leaving pills for aging Mother Merle and drops for Baby Blue

Eye's eyes—Katie sought the man's opinion of keeping sheep to manage the grasses growing tall across the uneven terrain. He suggested Baby Dolls: their wool was no good, and they were too small for meat, but they were relentless grazers who would subdue the weeds. However, they would be little help keeping down the blackberries, coyote bush, and poison oak—better leave those to Bamboo Billy—and sheep were prey to coyotes and Santa Cruz Mountains' packs of domestic and feral dogs marauding off leash, so she would have to pen them every night. Although the vet said he could equally picture pygmy goats leaping from stump to stump, they too would need warm, safe shelter come dark and during stormy weather; both sheep and goats would require some serious fencing. Katie reported that she had already witnessed several massacres of mourning doves' eggs and hatchlings after raccoons learned to manipulate the hook-and-eye catches on the former rabbit hutches attached to the barn. If she planned to reuse those cages, the vet advised, she must change out the old hardware for spring-lock latches, disinfect the wood, and replace the bedding material before letting any birds or hens turn those into new homes.

*

Whenever the Redwood Coast Nursery's pickup truck pulled into the parking lots of the independent retail nurseries in and around plant-crazy Santa Cruz—displaying its load of irresistible eye candy—the wholesale buyers always trusted their impulses, grabbed the best and marked up the price, knowing that their own shoppers would be indulging in their fancies shortly thereafter. Before any weekend—spring, summer, or fall—when fair-weather Saturday and Sunday shopping traffic guaranteed that the garden centers would turn a quick profit reselling Katie's affordable plants, the buyers were always happy to make on-the-spot purchases of her colorful, pest-free, robust dwarf dahlias, flowering ivy geraniums, Shasta daisies, and brown-eyed Susans. Katie was tempted to blow the last of the family's meager financial reserves on payment down for a new working vehicle that would support her growing business. Insisting that she was just looking, Katie fended off salesmen at dealerships in Santa Cruz and Half Moon Bay, where she had her eye on a 1970 long-bed Ford F-250 with 4-wheel drive. Plain styling would be fine; manual transmission and manually operated features would be optimal: more control of a simplified gearbox; less to break down; easier to repair. The retired Finnish metalworker, who used to work out of Fern Garage, could construct a tall, removable aluminum shell in which, on cross planks, she could shelve her plants for delivery in flats and cans.

When the Lowries' spending spree was over, the Redwood Coast Nursery again became the household's sole source of revenue, and they didn't know when the balance of Jan's cash estate would come into their hands or how much it would amount to. They could not afford to run out of water. The last droughty year, Katie had hooked up a hose to their potable water tank, but what if the well itself ran dry? After admitting that the millpond's overflow into Steep Creek could no longer be relied upon to deliver freshwater to her increasing inventory of plants, the Lowries decided to act in advance of dry season: if one of the two old redwood cisterns located along Upper Steep Creek could be repaired, pumps could be submersed into its stored water to help get through until winter rains bolstered the spring-fed reservoir again. Ross was engaged to shore up one cistern in exchange for four burnt-out hens, fresh vegetables from the garden, several hot lunches, and the leftovers she packed every evening for him to take back to his Ben Lomond Mountain home—wherever that was now. It took almost no cash to have him and his helper, Donald Duncan Lowrie, replace some warped wooden staves and tighten steel hoops while replacing corroded ones. After banging away in the woodland above the house, they finally ran surface lines down to the redwood holding tank and called it good. [2]

One wet December night, gazing out the picture window, Katie studied the far end of the driveway, where the Fleetside sat bogged down in mud; following the moonlit traces of the weighted beads of condensation streaking the pane, she didn't feel rich. The beat-up Ford—having performed honorable service over many years—kept

49

acting up, and repairs promised to cost more than the 1961 pickup was worth. Katie conjured up a time when she wouldn't be scraping its low-clearance bottom on the levee-like easement out to Grade Road or—for fear of getting stranded when driving out the next morning— she wouldn't have to park the Fleetside out-of-sight in Cliffport Town, loaded with budded and blooming plants, having to worry about merchandise being stolen overnight. Whenever the inheritance money arrived, she decided, she would shore up that driveway and buy a new truck too—unless her mother changed her mind and elected to undergo surgery, in which case there would be no funds to draw upon and no new truck. She pictured the garden center staffs delighted to see the North Coast's native daughter peddling her wares in a brand-new F-250 with Baby Blue Eye hanging out the passenger window, barking hello.

As February's onshore winds pruned the forest of its high dead-wood, Katie announced that if they could afford it, she also wanted to use the upcoming inheritance to build a greenhouse—a glasshouse with a gas furnace, evaporative cooling, crushed granite flooring, concrete aisles, and an automatic irrigation system with timed misters. She had taken long looks at plenty of greenhouses in South County, but she only needed one, and construction costs could be paid in full along the way. When renewing her license to sell nursery stock in Santa Cruz County, she anted up, applying for status as a producer, a wholesaler, and a retailer, no longer passing herself off as another hobby grower with some incidental sales. The Lowrie women agreed that with any monies left after the glasshouse was built, they would make repairs to the house itself. Why, what else should they do, being who they were? Was there a better place on earth for them to live?

———

Katie was squashing slugs with a trowel and using a pair of kitchen tongs to pick up snails, which she deposited in a plastic pail and tossed into the chicken coop when she was done.

"Hallo there."

She rose to her hands and knees, stepped to the central aisle, hiked up her jeans by two belt loops, and stood straight. "I didn't hear you drive in. The dogs must be in the house."

"*Jaja.* • Is Mister Lowrie perhaps around?"

Katie assessed the intruder from the ground up. He appeared to be around sixty and definitely overweight, with pink cheeks framing a red-complected nose. Pure white hair stuck out from under the hat that sat like an inverted, badly dented canvas bucket on his head. A thin white moustache conformed to the contour of his upper lip. He wore round-toe work boots and carpenter pants with a pair of pruning shears sticking out from one side-leg pocket. A goose down vest enclosed his barrel-like chest. Eyeglasses were suspended from a cord around his neck, and a compact, folding, handheld magnifying lens hung there from a lanyard. In one fleshy hand, he gripped a clipboard protected inside a soiled plastic sleeve. His heavy-lidded eyes looked almost closed as they searched for some wooden surface to rest the knuckles of his free hand, giving her the impression that he would gladly take the weight off his feet if the opportunity arose.

"What's the nature of your visit, Mister...?"

"Tuelling. Like working with a tool. Pieter Tuelling."

"I'm Katie Lowrie and by the way, there is no Mister Lowrie."

"I see. So ... I'm from the County Agricultural Commission."

"Yeah...?"

"They showed me your application, the girls in the office did."

"Oh?"

"So, they asked me to pay you a visit and all like that."

"They asked you or told you?"

Pieter Tuelling's smile exposed teeth neither straight nor white. "*Jaja*, you're right there." He pulled a wadded handkerchief from one vest pocket and rubbed the end of his nose. "They told me, that's it alrighty, sure."

"So, this is like an official visit. You want to take a look around, right? What part of County Ag did you say you're from?"

• *yes yes [pronounced "yaya"] (Dutch)*

"Nursery inspection."

"What are you inspecting for?"

"Oh, we help growers like you with pest control, vector control, weights and measures, all like that."

"You're not part of Co-op Extension...?"

"Oh no, Missus Lowrie. That is the University of California. I'm with the County of Santa Cruz."

"So, let me get this right. You're a regulator, right?"

"A regulator, *jaja*, if you say so. But there's more—"

"... I'm sure there is," she cut him off. "But what more do you need from me right now? Didn't my application make sense?"

"*Nee nee*, looks fine to me. But the girls in the office, they do the paperwork and all like that. Today I come to say hallo and see if you need perhaps more information, eh?"

"You sure picked a rainy day to make a field call."

He chuckled, scratching his white hair then reseating the formless hat toward the crown of his head. "*Jaja*, that's what I do. I make the field calls on rainy days, sure enough." His eyelids opened wider as he spotted a metal barstool tucked under her propagation table. "You mind if...?" he inquired with a pleading glance; she took a rag from her back pocket and wiped the moist dirt crumbs off the seat.

"There you go, Mister Regulator. Have a seat."

"Tuelling," he corrected her, settling down with a sigh. "Nursery folks call me Pieter, or Piet, if you like."

Katie opened a waist-high spigot until the piped water came trickling, then grabbed a dirty bar of hand soap off a ledge. After she had rinsed and dried her hands on a clean bandana, she hitched up her jeans again, leaned back against a post, crossed her rain boots at the ankles, took a pinch of sunflower seeds from an open package in her breast pocket, and began nibbling away, splitting the shells between the recessed incisors of her front teeth. "You sure don't seem to be in any big hurry to make your inspection."

"*Jaja*, that's right," he agreed, removing a square, hinged tin from one of his flapped shirt pockets. "You mind if—"

"... I don't care."

His pudgy fingertips with short-clipped nails got hold of a thin, dark brown cigarillo. "*Jaja*, I'm in no hurry now." He lit his little cigar with a strike-on-the-box wooden match. "Took me fifty-four years to get here, see? Now I got time."

"What's the deal?"

"*The deal?*" he echoed, puffing the tip to a glowing red ember while inhaling shallowly if at all.

"What do you need to come all the way out here for anyway?"

The county agent balanced his clipboard on the nearest dry surface and slowly scanned the worktable: jars and crocks stuffed with pencils and markers; dibbles, screwdrivers, pliers; dozens of whittled bamboo pegs; papers coated with specks of moist soil. A dollop of water from the ceiling struck his shapeless oilskin hat. "Tell the truth to you, I don't want to inspect anything, Missus Katie, but I got curious. Sure, twenty years on this job, I been all over North County, but I never knew any nursery up this way. I guess I been in the habit of turning around in Davenport, sure enough, or heading up that Bonny Doon Road."

Changing the crossing of her legs at her ankles, Katie continued to bring sunflower seeds to her mouth, one by one hulling them between her teeth then spitting out the husks or using long fingernails to flick them away.

"A little town is perhaps up that Grade Road, eh?"

"Fern's six miles up, if you want to call it a town."

"*Jaja, Fern, dat es het,* that's the one. That Grade Road must be the only paved road between Aptos and San Mateo County line I never drove on ... if it's paved."

"It used to be paved all the way through the mountains. It was one of the old ways to get to Saratoga."

"One of the old long ways, I bet you."

"Oh yeah. Nowadays you'd need a bulldozer to get through to the other side. County stopped maintaining it twenty-five years ago. So, is that what you do for a living, driving all over Santa Cruz County checking out nurseries?"

"*Jaja*, from Pajaro River to ... well, all the way up to Cliffport now," he added, grinning as he checked the end of his burning cigar. "Sometime I get a call from a nursery. Sometime the office gets a call. Sometime the shipment comes from out of the state and got to be held up, Missus Katie, all like that."

"You mean quarantined?"

"At garden centers and nurseries, *jaja*. At post office, the UPS. But most the time, I just talk to the nursery folk."

"Enforcing rules and regs, you mean."

"*Jaja*, there's that. Say for instance some peoples in some place I never hear of called Cliffport applies for a license to produce and sell nursery stock—*dat is goed!* So, I got to go see they got the information they need. Three, four more months more, I'm the county ag agent what got to talk to those peoples."

"Peoples like me, is what you mean. And I guess we have to talk to you, as we enter the quote system unquote."

"Some peoples, they like to talk to me." He took a final puff upon his little cigar, looked about for an ashtray, then just dropped it to the dirt floor. "Okay," he announced, lodging his brow-line eyeglasses on the bridge of his nose and retrieving his clipboard. "Now I inform you about resources." His swollen fingers worked open the stiff flap of the plastic envelope and pulled out a handful of pamphlets and bulletins. "Take these, please, then Pieter Tuelling can tell those girls in the office he did a good job, eh?"

She took hold of the papers and glanced at the titles: *Specifications for Securely Storing and Handling Controlled Substances; Protocol for Sale of Seed by Weight; Registration and Calibration of Certified Scales; Proper Labeling of Plants at Retail.* She turned the bundle upside down and slipped it under a transistor radio that sat on a nearby shelf. "Thanks, I guess."

"You welcome. I seen so many mom and pop operations go up, Missus Katie. And I seen so many mom and pop operations go down. I want to see yours go up, sure, and stay up."

"Well, this is a mom operation, Mister Tuelling. A mom and son operation, sometimes. And the Redwood Coast Nursery is going up."

"That's good, Missus Katie, that's real good."

"Know what else? I'm going to build a greenhouse someday, a real glasshouse."

"*Oh ja?* That's swell!"

"I suppose you'll be all over the construction details on that one."

"*Nee nee,*" he replied, wiping his nose with his balled, soiled handkerchief. "That's the building department. I got nothing to do with that monkey business. I'm for the plants. The plants and ... the peoples...." He paused, catching her eye and blinking twice. "Building, labor relations, taxes, all like that? That's not my job, *Godzijdank.*" •

"As for labor around here, you're looking at it." She glanced back to where she had been hunting down the mollusks hiding underneath the two-by-six planks of fir holding down the polyethylene sheeting along the inside perimeter of the hoop house.

"Do you mind if I ask you perhaps one question, Missus Katie?"

"What's that?"

"Why you don't get a big bag of snail bait for those sonsaguns? You don't need any permit for the metaldehyde."

"I don't want to be spreading poisons around, okay? We've got chickens pecking everywhere and two dogs to keep alive and I don't know how many guinea fowl and half-wild cats that really aren't ours. I've got kids running all over this place."

"You raising goats too?"

"No, not those kids. There's only one Billy goat and I keep him on a chain. I meant children. We run a music day camp for kids in summer."

"But you got to keep those chickens out of here or else...." He waved toward the many trays of young, started plants causing the warped wooden table boards to sag.

"I can keep the chickens out of the hoop houses but lots of birds pass through in spring and fall and some always manage to get stuck in here. Hummingbirds are always zipping around. No, no poisons."

"And white fly on those geraniums and the bud worm? And aphis on those fuchsias? The mildew on those dahlias?"

• *Thank God (Dutch)*

"You know something? I only release clean plants, okay? Ask anybody. Come spring and summer, plants blow out of here so fast they don't have time to pick up pests. All I ever use is a little horticultural oil and soap."

"*Ach*, that's good, Missus Katie, that's real good to hear."

"Yeah? I guess most everybody you meet is into Malathion and all that other stuff."

"*Jaja*, most everybody. Malathion and worse. But me, I was raised like you just said: oil, soap, Bordeaux mix...."

"Where was that you were raised?"

"In the Nederlands."

"I thought I heard a German accent."

He flinched. "Dutch, not Deutsch. Is a Dutch accent. No German."

The rainfall had ceased, but a steady stream of water drops coursed along a bow in the PVC piping overhead until it met a main joint then dripped right between them into a depression in the ground filled with potshards.

"That's some nice Kenilworth ivy you got growing under there," he said, gazing toward the foliage enwrapping a wooden table leg and spreading out like a mat below the bench.

"Is that what that's called?"

"*Cymballaria muralis, jaja.*"

"It's pretty but kind of weedy when it gets up onto the tables and into my pots."

"I know plenty old timers up the San Lorenzo Valley would like that pretty weedy sonagun in their rock walls and shady corners. Old World people, like me," he added with a grin, a brief opening of his eyelids showing baby blue irises. "You can put that up in pots and sell it, see? There's some advice from your county ag agent for you." He chuckled. "And that there Labrador violet you got over there under that table, that's a good one too. Good for certain butterflies. You go ahead, put that one up and sell that one too, sure."

"If the snails and slugs don't get to it first," Katie remarked.

"*Jaja*, I let you go now," he responded, promptly tucking his clipboard under one arm. "I let you get back to work."

Shoving open the flimsy door, she exited first and spotted his light green, government-issue Ford Bronco pickup parked in the turnaround, the county's circular blue-and-green seal painted on its door. Standing side-by-side, they observed the loud, staggered entry of a band of Stellar jays into the branches of the centrally located oak out of which a dozen juncos immediately dispersed. As the jays reassembled in a sycamore, loud splats of water dropped onto the tree's fallen crinkled leaves.

"So, how long before I get my nursery license, officially?"

"I have no idea. That is *bureaucratie*. Anyway, you got six months from when they mail it out, eh?"

"Six months for what?"

"To come into compliance with—"

Her laughter stopped him short. "So, you really are a regulator after all," she declared, almost slapping him on the back but thinking better not to.

"If you say so, it must be so," he replied, smiling and exposing some of his imperfect teeth. "But only *drie, vier* more months, eh? June 31st, 1971."

"That your last day?"

"*Jaja*, that's it, sure."

Katie observed the man's upper eyelids lift as he faced in the direction of the ocean, contemplating the sweep of darkening skies.

"Do you have a business card or something?" she asked.

"That I got, that I still got. "

She followed him down to his truck—his gait surprisingly spry for a larger, heavy, older man—where he jammed the clipboard between the narrow dash and the flat windshield and forced open the glove compartment with the tip of his closed shears. While he rummaged in the clutter, a green, plastic, pint-size flask in the driver's door pocket caught her eye: she made out its label—*Zee Wind Mondwater*—before he passed her a plain white card printed with his name, title, multiple phone and fax numbers, and the county seal. As they stood under the evergreen oak's wide-spread canopy, she looked up and made contact with the sky-blue eyes partially unveiled between their lids.

"Too bad I won't be here to see your glasshouse go up, Missus Katie, but I wish you the best in your nursery business. You got the makings of a real plantsman, you do."

"A plantswoman," she corrected him, almost patting him lightly on his forearm.

He furrowed his wiry white eyebrows then chuckled. "*Jaja*, now I see," he said. "A real plantswoman, like you say, that's it alrighty. Now you got to get you a good advisor on taxes and all like that. You got to get you a resale license too if you not charging tax to those ones what call themselves gardeners and horticulturists and all like that. You make them show you their C-27's, see? Make them fill out a Franchise Tax Card to keep on file. Why then—"

"... there you go again, Inspector!" she interrupted him, laughing. "Always warning me about something!"

"I'm not warning you, Missus Katie," he protested. "I'm informing you."

"Yaya," she uttered quietly, sticking her palms in her jeans' back pockets and grinning while stepping back from his truck.

When he heard her making light of his speech, he paused before cracking a smile revealing his ill-aligned, yellow teeth. "Informing," he reiterated, "not warning." Chuckling, seemingly pleased with his own rhyme, he ducked his head and dropped backwards into the driver's seat.

"I was just kidding," Katie apologized.

"*Nee nee*," he volunteered, "I'm one mean old man. You ask all the folks what I know for twenty years. *Oh ja, es de duivel, dat Pieter Tuelling!*"

His smile faded as he looked past her and beyond the upper meadow, gazing to the top of the hillside where the oak and bay woodland gave way to redwood forest rising up and over the first ridge until his sight settled on the taller treetops trending in the direction of Chapel Grove. He seemed to disregard her altogether as he spoke: "*Nee nee*, I'm not worried one bit about this Redwood Coast Nursery."

Katie shivered as goose bumps registered her recognition that the eccentric, veteran, foreign-born field man had just pronounced his blessing upon her property, her project, and her person. "Hey, wait!" she said. "I mean, please, Mister...."

"Tuelling."

"Mister Tuelling."

"Or Pieter," he restated, as if introducing himself for the first time. "You call me Pieter, eh?"

They made eye contact again and Katie regained her composure. "Do you know anything about weeds?"

"*Jaja*, I know the weeds, sure. Why you ask?"

Katie bolted, scrambling down the bank into the driveway ditch where she sliced off a handful of greenery from amidst a tangle of rusted iron and held it up in the air. "What's this stuff here?"

"That one?" he responded, leaning his elbow on the windowsill of his cab door. "What nutgrass you got there, eh? Bring that sonagun over here."

She clambered her way back up the gravel bank and plopped the wet sample down on the snub-nosed hood of his box-like truck. He got out of the car and adjusted his glasses, using his loupe to examine one leafy stalk. "Is *Cyperus*, sure, sure, but yellow ... purple ... *ensulentus* ... *rotundus*...?" He dislodged his rumpled hat from the crown of his head then recentered it after scratching his scalp. "Which one is this, eh?"

"You tell me. I can't stop that sucker from spreading."

"This I find out for you, Missus Katie. But you listen to me now. You cannot sell nutgrass, not yellow or purple. You understand me? You can't get rid of it, I know, I know, but you cannot dig this up from the ground and put it in any old can for sale."

He scanned some nursery stock rowed out in level gravel beds cut into the slope above the meadow.

"So, you can see what I've been up to, huh?"

"*Jaja*, I can see. And when I saw that assemblage at the gas station down thataway," he said, tilting his head toward the ocean highway, "I said *O boy! Now what we got going on here?* Okay, I go now," he concluded, stuffing the greenery under some collapsed wet cardboard in his truck's short bed. "I find out what you got growing there and I let you know, sure enough."

"Thank you."

"It will give me a reason to come back before I hang up these," he said, tossing his Felcos into the clutter on the passenger seat before fitting himself all the way in behind the steering wheel and closing the door.

"Do. I mean, please, come back."

He rolled down his window and looked right at her. "What'd you say?"

"When you find out about that stuff," she said, lowering her voice, "please come back."

The county agent winked both eyes twice then faced forward, his meaty hands gripping the wheel, but he didn't start the engine. "You know something, Missus Katie ... I got to tell you something now." He paused and heaved a sigh, still avoiding her eyes. "My wife, Ellen ... 'Drika' I called her ... she's gone now. But Drika and me, we used to picnic at that Waddell Beach up that-away. We used to walk up that creek...."

"Waddell Creek's only about five, six miles up the coast from here."

"I know that, I know. Maybe that's why I been turning around in Davenport the last two, three years, eh?"

"Is that when your wife died?"

"*Drie jaar geleden, jaja.* • Is okay," he barked, shaking his head as if to dismiss any further thoughts and turning the key. "I go write up a great big long field report and send you a copy."

"No, don't! Don't send it, I mean. Just bring it back with you ... when you come."

• *Three years ago, yes (Dutch)*

"I just joking you, Missus Katie. I wrote enough sonsagun reports. *Nee nee*, I tell the girls everything's okay in Cliffport California and that's that. But I come back, sure. Say, do you think it's going to rain?" he added as the first fat drops smacked his windshield.

"You think?" she replied, turning up her collar and looking up into the windblown oak.

He raised one hand goodbye, cranked his window closed, turned on the headlights and wipers, and eased the Bronco onto the lane leading out to Grade Road.

During lunch with her mother, while recounting the inspector's visit, Katie regretted she had treated him as a governmental pest, and Elise commented that, from what her daughter relayed, she thought he sounded like a man weary of his work, a sad widower, and a rather kind, patient person with a bit of mischievous twinkle left in his eye. Katie asked her mother if she knew what *mondwater* meant; Elise thought that the word was probably related to *Mundwasser* in German—mouthwash in English—but that was only an educated guess.

*

Baby Blue Eye barked twice; Katie paused on the railroad ties leading uphill.

"You put down gravel!" Pieter Tuelling called out after turning off the Bronco and opening the door.

"Didn't make a dent in it," she shouted back, shifting her flat-brimmed straw hat farther back on her head, crossing her arms, and contemplating the quirky county agent's ascent. He was wearing an unlined duck canvas jacket and a checkered shirt with a slot in the left breast pocket for his pencil. Horn-rimmed reading glasses and a loupe hung around his neck. Coming level with her, he touched the narrow visor of the flat, leather newsboy cap he sported on his white-haired head and bent forward to pet the dog between her ears as—wagging her rump—Baby Blue Eye sniffed at the return visitor's scuffed boots and frayed pant cuffs.

"I'd lay twenty times that much gravel, but we don't even own that road."

"No?" he replied, catching his breath.

"Our property only goes to about the far drip line of the oak. You have to be careful driving in and out or even your little rig'll end up in the ditch."

"*Jaja*," he declared and left off scratching the top of the dog's skull. "So, Missus Katie, I found out about that sonagun nutgrass down there."

"Yeah?"

"Is the yellow one. Is a bad weed, sure enough."

"I could've told you that much, doc."

The man bobbed as if dodging a near-miss to his chin.

"No, no," Katie hastened to add, "I mean, thank you. I appreciate it, I do." She tried to get him to make eye contact. "I mean it, really ... Pieter. And I want to say I'm sorry I was so bitchy last time." Now he was looking right at her. "I was. You caught me on a bad day, I guess."

He smiled. "*Jaja*. I been thinking that, Missus Katie. We got off on the wrong feet there. I been thinking that too."

"Well, I'm not killing snails today so if you want to come along while I let some fresh air into the hoop houses, you can do your snoopin' at the same time. Just kidding again," she added, then noticed him fidgeting with a piece of paper rolled up in his hand. "Is that for me?"

"*Jaja*, sure," he said, passing her the page. "Ever seen one of these?"

She glanced at small print typed in multiple columns on the two-sided sheet. "What is it?"

"*Nee nee*, you got to hold onto that," he insisted, refusing to take it back from her.

"Why?"

"That's the noxious weed list for Santa Cruz County. Your county ag agent got to give it to you, eh?"

She grinned, folded the page lengthwise, and stuck it into her back pocket. "Guess I got to keep it then."

"And this," he added, presenting her with a leaflet taken from one of his jacket's outside pockets. "This one is about eradication of that nutgrass. It says you can get rid of it, but I don't know. I seen farmers walk away from fields when that sonagun shows up."

"Thanks again." She stuck the leaflet into her other back pocket. "What are you, a walking library?" she added as he pulled a third piece of literature from his jacket's other outside pocket: a booklet with an annotated list of government publications available. "Anything else?"

"*Dat is alles,* I'm done."

"Then come on," Katie said, starting to secure all three documents under a rock then, after shooting a glance toward the cloudy sky, lifting the tail of her outer shirt and inserting the printed matter against the small of her back. "I'll look at them later, Pieter, I will. Now let's see if the squirrels got in again."

After she had dragged open the doors at each end of the three poly houses, they reached the northwest trending rise of the hillside's southwest facing slope. He agreed it would be wise to site her future greenhouse right there and began a discourse on glasshouse design, rattling off specifications for heating and cooling systems; typical floor plans and optimal ratios of widths to lengths to heights; equipment, models, brand names. He encouraged her to overdesign for ventilation, insisting that inadequate heat release was the most frequent flaw in greenhouse design and ought not to be overlooked. And he launched into a lecture on irrigation systems for inside the glasshouse and out. "You don't want to be spending the rest of your life at the end of a hose."

"So, you are an educator," she said, "not just a cop." She detected a blush rising to his already rosaceous face. "Come on, I'm just teasing you again. I can't help it. I like you. Come see the rest of my place or don't you have time?"

"What's all that over there?" His gaze had fixed on the lodge.

"What about it? That's what's left of the Mackenzie Lodge."

"*Nee nee nee,* I mean all that bamboo there."

"That's bamboo, for sure."

"Does that grove belong to you, Missus Katie?"

"Nah. That's the neighbor's property, whoever the neighbor is."

"Can we have a look-see?"

"Sure. You'll see where I source some of my special product line."

As they meandered through the overgrown bamboo, he asked her if it would be permissible for him to return—before or after his retirement—in the company of an officer of the Northern California Chapter of the American Bamboo Society. He certainly did not want to jeopardize the Lowries' relations with the rightful owners, but a bamboo enthusiast ought to have a look at the collection. "Even I can see there's the sooty, the smoked, the tiger, all like that. Those there are some very special bamboos, Missus Katie."

"I don't even know who the rightful owners are. Some real estate speculators."

"Well, would you look at that!" he declared, stopping in his tracks and staring toward the ground as they emerged from the grove.

"What is it, a snake, where? Have to watch out for baby rattlers this time of year. Blue, you come here!"

The sheepdog came to Katie's whistle and—ears perked—went down on her haunches, watching as the man picked something from the grass. "Here there, little one," Pieter Tuelling whispered, cradling something in one hand. "Is a baby possum been separated from its Mama." He stepped over to where Katie's legs were straddling the dog; a pink, hairless, recently born possum squirmed in the man's white palm. "It can't open its mouth. See where its lips are still all stuck together? Poor fellow's been evicted from Mama's pouch."

"Wow," Katie murmured. "Weeded out."

He rolled the tiny, close-eyed creature into Katie's open hands and withdrew his pocket knife, opening its single blade. "We're going to give this little guy a fighting chance, we are."

"What are you going to do to it?"

"Is a lost cause but we going to try."

He slipped the point of his blade into a crack between the joined lips and with one swipe opened the pointed snout. Pocketing his knife, he took the possum back into his hands. "Now you go on home to Mama," he whispered, checking to see that Katie's calves had a firm squeeze on the dog before setting the creature back into the grass. "Go on now, you poor little exile you."

Pieter accepted her invitation to a mug of coffee reheated in a pan over a camp stove at her tented workstation. Lighting up a little dark cigar, he drifted inside the door of the nearest poly house where an L-shaped counter, fashioned from plywood on sawhorses, supported the vintage brass cash register which had once rung out in Cliffport Store. Katie explained how she had hauled the contraption up from the Guild's vacated gallery on Route One; the bell no longer rang, and a rusted NO SALE tab remained permanently stuck, but its till drawer could be tugged open and jammed closed with a hefty shove. Nibbling on her sunflower seeds, she watched the man poke about her informal display of nacreous abalone shells, knob-cone pinecones adhering to a broken branch, and raptor flight feathers stuck upright in a bowl of sand. He seemed drawn toward three flat-bottomed glass penny jars holding bulk seeds, permanent ink marking the metal lids of each: RED VALERIAN; POOR MAN'S ORCHID; ROSE CAMPION.

"I'll be," he mused, sipping his mug, puffing on his dark tobacco. "Where'd you get these?"

"Those seeds get me. Those three plants sprout up like weeds around here. I hoe out the plants after I collect the seeds, but they keep coming back."

"So, you sell these seeds too, *ja?*"

"Yaya," she replied. "Is that against the law? The plants come up everywhere. That's what folks like. They're so easy to grow, you just throw the seeds out on the ground. All you have to do is press them under your foot, stand back, and they're up."

"Is this Campion the *coronaria* or *chalceldonica?*" he mused aloud, switching his tiny cigar to the hand holding his mug, donning his eyeglasses, sticking his paw into the jar, and rubbing a pinch of seeds between finger and thumb. The man's thin white moustache and wiry white eyebrows changed shape, following the pursing of his lips and furrowing of his brow.

She cracked some shells between her teeth. "Beats me ... *Inspecteur T.*"

Replacing the lid, he lifted a metal measuring spoon. "And this here is how you sell the seeds, by the spoon?"

"Twenty-five cents a scoop. Is that illegal too? Now don't tell me they're noxious weeds too," Katie moaned, rolling her eyes and placing her hands akimbo on her narrow hips.

"*Jaja*, in a field of Brussels sprouts, in a field of artichokes, these are weeds. But in a shady garden along the San Lorenzo River, in a country garden? *Impatiens balfouri*—nice! But, Missus Katie. You could get more money for these. Twenty-five cents a spoon, you giving them away."

"You're probably right there," Katie replied, retrieving her mug of lukewarm coffee. "But all I do is spread a tarp under the plants when the pods start popping on a hot day. If there's no breeze, I use some newspaper. They're free to me. This coffee's kind of cold, sorry about that."

He lifted his mug, took a sip, smacked his lips, and smiled. "Bitter and cold. That's how us real coffee drinkers like it, eh? But what about this *Centranthus*?"

"The valerian?"

"The bees and the butterflies, oh, they love that *Centranthus rubra*. But you know that's not *Valerian officinalis*...?"

"I think I learned that from my mom once. So, that's another freebie. That stuff'll grow upside down from a rock wall. I just put brown paper bags around the flower heads when they start going to seed, or cheesecloth if I have any around. One out of ten blooms white but I never know which ones, so I don't try to sort them out."

"Twenty-five cents a scoop," he mumbled. "That's one good deal. But you're losing money, Missus Katie."

"Maybe I should get a calibrated scale, huh?"

"Aha, you didn't burn those pamphlets after all!"

"Not yet. I read them ... most of them."

They descended to his parked vehicle; Baby Blue sensed the onset of a ride and positioned herself by the tailgate until the dog's mistress ordered her to back away and sit. Katie wondered what the curious man was taking from the cab and stepped into the shade, letting her straw hat fall back, suspended from a cord passing under her chin.

"I try to help good peoples stay in the nursery business," he said, handing her a much-read hardcover book with a dogeared dust cover; his blue eyes twinkled beneath their upper lids' overlapping skin. "Looks like your Redwood Coast Nursery is going to be my swan song, so ... that is for you, Missus Katie."

"For me ... to keep, you mean...?"

"*Jaja*, to keep. To read, to study, to learn."

She wiped her hands on her jeans and opened to the title page. "1936. That's the year I was born."

"*Jaja....*"

She stood speechless, puzzled by this sort of man, one who stopped to doctor a deformed newborn possum, who stood still stroking the crown of a baby redwood, and who bequeathed to her a book that had obviously meant so much to him. Whoever he was, he was getting into the Bronco and preparing to drive off.

"Thank you!" she burst out, rushing to stand beside his window. "Thanks ... for everything."

"You welcome, Missus Katie."

"You'll be coming back with that bamboo guy, right?"

"*Jaja*, that's right, I do that. But I got to call him first."

"Well, you know how to get here, and you can come back anytime, on official business or not. If that sign's standing up down on the highway, I'm open for visitors, okay? Just do come back ... okay?"

"I do that," he said, winking both eyes and patting the backs of both her hands that had found their way to the frame of the lowered open window. "I do that, Missus Katie, sure enough. I come back."

He turned on the ignition, put the transmission in gear, and slowly steered down the center of the elevated lane on his way back out to Grade Road.

*

On the ag agent's third visit, Baby Blue Eye didn't bother to bark and even led Pieter T. up the path to where Katie was mixing a batch of planting soil on top of a four-by-eight plywood sheet. She smiled hello and draped her wrists atop the shovel's D-grip wooden handle. "You're on a postman's holiday, coming up here on a Saturday."

He chuckled. "*Jaja*, a postman's holiday, that one I know."

"What's that you're driving today, a Dodge Dart?"

"That's a Dart alrighty." He neutralized his face. "Was my wife's...."

Katie let the square head shovel drop across the mound, freed her hands, and hoisted her jeans higher up around her middle. "What was her name again, Pieter?"

"I called her 'Drika.' Ellen was her name."

"That's right."

"Short for Hendrika."

"Oh...."

Even on his day off, he wore work boots and pants, carried holstered shears in one leg pocket, and dangled the reading glasses and folded magnifying glass around his neck. But he wore no vest or jacket, carried no clipboard, and had no hat on his head; his longish white hair moved in the breeze, and he periodically brushed it back with a big hand.

"You must be getting pretty close to retirement. Or has it already happened?"

"*Nee nee.* Six more weeks, Missus Katie. *Één, twee, drie, etcetera. Zes.*"

"You're a short-timer then. Hey, I want to thank you for that book. I've been reading it. Is that Roundtree still alive?"

"Rowntree," he corrected her.

"Oh, well, I was close," she said, idling the sole of her boot on the lip of the shovel's scoop so that its long handle teetered over the dirt pile. "If it were easy to remember, I guess everybody would've heard of her. But really...." She paused, searching for eye contact. "Thank you. I can learn a lot from her, for sure."

Pieter Tuelling explained that the man from the Bamboo Society was traveling from Marin in a separate vehicle and should arrive at any moment. They would be on their own, she apologized: between customers, she needed to build up enough mix for a landscaping firm's order of plants to be shifted up into gallons ASAP. He encouraged her to keep at it and, as if to underscore his point, put on a pair of drugstore sunglasses and turned his back, lighting up a small cigar. Yet soon enough he was again observing her work and seemed to be studying the recipe: two shovelfuls of native soil dug from the hillside cut behind her; one shovelful from a pile of finished compost hauled to the site; half a shovelful of the sand spilling out onto a tarp from a contractor's wheelbarrow left tipped on its side. After the twelfth shovelful, she turned the ingredients then tamped the mound to shore up its conical shape.

"So, what do you think of the Redwood Coast Nursery's basic planting mix, *Inspecteur*?" she asked, leaning on her shovel again. "Off the record, of course. Any recommendations?"

"That looks real good, Missus Katie," he replied, replacing his sunglasses in a soft pouch with a pocket clip and bringing his smudged reading glasses to this face, looking closer at the piles.

"But ... what?"

"Well ... have you got some bone meal ... maybe a little bone meal...?

"I think I have a bag somewhere, yeah."

"And what about oak leaf mold? Aha!" he exclaimed, raking off a handful of leaf litter from the top crust of the closest soil bank. "This here looks ready to go," he proclaimed, crumbling the material underfoot. "And you sure got plenty of it!" he proclaimed, letting his eyeglasses fall to the end of their cord as he swept his arm toward the upland. "Why, wait a minute! That was one big tree there, sure...." he said, resting his gaze on the hillside.

"That oak went down in the Christmas storm of '64."

"I know that sonagun Christmas storm. *Jaja*, I know that one alrighty."

"That was the biggest oak on the whole place," Katie stated.

A pearly-white car drove in from Grade Road and parked behind P. Tuelling's two-door sedan.

"What the heck kinda car is that?"

"That's Leonard's Volvo Sport B-18. That's a Sveedishah auto, Missus Katie. Oh boy, he likes his automobiles. You just ask him. Okay, I go say hallo."

"I'm keeping on with this cuz'—"

"... *jaja*, we two big boys. I show him the bamboos and we see you later on. Ho! Leonard! Up here!" he hollered, scampering down the path. "No worry, Leonard! I'm coming! That dog's fine! That dog doesn't bite."

*

She could see that Pieter T.'s associate seemed uncomfortable with her ramshackle operation and, when introduced, she knew by his handshake and his manicured fingernails that he was no nurseryman, at least not as she understood the term. His hard-sole moccasin loafers—worn without socks and tied with a bow—and his pleated khaki shorts suggested to her that Leonard Svenson was accustomed to a more refined form of plantsmanship than the applied horticulture which was her practice and livelihood.

With a native or acquired affectation of British enunciation, the nervous man's chatter took off at a quick, cleanly clipped pace. Katie sensed wholesale pretention and felt repelled. He sported a spotless Breton fisherman's cap like the ones she had seen real fishermen wear in Nova Scotia. His round, wire-rimmed John Lennon glasses seemed as costumed as his fly fisher's vest with its zippers, snaps, and flaps. Waxing rhapsodic over Bamboo Bill McGrath's plantation, the specialist described species and cultivars as variegated, satiny smooth, golden, pale green, inky black; since childhood, she had known them as beautiful beyond words and was turned off by his recitation in Latin, Greek, and Japanese.

"Don't worry, Katie," Pieter interjected. "I don't know exactly what he's talking about either."

"But, Pieter!" the visitor protested, wringing his hands. "You saw them! Good Lord, man! Do you know what that colony of black bamboo alone is worth, dead or alive?"

The off-duty county employee assured Katie that he had already explained to his companion that the groves belonged to someone else. "*N'est-ce pas*, Leonard?"

"Yes, yes, but to whom, to whom? Do you think ... just for a moment...?" he hesitated, holding a forced smile for a moment longer than usual. "What I mean is, do you think.... Well, let us just for one little moment imagine that as a representative of the American Bamboo Society I were to contact the property owners, hmm? What if that were to come to pass? Why, they may not even be aware of what an exceptional collection they have acquired. But I know weavers, cabinetmakers, furnituremakers—oh, so so many artisans throughout Northern California no no no, up and down all the Pacific States— artists and craftsmen who would die for this material." He shot his eyes back and forth between his auditors, awaiting a response. "But I'm afraid you don't really understand. Something like this just doesn't happen that often. If only to harvest a culm of each as a sample and leave the rest of —"

"... Leonard," Pieter Tuelling interrupted, as if addressing a misbehaving child.

"But, Pieter! Well I know, I know.... But isn't some party or other already helping herself to the plants over there ... hmm?" He paused. "By any chance, Miss Lowrie, by any chance does either that mattock or that spade left on the old back porch over there belong to you?"

She wanted to run for cover from his last fast-flashed, fast-erased smile. "It's Ms. Lowrie!" she declared, lowering her head, realigning her grip on the shovel's handle, and focusing her attention upon tidying up the mound's circular base.

Leonard Svenson closed his gaping mouth, dismissed himself without further ado, and headed down the railroad-tie steps.

"Be right with you, Leonard!" Pieter T. called out before clearing his throat. "I'm sorry, Missus Katie. Leonard's ... okay ... once you get to know him."

"No thanks."

"He's supervisor of the air traffic controllers for a large amount of air space in the Bay Area and, well, I guess he's used to calling shots, eh? He does know a lot of folks in the plant trade and—"

"... I'm sure he does. But like I said, no thanks, Pete."

"Okay, okay, I understand. So. I guess we'll be going now. We're headed to that roadside stand to see if they have any Olallieberries left if—"

"... they did last week but they're all gone by now. Anyway, you have to know who to ask for those Olallieberries."

He smiled. "*Jaja*, there's that. Oh, did you receive the permit papers? I signed my part right away."

"I got 'em."

"That's good."

They both turned toward the sound of a slammed car door; Leonard was apparently sulking in his Volvo.

"So, will I be seeing you again, Pieter, or will your replacement be checking to see if I'm ... in compliance?"

"That's right, that's right, they got my replacement now. Her name is … *wat es het…*? Nancy, Nancy Borkowski. But you may not see her for a while."

"That's fine by me but … I'll miss you, Pieter. I will." They exchanged a glance then averted their eyes. "So, does this Nancy B. go by the book or is she more … you know, laid back like you?"

"Lazy you mean. *Jaja*," he chuckled, "I got lazy."

"You got open-minded is what you got."

"I don't know her. She may be a stickler or—"

"… oh great! A real nursery cop!"

"Oh, I'm sure she can give you good ideas about your glasshouse when you get that built. And don't you worry. I will tell Leonard not to bother you. I'm sorry, Missus Katie. That man just likes to get his way."

"Who doesn't?" Katie posited. "I'm a nice person too, so long as I get my way."

He pulled the memo pad and a ballpoint pen from his pocket, wrote down a phone number, tore out the page, and gave it to her. "That's my home telephone, Missus Katie. You call me with any questions, see? If you like…."

"I just might. I mean, I will. Thank you … Pieter."

Tempted to embrace his barrel chest, she instead extended her dirty hand; he showed no hesitation shaking it with his own calloused mitt. "If an old ag agent can help this Redwood Coast Nursery grow, you let him know. But you got to call me, sure."

They released their mutual grip. He blinked his blue eyes then hid them behind the cheap sunglasses and descended the path; halfway down, alarmed by a screeching noise from the distant barn, he stopped. "What was that?" he called back uphill.

"I guess my son's waking up!" Katie cried out, shaking her head under the brimmed straw hat.

Pieter Tuelling looked at his wristwatch then over to the barn then back up at her.

"That's one loud guitar!"

"You're telling me! I don't know what I was thinking when I got it for his birthday."

"He's learning how—"

"... to raise all kinds of hell is what he's learning!"

They stood looking at each another, listening to a shattered, jagged, fragmented curtain of amplified sound, and shook their heads at the same time before he proceeded downhill, and she resumed shoveling her planting mix into a barrow. 3

Chapter 3

New Rules of the Game

KT   Hey, leave that on!

DD   Mom, if you play this album one more time—

KT   ... one more time, what?

DD   You're wearing out the grooves! You say I'm obsessed with my music but look at you. BLUE? These songs are all so sappy.

KT   There's not a trace of rock 'n roll in there?

DD   Why doesn't she just slit her wrists and record herself dying?

KT   You should hear yourself talk, DD. That's so sick. You don't have to appreciate my taste in music, but you don't have to be cruel.

DD   You dig Joni Mitchell. I dig Van Halen and Jimmy Page and Jimi Hendrix. I dig Jim Morrison—

KT   ... of The Doors? I hate to see creeps like him become heroes for young people.

DD   Creeps like who?

KT   Jim Morrison.

Silence

DD   Mom, is it true I remember sitting in your lap in a rocking chair and you singing *Danny Boy*?

KT   You remember that?

DD   I didn't know who you were singing to. *"Danny."*

KT   I was singing to you, silly. Probably trying to get you to sleep.

DD   That's like the first time I remember hearing you sing. How old was I?

KT   I don't know, two, three. It must've been before I went back East so you weren't three-and-a-half yet.

DD   Wow.

KT   That's the rocking chair in your grandma's room, Donald.

DD   It's that's old...?

———

Katie hired Jim Parker to design and construct the glasshouse and, while applying for the building permit, he learned that the Santa Cruz Buyer's Association had sold the surrounding land to an entity called YO-MIZO-SATA, INTERNATIONAL Ltd. In further conversation with Señor Morales at Coast Ranch Realty in Half Moon Bay, Katie found out that a number of undeveloped properties in the region were being off-loaded onto unwary foreign investors. The popular will to create a new regulatory body mandated to enforce coastal zone conservation had gained enough political momentum—locally, regionally, statewide—that it seemed to stakeholders with foresight that the days of lucrative, freewheeling "progress" at the expense of the natural world might soon be coming to an end along the California Coast. Throughout the Sixties, the Santa Cruz Buyers Association LLC had been one of many ad hoc investor groups cashing in on the relentless development of the California coastline, but to those keeping tabs on issues of governmental policy, it had become plain that a ballot referendum empowering a single agency to monitor and effectively nix the further subdivision of coastal land by wealthy corporate capitalists could cause the fair market value of their prime real properties to plummet. After a phone call and conversations with his colleagues in the office, Morales verified that, despite knowing better, marketers continued to broadcast the potential of North Coast Santa Cruz as another yet-to-be-improved-upon landscape, muting mention of the widespread grass roots campaign to rein in rampant, reckless growth.

Surveying, grading, and excavation at the nursery's greenhouse site had transpired by late summer 1971 when a gentleman came around, almost apologetically introducing himself as a representative of the Lowries' new landowning neighbors, YMS Int'l. He shared copies of documents pertaining to property lines and easements, reiterating the very terms that, five years prior, Katie Lowrie, Jan's attorney Gerald Hudson, and Coast Ranch Realty had successfully negotiated when Jan McLoughlin agreed to let a parcel be carved out of her acreage. Now boundaries and protocol pertaining to the Lowries' water rights, trail access, and use of the driveway linking their place with Grade Road were being recited to Elisabeth and Kaitlin Lowrie as if YO-MIZO-SATA Int'l had itself generated the easement stipulations attached to the deed. The man left information reprinted from the new purchasing agreement between the Buyers Group and YMS along with other dressed-up documentation—cc'd to multiple parties, including several departments of Santa Cruz County and two law firms. He concluded his presentation by announcing that in addition to delivering the paperwork, he had been hired to post NO TRES-PASSING signs, which he accomplished that afternoon. While Katie kept both dogs leashed on the porch, he drove a dozen freestanding metal stakes into the ground of the otherwise unfenced and unmarked border surrounding the twenty acres within which the Lowries lived and worked; words of warning on the attached yellow metal signs faced the house and grounds:

The next day, she discovered that the same notice had been nailed to trees and fence posts at the customary intervals along the outer perimeter of the larger eighty-acre parcel.

—————

KT   Look at me. Look me in the eyes, DD! You're stoned. And I heard all that stupid muscle car talk with your friends, talking about cars—"she this"—"she that." That's so Southern California.

DD   So fuckeen what? I just started like really listening to the Beach Boys for the first time after seeing *2 Lane Blacktop*. They're cool!

KT   What makes you think you can skip school to watch a movie at the Sash Mill? Are you smoking dope every day, DD? Are you?

DD   Mom, I told you before. I'm not talking to you when you call me DD.

KT   Okay, Donald then. You and your friends are smoking an awful lot of pot.

DD   What's an awful lot and how would you know?

KT   I hope you're not smoking anything unless you know exactly where it comes from. I know you don't trust me anymore but trust me on that one. I've seen too many minds blown—

DD   ... oh, Mom, come on.

KT   No, Donald, you come on! God! Can't we get through this together till the end of the school year?

DD   Then what?

KT   Then something else. Listen, I got a call from the Fern Store. They said you and your band are becoming regular nuisances up there after school. Maybe you better come right home from school before there's any real trouble.

DD   Who told you that, Missus Jenkins? Screw her.

KT   Donald!

DD   Oh come on. She's a fat idiot and you know it.

KT   You really are fifteen, aren't you?

DD   Not for long, Mom. And since when did you care what small-minded people like Missus Jenkins think about you or me?

KT   I care what Sherriff Pendleton's men think about you. You're in trouble at school. I don't want to see you in trouble with the law.

DD   What trouble?

KT   She says you guys are passing joints right out in the open.

DD   You used to smoke dope. Maybe you still do. Didn't you even run away from home once? I grew up listening to you and Josie harmonizing on *Four Strong Winds* and now you're telling me to sit through the rest of junior year at Regional High? That's fucked.

KT   But I did finish high school, Donald.

DD   Big deal. The North Coast Regional High. Rah-rah-rah. Hey, was Gran'ma the librarian there or something?

KT   How'd you know that?

DD   She told me.

KT   She volunteered in the library when I was a junior and most of my senior year. Mostly to keep her eye on me, I think.

DD   See what I mean?

KT   After that she was probably too ashamed of me to show her face there.

*

Katie nudged the door open and peered into her mother's bedroom.

"Come in, dear, I'm awake. Good morning."

Katie set the mug of tea on the nightstand and drew the curtain to one side.

"Crack the window for some fresh air, please. Is it nice out?"

"It is."

"I suppose you've been up since dawn."

"I have."

"What time is it?" Elise asked.

"Almost nine."

"Oh, my goodness. Almost nine and still in bed! That's horrible."

"Take it easy, Mom. It's Sunday. Enjoy your tea in bed."

"I may as well and thank you," she replied, propping herself up against the brass bed's headboard, "but this is getting ridiculous. I'm not sick. I should be up."

Katie watched her mother aligning her long white hair down the front of her cotton nightshirt and fiddling with the buttons on its panel.

"Lying in here, not knowing if I'm awake or asleep or in a dream. I best start setting the alarm if this goes on, as if I'd hear it ring. How long has it been, Kaitlin?"

"How long has what been, Mom?"

"Since the Guild broke up."

"Ten years, Missus Lowrie. Ten, eleven years."

Katie tied the curtain back and watched the incoming light illuminate the pillowcase creases impressed upon her mother's cheek.

"Get your coffee and sit a while, Kaitlin. I'd like to talk with you if you have time."

"I've had so much coffee I could burst. I'll sit though." She pulled the wooden rocker onto the braid rug and reset the throw pillow against its cracked leather back; it creaked as she settled in.

Katie surveyed the nightstand: bottles of pills and a water glass; the box of Kleenex and a jar of skin cream; a well-worn edition of THE COMPLETE POETRY OF EDNA ST. VINCENT MILLAY and— lying side by side—her mother's two Bibles. The St. James Version was frayed along its edges, and the corners of its hardbound cover—a dullish, indistinct color difficult to name—were crumpled and bent; multiple generations of yellowing cellophane tape held the spine intact. After almost a century of use, the pebbled soft-leather cover of

LA SAINTE BIBLE was cracked but pliant. A rectangular flat mat of braided grass, index cards with Liliane Piagère's handwritten notes, and Jody's felt cutout bookmark of a tree were inserted between its thin, fine paper leaves.

"Is the construction progressing to your satisfaction, dear?"

"It's coming along," Katie replied. "But I'm worried. Ever since I stopping putting out the sign down on Route One, nobody who didn't already know about the nursery drops in."

"You know what they always say: one must advertise."

"I hope I'm not losing regular customers by skipping this season's crops."

"They'll be back once the greenhouse is up," Elise assured her, blowing steam across the top of her mug. "They'll be back and with plenty of pent-up demand."

"What was it you wanted to talk about, Mom?"

Elise ceremoniously placed the mug back on the night table. "Where are my glasses?"

"They're on your face, Mom."

"They are? Oh my!" She adjusted the spectacles on her nose and considered her daughter's eyes before repositioning the pillows between her back and the headboard.

"Come on," Katie said, crossing her arms and kicking the chair into a slow, rocking rhythm. "What is it?"

"Well, I know you're forever accusing me of being a worrier—"

"... you mean a warrior, Mom, in your own way."

"No, let me speak, please, don't make fun. I am worried, sweetheart. About Donald."

"I know you are. So am I."

"Yes, I know you are. I do so want the boy to avoid the worst consequences of teenage ignorance."

"Me too!"

"Boys will be boys and all that, but not finishing his junior year in high school...? That's more than tomfoolery. That's extreme."

"I know it is."

"Your brother Jody—"

"... don't start, Mom." She brought her rocking to a standstill. "Just don't. You know it won't do us any good."

"But, Kaitlin. Perhaps if you and I can completely understand each other, we can help Donny get through this ... this ... whatever he's going through. Of course, at his age most boys will rebel against their parents—"

"... or parent—"

"... and their grandparents—"

"... or grandparent—"

"... now just stop that, would you, please?" She paused and took a sip of her tea. "I have enough trouble keeping track of my thoughts without your interrupting me. Oh, Donny used to think the world of me, Kaitlin. Even when he became so critical of you, he always held his 'Gran'ma' in high esteem. Until a year or so ago."

"I know. We've talked about this already, right? How I was even jealous sometimes."

Elise removed her glasses and re-knit her brows. "I know too much about such things. We both do. Jody, so full of mischief from the minute he was born. Breaking his leg in that fall from the old railroad trestle while showing off to his friends—that's all it was, showing off! Dislocating his shoulder in the high surf! That was so unnecessary and all before he was fifteen! At the age of ten sneaking out to join the night brigade on the ridge watching for the Japanese—"

"... Ma'am! You know what happens when you start to—"

"... what? Oh, I know, I know, you're right. I go into a funk. I'll stop now. And this isn't about your brother. This isn't about me or you. This is about Donny and making sure he outlives this streak of reckless behavior he seems bent upon."

"I don't know what to do with him, Mom, I don't. I'm hoping when Mike and Suzanne come down for the Fourth, Mike can knock some sense into DD's head."

"That's still two weeks away. Oh, I hope and pray my back doesn't go out when they're here. But I'm not sure about Mike knocking Donny in the head...."

"I don't mean actually hitting him. I just mean, Mike can do DD good just by being Mike, by being around him. You know he still thinks 'Uncle Mike' is 'cool.' At least I hope he still thinks 'Uncle Mike' is 'cool.' Mike's going to help me go buy the new truck—I told you that, right? He wants to. He loves doing stuff like that and DD'll love coming along. After that I'm sure Mike will be happy to help DD take possession of the old Fleetside."

"Are you sure that's wise, dear, giving Donny that old truck? I know you promised it to him for his sixteenth birthday but so much has happened since you made that promise. He won't drive it without a license, I surely hope."

"He's getting his learner's permit. That's what he says anyway. Let Mike Crogan be the first adult to ride with DD behind the wheel. I sure don't want to!"

"But how will he learn to drive?"

"He says Ross is teaching him."

"Ross Stewart?"

"That's what he says. I can believe that."

"I certainly hope the man stays sober when he does. Donny doesn't need any more bad examples, heaven knows."

"So, Mom. Maybe Uncle Mike can help out. You know Mike can't sit still except for meals. I can't believe DD'll sit on his butt watchin' TV when Mike starts tackling every project at loose ends around here. Mike's always been his superhero, you know: Mike the wildfire fighter. If DD doesn't shape up soon, I don't know how we'll make it around here through his senior year."

"But will he even be welcome back at the high school if there's more trouble? Will they just keep letting him back in?"

"I have to go see the principal about that. They sent us a notice. He's what they call an 'habitual truant' now. DD told me it'll be okay but what does he know? It's on his record so if he gets in any other trouble he'll go to Juvenile Court for truancy too. I have to go over and talk to the principal in person. DD won't go with me, not the first time."

"Remind me of his name, dear."

"The principal? Pierson."

"Pierson? No. No, I don't think I know of any Pierson."

"Maybe he'll know of you. I may not have left a great legacy at North Coast Regional, but you did."

"Oh, nobody remembers one thing about a volunteer librarian from twenty years ago."

"Anyway, I hope Pierson'll listen to me."

"Maybe there are studies Donny can catch up with, Kaitlin. Some summer school or something before his senior school year begins. Do you think Mike can make him do homework?"

"To catch up with what, straight D's?"

"Oh, my...."

Elise sniffed at her tepid tea and set it aside; Katie resumed her rocking.

"Where is he spending his free time, dear? I know he sleeps in the barn. And I see his friends come and go out there."

"The band, you mean?" Katie smirked.

"Jody was fifteen when he moved into the attic—no, wait, dear. I'm just saying that teenage boys do that sort of thing. But where is Donny when he's not out in the barn? I can see he eats out of the Frigidaire—"

"Oh yeah, he still does that just fine!"

"But I never know when he's here on the place and when he's not. Unless that noise of theirs is blaring from the barn, of course. Then I know where he is. But when was the last time the three of us sat at supper together, for goddess sake?"

"You're asking me? I didn't know where he was last night so when I caught him wolfing down cereal in the kitchen at five-thirty this morning I asked him."

"And?"

"He said he and the guys were hanging out all night outside some music joint in Half Moon Bay waiting for Neil Young to show up."

"Neil who...?"

"His latest music action figure, Mom. Actually, he's a pretty famous musician who bought a big spread up at the end of Bear Gulch Road."

"Bear Creek Road...?"

"No, Bear Gulch Road. Off 84, south of San Gregorio. It winds its way up into the Woodside Hills."

"Well, he must be famous if he can afford a ranch up that way, what with land prices gone so sky-high."

"I guess Neil Young occasionally shows up at some surfer's road-house and jams with the house band. Or maybe he brings a band with him and they rock out with whoever's playing there, I don't know."

"Oh, I see ... I think...."

"I'm telling you, Mom. I'm pulling my hair out. DD says I sound like a cop, always telling him what not to do. Don't do this, don't do that."

"Haven't you and I have been on that same sorry carousel, Kaitlin?"

"Wasn't it more like inside a not-so-funny fun house? So, what can I do, Mom? I can't come up with any ideas."

Elise folded the hem of the top sheet over the edge of the blanket and smoothed it beneath her palms. "That club in Half Moon Bay, Kaitlin. Do they serve alcohol there?"

"You can bet on that, Gran'ma Lowrie. I've never been there but it's pretty obvious. Rock 'n roll, dancing and what, root beer?"

"But Donny and his friends are far too young to be served alcohol in any establishment."

"Legally, they are. But it may come as no surprise to you that when I was growing up there were plenty of places up and down this coast where underage people could get something to drink. I'm sure there are only more today."

"But he's only just now turned sixteen years old. He isn't really drinking, is he, Kaitlin? You're his mother. If anyone would know, you would."

"I might be the last one to find out though. Listen, Mom. Has he ever? Yes. Will he again? Yes. Is he now? I don't know. I can't just kick him out in the cold, can I? I really don't know what to do."

They sat in silence.

"I'm afraid I have to get to the bathroom, dear. Can we keep talking when I come back?"

"I'm confused, Mom. I should be able to think of something."

"You're doing all you can, Kaitlin. You have to leave the door open, so to speak. I think you must be getting a better idea of what I mean when I say that sometimes all we can do is pray."

"Am I down to that now too?"

"Kaitlin. A mother's love and God's forgiveness never go out of fashion."

"But we're all blind, Mom! It's like we belong to one big Mother's Blind Love Club. They're ought to be a diagnosis for it, like for paranoia or depression or something: Mother's Blind Love!"

"If only Donny would pick up a hammer and let the men in that construction crew show him how to properly drive a nail."

"How about just picking up a shovel on the dirt pile? Working in the nursery's always been an option but he won't do it, Mom."

"Well, maybe Mike can talk some sense into him. They're bringing their horses, you know. Suzanne is dead set on getting me back up into the saddle. She's dead wrong, I'd say. But Mike should have lots of opportunities to get at the boy when they're alone."

"I hope so. I have to go pee now too, Mom. Too much coffee."

"Okay, you go first. Hurry up. But let's not make this a routine."

Katie rocked up out of her chair and stood on her feet. "Not make what a routine?"

"I don't mean talking like this, not that. I'm all for that. I mean letting me lie in bed and sleep half the day away. Maybe it's that new medication for—"

"... don't worry. Jim's crew will be back first thing in the morning banging away, yelling at each other like lumberjacks. That'll wake you up."

"Go on now. Better hurry up or I'll pee in this bed!"

*

DD   You call that open tuning? I call it out of tuning. Don't you ever get tired of fucking folk music?

KT   And don't you ever get tired of Led Zeppelin and Pink Flood?

DD   It's Pink Floyd.

KT   Pink *Floyd* then. Donald. Does that motorcycle out there belong to one of the guys in your band?

DD   It's Steve's.

KT   Is he in the band? Or is he just hanging out? Is he the one supplying the weed?

DD   I don't know. Why?

KT   Because I don't want you getting on any motorcycles.

DD   I've never been on it.

KT   Well, I forbid it.

DD   You what?

KT   I forbid it. You know why? Do you want to know why? I'm going to tell you why.

DD   Because it's not safe.

KT   Because when my brother was exactly your age he got on a bike that was too big for him and killed himself on the big S-curve between here and Fern.

DD   What? Uncle Jody did that?

KT   He did. So, that's why.

DD   How come you never told me that's how he died before?

KT   You think I like to talk about it? If your grandmother ever saw you on a motorcycle she'd probably have a heart attack and I mean that literally, Donald.

DD   Why?

KT   Because Jody was her son, you big dope. The same way you're my son. Jody was fifteen when he took some guy's Indian for a ride up Grade Road.

DD   That's so heavy, Mom.

KT   No motorcycles, okay?

DD   My uncle died on an Indian? I never knew that. This is getting weird.

KT   Why?

DD   Because I was about to ask you about Uncle Jody's boots.

KT   What about them?

DD   I don't know. Can I try them on?

KT   They're not just another pair of boots, Donald.

DD   I know that. Now I really know it. Wow. Are those the boots he was wearing when...?

KT   Tell you the truth, don't try them on. They might fit.

*

When the Crogans drove down from Cloverdale for four nights and five days, they hauled their two horses and Mike brought tools. First, he helped Katie navigate the dealership's FOURTH OF JULY FORD-A-RAMA SALE, where she ended paying in full for the long-bed, F-250 Series pickup truck she had been coveting for almost a year. She drove it off the lot, and Mike took the passenger seat in the 1961 Ford Fleetside while Donald jumped in behind the wheel to drive them home from Half Moon Bay—his longest legal driving experience to date.

Back at the place, the males set up shop under the oak and gave the old Ford workhorse a thorough going-over, changing out the plugs, replacing the belts, adjusting the timing. After a second run for auto parts, when Donald purchased new floor mats, cleaning supplies, and a "suicide knob" for the steering wheel, Mike left the boy alone to change the oil, top off the fluids, and spruce up the interior before washing and polishing the Fleetside's dinged and dented body as best he could. The following day, Donald grabbed at the chance to tackle some serious cross-town traffic when Mike requested a ride to Capitola, where full-length wetsuits were being offered for sale at O'Neil's Surf Shop for the first time. Mike Crogan didn't surf but he did regularly dive for abalone in the cold Pacific Ocean off the Sonoma Coast, and the innovative water wear promised greater warmth during longer dives. On their forays to and from Santa Cruz, Half Moon Bay, and Fern, Mike was impressed by the junior driver's confident handling of the refurbished pickup, and Baby Blue was ecstatic about riding around in the bed. Mike suspected that his mentee had already clocked a good number of miles illegally driving off-the-beaten-track under the tutelage of Ross Stewart.

Suzanne spent the entire holiday visit next to Elsie—in the house, on the deck, in town, and on a half-day horse ride over the varied terrain of the former McLoughlin landholding. Suzanne announced that this was the last time Rocky and Roll would be leaving home, for the vet advised against any further trailering for the aging horses. Elise responded in kind, declaring that this would be her last time on horseback too. Elise couldn't help but unburden her worries about her grandson to her closest friend, as well as voice her concerns about her daughter's mounting stress, reporting how in the past week her grandson had gained then promptly lost a lightweight summer job at the old Grange Hall in Fern. After the part timer's two evening hours of custodial duties were accomplished, rather than turn off the lights and lock up the building, the boy had been ushering his friends into the basement via a back door and, with a skeletal drum set and small portable amps, practicing music late into the night; Donald was caught at it twice and let go. Since the facility manager suspected that the released employee might never voluntarily explain the termination of his exceptionally brief career as a janitor in Fern's Community Center, the Lowrie family was notified.

*

KT   Okay, Donald, here's the deal and I mean it. If you don't go back to school on a regular basis this coming spring, if you keep eating out of the fridge, if you keep using the bathroom and leaving one helluvah mess in there and mountains of dirty laundry in your room—you'll have to start paying rent until you're eighteen.

DD   When I'm eighteen you won't have anything to say about what I do.

KT   Don't be an idiot. You're not an idiot, are you? Did I raise an idiot? Don't be one, okay, because you're not one.

DD   Pay rent for living in a barn? How much is that supposed to be worth?

KT   And while we're at it, why'd you put a lock on the barn door without asking me? You think I don't already know about your PLAY-BOY and HUSTLER magazines? Big deal. You think I can't break the lock to get into that pigsty you're living in any time I want to?

DD   Stay out of my stuff, Mom. If you break that lock I'll never talk to you again in my life. Can't you just let me alone?

KT   You want me to leave you alone, but you don't know who you are yet. Now either finish high school or start paying rent. Or we can figure out how you can work in the nursery but I mean really work. Not half-an-hour or so every couple of days. Or twelve hours a day like I have to. Eight hours a day, and not just when you feel like it. We could do a trade instead of rent money. School or work, one or the other.

DD   Mom! Why are you freaking out on me like this?

KT   You left the barn door open, Donald. You know the smell of skunk coming out of there? Empty beer bottles lined up in a row up on the beam. Is that supposed to be original or something? You're going back to school or getting a job or getting out.

DD   So, you went into my studio?

KT   You call that a studio? I was passing by and I smelled weed and I looked in. I actually have other things to do around here, Donald. I didn't have to go inside. Those centerfolds on the wall. Car parts lying all around.

DD   I can clean it up.

KT   You can but you don't.

*

On day four, Aunt Suzanne took Katie on an extended version of Suzanne's itinerary with Elsie the day before. Sitting the horses beside the millpond, the older woman finally broached the subject of the challenges facing Katie and shared her understanding of the stress load in Cliffport's only household. They dismounted at the trailhead to the spur path leading to Lookout Rock, tied the horses, and walked to view the sea. There Suzanne listened to her "niece" confess her utter confusion and alarm. Except for progress on the glasshouse, Katie admitted that there were no bright moments in her everyday life. She had not played guitar since her best friend and music partner moved to Seattle; her love life was drier than droughty; her mother's capacities were diminishing daily. Worst, her son's juvenile delinquency baffled her. After Katie had enjoyed a long, good cry in the arms of her mother's best friend, Suzanne popped a proposal that took Katie by surprise: what if Donald Duncan spent the rest of the summer in Cloverdale? The camaraderie between Donald and Mike was obvious and, just as obviously, the mature man exerted a good influence upon the immature boy. Mike was game—on the condition that the boy obeyed basic rules: no drinking, no smoking of any kind, no law breaking. Also, as a way to build his self-esteem, he would have to perform a modicum of chores and/or pay them a token fee in exchange for room and board.

Katie was flabbergasted by the couple's generosity, but she wondered if Donald would accept the plan. What if he insisted on taking his new truck and disobeyed curfew? What if he refused to return by Labor Day in order to start his senior year on time—if he was even let back into the school? Suzanne acknowledged these concerns and felt obligated to run the scenario by Elisabeth before anyone took it up with the boy. As the horses ambled along the cool, shaded lane of the panhandle leading out to Everson Road and back, Katie kept coming up with arguments in favor of the arrangement; Suzanne could see nothing but benefits all around. And, with his connections at the fire equipment factory and his years with the volunteer fire department, if anyone could get Donald a temporary summer job in Cloverdale, Mike Crogan could. Besides, Louisiana Pacific Lumber was always hiring—and firing—local high school boys for summer shifts on the green chain and as general helpers in the yard. If a paying job didn't pan out or appeal to their summer guest, Suzanne would welcome his help around the place, not minding at all if someone else watered the vegetable garden, collected the chicken eggs, fed the horses and cleaned the stalls, belched the pygmy goats, or shampooed the dogs. There was dry grass to clear away from the outbuildings before wildfire season, and wood to be split before winter.

*

DD   I asked for a job at Union Ice down in Santa Cruz today.

KT   What'd they say?

DD   They're not hiring. I guess they think sixteen's not old enough to fork spinach out of a railroad car. How fucked is that?

KT   You can still work here in the nursery.

DD   Doing what? Scrubbing cans in a garbage can full of bleach? Bitchin'!

KT   You have no idea what's going on, do you? Do you know how much money I save by recycling used containers from the nurseries? But they have to be disinfected first.

DD   Is that another one of the laws?

KT   Whether it's one of the laws or not, I have to prevent disease from spreading to the plants.

DD   I don't even care about your plants, Mom. [1]

Chapter 4

Karmann Ghia Lita

Sea-to-Summit • 1 Embarcadero Plaza, Suite 1111 • San Francisco CA 94106

August 1, 1971

Kaitlin Lowrie
One Grade Road
Cliffport CA 95017

Dear Ms. Lowrie:

Allow me to introduce myself, a member of the community liaison team at Sea-to-Summit Associates, the San Francisco-based development firm specializing in the conception and realization of large, upscale projects along the coastline of the Pacific Coast States.

The purpose of this letter is to reach out regarding your parcel in Cliffport, California. Sea-to-Summit is in contract with a client actively seeking to purchase real estate in your area. If you have ever considered selling your property at One Grade Road, please give me an opportunity to discuss this possibility with you in person at the earliest date. Our client is willing and able to pay top price for real property in a suitably situated location such as yours.

The "dog days of August" is an expression that may apply to some sectors of the business world, but at Sea-to-Summit we are committed to maximizing the benefits for all parties engaged. In today's extremely active real estate market, communication between all parties is urgent and vital. Feel free to call me during normal business hours at 415-541-1111 X 17.

I look forward to visiting with you soon.

Respectfully yours,

Angela Salomone
Community Liaison

*

Katie was delivering a pitcher of fresh-squeezed iced lemonade to Jim Parker's three-man crew when Baby Blue Eye sounded the alarm and raced downhill to meet a waxed, polished, plumred, hardtop Karmann Ghia coming in from Grade Road. A trim brunette dressed in a dusty-rose business suit emerged from the streamlined sports car. Electrical saw blades and metal fastening drills fell silent. The stranger lifted her round sunglasses away from her face, looked about, then closed the car door and stepped out from the shade of the oak; shouldering a strap leather purse and clutching a slim portfolio, she headed in the direction of the house.

"Get your own lemonade!" Katie exclaimed, setting the pitcher and glasses down on a railroad tie step. "I better see what this is about."

"We're just looking at the sports car, Katie!" yelled the man on the peak of the glasshouse frame.

"Sure you are!" she shouted back and the three men laughed.

Katie cut across the hillside in order to intercept the unidentified visitor at the fork in the path leading visitors either to the front porch steps or the staircase to the redwood deck on the house's north side. As the dog quieted down, the woman became aware of Katie's approach and with a free hand shielded her eyes. Her scarlet, low-heel pumps gleamed below the cuffs of her creased, ironed slacks.

"Hello there! I'm Angela Salomone from Sea-to-Summit." Her voice reminded Katie of the animated tone and upbeat inflection of the shapely, high-strung weather report lady on San Jose TV's evening news. A thin gold chain worn on top of the woman's silky blouse slid back and forth over an unmistakable bustiness. She pulled a business card from a flap pocket set at a slant in the two-button jacket nipped at the waist. "And you are Kaitlin Lowrie?"

"That's me," Katie replied, wiping her palm on her jeans before shaking the other woman's extended right hand with its fingernails painted bold red. A thick gold bracelet dangled off the wrist; she wore a narrow watchband on her left arm but no finger rings. "Baby Blue Eye, go away!"

"Oh, that's okay. I love dogs, especially smart ones like you, huh, Baby Blue?" she said, using the tip of one sharpened fingernail to scratch between the dog's ears. "Well, did you get the letter?"

"That was from you?"

"That's right," the woman replied, perching her sunglasses atop her hair. "I'm the one who sent it."

"We got it."

"We didn't hear back from you ... and I was in the neighborhood. I hope you don't mind my dropping by like this...."

"As long as you're here, let's go where it's shady."

As soon as the female caller passed out of their sight halfway up the staircase to the deck, the construction crew's racket resumed.

Katie offered the unsolicited guest the tall glass of lemonade she had already poured for herself. "I'll get another glass."

"Oh, thanks! Say, can I come along and take a look inside?"

"No, actually."

"It doesn't have to be clean or anything. I just—"

"... no," Katie restated. "My mother's napping and I don't want to disturb her."

"Oh, okay, I see ... so, no ... let's not then."

Angela assessed the columns of debarked, lacquered redwood rounds that served as seats around the irregularly shaped stump-top table and finally placed her leather-like portfolio as a cushion on the nearest stack before sitting down.

"Sit, Blue," Katie said, "and be good." The dog sat and looked back and forth between them, awaiting further instructions.

"She'll be good," Angela volunteered. "Right, Baby Blue?"

In her view out the kitchen window, Katie verified that despite all her feminine accessories, the woman was no natural beauty. In the nude her figure might conform to the preferred tastes of the working men raising her glasshouse on the hill—and to Katie's son and the members of his teenage band—but in profile her nose was large and bulbous, and her heavy lower jaw jutted a bit out beyond the rest of her skull. Outside again, Katie saw that the woman's eyelashes were not false, just laden with mascara matching dark brown eyes. A brush may have tamed her shoulder-length hair, but with the slightest breeze its full waves asserted a life of their own.

"What is the name of this gorgeous dinnerplate dahlia? It's so pretty!"

"That's 'The Queen of Madeira,'" Katie announced, setting her own glass down beside the wide ceramic saucer in which the blossom floated. "It's off one of my mother plants, if you know what that means."

"Oh, I know all about mother plants," A. Salomone replied, zipping open her bag. "My grandfather raised trees and shrubs in cans for the nursery trade in the San Joaquin Valley. And Nonna—my grandmother—she had oodles of canna lilies and bearded irises and those pelargoniums—what do you call them?—Martha Washingtons, that's it! She had those planted all over their place."

"Really? I raise ivy geraniums. Fuchsias and dwarf dahlias too. I'm taking a break from propagating right now while everything's upside down. There's no place to put anything until that greenhouse gets finished."

"Hell, honey, I know all about the nursery business. My brother and I were working in Grandpa's nursery when we were this high." She lit a cigarette and blew out the match. "I paid my brother in candy bars to have dibs on working in the shade house."

"Where was this?"

"Other side of Modesto. Hotter than hell out there in summertime, not like here."

"There's your ashtray," Katie volunteered, indicating a chipped abalone half-shell full of cigarette butts from the workers' lunch break. "Is that still a production nursery?"

"No way," Angela answered, puffing a cloud of smoke out one side of her mouth before tossing the match into the shell. "That dirt's in tract houses now. When Grandpa Salomone died, Nonna let my father and his brothers get rid of the plant inventory, tear down the nursery, and sell the place. That land all went into subdivisions after World War Two. My father and uncles used the money to start a grocery store chain. Smart move on their part too." Angela exhaled and removed the sunglasses from the top of her head, revealing the narrow arching lines of her plucked, dark brown eyebrows.

"I'm sorry to hear that."

"What, that my uncles started a grocery chain?"

"No, what I meant is, I hate to hear about good agricultural land going into tract housing."

The woman flinched; Katie sensed that without having intended to, she had just watered the seedling of the profound, fundamental discord between them planted by Angela Salomone's introductory letter.

"That's progress, I guess," the woman said, flashing a smile of professionally whitened teeth. "This lemonade sure hits the spot," she added, glancing at Katie then looking away. "There's a breeze up here but it's pretty hot for the coast today, right? You can call me Lita, by the way."

"We're in the one spot on this hillside where the summer fog never really settles in. Right here around the house and that meadow over there." Katie pointed to the sunlit bank across the way, where she had dug and leveled primitive terraces for rowing out containerized plants. "The ocean fog mostly follows the creek up into the woods and hangs around up there. Above the redwoods is where you reach the banana belt once you get past the first ridge."

"Yes ... I know...."

"Besides," Katie added, "how hot you get depends on what you're wearing."

Sea-to-Summit's representative looked at Katie's batik tee-shirt, blue jeans, and sandals, and she chuckled. "I guess I'm a little over-dressed for Cliffport. But I'm underdressed for the office if you can believe that. But like I said...." she added, pulling on her cigarette, gazing vaguely about. "I was just passing by...."

Katie extracted the woman's business card from her pocket and looked it over. "Did you say you call yourself Lita? This says Angela."

"My friends call me Lita."

"That's not from Leticia?"

"No, and it's not Letty or Trisha. Lita. My given name's Angela, right? But once I got to parochial school it became Angie. Then in high school I got called Angelita by some of the older boys—that and other things." She tossed off a billow of smoke. "I go by Lita now, that's all."

The exaggeration of her smile reminded Katie that the purpose of Angela "Lita" Salomone's unrequested presence wasn't small talk.

"Kaitlin—"

"... Katie."

"Katie. Like I said, we were a little surprised when we didn't hear back from you, after we mailed you that letter."

"Who's we?"

"The outreach team at S2S—Sea-to-Summit—my colleagues and me.... I thought we made it pretty clear that this is a once-in-a-life-time opportunity you and your mother might not want to pass up." The speaker sculpted the tip of her filtered cigarette inside the scalloped rim of the shell and lifted her free hand to one ear, glossy fingernails toying with a round, gold-plated hoop; she laid a long, lingering, unabashed gaze directly upon her hostess. "You do realize you're sitting on a gold mine, right? I sure wish I were in your position right now."

In the silence that followed, Lita took one more drag then dropped the smoking cigarette to burn itself out in the shell; Katie reached forward and extinguished it completely.

"And do you realize it's less than a year since we finally secured the deed to this place?"

"I do," Lita countered.

"You do?"

"On about ... November 15th, wasn't it?"

"Sounds about right."

"I've done my homework, honey," she said, crossing her legs and bobbing one shiny, shoed foot.

"And you can see I'm investing in a whole new glasshouse for the nursery."

"I can see that, sure. So?"

"So, I'm planning to live and work here for a long time to come."

"Now listen to me, Katie, let's talk." She sat with her legs still crossed but lengthened her top leg straight out in front of her and held it there. "For what our client is willing to pay for your twenty acres—twenty point three, to be exact—you and your mother could relocate and build a dozen new greenhouses. Two dozen, out in the Central Valley."

"Who'd you say your client is again?"

"Did I say? A firm based in Singapore doing business all over the Pacific Rim."

"YMS, you mean?" Katie's declaration drew a pause from the developer's agent. "I thought they were Japanese. YO-MIZO-SATA sounds Japanese to me."

"I don't know that much about who they really are myself, okay? What difference does it make where they come from if they want to buy? You name your price, Katie. I'll bet you a nickel they'll round it up and pay you outright too. No need to repair a thing. As is. You won't have to prepare anything, inside the house or out. I'm telling you, hon', we're talking cash on the barrel-head, foreign currency or not. Just let me tell them how much you want and see if they blink an eye over there in Singapore. YMS has already enlisted the services of a regional realtor to represent them in this transaction."

"It's not Country and Town, by any chance?"

"Who?" Lita unzipped her purse but paused with it partway open. "Hey, wait. Are you saying they're your realtors?"

"Nope, they're not mine. That's a real estate company in Santa Cruz. Greenbrier's. I thought you might already be making arrangements with them too, on my behalf, of course."

"Town and Country? Never heard of them. But these local realty outfits up and down the coast are a dime a dozen."

"I'm talking about the one that's buddy-buddy with Cummings and those gangsters finishing the development up the road."

"Did you just say *finishing*?" Angela's shut her lips over her teeth, re-crossed her legs, and pretended to be focusing on the rounded toe of her pointed shoe. "You're kidding me, right? Because if you aren't, you are sorely mistaken. That's just Phase One they're finishing, Katie. They're lots more of those Vignettes at Monteflores to come. You didn't know that? Oh, yeah, there's lots more where Phase One came from: more homes, more golf courses, more vineyards. Swimming pools, tennis courts. I really can't believe you didn't already know that."

"I wasn't aware of all that. No, I didn't know. I've been so turned off by the way Fern just lets Cummings and his cronies do whatever they want to get that development built, I try not to pay much attention."

Lita took a swig of her lemonade, spat a melting cube of ice back into her glass, and resumed toying with one earring. "They told me you might be a handful, Katie, but nobody ever said you were dumb. Said you were smart, as a matter of fact, just maybe a little too ... independent...?"

"I suppose that depends on who you're talking to. Bill Cummings? He doesn't like me. His fawning admirers who now consider themselves the real fathers and mothers of the City of Fern? They don't either."

"Here I thought all his time you already knew all about the master plan for Monteflores." Lita Salomone nestled her sunglasses deeper in the thick of her hair. "And now you seem to be telling me you think Monteflores is Bill Cumming's doing? No way. Oh, he's profiting madly by it, and little by little that smart ass cowboy keeps raising the price for the land he sells to YMS. He greased the slide, sure, getting Fern to incorporate so services could be extended onto whatever new parcel of land he wants to sell. But that all becomes YMS property, Katie. Monteflores Inc. is YMS' deal. Bill Cummings and his cattle company are big beneficiaries, sure. And think of the increase in tax revenues for the new big little City of Fern. But Monteflores belongs to YMS. You didn't know that?"

"Not exactly."

"Bill Cummings likes to make it look like he's the one donating the new schoolyard and the new bus to that little Mountain School. And all the paving materials and labor to resurface the side roads of that cute little sleepy mountain hamlet of Fern. Passing out one hundred twenty-pound frozen turkeys last Thanksgiving. All from the bottom of his heart, I'm sure. My impression is that Bill Cummings Junior is a smart businessman but not quite as generous as all that. I met Marcy Cummings once too. I can tell you that lady's one bitch royale!"

Lita threw back her head and let loose a laugh; Katie observed the mercury fillings in her upper teeth.

"I'm surprised those hulks building your greenhouse up there haven't told you any of this. They're locals, right? They must know that half the able-bodied tradesmen in North County are working on the project up the hill."

"Not the half I know," Katie quipped. "None of Jim's crew is."

"Jim's crew who? Don't speak too soon, honey. When Phase Two gets the rubber stamp, Gath Construction's subs will be hiring on plenty and paying good wages for some 'non-union assistance' shall we say? What I hear anyway. There always seem to be plenty of good old blank-truck-door-tradesmen willing to be paid hard cash off payroll—and frozen turkeys."

Katie stood up and stepped to the railing; Baby Blue lifted her head from her forepaws, watching for a cue. "Listen, Lita or Angelita or whatever you like to be called. If Sea-to-Summit is working with YMS and YMS is behind Monteflores.... I don't see why you and I are even talking."

"Oh, come on!" Lita exclaimed, whisking her glasses off her head and placing their frames spread-eagle atop her raised knee before passing her fingernails back through both sides of her hair as if simultaneously trying to fluff the waves and compress them in place. "Be reasonable. Shouldn't we be talking about the possibility of making some sort of deal that would benefit all parties involved?"

"You mean you want me to join Cummings and the money-grubbin' citizens of Fern at YMS's feeding trough?" Katie let the small of her back come away from the railing and stood free, hiking up her jeans and placing her arms akimbo; her dog rose up on all fours. "I know what you and your so called outreach team at Sea-to-Summit want from us. What you mean by being 'reasonable' is clearing out so some foreigners can have bragging rights about owning every last inch of Cliffport, California ... from sea-to-summit, like people like you have been saying around here for a hundred years."

"*People like me?*"

"Salespeople, promoters, drummers. I don't know exactly what YMS plans to do with the land they own that already completely surrounds us down here. Maybe they'd like to open a new lodge over there."

"That's a damn good guess, Katie," Lita mused aloud. "They just might do that someday."

"So, you can go tell Sea-to-Summit and YO-MIZO-SATA and Gath Construction this: the Lowries aren't selling. Okay? Now what kind of a deal can you make out of that?"

"And I thought my people got overdramatic!" Lita drank the last liquid from her glass and wiped her mouth with the back of her hand. "Lowrie's not an Italian name by any chance, is it?"

The dog followed Katie to the head of the stairs and waited for the signal to descend but Katie stayed put, one hand on the banister and the other stuck in her back pocket. "You can go now."

The visitor lodged her sunglasses back on the bridge of her nose and shouldered her purse. "I have a question for you then I'll thank you for the refreshment and be on my merry way."

"What's that?"

"I still haven't figured out how you were related to that McLoughlin lady who gave you this place."

"What business is it of yours?"

"Just wondering. You were born and raised here, right?"

"So they say. Ask your friends in the newly christened City of Fern. They might still remember who the McLoughlins were—and who the Lowries still are."

"I'm sure they do. Oh, there's one more thing."

"What's that?"

"Can you people claim responsibility for those things at the end of the driveway?"

"That dump across the road's not our stuff. Don't look at us."

"Because YMS expected all the junk in the ditches along the driveway that came with the purchase of the eighty acres. They'll clean that up one day or another. But what I'm asking you about now is all that crap out on Grade Road. Looks like a burnt-out VW bug and a picked-over Camaro. There's a Sears warehouse full of old appliances and—"

"... you can't pin any of that stuff on us," Katie interrupted. "Haven't your private investigators tracked down that information for you by now?"

"Then how about the mess in front of those old buildings down on the highway? All that shit piled up against those broken-down wooden buildings—that's a fire hazard and an eyesore too."

"Oh, come off it," Katie scoffed, hitching up her jeans again and crossing her arms. "You aren't trying to hold us responsible for that crap down on Route One, are you? That stretch of the road went out of anybody's control years ago."

"Are any people actually living down in here?" Lita asked.

"I don't know. Put your private eye on the case. Besides, if your allies in the real estate industry own it now, have them clean it up. I don't have a dog in that fight."

Lita looked from Katie to Baby Blue Eye and back to Katie. "You know there's such a thing as a county ordinance against abandoning vehicles and dumping trash by the side of a public road. And Caltrans is responsible for maintaining that length of Highway One along the frontage road of quaint old Cliffport Town or whatever the original Forty-niners used to call it. Caltrans might like an address where they could send an invoice for getting that stretch of roadway back into compliance with state law."

"Have them send the bill to Sea-to-Summit or YMS. You know their address."

Lita planted her soles on the decking and pushed down on them to stand up. "Oh, girlie, will you just listen for a second? I don't really give a shit about any of this, but I don't understand how someone smart as you are, someone who can grow this big, beautiful dahlia—what'd you call it, 'The Madeira Queen?'—how can you stand looking at all that trash in the ditches every day and that dump out on Grade Road? I'm an old country girl myself. I know about junk lying around the farmyard and all, but that's a disaster out there and down on Route One. God! Here, I'm leaving these with you," she said, yanking two binders from her portfolio and plopping them down on the table: a clear plastic binder showed some Asia language characters on its front page; the white cover of a second binder displayed the embossed S2S logo—a black silhouette of a steep, multi-peaked mountain with a wavy, aquamarine shoreline at its base. "In case you ever come to your senses, you can read those."

"Take those with you," Katie said.

"Don't you want to find out more about your new neighbors? They're here to stay, you know."

"My neighbors? I thought they lived in Singapore."

"Very funny. Okay, Katie, have it your way. YMS International just happens to be one the best-capitalized and most powerful enterprises operating in the Eastern Pacific Rim."

"Bully for them. Take those with you, I said. Take 'em!"

Lita smirked, stashed both items back inside her portfolio, and headed down the stairs with Katie following behind. Halfway down, the construction noise ceased, and the sound of high heels clacked in the silence. Upon reaching the shade below the wide oak, Lita raised her arm and made a wide, sweeping gesture, waving in the general direction of the hilltop. One long, lone wolf whistle sounded then a volley of hoots. Opening the car door, searching for her keys in the depths of her bag, she was about to get in when Katie—still standing outside the shaded zone—raised her voice: "I want to ask you something, Missus Salomone."

Angela found the keys, sloughed the strap off her shoulder, and tossed the purse into the passenger seat. She resecured her sunglasses on her face and turned Katie's way. "And what's that, Missus Lowrie?"

"What do you want to be doing this to other people for a living for anyway?"

She snorted. "Because I need to make more money, honey, that's why." She folded herself into the driver's seat. "And you know? I think it'd be a good idea for you to have a look at these. Here...." She dropped the binders on the gravel right beside her car, closed the door, started the engine, and put it in gear. "That's what I think."

Jim's crewmembers yapped like a pack of coyotes as the Karmann Ghia's tires spun in place then kicked up a rooster tail of dust while traversing the levee-like lane running between the two junk-filled ditches. Katie turned about and, facing downward, stiffened her raised right arm as if readying her shoulder to receive the recoil of a discharged pistol and flipped the men the bird before striding up the path to the house. To the sound of their laughter, she climbed the front porch steps and let the screen door slam.

*

Katie saw the sports car scoot up the driveway and Angela Salomone pop out. She was dressed in a short, pleated, white tennis skirt and a white polo shirt top; her wavy hair was constrained by a high-paneled white cotton visor, and its ponytail wagged as she dashed up the path—two steps at a time—yapping right back at Baby Blue Eye. When the panting woman landed her chalk-white sneakers on the deck, she broadcast a toothy smile and kept chewing gum. Katie couldn't see her eyes through the mirrored sunglasses, but she was impressed by Lita's melon-size, bra-bound breasts compressed beneath the short-sleeved shirt boasting Sea-to-Summit's schematic logo embossed in green thread. The same green logo was stitched into the visor's crown and the manufacturer's fainter white label— Sportive™ —was sewn into the adjustable side strap. Katie detected sweat beading in the irritated area above her lips, where Lita appeared to have recently waxed off any telltale signs of facial hair.

Without waiting for an invitation, Lita perched on a stool, crossed an ankle onto the opposite knee, and launched into an explanation for her sudden appearance. The white nylon shorts gripping her tanned, smoothly shaven thighs were of a piece with the skirt of her golf outfit, and her supple limbs glistened with sunscreen, suntan oil, or both. She said she was on her way to the first Marcy Cummings Annual Golf Tourney to be played at the newly opened Zinfandel Course at Monteflores, and she insisted that this time she really was just dropping by. "I wanted to tell you," she declared, lowering her leg and dropping her shoulders as she tossed her white-framed sunglasses onto the tabletop and let out a sigh, "it's too bad I made such a bad first impression."

Katie turned off the transistor radio weighting down the Sunday Chronicle. Without a word, she extended her iced tea to the breathy visitor who said thanks and drained the glass. "Well?"

"Well, what?" Katie asked, picking out some shreds leftover from the sunflower seed shells she had been whittling down between her front teeth.

"Hey!" Lita burst out, slapping both thighs. "How come your Christmas lights are still up on the roof of the barn?"

"They are?" Katie replied, leaning to see the barn from where she sat. "I guess they are at that."

"That's crazy! It's the middle of August!"

"My son never did get around to putting them away like I kept asking, so I gave up. I promise not to turn those on until Christmas-time, okay?"

"I guess he gave up too," Lita said. "That's one way to resolve a dispute. Hey, when can I meet him anyway?"

Katie ignored the inquiry and noticed that the ball of Lita's sneaker stay pressed against the deck's wooden planks, but her heel was bouncing up and down. Lita caught herself and set her other ankle on the opposite knee, tweaking the rolled top of her white quarter sock with fingertips newly painted pink.

"So, what about it, Katie? Did you look at those brochures?"

"I looked at 'em."

"What do you think?"

"You can have them back. I'll go get them if I didn't throw them away."

"I don't want them back, damnitall! I want to know what you think about doing some business."

Katie stuck a pinch of sunflower seeds into her cheek.

"Oh, come on! Don't roll over and play dead on me, girlie. I know I'm all worked up right this second—I'm running late for the opening ceremony. Anyway, you know exactly what I mean. And by the way, there's no Greenbrier Realty or Town and Country involved in any of this. I looked into that. Greenbrier's Country and Town in Santa Cruz?

Big fish, small pond. But our realtors will come down from the City and work with the listing agent of your choice, of course."

"Maybe you didn't hear me the last time. There's not going to be any listing. Now if you're here to play golf, go play golf, and I'll get back to listening to the Giants finally beat the Dodgers on a nice, quiet Saturday afternoon.

"I just had that game on—shit!" Lita jumped up. "I left my cigarettes in the car. I'll run go get them."

"No!"

Lita lowered her foot to the deck and scooped her glasses off the table then came to a halt. "What'd you just say?"

"I said no. Just run. Go. For good."

"Go? For good?" Sea-to-Summit's agent in the field stuck one arm of her folded sunglasses into the V-neck opening of her tight, white shirt. "I don't think so, hon'."

Baby Blue Eye tilted her head and gazed at her mistress as the visitor rose and began pacing the perimeter of the deck, her fists plunged into her miniskirt's deep side pockets, her jaw muscles clenching and unclenching as she chewed harder on her gum. "Katie, you don't know what's going on—or do you? The boys I work with ... the boys I work for ... they play hardball. You know that mess down on Scenic Route One we were talking about? Our lawyer says it sounds like the origin of that rubbish pile could very easily be traced back to the Redwood Trees Nursery—"

"... the Redwood *Coast* Nursery," Katie corrected her.

"Okay. Anyway, I just now took a closer look at that hobo-ville down there and it does look like it's got Redwood *Coast* Nursery's name written all over it. I love the pink flamingos, by the way—very classy. Same goes for the dump at the end of the driveway. I have no doubt at least some of those big-ticket items once belonged to the Lowrie household. And I have to tell you, it wouldn't take a certified nurseryman to notice the resemblance between the landscape plantings all around the old lodge and the plant material in those five-gallon cans you've got rowed out over there above the meadow. You've been helping yourself to someone else's plants for some time now. That's called stealing private property, Missus Lowrie."

"You've got to be kidding! Are you trying to blackmail me over some old, forgotten bear's breech and bush impatiens?"

"Come on, Katie! You don't think the suits at YMS really give a shit about a bunch of bushes stuck into rusted-out egg cans—of course they don't. You and I don't have to pursue that angle. I'm just trying to get you to see the light, honey. You've got new neighbors now and—"

"... I thought those suits you're talking about live in Singapore or Japan or someplace far away like that."

"Then let's say they're not your immediate neighbors. Or residential landlords. Let's just say they're your overlords and the sooner you realize it the better off you'll be. If we can't beat 'em, girlie, we better join 'em."

"Get off my property. Go on, get out!"

"Okay, okay, I'm going. Jesus! Oh and hey, Missus Lowrie! Better not let those studs building your greenhouse get caught taking the driveway up to the old lodge anymore. Cutting across private property to drop off their building supplies and all? Nuh-na. No trespassing, remember? Okay, I'm going then. I'll send your best regards to Bill Cummings when I see him in about fifteen."

"YOU SNAKE!"

Sea-to-Summit's representative paused halfway down the stairwell and turned around; Baby Blue Eye growled. "Are you completely out to lunch or what? I can't believe you! And you want to know something? We can't beat 'em. Don't fool yourself. We can't." Lita Salomone took the bottom two steps in a single leap. "Bye now, sister!"

"Stay, Blue, stay!" Katie ordered the dog, and they watched the woman loping the rest of the way to her compact car.

*

Elise called her daughter to the picture window. "It's her car again, isn't it?"

"Looks like it."

"Why is that horrible woman coming back here again?"

They watched Angela Salomone park in the cul-de-sac and head toward the house, carrying only a beaded clutch purse. Her hair was loose and stringy, as if she had showered and, without stopping to dry it, changed into her cowboy boots and a beltless, spaghetti-strapped country dress before hopping into her car.

"I guess we're about to find out."

"You be careful, dear. She doesn't seem like a very stable human being, emotionally. Look how she's walking."

"I think she's drunk, Mom."

"Oh no! How can she make such a spectacle of herself! Then just tell her to go away or we'll call Sheriff Pendleton."

"I already told her to go away, twice. But here she is again."

Elise groaned and retreated to her room. Baby Blue Eye barked half-heartedly as she accompanied the familiar stranger up the steps on the north side of the house. When Katie came out the pantry door, Lita was gaining her bearings after the climb.

"Hi there."

"What's going on?"

"I came t'pologize. Feel shitty 'bout z'afternoon."

Katie noticed how the exaggerated motion of her mouth while slurring her words almost curled her lips into a snarl. She wore no make-up. The cerise highlights on her cheeks, nose, and bare shoulders, as well as the raspberry blush across her uppermost chest, suggested the aftereffects of a hot shower, sunburn, or alcohol—or some combination of all three.

"Not going t'lie t'you. I'm not in great shape, 'kay?" She steadied herself with one hand on the railing while gauging the distance to the closet stack of redwood rounds. "But I know what I'm saying and I'm sorry."

"What for?"

"Everything, damnitall!"

Lita bucked up in a visible effort to hold her head high; Katie expected her to topple over. "And I know I look like shit so don't look at me that way. I had to get out of there fast!"

She made it to a redwood seat where, closing her eyes, she sat, her head wobbling. Katie went down on her haunches and looked up into the other woman's face.

"Some face, huh?"

"Did something bad happen to you up the hill?"

"D'you say *something bad*? Listen, 's no good. I've had it up to here with all of 'em. I don't feel well. I'm going home." She fished a cigarette out of her purse and with difficulty aligned her lighter's flame with the cigarette's tip, widening her eyes. "Listen, Katie, listen t'me now. I couldn't go back t'San Francisco without telling you I'm sorry and I mean it. I know lots of people think I'm a snake but you ... you ... you had the balls to say it to my face."

"I guess I did say something like that," Katie said, scratching Baby Blue's head then standing up straight.

Lita smirked and placed her cigarette in the corner of her mouth while raking her fingernails through her unkempt hair. "No, wait, what am I doin'? I can't be here," she muttered, looking around as if she were waking up. "Lemme get on the horn to my roommate. We're supposed t'go out tonight but I'm goin' to bed soon'z I get home."

"You can use the phone, but you can't take that with you into the house," Katie said, indicating the burning cigarette.

"Gotcha." Lita started up but teetered and reseated herself, elbows on the stump table, forehead cradled in her palms. "God, I'm sick of everything."

"Maybe you better rest here a while. I don't think you should drive back to the City right now. Have you eaten?"

"Eaten? Oh god have I eaten! And drunken! No, I need t'get t'bed. Doesn't off'-en happen t'me, not this bad. Mus' be the combination...."

"What combination?"

"I couldn't sleep last night. All wound up about this gold thing—*golf* thing. Marcy's Golf Tournament. I can't hit a stupid white ball straight when I'm stone sober! So, I took a pill to sleep but this morning I overslept so I took some uppers lying around th'apartment. That and a couple espressos woke me up then—hey, maybe it was the sake! Yeah, sure, it was that sake!"

"You've been drinking sake?"

"Some Jap jerks were up there for the opening ceremony, reps from YMS or something. A traditional sake ceremony—what a joke. There was this big old crock, and somebody took this big old sledge-hammer to it—Kampai!—broke the fucking thing wide open! Then came the bullshit speeches and toasts and hors-d'oeuvres and this was before we started playin' golf. God was I not in the mood for golf! After our little cat fight? Shit on a stick, I wasn't in the mood for anything. And all those wolves ogling my only assets...." She paused. "Oh hell, sis', don't look like that. My older brother and cousins taught me what my assets are a long time ago and it's sure not this," Lita said, digging a painted fingertip into the cleft of her chin, tilting her head sideways, and fluttering her eyelashes in a Shirley Temple parody. "This is no pretty face, but I learned t'use th'assets I do have—my ass and my tits, that is, if I have t'spell it out to someone like you. God, you must hate me, but I don't hate you, Katie, I don't. And I sure don't have z'inter-esting face like yours either."

"Interesting." Katie chortled. "That's one way to put it."

"Oh, come on, girlie. You're cute as a bug's butt and you know it."

"I don't exactly have your curves," Katie responded, hitching up her pants by the belt loops.

"Ha! Maybe God'll figure out some way t'spread out the wealth one of these days! Isn't that what they always say in Berkeley? 'Redis-tribute the wealth?' Right! Rots a ruck with that one, boys and girls! Hey, lemme get on the horn. I gotta go."

Katie led her to the telephone on the kitchen counter and saw her mother crack open her bedroom door to sneak a peek. While the visitor fumbled with the phone piece, Katie went back outside and took the car keys from the diminutive purse then waited, anticipating Lita's return before wondering if, even in her condition, Sea-to-Summit's ambassador might somehow start snooping about inside the house. Upon reentering, Katie discovered the woman had instead found her way into the oversize club chair where—eyelids drooped—she had collapsed.

"Did you tell her?"

"What's that?" Lita forced her eyes open. "Wasn't there ... I'll just ... go soon...."

Katie watched her eyes stay closed and spread the afghan from the sofa across the thin print dress before pulling off the boots stamped with colored, floral cutouts. After informing her mother of the situation, Elise took one long look. "It's the ghost of Jan McLoughlin." Katie slipped outdoors and, after completing her end-of-the-day yard chores, she found her mother occupying the red upholstered chair in the main room, pretending to read but obviously sitting guard over the snoring intruder.

*

Katie had returned the car keys to the clutch purse, and Elise had retired to her bedroom for the night by the time Lita stirred awake. Yanking on her boots by their pull-tabs, standing up and stomping once on each stack heel, Lita make a trip down the hall then accepted the coffee Katie served her outside, where she could smoke.

Katie fetched a flannel shirt to drape over the shivering woman's bare shoulders. Coming more fully awake, Lita apologized for having shown up "in the bag" and asked Katie to stop her if she had already told her about the ridiculousness of some priest's blessings before the mallet hit the ceramic sake barrel and cries of Kampai! Kampai! Kampai! had broken loose. Still partially inebriated, Lita recapped speeches made by the notables from Sea-to-Summit, YMS, Monteflores, and the City of Fern, and she recounted how she had been teamed up for golf with the guys from Coastal Property Management; how she had plowed through the offerings of the roving bar cart and the sushi bar in the shade tent at the seventh hole; how the tournament's namesake had made a cameo appearance on the sidelines once the game was well underway. As if in a fairy tale, Marcy Cummings—dressed like Dale Evans—had shown up astride a platinum thoroughbred and stationed herself atop a grassy knoll in the shady rough at the nineth hole. She had waved but not gotten down from her horse. Of course, the animal's hooves would have torn up the fairways and greens—Lita understood that much; but the dame's haughty smile and the newsreel waving of her gloved hand had sickened her. When her foursome had finished one round of shoddy golf, she had rushed through her paces in the ladies locker room and fled before the big barbecue began.

With more coffee, she became even more talkative; Katie wondered whether Ms. Salomone had lost all track of her audience as the woman recapitulated YMS' pitch for its Pacific Rim developments in general and the virtues of life at Vignettes One at Monteflores in particular: a gated community of luxury homes built around a golf course—with the Scotts Valley Airport, the medical facilities in Santa Cruz, and the cultural opportunities represented by the University of California located near but not too nearby. Lita stopped herself: "Hey! How come I haven't met your mother yet? Are you hiding her from me? God bless all moms. You're older than me I think—what year were you born?"

"1936."

"Me, '41. See? But I feel like you're my little sister or something."

"Age has nothing to do with it," Katie stated.

"If you say so.... Hey, can I borrow a comb or a brush or something? I must've left mine back in the locker room. Anyway, don't we both have about the same color hair? No, I guess not really...."

Katie returned with a hairbrush. Attacking her tangles, a newly lit cigarette stuck in one corner of her mouth, Lita went on absent-mindedly. "By the eighteenth hole I figured out those cads with Coastal Property think I ball every junior executive in Sea-to-Summit to keep my job. Oh God! That must sound slutty to somebody decent like you. I'm really not like that. And I'm not up to pulling any fast ones on you either, Katie. I'm off-duty and this is off-the-record. But I've had it with this whole business so I'm telling you the truth."

"And what's the truth?"

"The truth is, if you and your mother don't come around to their way of thinking—now just listen a sec'—don't freak out. I swear to God, they're people at Sea-to-Summit who'll just go around you—and me. And you don't know how miserable those people can make the lives of anybody resisting the power of their persuasion."

"Their money, you mean."

"Of course, I do. And other things...."

"Those hardball players."

"That's right, honey. Say, have you got anything stronger than this to settle my nerves? 'I'm so dry I'm spittin' cotton.' Ever see that one with Marilyn Monroe?"

"What, a movie?"

"BUSTOP."

"No."

"Well, I did. I saw it when I was fifteen. 'I'm so dry I'm spittin' cotton.' I've always loved that line. Marilyn Monroe."

"I have a question for you, Angela? Why do you need to be making so much money?"

"It's not so much to some people but it's more than I have right now. And I do need to make more. I want my Porsche too, you know. But you really don't have anything to drink around here?"

"A six-pack of Lucky Lager's all we've got in the house."

"Well, get me whatever you've got, then I'll tell you what those sharks have in mind for Cliffport's sea-view acreage."

"I do want to hear that part," Katie responded. "I'll have a beer with you."

"Fine. Then I'm driving back to San Fran. If my bosses knew I was talking to you like this, I'd be out of a job. Maybe I already am. And don't tell me that'd be a good thing. I've got bills to pay."

"Be right back."

While returning with two beers, Katie flipped on the outside light switch, but the bulb went out.

"Thanks," Lita declared, taking hold of a bottle's neck. "I need this. Kampai!"

They sat and drank in moonless darkness.

"Don't you ever get lonely out here all alone? I couldn't stand to sit alone at home on Saturday night. It's Saturday night, right?"

"Who said I'm alone? My mother's here and my son when he's around."

"How come you've never introduced me to him either? Not that they'd like to meet the snake-in-the-grass Sea-to-Summit put on this job. But really, don't you want a man sometimes, you know what I mean? You've got a kid, so I know you're not the Virgin Mary! How old's your boy anyway?"

"Sixteen."

"Oh boy, sixteen. That's a handful! Anyway, I can't remember the last time I sat at home on Saturday night. What time is it? I can't read my watch in the dark. Anyway, it's too late to call my roommate. She's probably already out dancing around the City."

"I've been out enough Saturday nights to last me the rest of my life. Better no company than bad."

"I sure's hell hope you're not referring to me, hon', though I don't blame you if you are. My best behavior is never very good. And I haven't exactly been making your life any easier. Funny thing is that's all I really want."

"What is?"

"To make it go easier for you—but no more real estate business, goddamnit. But tell me the truth about it."

Katie watched the butane flame light up another cigarette.

"About what?"

"Don't you ever get horny? When was the last time you ... you know ... made whoopee, as my Nonna used to say?"

Katie confided that she had last had some loving when her best friend's cousin-in-law came from out of the area as the Wiltons were leaving for Seattle; he had helped them pack up then stayed on in their empty house for a week.

"And before that?"

"I don't know, a long time ... years, maybe...."

"So, how was it, fun? I mean, was he ... any good?"

"He never had any trouble getting it up, if that's what you mean."

"Told you! A girl's got to go for a roll in the hay every once in a while."

"Well, we never set any hay on fire. It was ... okay." Katie wondered why she had risen to the other woman's challenge and what she had to prove to Angela Salomone. "But you were going to tell me what those people have planned for Cliffport."

"That'll cost you one more Lucky, darlin'. And you can't tell anybody I ever told you anything."

"Okay. Be right back."

"Hey, you promise?"

"I promise."

"I gotta be crazy. Go get that beer."

Katie returned wearing a fleece vest and set down two opened bottles.

"Thanks. Well, what can I say? The Monteflores master plan has been all mapped out, Missus Lowrie. And there's no end to the parcels that Cummings Land and Cattle Company will be happy to sell, especially when beef prices go down. I'm serious, sis'. The number of trophy houses those guys are going to be building out up the road? Vignettes One, Two, Three, etcetera. And once your little twenty-acre holdout gets acquired—by whatever means it takes—Sea-to-Summit's services will no longer be required. Acquisition of this last twenty acres will mean S2S has delivered on its contract with Yo-Mizo-Sata and be movin' on to greener pastures. That's the deal: all the acres from Cliffport Beach to the first ridge and inland from there. Get it? With Cummings and the good folks of the City of Fern, they'll be nothing to stop them from building out this west side of whatever you call that mountain up there and offering very wealthy people their overpriced sea-view estates. They just have to find a way to buy off those Coastal Commissioners if they come down this far. That's the plan anyway. Maybe that Cliffport Hotel down on the highway'll be the site of a new realty center. Where that old gas station is, they want to put in an art gallery or something like that. On the corner where that store was, that'll be the 19th Hole Bar 'n Grille or some bull like that. Maybe the links at Monteflores will eventually include one final spectacular drop to Scenic Route One. God knows if that'll happen, but it might. Just a matter of time and money. So, there it is, girlie. That's why they want this place so bad, for their Western Gate to Monteflores. Swear to God, they call it that too: The Western Gate to Monteflores. Where that old lodge is over there in the dark—you guessed it right the other day— they want to build a new lodge with a golf shop, white linen restaurant, I don't know what else. It'll all be one fancy sales center with a hotel for your out-of-town prospects. So now that I've told you what I know and I don't know why, I'm screwed."

Katie sat on in silence. She now comprehended the significance of eliminating the eyesore of the impromptu public dump at the end of the driveway as well as razing the accretion of squalor down on Highway One. She visualized their clearing the Mackenzie Lodge ruins after that, along with the original Mackenzies' first hillside house—her home. The last of the redwood timber that had built Cliffport—all of it would be eliminated to make way for an art center, a gift store, a bistro, an expensive restaurant, a swanky sales office. If no one stopped them, they would use old growth redwood to build their Western Gate to Monteflores, she thought, and leave no memory of the Mackenzies or the McLoughlins or the Lowries. Even Chapel Grove's ancient redwoods, all of them, might be erased, obliterated, no trace left.

"So," Lita took up again. "You want to kick me out now or you want to know how I got to be such a bad girl?"

"This thing's bigger than both of us."

"That's what I've been trying to tell you, sister. So, do you want to know why I've sold my soul to the devil or don't you? I know why, I do. I can tell you too if you care." Lita chugged at her beer. "Get me one more of these and I'll tell you my whole sorry story if you want to hear it. May as well, I'm screwed now, tipping you off to everything I know. Then I'll get out of your hair for good, I promise."

"I've known bad girls before you. Maybe I was a bad girl once myself."

"Yeah? Tell you my story, then you tell me yours."

Katie went for the last two beers in the fridge. [1]

*

During Elisabeth Lowrie's midnight tour, she discovered the intruder sprawled out facedown atop the mattress in Donald Duncan's former bedroom, stripped to her bra and panties, her boots and summer dress dropped on the floor. Elise let the dogs out to pee and in the grainy darkness made out six empty bottles on the table. She fed the dogs some kibbles and went back to her room with a cup of chamomile tea. Unable to read, closing her eyes, gently rocking, she heard Liliane Piagère Lowrie's voice reciting the Lord's Prayer in French between her ears.

———————

- Hello.
- *Hello, Kate.*
- Who is this?
- *It's me, Kate. Dick.*
- Richard?
- *Blowin' your mind, or what?*

Silence

Hey, Kate.
- What do you want?
- *What do I want? I want to say hello.*
- Why?
- *I want to tell you something.*
- What?
- *I'm sorry. You know what I mean?*

Silence

You hear me?

Silence

Kate, come on.
- I don't want to talk to you.
- *What the hell? You won't accept my apology? Come on!*
- What do you want from me, Richard? It's been like fifteen years since

I've heard from you. You call up: *I'm sorry.* Nah. I don't want anything to do with you.

Silence

Did you hear me?

Silence

- *I want to see our son.*

- WHAT?

- *Our son. I want to see the boy.*

- You've gotta be kidding me. *Our son. The boy.* You asshole! I've worked my ass off for fifteen years raising our son without a word from you and not a penny.

- *But I want to change. I want to try but I need your help.*

- Don't bullshit me, Richard.

- *Jesus, Kate! Give a guy a break. You won't even let a father who fucked up once try and make it right with his kid?*

- How are you going to make it right? Where are you anyway?

- *Marina.*

- You're living in Marina?

- *Sort of.*

- What's that mean, *sort of*?

- *I'm in this program. The county puts me up in a motel here so I have to pay like next to nothing. As long as I show up for the appointments and all, everything's cool. But I'll have to find another living situation....*

- Nuh-uh, no way, you're not living here.

- *Jesus Christ! I'm not asking for that.*

Silence

I'm asking for your forgiveness.

- And permission to see Donald? No. Who's writing your script? No, Richard. Leave us alone.

- *Goddammit, Kate. I'm finally in fucking treatment, cleaning up my act and SLAM BAM THANK YOU MA'AM you shut me down like a motherfucker.*

- *Like a motherfucker?* No, Richard, no. You can't see Donald, the answer's no. You can't talk to him. You can't visit him. It's not going to happen. Don't step foot on this place. You hear me?

- *Did you even hear what I just said? I'm in rehab. I'm going to change. I am changing.*

Silence

- What rehab?

- *You know, rehab. Counseling. Physical therapy too. I had a little accident.*

Silence

- Have you been in prison?

- *No.*

- Jail?

- *Yeah, sure....*

- The penitentiary?

- *No.*

- State prison?

- *I just told you no, goddamnit. The Monterey County Jail. But I'll be off probation soon. I've cleaned up my act, Kate.*

Silence

- You had to clean it up, you mean. I guess I should say good for you, but I can't. No, Richard, it won't work. After what you did to me, screwing up my life? You used me, you rotten son of a bitch.

- *I loved you, babe. We were—*

- ... don't you use that word love with me, you creep, and don't call me babe! If you walked in here right now I'd scratch your eyes out!

Silence

The damage you've done to Donald dropping out on him before he was even one! Do you hear me? And now you want *to make it right with the kid.* I can't believe it. Who writes your lines, your rehab counselor? I don't trust you. I don't believe you. I don't even like you.

- *I get the message.*

- Then stay away. I'm hanging up and don't call back.

- *Wow. I didn't expect this comin' from you, Kate. And you wouldn't have to scratch my eyes out, sister. I already got a scar on my face like fuckin' barbed wire. If you had any idea what I've been through.*

Silence

You don't even want to know what happened?

Silence

I almost died, Kate.

-By an overdose?

Silence

-*No, not by an overdose. I had a car accident. Make a long story short, I had this job driving this Audio-Visual van for all the community colleges in the Bay Area, both Bay Areas: Monterey and SF. I was handling the best damned portable A-V equipment available. State of the art. You know what I'm talking about?*

Silence

So, I'm driving that van from college to college. Even Cabrillo. Hey, you still there?

- Yeah.

- *For almost ten years straight it was goin' pretty good. Too good. Settin' up equipment, solving technical difficulties, runnin' the sound system on all their shows, shit like that. Then I don't know, I got to dealin' a little booh. It was just too easy, you know what I mean? Those college kids will buy anything: stems, shake, no big deal. A nickel bag of Mexican here, a dime bag there. Then it got so there were these side orders for harder stuff. Like snow.*

- Cocaine?

- *I don't know how it got so out of control. I can see that now looking back on it, after counseling and—*

- Shut up, Richard! Whatever happened next, I don't want to hear any more. Just shut up!

- *Whoa, Kate!*

- Whatever you've been through, whatever you're going through now, whatever you're going through next–count us out. I'll call the cops if you come around here. When I was young and gullible you hit on me, Dickhead. And then you fucking used me. You're a user. You use people and you use drugs. Give me a break, you shit! You used me then you threw me away. And you threw our son away too!

- *You're the one who threw me out!*

- And if I had let you keep on using me? By now you'd be pimping me on Market Street.

- *You're fuckin' up my head, Kate. I never knew you had it in you. You're one tough chick.*

- You called and you got your answer, okay? No. Don't call. Don't show up. Don't go around me trying to see him. I don't care what the law says about our situation. I don't care what visiting rights you may claim to have. Wasn't that next? Isn't that what you were going to lay on me next, how you have some legal right to see your son? Forget it. We were never legally married. Tell that to the judge. I'm sure you'll be talking with plenty of judges in the future.

Silence

- *You still makin' music?*

- What'd you just say?

- *Are you still playin' guitar, singin'? You were good—*

- What did you ever care about my music? You'd say anything now to get what you want.

- *But you had a great voice, Kate, and real performance potential—*

- *Performance potential?* I'm hanging up and I'm warning you, Richard Debruen, I'm warning you right now. You show up around here and I'm not responsible for what I might do.

- *We're all responsible for what we do. That's what—*

- SHUT UP! I see through you like fucking pane glass, you asshole! You think maybe I haven't been through a few things myself in the last fifteen years? I don't need you. I don't want you in my life. You're a user. DO YOU EVEN KNOW WHAT I MEAN? I won't let you mess up DD's life any more than you already have.

- *DD?*

- That's his nickname; Dickhead's my nickname for you.

- *Whoa. This is some serious shit.*

- I'm having enough trouble getting him though high school and—

- *High school, wow! What year's he in now?*

- Forget it, Richard. You're a loser. I'll kill you. I wish you had died in whatever accident you had.

Silence

- *He's my son too, Kate.*

- He could have been, once upon a time. Not now.

Silence

- *Are you married?*

Silence

You got a man, Kate?

- GO TO HELL AND STAY THERE!

(click)

Chapter 5

Violations

SZ   Hello?

EL   It's me.

SZ   Elise! I thought we might be hearing from Cliffport. I bet Mike you'd be first to call.

EL   Well, you won that bet. You can tell him Donald Duncan Lowrie's grandmother is on the telephone and she wants to know: how is the boy?

SZ   Doin' good, Ellie.

EL   Donny's doing well?

SZ   He is. I'd let you talk to him, but I don't where he is.

EL   What do you mean, you don't know where he is?

SZ   He's at work, Grandma! Don's been hard at work six days a week.

EL   *Don?*

SZ   Sounds more manly than Donny, doesn't it? Anyway, that's what he wants us to call him.

EL   Did you say he's working six days a week? That's something new.

SZ   He's a regular on a brush-whacking crew.

EL   What's a brush-whacking crew?

SZ   Every summer PG&E pays these rough-and-tumble contractors to clear brush out from under the power lines. Mike lined that job up for him.

EL   Where do they *whack brush*?

SZ   Out in the woods, up in the hills. A crummy picks him up at the bottom of the road at 5:00 AM every day except Sunday. Whether they get to the work site at five-thirty or six-thirty, they're paid for a full eight hours, and they drop him back off around two-thirty or three in the afternoon. Sometimes four. Some of those locations are harder to get in and out of than others. They go where big equipment can't. Lately they've been working on the ridge between Ukiah and Boonville so that's not far at all. The van pulls a chuck wagon and drinking water and a port-a-potty, and they spend all day out in the boonies, whacking brush. That's why I can't tell you exactly where he is. He should come staggering up the road in an hour or so if you want to call back then.

SZ   Why *staggering*?

EL   That's intense terrain, Elise. And it's been over a hundred degrees three days in a row now.

EL   It sounds like chain gang work. Is it safe?

SZ   He's fine, Ellie. Want to call back and talk to him then?

EL   Oh no, I'd better not. He'll thinking I'm checking on him—

SZ   ... which you are.

EL   He'd say I'm babying him or something. Don...?

SZ   Come on, call back if you like. He's in the shower by four-thirty and by five he's prowling my dining room like a starving wolf.

EL   Well, I wanted the real news from you. I don't want to get it secondhand from my daughter anymore, all filtered and watered down. Kaitlin increasingly seems to think she has to protect me from reality.

SZ   I'm talking reality, Ellie. You wouldn't recognize him. He went to the barbershop.

EL   Donny cut his hair?

SZ   After two days out in the brush, Donny did. The heat, Elise, he had to. The boy's learned to use gloves and ankle gators and goggles. It's rough country out there and it's just too hot. Not to mention the poison oak and the rattlers and the ticks—

EL   ... now stop it, Suzanne, stop it! I know you're just saying that to get my goat ... aren't you?

SZ   Too much reality for you, Granny? Listen, Ellie, your grandson's fine. He's young and he's strong and he's living clean as a whistle. Up before sunrise, in bed by dark.

EL   Are you and I talking about the same person?

SZ   That Lowrie boy does play it a little close to the vest with his old aunt and uncle, but I guess that's normal.

EL   What do you mean, he plays it *close to the vest*?

SZ   I mean, he doesn't open up much, at least not to us. Even when the boys drive into town, Mike says he doesn't talk about whatever's on his mind. But oh, he loves driving Mike's big truck!

EL   Of course he does. But I know what you mean about him holding back. Gone are the days when he would rattle on to Mom and me about what was on his mind ... or in his heart.

SZ   What do we expect? He's sixteen. He's a young man now.

EL   He's a boy, Suze.

SZ   They're all always boys, Ellie. But what I meant is, he's acting out the Marlboro Man.

EL   And how are you, Suzanne? How is Mike? Donny's guardian angels.

SZ   Life's good, it's good. A little too smoky with the grass fires adding to what the teepee burners put out.

EL   Are you already having grass fires?

SZ   Every summer, you know that, all that open BLM land. And I always forget how bad it can get. Cloverdale's annual summer smoke-out, although our little corner of the world's spared the worst of it. How are you feeling? Still postponing surgery?

EL   I am, and I am not. The chiropractor isn't certain surgery would have a positive effect.

SZ   Bummer.

EL   Kaitlin insists the last of our money be spent on repairing my knee or some treatment on my back or something. And when Kaitlin insists on something ... well, you know how that goes. But now I'm waiting for clearance from the cardiologist for any operation.

SZ   Right. So, have you burned through that money the old griper left you? What was her name? Jane...?

EL   Jan. The money Jan left Kaitlin, you mean? Jan McLoughlin never left me one cent, for heaven's sake.

SZ   She left you the house and grounds, didn't she?

EL   It's in Kaitlin's name. The lawyer claimed it was an expedient of some sort about taxes or something. Without my daughter ...? I'd be homeless or in some trailer park along a river somewhere. I wouldn't have gotten one square foot of property from that woman. But Kaitlin has been absolutely equitable with the money. She invites my partic- ipation in the big decisions. Her new truck, the big glasshouse, the irrigation—all of it. The plumbing is redone. Her greenhouse is almost finished.

SZ   The plumbing in the house?

EL   Not inside, but all around it. They laid new pipes and arranged the water system to direct freshwater to the nursery and the house. I don't understand exactly how it all works, but it sounds smart to me. I told her now we ought to have a new septic tank sunk in the ground— after all these years...? But that bullheaded daughter of mine says if it's a choice between a septic tank and fixing my knee then "no way!" That's how she speaks to me, Suze: "No way!" Headstrong, just like a teenager.

SZ   You gotta love that pistol-packin' Katie—I know I do!

EL   Well, I do too, I do too, of course I do. And beneath that tough hide of hers is one tender-hearted, extremely considerate human being.

SZ   She isn't right there by the phone now, is she? We have to figure out when to send your Donny boy back home. Mama wants him home by September 1st, right, to work something out with the high school? Hey, Ellie, if the dates work out, how about you all spend Labor Day weekend here with us? Let your daughter drive her new rig up here and you two spend a night or two? We have room. Who cares if it's one-hundred degrees when you're sitting in the shade gabbin' away with a glass of something cool to drink? Something non-alcoholic ... of course....

EL   Suzanne! Don't you test me too! But I'm not sure I'm ready for such a long car trip ... my back....

SZ   Okay, okay, so be that way.

EL   And Kaitlin's awfully busy, really she is.

SZ   Still, think about it. The brush crew will be done the last day of August. Mike'll probably still be putting out fires at work and out in the boonies.

EL   Thank you, sweetheart. You're the dearest friend a person could possibly have.

SZ   Well, you did call me an angel a second ago, and I'll remember that. Oh, by the way, our lodger can keep his last paycheck. He doesn't have to pay us one thing more.

EL   Oh, Suze! See what I mean? That's so kind and helpful of you. Maybe the boy will gain a sense of the value of good hard work.

SZ   It was Mike's idea and I second it. Let Mister Don go home with some pocket change or pour it all into the gas tank of that old jalopy of his.

EL   Yes, he probably will. He'll probably do just that.

SZ   Okay, old gal, I better run. This call is costing you, unless you're flush, of course.

EL   We are not flush.

SZ   Anyway, besides the other animals around here, I've got two big boys to feed soon.

EL   Two big men, don't you mean?

SZ   Oh, Elise, you can be proud of your grandson. I know I am ... better than the grandson I'll never have....

EL   Oh, Suzanne....

SZ   Now let's not get all teary-eyed and sentimentalist at the same time.

EL   No, let's not. I'm so glad I called and so happy to hear the good news. Donny cut his hair! Wait until his mother hears that!

SZ   Have Katie call me, would you, about dates I mean? Before seven in the morning, after seven at night. That way she'll find me near the phone.

EL   Of course I will, of course. Thank you so much. And thank Mike, do thank Mike for me. Better not tell Donny I called ... do you think?

SZ   I won't tell him if you don't want me to. Anyway, everything's fine.

EL   Everything's fine.

SZ   Ciao, Elisabeth!

EL   Goodbye, dear.

*

Within a week of his return to Cliffport, his mother and grandmother were disabused of any illusion that Donald had permanently embraced reform. He refused to meet with the high school principal, and he resumed residence in the barn, which again became his band's default hangout-cum-practice studio. Katie gave him a list of jobs to accomplish: spreading crushed granite in the greenhouse's pathways; bolting steel benches in place; shoveling oak leaf litter from the forest floor onto tarps and dragging them downhill. After he had done a semi-satisfactory job of those tasks, she told him to bring on a friend to assist him in the repair of the simple post and beam frame structures covered in shade cloth; an afterschool helpmate could be paid in cash while Donald worked in exchange for room and board. That project progressed somewhat over three afternoons until Katie put on the binoculars and glassed them straddling some stacked two-by-fours, sharing a joint, occasionally striking their hammerheads on the lumber in imitation of hammering. She paid his friend for six hours work and let him go on his way before confronting her son with the ultimatum: work in the nursery, generate income elsewhere and pay rent, or find another place to live.

*

"Why don't you just sell this place? Did you even find out what they'd pay for it? Sell it, Mom! You wouldn't have to get up every morning and move plants around all day."

"Those plants are my friends, Donald. And they're our only source of income, for now."

"I don't want to be a slave to plants all my life. What are you going to do, Mom? Work here for the rest of your life and die?"

"Maybe. Probably."

"You could be living in a new house, Mom. This house was old and funky before I was even born."

"Before I was born too."

"So? After that, then what?"

"After what?"

"You stay here after Gran'ma dies. Then you die. Then what will happen to this property?"

"I don't know. What kind of a question is that to ask like that? Anyway, right now nobody's dying."

"Well, are you going to pass it on me? It's my right to inherit it, right?"

"What for? So, you could flip it off at the first opportunity? The ways things are going around here, Donald Duncan, I'd probably donate it to some non-profit organization before I'd pass it on to you, if I thought you were just going to liquidate it the day after my funeral."

"Are you shittin' me? You'd give the only thing I'll ever inherit to the State of California?"

"I didn't say that."

"What do you think this should be, the new Little Big Basin Park or something?"

"I never said that. But I know Chapel Grove will be preserved. Those trees are protected. The cemetery is protected forever. At least I hope it is."

*

In clean clothes, with his hair tied back, Donald Lowrie spent a full day looking for work at the cement plant in Davenport, the tannery in Santa Cruz, and the San Lorenzo Lumberyard in Felton. All three personnel offices basically told him the same thing: We're not hiring, and you belong in school. Back home, he turned on his mother, blaming her notoriety for the blanket refusals to let him submit employment applications. He attacked her "weirdo ways" and her reputation as a "hippie nature girl" for having cursed his prospects for work on Santa Cruz County's North Coast forever. She laughed at his flailing argumentation and delivered him a new list of chores in the nursery. In a pique of adolescent fury, Donald threw his acoustic guitar into the Fleetside's cab and filled the pickup's bed with a carton of clothes, a milkcrate full of hand tools, his sleeping bag and a tent, and miscellaneous car parts. Locating her on the hillside, he told her hated her and was tired of her fucking up his life. He said he would be back to see his "gran'ma" and the dogs—but not her. If he thought he stood a chance, he said, he would be applying for work on the Monteflores project, then he left without letting Baby Blue Eye stay on board.

On the second night without word from him, Katie felt her right eye spasming and, after breaking the padlock on the barn door—looking inside for she knew not what—she telephoned her Aunt Suzanne to find out if her son had taken refuge in Cloverdale. Suzanne promised to inform her if he did show up there and pledged not to make any living arrangements with the boy without his mother's foreknowledge and approval. Katie then followed her mother's advice and left a message in Sherriff Pendleton's office requesting that he call the Lowrie residence in Cliffport. He did so and, off the record, agreed to put out the word with his men in the northern coastal and mountain region, especially with the one patrolman who passed through Fern, Davenport, and Swanton once or twice a week. But running away from home wasn't a crime in California, and the sheriff—familiar enough with Cliffport's sole residents—declared that if the boy was sixteen years old and in possession of a legal driver's license, his flight from home after a family fight was no good reason to notify the CHP or broadcast an all-points bulletin to the entire police force anytime soon.

Donald had run away but not far, having joined Ross Stewart living in an cluster of older recreational vehicles parked in an unplanned, unlit, unsupervised dirt lot on the outskirts of Princeton-by-the-Sea north of Half Moon Bay, where Ross was subletting a trailer with three good tires on a week-to-week basis from someone who claimed to know its rightful owner. Ross appreciated the ten dollars Donald kicked in per week and pledged not to betray the teenager's location if anyone came around. Donald learned to take outdoor showers at the unlocked bathroom on the public beach and to take advantage of the establishment next door, a legitimate community of stationary mobile homes boasting a Coke machine, an unlocked bin of crushed ice, a washer and dryer, and some plastic chairs on Astroturf.

The teen steered clear of the Coast Guard Station at the end of the dock but didn't avoid the hobos and winos huddling in Pillar Point Harbor. When he went looking for work, the manager of the commercial dockyard's Marine Supply & Hardware sent him packing, and when he wandered through an open door into the Seafarer's Hall of the Commercial Fishermen's Wives Association, an older man barked, 'Stay the hell outta here, you little wharf rat!' But after he did a fair job repainting the wooden sea goddess riding the wooden shark at the entrance to the Pink Mermaid Bar & Grill, he began picking up day jobs: restacking wooden pallets, scraping out plastic tubs, powerhosing the concrete pad and picnic tables at the Crab Shack, where the owner gave him a butcher-paper cone full of fish and chips whenever the kid performed some menial chore. People grew as accustomed to the familiar figure of the "long hair" as they were used to the feral cats and the trailer park's impoverished elders who, on their regular rounds, turned over promising scraps at the ends of sticks while walking their dogs and collecting empty bottles and cans. Sometimes Donald would pinch a wad of Ross' stash and sit on a stockpile of interlocking concrete jacks, enjoying the clear fall weather and listening to the hypnotic swaying of masts in the marina, clicking and clacking like a stick forest of deciduous trees. To the regulars, his silhouette became as unremarkable as the shapes of the pelicans, the cormorants, the pigeons, and the gulls lined out along the jetty.

Donald's only brush with authorities occurred one Saturday evening at the end of the main pier, where he had strung trap lines to crab pots salvaged from a neglected pile of debris. A pair of uniformed Fish & Game officials—who had spent the day using portable scales and specially marked planks for weighing and measuring the sports fishing boats' hauls of Dungeness crab—cornered the youth for a chat. Officer Merriam studied his driver's license and ended by issuing a citation for fishing without a license, ordering him to gather up his traps, and warning him not to show up on the pier again without carrying on his person a current season's license. Donald feigned following orders slowly enough that, once the men had packed up their gear and driven off the day, he simply cut the poly lines, abandoning the worthless, ineffective pots on the water bottom.

That year the Central Coast's Dungeness commercial crab fishing season was scheduled to start on the second Tuesday of November; the fleet was gearing up. Recreational fishermen had been landing huge male adults, and the industrial harvest promised a bumper crop. Donald's willingness to do any work on short notice and a cash-only basis started paying off: he spent a week loading crusty, wire-wrapped, 12" × 40" rebar crab pots onto pallets then offloading them onto boats. Ross Stewart was not excited about returning to the cold shed for another season shelling crab claws coming fast at him down the chute. He could eat as much meat as he liked—that led to loose bowels in a hurry—but the processing plant paid poorly, regardless of the position. Wages on the dock—operating the hydraulic blocks that lifted traps or forklifting on the all-night shift when the season reached its peak—didn't amount to a huge step up the pay scale either. What Ross wanted was a profitable job on a boat: setting lines, pulling in traps, working the live tank when the steel screen raised the fighting-mad monsters up to be wrested apart from one another by hand, the keepers thrown into plastic bins, those of questionable size tossed into pails for individual measurement. The work on a crabbing boat was cold and wet and often nocturnal but, with coffee and pills, Ross knew how to make it bearable, for he had spent two seasons in Alaska, where the king crabs had torn his first pair of rubber gloves to shreds before he learned to work fast enough. When Ross met someone who knew someone in Fort Bragg looking for a seasoned deckhand on the CRAB MAGNET—a forty-three-foot wood-hull vessel with an 180 HP engine slated to fish out of Noyo Harbor starting November 9th—Ross was hired on. Donald begged to tag along; Ross made no promises but agreed. Before caravanning with the older man to Fort Bragg, the boy managed to trade his guitar and amp for a duffel bag of new-crop Santa Cruz Mountain marijuana and to drop off a Hallmark card in the Lowrie mailbox for his grandmother's sixty-ninth birthday. At Noyo Harbor, Ross vouched for the youth's strength and capacity for hard work and the skipper said okay: if the greenhorn would do what he was told and make himself scarce when not wanted, he could come on board as bait boy and general help.

Renting yet another broken trailer parked on Noyo Flat, Donald again shared expenses with Ross. He sent another drugstore card home at Christmas and, on his seventeenth birthday in February, he sent a postcard. At sea he was exhilarated by the sheer sensations that commanded his nights and days; on shore, he separated more buds and leaves from stems and, when he had sold out, went inland to explore the scene in Mendocino County. Mid-May, when the skipper called it quits for the season, Donald's wallet was swollen with twenty-dollar bills, and he wasn't inclined to go back to Santa Cruz. He mailed a letter home announcing that he was headed north to look for work in the fisheries of Puget Sound: not to worry, he was stoked, having great time, no big plans. If his DMV registration renewal arrived in the mail, forward it to PO Box 179 Fort Bragg.

————

In anticipation of Thanksgiving's annual private pilgrimage to lay the wreaths in Chapel Grove, Katie sought a roundabout approach, which might provide an alternative to the steep, uneven path up from the trailhead at Jan's bench; that trail was a tough trek on foot even for her, but now it would be prohibitively strenuous for her increasingly lame mother. Driving up Everson Road, ignoring all NO TRESPASSING signs at the turnoff, Katie cruised down Cuesta Ridge Lane, peering into the woods to detect any former overgrown access. She seemed to recall, from her childhood, that an extinct logging road—abandoned even before she was born—took off from the old Mackenzie panhandle, skirted the millpond, and intersected with the main footpath dropping down into the congregation of giant redwoods under which Cliffport's pioneer families lay at rest. At the gashed mouth of an entry punched into the forest, she stopped the truck: between heaps of soil, stone, and branches, a newly plowed surface ran the length of the course she had been looking for.

Turning a blind eye to more PRIVATE PROPERTY signage, she eased the pickup down a bulldozed passageway, the raw, fresh seam of a forest wound with slash and construction refuse banked to both sides. Within one hundred yards she encountered a tubular cross bar of yellow steel blocking vehicular traffic. Midway across the bar, a framed, laminated notice was suspended by metal bands:

The barrier's locking mechanism included a padlock tucked deep up inside a steel box so as to prevent it from being picked or cut. Katie cursed, locked Baby Blue in the cab, ducked under the bar, and continued on foot down the corridor hacked through the second growth redwood and fir.

Within another hundred yards, she came upon an eight-foot high security fence installed around the old millpond. Walking the perimeter of the reservoir's caged one-acre, kicking at debris the construction crew had left behind, she tested the chain-links' capacity to hold her weight: the mesh openings afforded her no toehold, and the horizontal tension wires along the bottom limited the play of the fencing at its base. She realized that it would take an agile, lightweight individual wearing special shoes to scamper up the poles rooted in half-buried balls of concrete set ten feet apart; even then, the prickly ends of galvanized steel along the horizontal top border—although not strictly speaking barbed wire—would offer mean welcome.

She was deep in enemy territory now. No more threatening signage was required, yet she found a crudely spray-painted plywood board leaning against the new fence's padlocked gate:

Katie didn't comprehend what the millpond needed protection from. Deer, lengthening their necks to drink? Raccoons, washing their hands in water? Swallows on the wing, skimming the surface while dropping down for a sip or to scoop up insects? From now on, local youth would be prevented from taking a dip in Mackenzie's Millpond, and the next generation of young lovers would be dissuaded from lingering in the vicinity let alone lounging there. While the chain-link fence might not break the younger ones' hearts, the insult would surely hurt older lovers who relished memories of earlier encounters in the secretive glade. Katie decided her mother need not learn of the new proprietor's encroachment upon the source of her nursery's irrigation water and this extirpation of collective memories going back at least one hundred years.

*

Two days before Thanksgiving, Katie filled a burlap bag with fragrant wreaths made from Douglas fir, bay laurel, and the needles and cones of redwood, and escorted her mother to Jan's bench. Baby Blue Eye policed the area while the Lowrie women settled on the wooden ledge of the downed redwood log out of which a quarter section had been cut more than a century ago; they surveyed the meadow below and the hillside they were now forced to share with YMS INT'L Ltd.

Since Angela Salomone's last appearance, the absentee landowners had made their presence known in various ways. Toward the end of October, County Public Works—presumably under pressure from Coastal Property Management—spent three days employing heavy equipment to remove the auto bodies, scrap metal, mattresses, appliances, and other garbage from the unlawful public dump at end of the driveway, and the ground was scraped bare; the Lowries predicted that the overhead canopy of Tasmanian blue gums would inhibit any plants from volunteering on that far side of the road. The following week, without forewarning, Gath Construction dispatched a twenty-five-foot gooseneck flatbed trailer to One Grade Road, offloaded a backhoe and a front loader on the gravel lane leading in and out of the Lowries' residence, and drove off without a word. When Jim's construction crew arrived to work at 8:00 AM, they discovered their access denied, parked their trucks down in the whale watch turnout on Highway One, and hiked the quarter mile up Lower Steep Creek trail. That afternoon, a second Gath employee stationed a mid-size gondola at an odd but serviceable angle right where the scrapheap had been removed from the far side of Grade Road, and over the next three days a six-man crew deployed a grappling arm and a Bobcat to clear out the driveway's ditches, loading the junk into the gondola to be hauled off to the dump. The men refused to answer Katie's questions concerning this unannounced roadblock, and she made several attempts to reach Gerald Hudson in order to seek his advice about the Lowries' legal recourse; the San Francisco attorney never picked up, nor did the Sheriff's office send an officer to investigate as promised over the phone. The Lowrie women hunkered down to wait out the siege until, three days later—having chewed up the banks of the levee-like roadway—the equipment was carried away on the gooseneck trailer and a truck-tractor retrieved the gondola. Within weeks, green spears of nutgrass and horsetail were visible re-emerging from the torn-up ditches.

After that week of noise and confinement, the Lowries witnessed a two-man crew built a mortised, three-cleft-rail fence along the north side of Grade Road—running from the corner at Highway One, up past the entries to the Lowries' lane and the old lodge, tapering off where wide-spread evergreen oaks overarched the darkened road above. When they saw that the barrier had been left open at the entrance to their driveway as well as between the tall, twin-redwood portal to the old lodge, the Lowries assumed that those two gaps would remain unfenced, but wire mesh gates were soon installed spanning both spaces, and chains with padlocks were permanently attached to the latch posts. The lodge gate was locked; the padlock secured to the chain on the gate to the Lowries' driveway was not.

From where they sat on Jan's bench, they could survey long stretches of the fence, and Elise voiced her opinion that the oakwood rails running parallel to Grade Road at least blended into the rural scene. "You must admit, dear. It all looks so much better without the boneyard in the ditches and the junk dumped out on Grade Road."

Katie suppressed mention of the ugly cyclone fencing around the millpond, which did not fit into the natural surroundings at all; she didn't want to distress her mother with further evidence of YMS' brand being stamped on the land. "Yeah, it does. But they didn't have to go about the whole thing the way they did."

"I do still have to wonder why they're going to such great expense," Elise mused aloud. "Whatever are they trying to keep out or in? That sort of fence won't keep an animal from going or coming, except perhaps some old milk cow we haven't seen around here for forty years. Whatever is it for, Kaitlin?"

"They want to make a statement."

"But to whom?"

"To you, to me, to the new residents of Vignettes One at Monteflores. To the greater citizenry of the North Coast. At least it's not one of those vinyl white horse fences they've got up the road."

"Oh? Do they have that fake plantation fencing up there?"

"Miles of it. The part of the golf course you can see from Grade Road is lousy in pure white plastic. I must admit if you blur your eyes it looks pretty sharp against the Kentucky bluegrass or whatever they've got planted. Wide, weed-free lawns, 'as seen on TV.' But what really bugs me is that lock on our gate. They aren't locking it yet, but they could."

"But they haven't given us the key, have they?"

"Nope."

"Well, that's not right then. It's not legal. We have a perfect right to use that easement in and out of our property anytime we want to. What about in an emergency? All that is written into the title, isn't it?"

"Of course, it is. But you know how it goes with locks. Keys get lost. Combinations get changed, forgotten. The first time I find that locked I'm taking bolt cutters to it, I swear."

"Now, dear, don't do anything rash. Perhaps they had to put a locking devise on our gate to satisfy the letter of some law or some code or other. For their insurers, perhaps."

"You can see from here how their machines tore up the banks. That silly little gravel levee wasn't built to hold the weight of all that heavy machinery."

"In any event, they're gone, it's done, and the gate isn't locked—for the time being."

"But what's next?" Katie rejoined. "When the nursery gets busy in spring, I can't be dealing with locking and unlocking any gates."

"My, my, my. You're getting to be the worrier in the family now, aren't you?"

The sheepdog popped out of the bushes to check on their laughter then disappeared.

"Does that huge old redwood trunk still block the trail up ahead?"

"It does."

"Then you best go on ahead, Kaitlin. The steps up and over that fallen log alone are too much for me. If you still can't go under it and you still can't go around it, well ... I'm afraid this old potter can't go over it, even with your kind help. We both know I can't make it up all the way to the grove anymore, so you go on ahead, please."

"But there's no hurry."

"No, there's no hurry," Elise concurred.

Baby Blue Eye swung by to check on their silence.

"I must say your new glasshouse looks very pretty shining in the sun. Are you happy with it?"

"I am, and just wait till I put some whitewash on in the spring. It'll look as spiffy as one of those Vignettes they're offering for sale at Monteflores for a quarter million dollars!"

"A quarter of a million dollars?" Elise echoed. "Why ever do they call them 'Vignettes,' I wonder."

"I think because of these fake little vineyard blocks that separate the house lots. I've heard they might be ag tax write-offs for somebody but I don't know. It's all some snotty scam, for sure."

"I can't get over it," Elise mulled, looking about. "Old Mother Merle is the only dog we haven't buried somewhere on the place. I understand why you left her at the vet, I do, dear."

"But what?"

"I do wish there were some special place where Donny could go to pay his respects to Merle when he comes back home."

"If he does come back home."

"Oh, he'll come home all right—just as his mother did before him. He'll come home. Maybe we ought to build a bit of a shrine or something. After all, after Jeffrey Wilton, Mother Merle was Donny's best friend growing up."

"That's true too."

Baby Blue Eye looked for a place to land between them on the bench and leapt up as soon as Katie scooted over to make room.

"Can we talk another moment, Kaitlin?"

"Sure. About what?"

"About what you're going to do with my remains when I'm dead and gone."

"Ma'am! Do we have to talk about that right now?"

"Seems to me there's no better time nor place. This is as close to Chapel Grove as I'll ever get—alive, that is. And I'm too heavy to be carried up there, either now or later in a coffin."

"I suppose you're going to get super practical about this too?"

"Yes, I am. I don't want to be a burden on anyone, least of all on you, Kaitlin. You do know, there's nothing in my understanding of what the Lord wants from me that says I must have a formal Christian burial. You know that much about me, or don't you?"

"I read your memoirs, Mom. You never wrote any more of those, did you?" [1]

"No. No, I didn't. I suppose I've just been living my memoir from where I left off. And now that we talk...."

"Mom, listen to me. All your friends from the Guild and the folks in Fern who've forgiven you for spawning me—"

"... pshaw!"

"They'll want to have a memorial service for you. They'll want to gather together somewhere and sing songs and shares pictures, to eat food, to celebrate your life."

"Well, let them, for goodness' sake! And you must lead them in those songs, Kaitlin, please. Gather in the meadow there or down at the whale watch or up in the Grange Hall, I don't care where. I'll have traveled beyond all my worries and woes by then, now won't I?"

They sat in silence. Katie's fingers tested the springiness of some conifer needle tips sticking through the burlap weave. Elise reached over the top of the dog and laid her hand on her daughter's hand.

"And when you do have that gathering, you will let them all know that without them—and you—I never would have made it through some hard times. Let there be absolutely no doubt about it: without their kindnesses and generosity and yours, I would not. Speak it for me, dear, please. Let them know how profoundly grateful I have always felt." She retracted her hand. "But back to my initial question. How would you feel about having me cremated and scattering my ashes in Chapel Grove?"

"Is that legal?"

"If a doctor completes a form it is. You'd have to follow the rules."

"Does it cost money?"

"I think the funeral director collects a fee. I don't know how much."

"How do you know about all this, Mom?"

"I checked it out once ... in Jan McLoughlin's case, as a matter of fact. I must still have a booklet somewhere on state and county regulations about spreading ashes at sea or on private land." She paused. "You never did collect Jan's remains, did you, dear?"

"No, I never did. She really didn't care what happened. At least she didn't leave any instructions."

"Well? So? In answer to your earlier question, this is exactly why we're talking about such practical matters on an impractically beautiful day. If possible, I'd like you to spread my ashes over the graves of Dorothea and John. And sprinkle a portion over your brother's grave, like a gentle rain. That's all I want. I don't need to be buried in a coffin. Do you suppose the road from above is all grown over by now?"

"Yeah ... most likely."

"Then how is anybody going to get a coffin up there now? That's how they used to bring the boxes in, you know, on a horse drawn cart on that logging road that led to the pond. I'm too heavy as it is, even without a coffin. You couldn't have carried Mother Blue up there and you surely can't carry me. Besides, you shouldn't have to, there's just no need. There, I'm done now. Enough about coffins! I'll put it in writing and Mike and Suzanne can sign it as witnesses when they get here tomorrow. Now, is there anything else we ought to go over before you go up there and do what's right? I thank God every day that you've saved those big trees up there and the sacred ground beneath them."

"Oh, Mom, I love you so much."

"Oh, Kaitlin. What else can we do but love one another? What else is there?"

The women watched the clouds' shadows shifting across the land and passing over the stippled surface of the sea.

"I sure hope we really and truly have all that saved, the trees and the ground, I mean. I'm going to have to review the details one of these days before Hudson is no longer around to help me out."

"Oh Lord, yes, you must do that. You mustn't let anyone on earth ever desecrate Chapel Grove."

"I won't. I swear to God, Mom. I won't."

"I know you won't. Kaitlin Liliane Lowrie. Do you have any idea in the world how often I have thanked the Lord that you and I got through that awful period of your rather prolonged adolescence? And I hope and—"

"... pray that DD gets through this period in his life his too. Is that what you're getting at?"

"I suppose, I suppose it is. For a while—now you must remember this—there was a time when I thought I'd lost you forever."

"I came darn close to losing myself. When I was back East, I wouldn't have blamed you if you'd swapped me out for Josie. I was so confused."

"And Donny's confused about all of it now. But you can bet wherever he is, on land or at sea, in his heart of heart he misses his mother—"

"...his grandmother, you mean."

"One day, when he comes to his senses, as you did—no, wait now, let me finish. You did, darling, and now look at you: a fine fine fine human being. I may never know what all happened to you on your big trip back East, but I believe I know why you left and why you came back, whatever happened in between—"

"... you don't want to know."

"Perhaps not. Oh, why is raising children always such a difficult thing to do well? But that was all so long ago. It's getting on in the day now. Hadn't you better go on up?"

"Do you want me to take you down to the house first, Mom?"

"Oh no. Baby Blue will keep me company while I sit right here. You just go and do what has to be done. Don't forget to pull the dry grass away from Jody's little wooden picket fence."

"I won't forget. What about the Mackenzies' plot?"

"What about it?"

"Shall I straighten out their part too?"

"Oh, perhaps just drag any large fallen branches aside. If their own people can never once tend to their family plot, it serves them right." She cupped her mouth with both hands. "Oh, what an awful thing to say! Shame on me, shame! Why, don't be alarmed, Baby. That's a good girl. Go on, Kaitlin, go. Do you miss Mother Merle, Baby Blue, do you? Go on, sweetheart, we'll be just fine. Baby Blue and I will be sitting right here having a nice conversation with Aunt Dorothea and Uncle John and saying hello to Old Mother Merle, should she show up. You see, Baby Blue's already listening closely. You'll stay with me, Baby, won't you?"

*

Telephoning Cliffport on Thanksgiving Day, Josie Wilton announced that—on condition he finish his senior year in good standing—her son, Jeff, had been granted early admission to Reed College for the 1972 academic year. Katie reported that DD had dropped out of high school without finishing his junior year and was supposedly baiting for crab somewhere up the California Coast. Once Katie had done reporting the harassments executed by Sea-to-Summit and Coastal Property Management on behalf of Yo-Mizo-Sata International, she started crowing all about the changes at Redwood Coast Nursery, where she was expecting to take delivery of a custom billboard-type sign that would be visible from Route One. The two friends confessed to each other that they were not playing their guitars, although Josie said the singing and songwriting scene in the Pacific Northwest was flourishing; Katie assured her that, while she kept up with all the new releases by Joan Baez, Joni Mitchell, Judy Collins, Carole King, and Laura Nyro, she still loved listening to classic renditions by the likes of Ola Belle Reed and other Southern mountain singers. True to form, Josie insisted on wishing Elise a Merry Christmas directly; while her mother and her friend prattled on, Katie grew leery, anxious to take back the phone piece and finish the call, for what if Josie asked her mother about the prospects for any further developments between Katie and her husband's cousin after whatever happened between them during that week after the Wiltons left Santa Cruz? To Katie's relief, Josie never brought up the subject, and their call ended on sad, sweet notes, with mutual pledges to pay each other visits the coming New Year, either in California or Washington State or both.

*

The mid-December completion of nursery improvements warranted a celebration, and Katie invited Jim and his crew back for a New Year's Eve Day spread of chips, salsa, chili con carne, and quesadillas. Elise put on her new holiday sweater, blessed the festivities, made herself a cup of tea, and retired to her room before the cork popped from the first bottle of sparkling wine and the first of many toasts was made. Jim phoned before noon: he was running late—better start eating without him—so the men dug into the spicy meal and polished off Katie's six-pack of Dos Equis. She kept the tortillas coming and the hot sauce bowls full, glad to be up on her feet serving them for she felt their inarticulate affection—disguised in gentle jibes—toward her, and she hoped they sensed the appreciation she had acquired for each of them over the last half-year.

Through the fogged picture window, Katie spotted the incoming utility truck Jim often used when delivering building supplies, and she wondered about the rustic hut strapped down atop the flatbed, figuring the master craftsman must have contracted to build and deliver a fairytale folly to satisfy some client's whim. He parked the truck with the other vehicles and lugged a carton up to the house, where he was welcomed at the table and his men didn't hesitate to break into the case of Anchor Christmas Ale. Amid laughter and self-congratulatory revelry over projects accomplished across the hillside, the group gossiped about Vignettes One at Monteflores and shared rumors about developments to come. Katie interrupted their drinking with a tray of brownies and a pot of her strongest coffee and expected to be wishing them a safe and Happy New Year, bidding them adieu as soon as dessert was done. Then a metal flask appeared, and the men spiked their second mugs of coffee.

"You guys ready?" Jim queried.

They grinned, gulped the coffee, stuck the remaining unopened bottles of ale in whatever coat pockets were handy, and joined Jim on the porch, lighting up cigarettes.

"Come on out here, Katie!" Jim called. "The boys and I want to show you something."

She pulled a hooded windbreaker over her head and followed the leader down to where Baby Blue Eye—looking puzzled by the somewhat tipsy bearing of the four familiar figures—stood guard among the pickups herded under the oak.

"Well, Missus Lowrie. Where would you like us to place it?" Jim asked, opening his palm toward the curious wooden playhouse on the truck bed.

Katie stepped out of the drizzling rain, inspecting its single-slope roof, two-thirds in redwood shingles, one-third in glazed skylight. Flower boxes had been built below its two outside windows.

"The boys here figured the boss lady at Redwood Coast Nursery is going to need an all-weather office," Jim explained. "We're thinking this little building might do. We recognize it's a downgrade from your plywood sheets and sawhorses," Jim added, then waited for the guffawing to subside, "but we're pretty sure you'll get used to it."

Katie cinched her hood, trying to hide the tears welling up in her eyes.

"How about right here?" he proposed.

She nodded and moved back to let them go to work. Jim used a tape to measure the site; the men placed a dozen precast concrete deck piers with metal brackets. Lowering the hydraulic tail-gate, they lifted the mini-house onto four redwood beams set at cross-angles and muscled it onto the piers. Once they had it shimmed level, with the front door aligned to squarely face the wide landing at the Lowries' end of the driveway, they opened their beers and cheered, clinking bottles.

Baby Blue jumped inside, sniffing the interior's periphery and, apparently satisfied, sat on her haunches in the doorway. Katie hugged each man in turn before stepping into the empty booth, eight feet across and six feet deep. The freshly veneered planks of the walls and flooring glowed orange like the redwood forest floor after rain. The skylight was already collecting bits of moist leaves and twigs, and she could picture it—come late spring—blanketed in the spent, chartreuse catkins from the oak. Katie saw herself stationed on a bar stool at the slanted built-in desktop attached to the wall above a set of open-faced niches. While tending to paperwork, she could keep an eye on the driveway. Anyone needing to get out of the weather would have shelter. Perhaps she would run a phone line from the house, or at least an electrical cord, so that from her kiosk she could monitor the comings and goings at Cliffport's sole commercial enterprise.

As she stood on the threshold, conjuring up words to express her gratitude, Jim produced a carved, green-painted redwood sign from his truck's cab and held it against the lintel over her head. Raised letters were painted bright white. Katie ducked her head, stepping outside and looking back—OLD MOTHER BLUE'S DOGHOUSE—before bursting into tears. The men laughed. Baby Blue Eye barked. Jim hugged her with one free arm while she wiped her face with the back of her hand, trying to address them but giving up and taking a long slug from a second flask passed around. Jim said that when he came back to mount the billboard up the hill, he would secure the bottom of the building to the pier brackets and set up some steps.

Within a week, Katie was helping Jim use a posthole digger and two sacks of ready-mix cement to sink a pair of 6" × 6" treated redwood posts into the ground on the rise behind the greenhouse. After stabilizing the sign, they hiked down Lower Steep Creek Trail and crossed to the whale watch on the far side of Highway One.

The hand-painted 8' × 10' billboard proved visible and legible: [2]

After Jim left, Katie tacked up her license to sell nursery stock, as well as information charts about gardening and decorative posters of trees and shrubs. She also hung Jim's DOGHOUSE shingle above an enlarged, framed photograph of the deceased sheepdog lying on her side with one last litter of pups—including Baby Blue Eye—at her teats. Katie had ordered a second carved shingle to place over the front door, its raised letters also painted white against green:

With no customers or even casual visitors on rainy days, she wrote FREE across a piece of cardboard and stuck it into the lug of extra lemons on the temporary stoop of redwood rounds. 3

During a spell of February's false spring, Katie took advantage of fair weather to add gravel to the driveway, which Gath's heavy equipment operators had done a fine job tearing up while clearing out the bone yards parallel to the elevated lane. While making multiple roundtrips to the supply yard, where she suffered pains watching the #3 grade crushed stone beating up the inside walls of the truck's bed while being dumped from a front loader, the yard boss let her take one of his idling employees back to Cliffport, where he joined her shoveling, shoving, kicking, and cursing the rocks off the tailgate and spreading them on the surface of the road. Katie did her best to level the dips and potholes of the narrow thoroughfare running from the Lowries' oak out to Grade Road, but the embankments were steadily collapsing. 4

One morning she woke up knowing it was time to invite the retired field inspector back for a sociable tour, for he had believed in her dreams for the Redwood Coast Nursery. She could show off her new digs to Pieter Tuelling and at the same time pick his brain for fresh ideas about what to do next and whatever she might not have even thought of yet. The man didn't answer his phone for several days, so she mailed him a note. At the end of April, he telephoned from Boston: he was bound for the Netherlands but would be back in three weeks at which time he would—with pleasure—contact her about making a visit.

Chapter 6

Early Sunday Supper

Pieter Tuelling parked the compact 1967 Dodge Dart under the oak's drizzling tassels and stepped into the welcoming hut. He wore outdoor boots and toted pruning shears but carried no clipboard; one of his plaid shirt's two breast pockets was stuffed with a memo pad, his eyeglasses, and a pencil in the slot; the other held a packet of tissue paper and a tin of Nat's Select. After shaking her hand and bending partway down to pet the sheepdog, the heavyset Dutchman took to the spare high stool. Katie soon found herself reciting her catalogue of complaints about the neighbor's harassments, and she offered to share their offensive correspondence when they got up to the house. Outside, Pieter set one sole on the Ford F-250's rear bumper, leaned over the tailgate and peered into the high aluminum shell, shifting his cotton twill bucket hat back off his forehead. "That's the way alrighty," he said, expressing approval of the internal wooden frame she had built to hold removable plywood shelving. "You know what you're doing, Katie Lowrie, sure enough."

Winding up the main path, he walked with his usual light step, uh-hum's and aha's and *jaja*'s signaling his recognition of her visible accomplishments since his last visit. A fleeting tremor of his head, a brief widening of his puffy eyelids, a momentary pursing of his lips while he stroked his thin white moustache with the stub of a fat thumb—all his short-lived gestures and barely audible interjections left her no doubt that the experienced nurseryman apprehended the inventiveness of her homemade solutions; he especially expressed his admiration of the narrow, sunken, wood-lined troughs angled toward bags of sand placed so as to channel rainwater shed off the path into simple gravel catch basins.

As they stood on a compacted earthen landing with a direct sight-line to the lodge collapsing in upon itself across the way, Pieter lit up one of his natural-colored cigarillos while Katie bemoaned how the boundaries were now being reinforced by Coastal Property Management, completely thwarting her access to source plants on that adjoining land. The era of filching acanthus, bergenia, and bush impatiens—whether by collecting seed, cutting off pieces, or lifting entire plants for transplanting into her recycled containers, root systems and all—was over. By now she knew how to make those classic perennials—staples in her limited product line—thrive under her care, but with so many eyes spying on her activities, she had finally to give up tromping about, irrespective of boundaries, digging up plants. She confessed she was contemplating one last round helping herself to propagules from the relic plots of Shasta daisy, rudbeckia, scabiosa, and coreopsis growing in drifts on the new landowner's old grounds, but she would have to move stealthily, when no one was watching, literally covering her tracks. The lilies and hardy fuchsias naturalized in and around Cliffport Town were now also the private property of Yo-Mizo-Sata, and she lamented the loss of future sessions spent dodging humming-birds and bees while taking cuttings from Ida Mackenzie's fuchsias established between the remnant wooden walls of the Cliffport Hotel and its decrepit picket fence. There was even a chance she would be challenged by some authority on the far side of Highway One if caught backing up to the whale watch's guard rail, tossing offsets from the red hot-poker plants into her truck bed or scrambling around the bluff's gullies between the shoulder-less highway and the beach, stuffing burlap bags with seed pods from the yellow bush lupines that grew on Southern Pacific Railroad's posted property.

"You might poach a few more those succulents perhaps before you turn over your new leaf," Pieter suggested, grinding the little cigar butt under his heel.

"Which succulents are those?" Katie asked.

"Those coast dudleyas what look so good in those two trays you got there."

"You're right. Maybe one more round ... before I mend my ways...?"

"Now don't you tell anybody I heard that, Katie Lowrie."

"I von't tell dot to a soul, Inspecteur Tuelling."

They laughed.

"*Jaja*, is a shame you can't get at those bamboos. I know, I know, you and Leonard, cats and dogs."

"I was thinking about that guy. I think he's what my mom used to call 'a prig' but I'm not sure what it means."

"Okay, okay, but he does know the bamboos. He said that plantation over there is worth a small fortune."

"If the Air Traffic Controller can work a deal with Coastal Property Management, let him have at it. But it'll take a backhoe to get those clumps out of the ground. With a Ditch Witch you could get the rhizomes."

"You got any idea when those developers going to make their next move on you?"

"I don't. Maybe they're waiting to see if the Lowrie ladies will bite the golden carrot."

"The 14-carot gold carrot, you mean. Don't you worry, Katie. There are plenty other sources of good plants—cheap too."

"Like where?"

"I show you where, Miss Katie. I take you where, sure, if you like."

They resumed their ascent and, after arriving at the wide concrete apron in front of the glasshouse, stepped inside. "Isn't it beautiful!" she exclaimed, immediately regretting having spoken so loudly as soon as she saw the old plantsman crushing his hat between his hands, his head bowed in reverential silence. When he raised his face, she couldn't detect if his eyes were tearing up or just ordinarily rheumy.

"*Jaja,*" he whispered. "I cannot feel out of place inside such a glasshouse for the plants." Resetting the floppy hat over his white hair, he cleared his throat. "So, do you miss the Kenilworth ivy and the violets yet?"

"I do, but not the slugs and snails...."

"They'll be back," he quipped, "if you don't spread the poison."

"Nobody's spreading poison in here. You know that, Pieter," she reminded him. "So, take a look around. Tell me what you think."

Every few steps he paused to assess some feature of the structure or acknowledge the idiosyncratic way she was arranging her new workspace.

"No ideas for me?"

"Everything going on in here is good, Katie," he said, pinching a fragrant pelargonium between two ridged, spilt fingernails and bringing a leaf to his reddish nose. "*Het is al goed.*"

"I'll fire up the furnace," she declared, striding down the aisle. "Wait till you see this!"

She turned a dial and stood back waiting for the definitive THWOCK of the pilot light's ignition. Pieter Tuelling applauded; Baby Blue Eye barked. She shut it off and they exited through the rear door where, from a smaller concrete pad on leveled ground, they surveyed the shade frames in the upper meadow. She explained the workings of the new irrigation system, how water could be channeled from Steep Creek into the refurbished cistern and, in a drought year, potable well water could be redirected from the tank serving the house. While passing back through the glasshouse, the man casually bobbed a four-inch pot up and down in his hand as if evaluating the quality of the planting medium by its weight; before exiting, he plunged both hands into a tin bin, scooping out two cupped palmfuls of the planting mix and raising it to his nostrils—inhaling, nodding, winking both blue eyes at her, and releasing the material back into the bin.

"Don't you find anything wrong, *Inspecteur*?"

"There is one thing...."

"Which is...?"

"Where you going to put all your tools and supplies perhaps you got to keep dry? You got a shed or something in mind, Missus Katie?"

"I'm thinking of throwing up a mini hoop house for all that."

"Jaja, dat werkt."

"I wouldn't have to call in the Planning Development Department or the National Guard to get a permit for something like that. I've had enough of our Santa Cruz County bureaucrats for a lifetime—and I don't mean you, Pieter. Anyway, you're officially retired now, right? But not everybody working for the county is like you. At least nobody I've run into is."

He smiled then pulled out another short, thin cigar. "Is okay...?"

"Sure. Just don't smoke any of your Amsterdam hashish around my mom!" she cracked; he bristled. "Just kidding, come on. Let's go see if my mom's awake, and I'll show you the documents from my jail-keepers."

"Jaja," he muttered, waving his wooden match dead. *"Het documentatiemateriaal."*

Cutting their way through a passel of the free-ranging guinea fowl, they reached the deck, where Pieter settled into a weathered wooden chair on the deck and smoked down his cigarillo while, finding Elise asleep in the club chair, Katie simply retrieved the papers chastening her about her baby billboard signage and her minor easement repair work. He slipped his hornbeam spectacles from a soft pouch and focused upon the letters. She went back inside to heat coffee and, after serving it, sat cross-legged in an ephemeral patch of sunlight, waiting until he had the pages weighted down under the abalone shell.

"Is a darn shame," he said.

"What is?"

"Peoples got to be that way. Did they ever talk to you?"

"In person, you mean? Face to face? No. Oh, wait a sec'.... There was one gal who came around a couple of times. I don't know if she still works for them. She waved some money in my face to entice us to move off."

"I bet she did that, *ja*. That's their carrot and those there," he added, indicating the letters, "that's their stick."

"If what they're doing to us was illegal, I'd be fighting them with all I've got!" Katie declaimed, realizing she had yet to mention the indignity of being locked out of the millpond.

They both turned toward the squealing of a red-shouldered hawk at the woods' edge—or a Stellar jay doing a good imitation; Baby Blue's ears remained perked until the persistent keeyur keeyur keeyur stopped cold.

"And here I was fantasizing about one day turning this place into the Steep Creek Bed and Breakfast Inn in Cliffport!" She tossed off a laugh. "Not much chance of that happening with their new border patrol out in force."

"That's funny." He chuckled. "I was thinking of a *biergarten*."

"A beer garden?"

"*Jaja*, I was! All those shade houses you got over there...? Or put tables maybe up in the old orchard terraces.... *Ach*, I'm joking you, Katie. But maybe I did imagine such a terrible thing as a *biergarten* for just a second, when I was daydreaming."

"I can see it now: The Redwood Coast Nursery Beer Garden, with Elisabeth Lowrie checking in guests and waiting on tables!"

"*Dat es het!*" he exclaimed, snickering. "*Ach*, we so bad, Katie, so bad."

Hawk or jay, the bird had flown away or stayed in place, quieted down.

"One day those idiots'll send me a letter telling me to get Bamboo Billy the Goat down there out of the stump field even though he's keeping their weeds down and reducing the risk of fire, for free. It's so weird. I'd voluntarily build up the banks of the driveway without asking them for a cent, but they won't let me. Which means no big trucks can get in and out of here. I don't even know if my delivery trailer will make it when it's loaded with plants."

"*Jaja*, you got to do some *mathematica* before you load that up, Katie."

"But what should I do? Tell me, please," she said, rising to her feet, hitching up her pants, and leaning back against the rail. "I can't devote my whole operation to crop after crop of four-inch color and a few one-gallon perennials. I don't have the space or outdoor heat to grow the kind of shrubs the bigtime landscapers buy. You know, those rhaphs and escallonias. Our old roses, Cecile Brunner, Lady Banks, they grow fine here—you'll see that when we go below the house. But they'd take too long to turn a crop and I have to start making money. The well's almost running dry."

"*Vhot?* You running out of well water?"

"No no, the money well, I mean, not water. If you have any ideas, I'd really like to hear them, Pieter. More coffee?"

"If it's cold and bitter," he replied, "sure."

"It sure is good to see you," she said, refilling their mugs. "I'm sorry I get a little overexcited sometimes. It's not your job to be my advisor anymore. Hey, I just remembered I have to check on a broken timer."

"*Jaja*, you do that, sure, but before I forget: you got to add that '*Gartenmeister Bonstedt*' to your nursery stock, Katie."

"The what?"

"Is a fuchsia. You get that '*Gartenmeister Bonstedt*' into production, you never going hungry, Missus Katie. I saw it so much in my last travels. Okay, go on now, go on. I be here ... thinking ... ideas," he said, tapping his head, chuckling, snuffing out his spent little cigar.

*

"Oh, there you are," he said, coming awake.

"You sure you want to see the garden today? We could save that for—"

"*Nee nee nee*, let me see, let me see. I just closed my eyes ... to listen to the trees ... the wind in the trees. You show me what flowers and vegetables you got growing down there, eh," he said, shifting his weight while preparing to rise to his feet. "If you got time...."

"I do."

"When Pieter Tuelling no longer accepts the invitation of a smart young nursery*woman* into her garden, well ... you shoot him, Katie Lowrie. You just shoot the fat old man."

Rounding the back of the house, ever the educator, Pieter paused to inform her that the Meyer lemon bush before his eyes was a surprisingly healthy relic of the original plants introduced to the United States in 1908 by Dutchman Frank Nicholas Meyer, a naturalized American citizen in the employ of the USDA collecting plant specimens on excursions into China; Meyer had brought the first Hachiya to the West too, he added, throwing a glance at the nearby persimmon tree. The pair passed through the informal zone where herbs and flowering bushes had been growing between the porch and the pump house since before Katie was born—upright rosemary, sprawling oregano, fragrant mounds of sage and spearmint and thyme, all laid out by usage rather than design. Cosmos, alyssum, and borage reseeded everywhere at will. Hummingbirds fed on butterfly bushes and Monarch caterpillars on milkweed. Framed, removable wire domes fit over the tended asparagus beds. With a twinkle in his blue eyes, Pieter worked the ends of two stubby fingers through bird netting over raspberries, tweaking a few berries off an older brown cane and teasing them through the nylon mesh before popping them into his mouth.

She unlatched the gate to the vegetable garden enclosed by a framed hog-wire fence high enough to dissuade deer from taking running leaps downhill. Patches of marigolds, nasturtiums, and calendulas volunteered outside the fence line and, where not hoed out, popped up in the paths between raised beds ringed by moats of trampled soil. Katie knew that silence on Pieter T.'s part implied an understanding of his keen observations. Stopping, stooping, muttering something about rabbit damage, she complained that there wasn't a fence she knew could keep out the rabbits, possums, skunks, and raccoons. "See those redwoods over there?" she said, without removing her gaze from chewed carrot tops and chomped-down parsley. "That's where they live, and this is where they dine! If not for the cats and the owls and the hawks—and my Macabee traps," she interjected, pointing out an array of lightweight chains staked into disturbed soil where a network of gopher tunnels ran on both sides of the fence—"there wouldn't be much left out here for the rest of us to eat."

A rectangular, L-shaped extension of the garden enclosure was devoted to a trio of bins fashioned from wooden pallets with framed, small-hole aluminum sheets laid on top. Pieter dislodged the lids and poked the piles with a digging fork. In the first, kitchen scraps and garden waste were still identifiable between layers of straw. Turning the middle bin released the steam of ingredients breaking down. The Old World gardener set the fork aside and plunged bare hands into the soft, crumbly, finished compost of the third bin, lifting it then letting its uniform, dark brown texture trickle through his fingers as he inhaled, closing his eyes. As he replaced the tops and put his drugstore sunglasses on, Katie wondered again if he was growing teary-eyed or simply protecting himself from the diffuse, bright light.

"*Dat verks?*"

"*Jaja,*" he stated softly and smiled, pinching his moustache between a soiled forefinger and thumb. "Is *Biodynamische*! From now on, I study under you, Katie Lowrie. I learn from you."

"Oh, bull," she retorted.

While they were parting in the turnabout, Katie invited the widower back for early supper that coming Sunday; yes, she assured him, Elisabeth Lowrie would be happy to attend.

"Until then I sleep with my thinking cap on," he pledged. "Maybe I get more ideas for the Redwood Coast Nursery."

————

Katie paused before entering the room. Without having heard the dog bark or anyone knock, she was surprised to discover their Sunday supper guest had arrived, and she watched her mother ceremoniously accepting a substantial bouquet. "Hi there," she finally said, clearing her throat. "What a great bouquet!"

"Hallo, Missus Kate." Pieter shook her extended hand with

a pseudo-theatrical dip of his head while proffering a thin, ribbon-wrapped box.

"What is this, a government bribe?" she said, accepting the house gift and smiling broadly while turning the white package over in her hand and holding herself back from hugging his keg-size torso.

"*Jaja*, is a bribe," he chuckled. "You found me out, Missus Katie. Is a bribe so you will like me...."

"Oh, she likes you all right," Elise remarked.

The threesome stood in silence, eyeing one another with open smiles. Each had dressed up for the occasion. Elise had on a pair of amply pleated dress slacks and sported an embroidered woven vest over a white peasant's blouse, puffy in the sleeves. She had brushed her long, thick, white hair back over her shoulders, gathering its central portion into one broad silver barrette worn at her nape. The male visitor was outfitted in a tan, long-sleeved, corduroy shirt tucked in at the beltline of his green velour trousers; below their cuffs, his oxfords shone bronze. Beads of green and blue turquoise dangled from Katie's ears. She had twisted her wavy chestnut hair into a ball above her neck, swept some back on the left, and let the rest freely cascade down on the right. Pieter had never seen her without a hat on her head or her hair free from any ponytail, nor had he had ever seen her out of work boots and jeans, but now she wore loose-fitting denim culottes, Mexican huaraches, and a sleeveless, French-cut, teal cotton top revealing long, bare, lean, lightly freckled arms.

"I sure hope you're hungry," Katie said, breaking the palpable silence, "because Mom has made us a feast."

"O *ja*, I'm always hungry, sure enough," he responded, patting the bulge above his cinched belt while his smile revealed the imperfect alignment of his teeth.

"Kaitlin's done all the work, Mister Tuelling."

"*Nee nee*, you must call me Pieter, please. Here in California, we're not so formal as the in Old Country, eh? 'Mister,' '*Monsieur*,' '*Meneer*,' and all like that...."

"Then you must call me Elisabeth ... or Elise."

"Jaja, Liesbeth!" The man's eyelids closed then opened wide and stared. "Elisabeth...." Her mother blushed and he lowered his eyes, shifting his weight left and right. "Is a beautiful name, sure."

Katie sensed the fait accompli of their mutual affection. "Uh ... excuse me," she volunteered. "Why don't you let me put those flowers in some water ... Mom...?" She took hold of the generous bouquet. "You two sit down, go on now. I'll bring the soup ... or shall I open my present first?"

"What you like, Katie," Pieter replied. "But you wait perhaps for dessert for that...?"

While the man exchanged a mischievous glance with her mother, Katie slipped away and took her time in the pantry and kitchen, as if to let two former lovers catch up on time lost, as if the couple must have met in some previous epoch before she had even been conceived. She set the simple yet sumptuous floral arrangement in one of Elise's tallest crackled-glaze stoneware crocks and placed it on a mat on the solid white tablecloth, over which the Lowrie women had laid an heirloom piece from the McLoughlin linen closet—an ivory-colored, cotton lace runner with a border of thistle patterns, handstitched. Each place had been set with Ida Mackenzie's finest silverware, and the rest of the dinnerware was of Elise's translucent, off-white, hand-built porcelain. Her teapot, mugs, and dessert plates were arrayed on the kitchen counter.

As soon as Katie had served the clear vegetable soup from the tureen and sat down, Elise clasped her hands, closed her eyes, and lowered her chin toward her chest: "For what we are about to receive, may the Lord make us truly grateful." Katie and Pieter barely had time to say Amen before the older woman gave the lazy Susan a slow spin so that the bread knife's handle ended pointing toward their guest. "Please, do us the honors of slicing off some pieces of Katie's fine, fine rye bread. Is it still warm in the middle, do you think, dear?"

"Let's see," her daughter replied, reaching for the butter plate. "Go for it, Pieter. I'll take the crust unless you want it."

"Oh, I like it all," he responded, handling the knife with dexterity.

"I like it all." Katie noticed he wore no wedding ring and, although he must have scrubbed his hands, the filed, tightly trimmed nails were still ridged and showed spilt ends. His freshly barbered white hair framed his round face, and his cheeks gleamed pink with a sheen of having shaved too closely. The bright white undershirt visible between the wide-open, buttonless lapels of his shirt looked brand new. On his previous visits, the Dutchman had always been polite, but Katie wasn't accustomed to his refined indoor comportment and his almost courtly table manners. *"Smakelijk!"* he declared, sipping his soup and buttering his bread, his chameleon-like eyelids opening wide to expose the sky-like color of their irises. "The vegetables in this soup are from the garden, eh?"

"You're right. Now tell us where you got that beautiful bouquet."

"Simply beautiful!" Elise added.

Three trusses of lavender, purple, and red rhododendron stood tall alongside two spikes of pink and white foxglove nestled in flattened, dark green sprays of fragrant incense cedar. All three diners gazed at the display, as present at the table as any fourth diner might have been and somehow sitting in for a missing party.

"I picked those at Nico's Nursery ... in Drika's garden there."

"Where's that?" Katie asked. "I've never heard of that one."

"Oh, is up Soquel Gulch Road, Katie. Up at the top of Soquel Gulch."

"But what a combination of colors and textures and shapes!" Elise gushed. "And just the right proportions! Wherever did you learn the art of arranging cut flowers? Or do all Dutch gentlemen know how to make miracles with flowers?"

"I learned from Drika. Was Drika taught me all like that."

"Drika...?"

"I told you, Mom," Katie whispered, "his wife." She raised her voice again: "Drika was her nickname, right, Pieter?"

"Jaja. Ellen was her given name. Ellen Hendrika...." He stuffed more bread into his mouth, chewing and swallowing before he spoke: "I taught her the Latin names of the plants and she taught me their

beauty. She was smarter than me, see? An artist too: she made wonderful plant illustrations, *jaja*. She left me with so many watercolors I don't know what to do. They don't belong in a museum or herbarium, *nee nee*; they aren't that kind. But so ... *schoon*...."

"The new library in the Strybing Arboretum might like to see them...." Elise essayed.

"The Strybing Arboretum...?" Pieter repeated. "*Jaja* ... that Strybing Arboretum in Golden Gate Park ... *jaja*...." he trailed off, focusing on his food.

They ate their bread and soup in silence.

"Perhaps Pieter would like a look at Mary McLoughlin's wildflower album, dear. Shall I—"

"... maybe later, Mom, not now. She's talking about a homemade album of colored pencil wildflower illustrations and pressed flowers we inherited," Katie explained to the guest. "All of them from right around Cliffport at the end of the 19th century—"

"... in the aughts of the 20th century, dear," Elise corrected her.

"In the what's?" her daughter asked.

"Nineteen-aught-eight, nineteen-aught-nine, somewhere in there before the First World War."

Katie rolled her eyes and checked on their guest's comprehension.

"I like to see that album, sure."

"But first let's eat," Katie reasserted. "I'll bring the food to the table and everyone can serve themselves."

"Would you like something besides water to drink, Pieter?" Elise inquired. "Do you want some lemonade? It's freshly squeezed. Or iced tea?"

"Thank you, but I'm fine. *Dit is goed water*. Is from the cistern, is it?"

"It's from the well," Katie answered. "We don't drink the cistern water; the plants do."

Katie passed her mother the platter of roasted chicken and began rotating the bowls of vegetables and potatoes. "Help yourself, everyone, there's plenty more. You know, all these plates and goblets, everything except the silverware and the tablecloth—my mom made them herself."

"Oh, Kaitlin, that was so many years ago."

"Still, aren't they beautiful, Pieter? 'Form and function,' she always said. Right, Mom? 'Form and function.' Aren't they cool, Pieter?"

"*Jaja*, the weight, the color, the shape. The mother provides the plates and the daughter provides the food!"

"Not all the food," Katie responded. "This isn't one of our chickens."

"No?"

"Nope. This one's store bought. The family butcher is away for a while.."

"And who is the family butcher if I may ask?"

"Oh, Kaitlin!" Elise protested.

"What's wrong?"

"Calling DD a butcher!"

"That's my son," she explained. "DD, short for Donald Duncan."

"I see. So, your son is ... away...?"

"'Gone fishin', playing hooky, something like that. He's the only one around here who can stand to kill the hens once they stop laying. I've never known him to put the axe to one of his pet roosters though."

"Kaitlin, please. Can't we talk about something else at the supper table?"

Pieter commented on the wonderful food: lemon-pepper "store-bought" chicken baked with fresh herbs and garlic; steamed broccoli with diced garlic and pine nuts; buttered new potatoes sprinkled with paprika and dill. "How do you get your new potatoes so early? Is not June yet, eh?"

"I steal the little baby tubers and put the mama back to bed."

"*Lekker!*"

"*Liquor?*" Elise echoed, pausing with her fork halfway to her mouth.

"Delicious! Is delicious!" he translated. "So, your son is perhaps in the military...?"

Katie gagged on her mouthful of food and clutched her throat, coughing, chortling.

"Kaitlin Liliane, please! Now be quiet for a moment. Drink some water."

She swallowed from her goblet and cleared her throat. "DD in the army? He probably should be but he's more like in the army against the army, if you know what I mean."

"Will you please let the man eat in peace?"

"He asked. You asked, didn't you, Pieter?"

"*Jaja*, I asked."

"Anyway, he's not in the army. He's not even Draft bait yet. Just turned seventeen in February."

"Sometimes I wish my grandson had been born a girl."

"What the heck does that mean, Mom?"

"So, he wouldn't have to register for that Draft."

"Oh, okay, I agree with you there. See, Pieter, I'm afraid we're not what you'd call a military family."

Elise rested her knife and fork on the rim of her plate. "I don't know how you view these matters, Mister Tuelling ... Pieter, I mean. But in my opinion.... Well, there's something not altogether honest about our presidents and congressmen in recent years. Everything seems to have gone out of whack in Washington. Oh, I would be loath to send a member of my family to fight in some foreign war for reasons I still do not understand, even after all these awful years. To go about killing people in Southeast Asia or being killed, based on faith in a government run by politicians practiced at pronouncing contradictions? I would be mortified if DD were drafted and shipped off to Vietnam. I know, I know. We're told there is only so much an ordinary citizen can comprehend. Top secret intelligence and all that information from spying. Yet in the last World War, in the Korean War, didn't our fighting make sense to most people? It made sense to me, even if human tragedy never completely 'makes sense.' But this war in

Vietnam is simply insane." She dabbed her lips with her cloth napkin and shook her head. "I'm sorry."

"*Nee nee*, no need to apologize. I learned early, is impolite to criticize my host country, eh? But the Dutch people also, they do not understand this crazy business in Vietnam and all like that."

"The Finleys just lost young Tom over there. You hear about that, Mom?"

"I did, and for what? I don't know those people well, but I wouldn't want to face that family in its mourning. Oh, dear, I'm afraid we're not doing a very good job of entertaining our special guest. I do want to express our appreciation for your interest in my daughter's nursery."

"I was paid by the County of Santa Cruz to give advice! Now you two are paying me with hospitality—and true talk. Being here like this, this makes me feel real good. You doing a fine job of entertaining, Elisabeth Lowrie. *Jaja*, don't you worry about that."

Katie cleared some dishes while keeping an ear on their conversation.

"My daughter has quite a challenge with the ball and chain being put on her leg by the Monteflores people."

"*Ja*, I understand so."

"I understand you've suggested she develop her nursery business along exclusively wholesale lines."

"That's the way alrighty."

"But how can she invite wholesale buyers here, given the limitations of that little road in and out?"

"Katie, your mother reminds me." He raised his voice. "I been thinking."

"Thinking what?"

"Maybe you got to get the landscapers and contractors to take delivery of your plants at the worksites, see? Or you secure some drop spots here and there, instead of them driving trucks in here. Could be you need to get a holding yard, eh? Or you make deals with the garden centers and pay a fee or a percentage—you got to do that, sure—so the contractors pick up the plants there, see? Forget about those sonsagun retail shoppers what want onesie-twosies and all like that. I know, I know about those ladies who lunch and have all the time—"

"... and money—"

"... in the world. How many times I waited, when I was in the outside sales, waiting for the boss to get done talking to those ladies—bah! More money than brains, most of them!"

"Oh, once upon a time I knew that crowd," Elise pitched in. "Where I grew up in Piedmont, there was a big carriage trade and real carriages too!"

"That's funny, Mom ... 'and real carriages too'! A carriage trade...."

"Well? That's what it was called, wasn't it, Pieter?"

"*Jaja*, I heard that before. So, Katie, I been thinking."

"That's lucky for me." She slid back into her dining chair. "Yeah?"

"You got to specialize, like I said. You know you can't get big—"

"... with Coastal Property Management boxing me in on all sides and four-fifths of our acreage too steep for production, I can't."

"And not working by yourself neither. Not even if you got a partner—"

"... what's that mean, a partner?"

"I mean, I seen lots of mom and pop operations go under, end up in divorce even. The man, the husband, he grows the plants, he does the landscape jobs. The plants she doesn't sell in their little garden center, he puts those into the people's yards, see? Sounds good. His wife, she runs the nursery and the gift store. She does the books. Maybe they got a daughter in high school what does the flower arrangements, like a florist only cheaper! But that family there, they work like dogs, and if he wants to keep a few good employees after busy season, why then the poor man got to find work just to keep those employees busy the slow half the year. Garden maintenance, eh? *Nee nee*, you got to stay small or get big or get out."

"Well, I can't get big and I'm not getting out."

"Then you got to stay small and—"

"... specialize."

"*Jaja, dat is het!*"

"My daughter does have a green thumb though, doesn't she, Pieter?"

"No doubts about that. That's two green thumbs she got there and a good brain."

"I think I see a little green," Katie said, examining her fingers, "below the brown dirt. My mom used to get her hands dirty too, you know. In the pottery and in the garden. And whatever she touched grew too!"

"Oh, Kaitlin. Everything I knew I learned from Aunt Dorothea. And my stepfather before that—he was an estate gardener in Piedmont, Pieter, from Scotland. And I mustn't neglect mention of a semi-mute Russian peasant too. I shall never forget old Sergei...."

"And everything I know I learned from her," Katie said, tilting her head toward her mother. "Where'd you pick up your gardening, Pieter?"

"I learned the kitchen gardening from my mother, sure, and my grandmother with her medicine plants. My grandfather, Klauss Tuelling, he was the bulb farmer. *Jaja*, tulips, why not? When I was a boy I spent summers in the Bollenstreek, where most those bulb fields are. We lived in Den Haag, but my father's father inherited the polder in Bollenstreek. So, after I graduated the Lyceum—"

"... the what?"

"Let's say ... high school...? After that I was not decided."

"About what?" Elise asked.

"I was confused, but in a good way I think now. *Ja*, I think so, Elisabeth. I was confused in a good way. I was a good student, see? But I wasn't ready for university, and I didn't want to become a bulb farmer, *nee nee*. So, during a *trekkende jaar* ... you know what is a *wanderjahr*...? A year off...? I stopped at a German-speaking community in the Alsace—to study the *biologisch dynamische landbouw*. Biodynamic agriculture, you say."

"That's going on over at UCSC right now," Katie asserted. "I took a weekend workshop once with Alan Chadwick."

"*Jaja*, that Chadwick from England. I heard of that man."

"Have you met him, Pieter?" Elise inquired.

"I know of him, sure. He does not know of me. Biodynamic gardening, I know that without him."

"It all comes to the same thing, right?" Katie asked.

"Maybe, maybe so. The raised bed, the double digging, the organic compost...." He broke off, lifting the curtains of his eyelids and looking directly at her, grinning: "No synthetic fertilizers ... no pesticides...." He blinked twice and let the curtains fall.

"So, you studied in Germany when you were—"

"*Pardon*, but it was in France, in the Alsace. I was in France when I was seventeen. That's the age of your boy now, not true? The one gone fishing."

"Yaya," Katie spouted. "Dat vun vhot got avay!"

"Stop that now, Kaitlin!" Elise declared, narrowing her gaze upon her daughter. "When was all that, Pieter, if I may ask?"

"Oh, gosh. 1934, '35, all like that. Gardening in nature ... 1935...."

"Speaking of gardening," Katie said, rising to her feet. "Is anyone interested in some organic greens with radishes, carrots, beets, green onions, and snap peas, all mixed up in three kinds of lettuce leaves grown ... *without pesticides or synthetic fertilizer?*"

They loaded their salad plates and took turns with Elise's ceramic oil and vinegar set.

"I can't remember any details from that workshop," Katie took up. "The compost recipe was pretty far out there. Dairy cow manure— cow manure, right? No rabbit or chicken or horse manure. Wood chips, oak mold—there's always plenty of that around here. How'd it go? Minute concentrations of chamomile, yarrow, valerian, stinging nettle, dandelion—"

"... oh, my goodness," Elise muttered. "I think I remember your telling me about some esoteric recipe...."

"I've always made out fine following what you taught me, Mom. Alternate layers of wet and dry, and greens and browns. Water the pile, turn it, add a shovel or two of finished compost for starters from time to time. That's simple enough. Maybe too simple for university students to understand. I don't know, you just have to let compost grow."

"You make it sound like baking bread, dear."

"Yaya," Katie intoned in pseudo basso profundo. *"Dat is het!"*

"I have asked you several times to please stop that now, Kaitlin." Pieter grinned while buttering the last end of bread.

"Did you eventually graduate from that program—whatever it was called?" Elise asked.

"Nee. After those Nuremburg Laws what passed in September of 1935...." Pieter broke off, his eyelids rolling down like a storefront; the Lowries looked at each other during their guest's long pause. "My parents, they called me home to the Nederlands," he resumed. "I enrolled in the university at Leiden, sure."

"Studying...?"

"Plant pathology, eh? I thought I could be like the great Alsatian, Albert Schweitzer, by helping the farmers to feed the people."

"And ultimately you did just that!" Elise proclaimed.

"Nee nee. What I did was help the greenhouse growers keep their carnations from wilting, Elisabeth, and the sonsagun white flies off their Christmas crop of poinsettias. I never kept anyone from starving, except my wife and me."

Katie again rose and cleared some items off the table. "Does anyone want dessert now? I'm stuffed. Pieter?"

"I ate like a horse. I got a sweet tooth, sure, but no dessert for me right now, thank you."

"How about some fresh mint tea? Would you like that?"

"Ach, I love the mint tea, Elisabeth."

"Better than my bitter coffee?"

"Kaitlin, you heard our guest. Please, dear, run fetch a handful of fresh mint and I'll use the lemon on the shelf. Do you prefer honey in your mint tea or sugar?"

"Fresh mint tea with lemon and honey? *Das is verse munt thée!* " •

"I think that means he prefers honey," Katie remarked.

• *fresh mint tea (Dutch)*

"And you know where the bathroom is down the hall, do you, Pieter? I'm afraid we all just leapt upon the food without a second thought. I'll bring out the wildflower album we were speaking of."

"Thank you," he said, rising, pulling out her chair, and assisting her to his feet. "After you, Madame."

When Katie observed the couple standing closely opposite each other, gazing into each other's eyes, she felt the tangible affection between them and winced, recognizing that her mother had for decades missed out on any such gentlemanly attentiveness and that, unless something changed course in her own life, she too might never enjoy living in intimacy with a kind man.

"Now, Pieter," Elise said softly, "when I return I expect to find you sitting in that big chair there by the fireplace where I shall leave the album and serve you your tea when it's ready."

"*Verse munt thée*," he whispered, watching the woman's halting, lopsided gait after she had turned away.

Katie had no way of knowing, but she suspected that at that very moment the widower might be watching both Liesbeth Lowrie and some imaginary composite of his grandmother, his mother, and his wife moving away from him down the hall.

*

Having taken occupancy of the leather club chair, Pieter pored over the wildflower album, his hornbeam reading glasses halfway down his nose until, after one cup of sweet tea, he relocated to the table in order to view the oversize folio with greater ease and in better light. Elise refilled his cup and dished out a piece of her rhubarb pie.

"I hope you'll like this," she whispered.

Absorbed in examining the pressed flowers and colored-pencil drawings, she made no response and, wondering if he had heard her at all, left him alone, handling the edges of the 12" × 15" sheets of vellum paper with great care, absentmindedly forking bites of pie into his mouth and sipping the tea without taking his eyes off the pages. Over their kitchen clatter, the Lowries could hear him vocalizing under his breath. When they were done cleaning up, Elise took the opportunity to retire to her room, remove her laced shoes, and rest her swollen ankles on the ottoman before working her feet into house slippers; Katie attended to some outdoor chores. Upon reconvening, the women found their guest gazing through the picture window with his dining chair angled away from the folio closed on his lap. Caught off guard, he fumbled slightly while squaring his chair off against the table.

"Now now, you just relax," Elise instructed him. "Would you like another slice of pie?"

He grinned and palmed his belly. "Thank you, Elisabeth. *Erg smakelijk*—very tasty. Now you found out I am gourmand. Oh, I like not gourmet food too but lots and lots of it! But first ... I'm fit to burst ... if you will excuse me...." he trailed off, rising to his feet and heading down the hall.

"Mom, are you sweet on our old Ag agent?" Katie asked, once she had heard the bathroom door close.

"Do I have a crush on the man, do you mean?"

"You two act like a couple of lovee doves, the way you melt just looking into each other's eyes."

"Oh, my gracious, Kaitlin. Don't be silly. You are a bit jealous, aren't you?"

"Jealous? No, I'm not jealous. But sometimes I feel like I should leave the room, the air gets so thick with all the billing and cooing going on."

"Oh, that's funny, dear. *'Billing and cooing'*? Now don't be silly. He must be closer to your age than to mine. Do we even know how old he is?"

"He must be fifty-six by now. I think he retired at fifty-five."

"But you're talking like a child, Kaitlin. I'm simply enjoying the rare treat of serving a man in this house, a gentleman who is ... appreciative."

"Yaya," Katie uttered. "A suitor of the old school, sure enough."

"Please stop it, Kaitlin. Shush now. I think he's coming."

Pieter took his place, consumed the pie, and sipped the warm tea. "What do you think?"

"Delicious, Elisabeth. Everything has been delicious."

"Thank you, but I meant about that album. Isn't it special?"

He let his gaze linger on the wooden cover and touched the brass hinges with one large forefinger. "I can't tell you how special. When my brother and my sister and I were children, we made such drawings and pressed flowers in our albums and all like that. All Dutch schoolchildren had flower books back then. Smaller than this one but is the same idea."

"They did?" Katie asked. "In elementary school, you mean?"

"*Jaja.* I don't know if they still do that but that was the way we learned the flowers. *De wilde bloemen in de natuur.* Then it was Latin names in the Lyceum and for me in university—oh boy, every little thing about the plants I had to learn then."

"Perhaps we better let our guest rest, dear. We've been badgering the poor man since he walked in the door."

"Is okay, is okay. I got to sing for my supper one way or other."

"Hey, wait a sec'. Where's my present?"

"I put the box on top of the refrigerator, dear."

"Okay, here we go!" She sprang out of her chair, retrieved the package, slipped off the ribbon and bow, and undid the white tissue paper. Inside she found a sampler of expensive, flat-backed, Belgian chocolates in thin gold foil. Molded Dutch clichés were stamped on all the pieces: impressions of a windmill, a pair of clogs, a dairy cow, a sailing boat, a tulip, a tulip glass for beer.

"Oh, these are so cute!"

"How thoughtful of you," Elise said.

Katie put the lid back on and pressed the box to her chest before letting out a big breath. "Would you like to select the first one, Maman?"

"No, thank you, dear. I really shouldn't. And I think those confectionaries are meant for you," she added. "I best go raise my legs. But don't you run off without looking in to say good-bye, Mister Tuelling. Please...."

"*Oke, Mevrouw Lowrie.* I come to say goodbye after I drink Katie's bitter coffee and eat up all her chocolates when she's not looking."

*

He picked out another chocolate and, without sharp fingernails to help, gently rubbed the gold foil off a tulip glass with the pad of his broad thumb.

"I bet you'd rather have a tulip glass with Heineken in it than a chocolate tulip, right?" Katie asked, setting the coffeepot and two mugs down on the stump tabletop.

"You know me too well, Missus Katie."

They sat, nibbling and sipping, waiting out a silence that admitted echoes of the distant surf breaking the rocky outthrusts defining Hidden and Cliffport Beaches.

"I think I talked too much maybe for your mother, eh?"

"Talked too much or too much truth?"

"Oh?"

"Don't worry about it. Sometimes I think she can only take so much reality, so I try to be careful. But then I realize she's a pretty tough old gal."

"That's good, that's good. I know you're one strong lady too."

"Strong or stubborn?"

"*Jaja*, like that too. The way you holding out here in Cliffport, doing what you know is right."

"We'll see how long I hold out. Maybe I'll cave in one day. Drink your coffee while it's hot. Wow, that was one good sailboat. Let's see how chocolate clogs taste. Want another tulip?"

"The rest is for you ... and your mother."

"So, what other advice do you have for me, *Inspecteur*, while I hold out here, doing what's right?"

He sighed and lit another petit cigar. "BAH!" he exclaimed, blowing smoke. "I give you ideas until the cows come home, Katie Lowrie. Listen, you be glad you're not stuck growing those red tips and viburnums. The roses, the Leptos, and ... what did you say? Escallonias? Rhaphiolepsis? Those big boys up the road there in Half Moon Bay, or down in Watsonville, or over in the Central Valley—they got you beat at that business before you start. They got the heat, and they pump those plants with fertilizer and then the darn fools, they cut their prices to get into the stores. Those sonsagun plants are footballs to the buyers at those Woolworth Garden Centers and all like that, footballs to kick around. You stay out of that commodity business, Missus Katie. There, that's my advice and it's free."

"So where does that leave the Redwood Coast Nursery?

"Okay. You listen to me then you do what you like. First, you keep your four-inch cash crops. Didn't you say you sell out every year?"

"You remember that? Every crop."

"Why sure I remember! I still got that disease of a good memory. So, now you got bench space up there to grow even more those darn fuchsias and dahlias and trailing geraniums—as good as any I ever seen coming out of anybody else's hothouse, Katie. Don't you give up on those pretties ... even if they do take a little synthetic fertilizer from time to time, eh?"

"Okay ... I get it."

"And you build up your inventory of those old-fashioned perennials you got a start on. You keep your eyes open and maybe pick up some of the variants too. Take that there basic Shasta daisy you got going. There are doubles and semi-doubles and frilled ones and quilled ones—*ach*, I forget all the darn names: 'Marconi,' 'Esther Reed,' 'Snow Lady,' Jane baloney, John salami—all like that, see? You see any of those old daisies in cans, you grab them, Katie. You already got that bush impatiens and the *balfourii*, what you call it ... the poor man's orchid? But what about some New Guinea impatiens, eh?"

"What about them? I don't even know what they are."

"*Ach*, sure you do, sure you do. You get some New Guinea impatiens, and you expand the line, see? Don't think a gardening town like Santa Cruz isn't going to want variety in their little cottage gardens. The old favorites, they never go out of style. There you go. There's another two cents."

"Don't stop now! What else?"

"What else?"

"Yeah, keep going."

"Well, you got to expand, sure, but be careful. Those tall delphiniums and flowering vines? The peoples like them, sure they do: 'So showy!' they say, and they are. But you try staking and tying and delivering a load of delphiniums all in one piece! Too much handling, working all alone like you do and all like that."

"What about tuberous begonias?"

"*Ach*! Vhot you want those headaches for? Antonelli Brothers and Brown Bulb Ranch, they got you beat, darnitall! And the fungicides they use! You need more than baking soda for the diseases those sonsaguns get and lots and lots of space for air to circulate around in the greenhouse."

"I could hang them above the benches. The colors are so beautiful...."

"I know they're beautiful, I know they are. You think an old Dutchman doesn't know a beautiful flowering bulb when he sees one? But what about those fungicides and all like that?"

*

They found Elise asleep atop her bed, a pillow below her outstretched legs, her hands folded on her chest—sepulchral. Moments later, as they said goodbye under the oak, Katie couldn't contain herself: "Are you sweet on my mother, Pieter Tuelling?"

"What's that you saying now?"

"Do you have a crush on Liesbeth Lowrie, I'm asking."

"You joking me, Missus Katie?"

"Yeah, I guess I am, sort of. But the two of you sure got along from the second you met."

"But Elisabeth is one fine person, Katie. You got one wonderful mother there. I think you know that."

"Then I guess you're both just two old flirts at heart!"

"Is maybe so. That's it: two old flirts, just like you say, *jaja*. But now I ask you something." He fiddled with the key ring in his hand. "Why you didn't get married again, Missus Katie?"

"I never got married in the first place."

"Okay, okay, maybe so. But why not ... later then?"

"I guess I never met the right person."

He waited, playing with the order of the keys on the ring.

"If you were twenty years younger, Pieter Tuelling, I might consider such a proposal coming from someone like you."

"Oh boy, there you go again! And twenty pounds lighter you forgetting to say!" He opened the car door. "If I was twenty years younger, Missus Katie, I think we both be considering that—but before you got pregnant with child, eh?"

"Why, *Inspecteur Tuelling*!" She scowled falsely, punching his shoulder. "Talking like that to a young unmarried lady! You are an old flirt, aren't you? I never knew you had it in it you."

"I did once," he said, getting into the Dart and pressing the lock on the door. "I don't now."

Without looking back, he started off, waving his ringless left hand out the window as he navigated the ramp-like incline onto the lane. [1,2]

Chapter 7

The Education of a Nurserywoman

Through chinks in the grape-stake fence running along an unmarked, unpaved lane at the top of Soquel Gulch Road, Katie spotted his Dart and realized she had overshot her mark. She backed up to the wooden sign lying in the blackberries—NICO'S NURSERY—then drove through the open, broken farm gate. At the end of a dusty, tree-lined corridor, she stopped in sunlight and parked next to the other car in front of a plain-timbered, one-story cabin. Across a clearing, where another lane presumably led to the site of the former nursery, a barn and a garage buckled. The sliding barn doors had slid off their rusted upper rails and been left that way, leaning against the peeled paint of once-red walls. On another side of the wide yard—front hoods gaping like the beaks of prehistoric birds—two wheelless flatbed trucks rested on empty axles raised on wooden blocks.

Pieter Tuelling, wearing his usual outdoor clothes, stood on the dwelling's threshold with a smile; Baby Blue Eye yapped at him from the passenger window and, as soon as Katie opened the cab's passengerside door, the dog escaped, tearing circles around the man, too excited to pause for his foiled attempts to pet her calmly. "So, you found it after all," he said, one hand brushing back his white hair and the other extended to shake.

"Where's the nursery, back there?"

"It was back there." he replied, waving beyond the buildings. "Maybe it should have been called the Hidden Nursery, eh?"

"Is this where your brother lived?" she asked, assessing the weathered, box-shaped cabin.

"*Jaja*, this where Nico lived. There's not much left inside," he added, holding open the screen door, "but come inside, take a look for yourself."

They stepped directly into the front room housing a potbelly stove; a four-foot tall refrigerator raised on cinder blocks; a table with a drawer and wooden legs; two kitchen chairs with cracked vinyl seats and rusty, pitted legs. Pieter's station at one end of the chipped enamel tabletop was obvious: a magnifying glass lay atop open newspapers along with a coffee mug, a pack of cigarillos, and an ashtray crowded with butts. Two drinking glasses stood upside down in an open-faced cupboard, otherwise bare. A one-burner propane stove supported a banged-up one-quart pan. "Go ahead, look back there too, go on. I know you're curious, sure." In a constricted closet, the washbasin had come away from the warped wall paneling; an inch of off-color liquid sat stagnant below the lowest ring of stains in the toilet bowl. The bedroom was devoid of furniture and decoration.

She turned back to the stark front room. "Did he really live here all the time?"

"*Jaja*, all the time."

"All alone?"

"All alone."

"He never married?"

"*Nee nee*, never married."

"It feels like a prison."

"*Jaja, dat is het*, Missus Katie. He lived like a prisoner, sure enough."

Making her presence known on the other side of the screen door, the dog whined. Instead of inviting Katie to sit down, Pieter stuck on his bucket hat. "Come on outside. This in here isn't what I got to show you."

As they crossed the clearing, he swept his arm toward a vista of unbroken forested mountains. "Most those there are the 'Soquel' race of redwoods, eh, of course. Those branches turn up. But back here," he continued, as they followed the hardened dirt track rounding the garage, "here we got those 'Aptos Blue'—that blue-green strain with the drooping branches. And that one over there...? Is 'Los Altos,' with the dark green branches arching and all like that."

"Unt all like dot?" she said, grinning.

"But you can see the difference, Missus Katie, can't you?"

"You're too much, *Inspecteur!*"

"Too much...?"

"Too much means pretty good. Go on, I'm listening."

Their route was blocked by a mound of soil twenty feet across and five feet high sitting in front of a row of open enclosures framed by cinder blocks, all empty but for scraps of windblown twigs, branches, and leaves.

"You want this pile of acid soil, Missus Katie?"

"What?"

"I say, do you want this pile? It's all yours, gratis."

"You're giving me all this? That's a whole dump truck load or more."

"*Jaja,* twenty yards, twenty-five, I think so. That's the acid soil ready for the ericaceous plants and for the camellias."

"Air-ah-kay-shush?"

"Ericaceous, like the ericas, eh? Rhodendrodrons and azaleas and all like that. Lots of forest humus in there, and sand, and peat."

"But...?"

"But what? Nico's Nursery is closed forever, Katie Lowrie. The Redwood Coast Nursery is getting started." He lifted a crusted canvas tarp off a piece of rusted machinery. "You want this too? Take this too and those screens what go with it. *Ja*, take it! This old four-horse-power engine will make your life easier, sure."

"What is it, a chipper?"

"*Nee nee*, is a mixer," he said, yanking the cover all the way off. "You never saw a gas-powered soil mixer like this before? Is loud, heavy, ouf! But oh boy, what a worker horse!"

She inspected the corroded steel contraption from all sides.

"You see the little plate there? Lindig Soil Shredder Model M-8. Those steel blades hanging down, they start turning and—don't you say 'flail'? Is that a word in English?"

"Yeah...."

"Good then: they flail! It says 'EZ Starting Spin' right on the side there but I don't know if that Briggs-Stratton going to spin so easy anymore. Take it home, give it a try. You got to clean out any gas, put in a new plug, all like that. And put some air in those two sonsagun tires. But come on," he said, leaving the tarp on the ground, "I'll make us some coffee. Instant is all what I got. Come on. That soil and this old worker horse, they still be here."

Katie called in the dog and they headed back toward the cabin. Along the way, he encouraged her to peek inside the buildings. "Why you don't take that easy haul cart in there too? And that can carrier, eh? 5-, 15-, 25-gallon cans, that thing can carry all those—pretty nice, eh?" She squinted into the darker space. "Go on. Look around in there. Take what you want, why not? I go boil that water."

Katie stepped into the cobwebbed interior and let her eyes adjust. Three upended barrels held a variety of long-handled tools. She gripped the cool steel handles of the hand dolly then those of the sturdy cart and kicked their flat tires. "What's with this guy, Blue?" she addressed the dog aloud. "Is he for real?" Walking back across the yard, she pondered the generosity of donations made without fanfare or any contingencies that she could detect.

*

Inside only long enough to fix their mugs of coffee and snatch some butter cookies, they retraced their steps back to the other side of the outbuildings. Circling the mound, they entered a pathless, park-like setting with mature trees and shrubs established in a rough lawn under a partially open sky. A single, slumped, gray bench sat at one overused picnic table in the shade of a Monterey pine.

"Over there that's a Giant Sequoia but it'll never get to be a giant: not enough freeze here. And that's the Dawn Redwood. You know the story behind that one, don't you? I tell you some time, *jaja*, I tell you that one. And those up there," he said, pointing beyond a high hedge of redwood that once upon a time had been kept tightly trimmed across the top and along its sides, "that's your good old 'Santa Cruz' redwood. So is this," he added, approaching the hedge. "This light green color ... these soft leaves...." His words trailed off as he caressed the foliage. "Poor thing, I got to give you a haircut one these days. *Jaja*, we planted this hedge here and those trees there, Nico and me, when we found out nobody was buying our redwood trees. Back then the peoples were cutting them down to plant their bluegrass lawns. I always wanted to get the 'Woodside' and 'Filoli' selections onto this place but...." He paused, gripping his chin between with his finger and thumb then shaking his head and removing his pack of Nat's Petit Maduros from his pocket. "Somehow that never happened."

"Wow," Katie whispered, turning around. "This is like a park."

"*Jaja*, is a park, a little parkland and not a woodlot, see? 1.6 acres. When you see these bushes in spring, then you going to say '*Wauw!*' Those camellias and rhodies and all those Japanese maples. That big old Pieris over there. And when those Exbury azaleas bloom...? Then you going to say, '*Wauw wauw wauw, schooooooooon!*'" •

"Aren't you going to tell me all their names, professor?"

"*Ach*, don't get me started, Katie. I can do that, and you know I can do that. I know their names, sure, these are my friends. But come on now, let's sit down."

"Wait a sec', where's Blue?" She whistled; the dog came in. "Is it okay if she runs around off leash like this?"

• *Wow, wow, wow, beautiful! (derived from Dutch)*

"Is okay, is okay. Maybe she runs down those sonsaguns wood rats down there." He gestured toward a weathered, wood-slat building no bigger than an outhouse. "Chewing up the wires and piling up their junk all inside the springhouse, the rascals!"

They rested, settling carefully at either end of the sagging raw-wood bench. During the extended silence, Katie stole a glance: Pieter T. seemed to have dropped into absentminded reverie after having lit a black cigarillo, its blue smoke vanishing into the dappled light. She felt the urge to put cool cotton pads over his puffy eyes and tuck the skeins of his soft white hair back behind his ears.

Pieter announced that he wanted to divulge his dilemma: he wanted to keep this *pied à terre* at the highest point on the ridge above Soquel Gulch but selling off Nico's three acres would earn him far more money than he would net for his modest ranch house on less than a quarter-acre off Pleasant Valley Road in South County. After his brother had died, he and his wife had intended to put the property up for sale and had even hired help to clean out the cabin, to level the nursery production area, and to haul off the clutter accumulated in the clearing and around the barn and non-working garage. However, this open-air grove of planted trees and shrubs looking out over a north-ward-trending section of the Santa Cruz Mountains had turned out to be the one place his wife could find peace of mind when she herself became terminally ill, and in the years since Drika's death, the petite park had become his own private sanctuary too. He did not want to witness some rich buyer from Santa Clara County knocking everything down in order to put up a trophy home or a vacation retreat behind locked gates. Lately, it had even occurred to him that the shrubs would make marvelous cutting material for some young nurserywoman looking for some free propagules. He paused, his eyelids parting widely before resting again at half-mast. "You know what I mean by propagules ... for propagation...?"

"Sure," she said, curious about this man who never made conditions or asked her for money. It seemed he wasn't even considering the possibility that she might reject any part of his offerings.

"Okay," he declared, exposing his oddly angled front teeth, smiling right at her, and blinking twice as if aware of her thinking and the involuntary quiver rippling up the back of her neck. "Go get your truck and we load up those things."

They improvised a ramp and wrestled the soil shredder, the hauling cart, and the can carrier into the back of her pickup. Pieter pressed her to take all the long-handled tools from the barrels—and a couple of ladders—but to leave him one spring rake and one shovel. She resisted, arguing that she had enough rakes, shovels, mallets, and pruning instruments, and that he would need the ladders for his own park maintenance; he countered that it was she who would need more tools outfitting the Redwood Coast Nursery's workers—maybe sooner than she thought.

"I thought you said I'm supposed to stay small. Stay small, you said that, Mister Tuelling. But you're not going to let me, are you?"

He grinned, blushed, and changed the subject, nodding at dozens of empty, restaurant-size food containers piled helter-skelter in two roofed stalls with horseshoes nailed across the rafters. "You come back for those old nursery cans too. They already got the nail holes in the bottom, eh?"

*

Moist red streaks ran across his brow where Pieter's hat's sweatband had left its impression. Opening the wobbly latch of the refrigerator door, he dragged three bottles of Heineken from the rear of the single wire rack. "The gas is turned off," he explained, "but I got to keep electricity running since I learned to drink my beers cold like Americans." Flipping off the three metal caps with his pocketknife, he passed her a bottle. "And to run the pump, to water some special plants out there I got to show you still." They clinked two bottles, and she sipped a stronger, bitterer tasting beer than she was used to.

"So, what are those special plants?" Katie inquired, shifting her rear end in search of some portion of the cracked vinyl seat that wouldn't bite at her through her jeans. "Is there still some nursery stock squirreled away up here somewhere?"

"I show you. I show you everything, Katie. But first we workers take a break." He paused, lifting his bottle to his lips and chugging down half its contents. "Is the law!" he declared and sniggered, reaching for another smoke.

Katie relaxed and watched him finishing his first beer within a minute and helping himself to a second. Sipping hers, she rocked back onto the two splayed rear legs of her chair and saw rose pink blotches blooming at his temples and on the highpoints of his cheeks. "How come your brother lived like this? I mean, was it always so ... simple in here, even before you cleaned up?"

"Simple ... *jaja*, that's it. No knickknacks. My Drika, down in Corralitos, she had enough those knickknacks for me and Nicholaas too."

"Were there any curtains when he lived there?"

"Oh ... *ja*, I think he had curtains...." Pieter mused, looking at the windows on either side of the room. "He was still Dutch, you know. *Ach*, if not for that woman's touch, this place would have been...." he broke off, hastily downing what was left of his beer and rising to fetch another. "A prison cell, like you say."

"He never got over what happened during the war, is that it?"

"*Dat is het*, Katie, now you got it. That's it right there. He...." Pieter stopped short and sat down, brooding over the unevenly smoldering end of his cigarillo while pinching a portion of short white hairs in the horizontal sliver below his nose.

"Yeah...?"

"My brother, he never talked about it much, Missus Katie. But one day he told me, he said, 'Nobody knows what I saw.' I believed him too. He didn't want people to ask him about it. He wore long sleeves all the time. Hot as the devil's house outside, he wore a shirt to cover the numbers on his arm, eh? And in the end, Katie, in the very end, seeing me—his own brother—it only made poor Nico feel worse. He didn't even want me playing with my special camellias up here anymore."

"What do you mean, playing with them?"

"Grafting scions onto rootstock. Pollinizing, hybridizing, all like that."

"I didn't know you did that sort of thing."

"*Jaja*, that's my hobby, sure. Or it was. But Nico, he wanted only *de productie, de productie, de productie.*" The man snuffed out his poorly burning cigar and sat silent.

"So, do you have a little greenhouse of your own in Corralitos?"

"There are lots of greenhouses in Corralitos, big ones too, but me? *Nee.* I used to grow cut flowers ... for Drika... that's all. But I got Nico's nursey production books in Corralitos. I give those to you too, Missus Katie, but they're all in Dutch! Say, you don't want another beer?"

"No, thanks. I better go soon. I've got some new equipment to deliver to Cliffport this afternoon."

"New used," he said and they smiled. "But first I got to show you those plants. Then I let you go."

He considered taking the beer with him, but left it unopened with the empties on the table.

"Okay, so show me."

The man donned his hat, and she followed him back across the yard and around the garage, where a narrow opening in the unruly redwood hedge admitted them to a sort of ampitheater whose crescent-shaped tiers stepped up a dry, earthen bank below the backdrop of the tall 'Santa Cruz' redwoods he had already pointed out. One level was covered by a dilapidated, three-sided, glass-roof structure that must once have provided cold winter protection for the now-skeletonized plants below. A second tier was surmonted by remnants of an open-work roof of wooden laths that had created shade for the specimens underneath it. At least one aluminum tag hung on each plant, accentuating the deformed anatomy of the individual bushes and the empty spaces between them. Branches were partly or completely denuded of leaves; whatever foilage remained showed signs of distress. Much of the unmulched ground had eroded away, exposing the tops of hardened root balls in irregularly shaped blocks protruding above the surrounding soil. Attached to several upright galvanized steel spigots, lengths of kinked, rigidified rubber garden hose lay about.

"What the heck was this?" Katie asked.

"Is my special collection of tender rhododendrons and camellias. What's left of them, after I sold off Nico's regular stock."

"So, what are you going to do with them now?"

"I'm going to give them to you, Missus Katie."

"What'd you just say?"

"I'm donating these plants to the Redwood Coast Nursery. With a little protection from the cold and wind, they will grow *wonderlijk. Fantastisch!* Sure!"

"But I ... I...."

"I know, I know, they don't look so good right now. But you scratch the bark on most those plants and you going to get green under those two green thumbs you got. They need a new home, Katie, that's all. New soil, new mulch. A new home in Cliffport."

"Are you crazy, Pieter Tuelling?" Katie spun around and threw up her hands. "How am I going to take care of them? I don't know the first thing about growing these kinds of plants, especially bringing them back to life."

"*Ja*, you do, you do," he countered, "and I know the rest."

"But where am I supposed to put them? Let's get real, Pieter."

"I show you where. You tell Mister Tuelling to go for a hike if you like. But ... if you want me to tell you...?"

"Oh sure, why not? This I've got to hear!" She plopped down on a shelf-like earthen bench between two ghostly, misshappen shrubs. "Go on."

The retired field agent also settled on the lowest ledge and described his vision for resiting the collection in Cliffport. First, the trees in the defunct orchard terraces up behind the Lowrie residence would be razed and their stumps removed. Next, the holes would be filled halfway with the finished soil for acid-loving plants; then they would build a shade structure over half the terraces and a frost-protection structure over the other half then set up an irrigation system. Finally, they would dig up these plants, transporting them along with some of the same special soil mix in porous burlap bags, and sinking them—sans burlap—into the prepared holes, setting them high, backfilling with native soil, and mulching with oak leaf litter or pine needles.

By the time he had wound up his presentation, Katie's elbows were on her knees and her foreheard was cradled in her palms. When she was certain he was done, she sprang to her feet, set her knuckles on her hips and, arms akimbo, turned her face to the sky to let loose a great horned owl's hoo-hoo hoo-hoooo; Baby Blue barked back from somewhere out of sight.

"What have you been smoking in those little cigars of yours, *Inspecteur*? I never knew you brought hash back with you from Amsterdam!"

"What's that you say, what's that you say now?" He rose to his feet. "I never smoked that stuff in my life! I smoke good cigars—'made in Holland'—when I can find them."

"Then you're just plain crazy, is that it? Come on, Pieter! I don't have the time and money to make all what you said happen. That'd be huge for me. Why not give these suckers to some plant freaks at the university? How many are here, fifty? How many do you think would even survive being transplanted—five?"

He clasped his hands on his abdoman and lowered his eyes. She stepped closer and touched the ruddy, reddish skin on the back of his uppermost hand, searching for a glimpse of blue between his narrowed eyelids.

"I'm sorry, Pieter. I don't mean to seem ungrateful. I'm not mad at you. It's just I've got so much to do before I start rescuing rare plants ... whatever you call them ... erica-ace-cee-us?"

"Ericaceous from Ericacea family. And the camellias from Theacea."

"Right, those too. Oh, man, this is nuts! What am I, an arboretum?" Katie strode alongside the bottom row of plants, turned around, and placed her boot on the ledge. "You know what I mean, right?"

"So, I can talk now...?"

"Yeah, sure, of course. I'm sorry. I guess there's some Irish left in me after all."

"When I have the money ... when this place sells, or the Corralitos place.... Well, then I have the money and the time, Katie. I already got the know-how. I can show you how to grow these plants, eh? You got two green thumbs and ... you've got the ground!"

"Shit! Okay, it's true. You are crazy, I see it now. Oh, I'm sorry but I'm not 'joking you' now. You better find somebody with more time on their hands than me. Besides, my mom would never in a million years let me chop down her Uncle John's fruit trees. He was like God to her, Pieter, or at least a godfather. That orchard is like a sacred grove to her, like this little parkland here was sacred to your wife ... and is to you. You've seen that tractor sunk to its belly up in the orchard, right?"

"*Jaja*, I remember, sure."

"Once I asked my mother how come she never got that dead tractor pulled out of the orchard. She said John McLoughlin died of a heart attack falling off that Farmall and that's where it should remain as a memorial to the man. You know what I think really happened? After she found him lying there, when it happened, she was so freaked out she couldn't do a thing on the place for a long time. Nothing. She could've had it pulled out of there anytime after that, but it's become like a symbol for her."

"I can understand that, sure enough. But can I ask you something else, Missus Katie?"

"Something else? Sure you can. You have another pet project in mind? Oh, Pieter, I really dig you, goddamnitall, you know I do! But right now you're freaking me out. Okay, okay, I'll shut up." She sat back down. "Go ahead."

"How many of those fruit trees in that orchard are still alive and productive? Ten? Five?"

"Maybe five out of fifty."

"And still producing edible fruit?"

"One."

"Aha! One out of fifty!"

"But that pear, Pieter, that goes back like seventy or eighty years. I can't ask my mother to give up those crummy little Bartletts it puts out. You wouldn't even think of it, if you knew her better."

"So, I got a proposal."

"You and your proposals!"

"We leave that tractor there and leave that pear tree there and Elisabeth Lowrie lets us take out the rest."

"And we grind out all the stumps?"

"Or burn them out, *jaja*, or.... By the way, did you see where DDT was just outlawed?"

"I did. At least in the US. It can still be made and exported, of course. Disgusting pigs!"

"Okay, so, no poisons in Cliffport. You get some roustabouts you got up that way to get those sonsagun stumps out of there and fill the holes halfway with the mix and then, one by one, you and me, we lift these plants here, roots and all. Of course, I got to take cuttings off each one first, in case they die, like you say, from the transplant shock, eh? I help you nurse these plants back to life, Missus Katie."

"I'm going to have to think long and hard about this whole thing, Pieter."

"I understand that, sure enough."

Keeping several yards ahead of him, Katie meandered back to the pickup in total silence and found Baby Blue Eye dozing in its shade; she rattled her keys; the dog rose. Katie squared off opposite her mentor, shielding her eyes from the sun, waiting until she could see both his narrow eyes. "Tell me why you want to do all this for me, Pieter?"

He blushed, disengaged from her gaze, crossed his arms, turned sideways, and heaved his upper-body in a sigh. "I got to redeem Pieter Tuelling, Missus Katie. I think so. Before the end comes, I got to redeem Pieter Tuelling, sure enough."

Reaching out to kiss his cheek—Katie decided not to and ushered the dog into the cab. Baby Blue positioned herself at the passenger window, forelegs on the frame; Pieter scratched the dog's head and blinked twice at the driver before stepping away.

By the time Katie was waiting for the first red light to change on Soquel Avenue, she was rehearsing the conversation with Elise.

*

On her return visit for the purpose of collecting as many empty plant containers as the Ford's shell could carry back to Cliffport, Katie arrived before Pieter Tuelling and—after slipping a bowl of freshly picked raspberries into his little fridge—wandered the grounds, letting Baby Blue Eye run free, sniffing out the place anew. The winter–spring flowering season in the garden park, succeeded by new green growth, had left behind pools of rotten, fallen petals, especially camelias in which towhees scratched and pecked. Sparrows and finches flew in and out of the muck, gorging on the bounty of insects, earwigs, pill bugs, and slugs populating the decay; thrushes and flickers flushed them out, then the jays moved in; ultimately the towhees returned, and the cycle repeated. Katie ambled over to the opening in the redwood hedge, took one look at the sickbay, and stood dumbfounded by her own willingness even to entertain the prospect of participating in Pieter's plant rescue scheme. She again fought the thought that he was nothing but a lonely, eccentric retiree using the project as an excuse to secure her presence—or her mother's—in his life, or else he was merely exploiting the Lowrie's rent-free land for his own idiosyncratic purposes.

Elise had shown no alarm upon learning of his proposal but rather blessed the former orchard site's conversion into a refuge for plant species and cultivars unlikely to be available in the ordinary nursery trade. Once she had been reassured that the tractor wouldn't be displaced and the fruit-bearing pear would be left standing— and there would be no significant financial burden placed upon the Lowries' shoulders—she agreed to the undertaking, intimating that if the Dutch expatriate were the source and backer of such a plan, it must be fundamentally sound. Katie's long-orphaned mother had even expressed her hope that, for the rare visitor who remembered John McLoughlin—forester, dairyman, egg farmer, orchardist; loving husband, father, and son—highlighting that abandoned piece of anti-quated farm equipment might in some way draw his name out from an obscure corner of their minds. Others, too young to know, might simply ask why an old tractor was left there and to whom it had belonged. [1]

Katie walked across the bumpy patches of turf and found a spot where she could sit and survey a deep, wide swath of the familiar mountain range and its waves of forested ridges receding hazily to the north. Ever more frequently, she would come upon her mother seated in the upholstered red armchair turned toward the picture window in the main room or settled in the stiff leather of Uncle John's old Western cowboy rocker in her bedroom—gazing inward, one of her two Bibles in her lap. Katie had once dismissed her mother's declarations of belief in Christ as instances of a silly, softheaded, deep-seated religiosity coming to the surface when the woman was most under duress; now Katie could acknowledge them as revelatory of the ground from which the woman drew her strength: a Christian-conditioned faith empowering Elisabeth Piagère Lowrie's resilience and providing her incomparable analgesia. Katie stood up, stretched, and laughed: if her mother ever witnessed the Dutchman plowing through his packs of tan-, brown-, and black-wrapped cigarillos while knocking back two or three Heinekens before 2:00 PM, she might reconsider the saintly status she seemed to grant him and reevaluate his seasoned, charming manner at that Sunday supper when Pieter Tuelling had showed up thoroughly scrubbed, nicely dressed, and bearing gifts.

She strolled over to the picnic table and sat down again, weaving pine needles in her fingers, questioning whether her mother would live long enough to enjoy peace of mind about her only grandchild. How many years would it be before Donald Duncan would be clearheaded and openhearted enough to pay his "gran'ma" her due other than in occasional lip service on long-distance phone calls or token postcards sent while living a style of life that flew directly in the face of everything Elise believed was right and true? Katie's own cross-motivations perplexed her: whether to forgive the growing boy his flagrant disrespect and tolerate his blatant immaturity, or to apply even greater strictures on the reckless self-indulgence she feared might do permanent damage to his body and mind. She knew the allure of unleashed rebellion; she had flirted with danger and suffered the consequences of self-abuse. Had she been wrong to lay down the law with her teenage son? For the time being, he was who-knew-where with who-knew-whom doing who-knew-what. Would she do it again if he showed up for a visit or expecting to stay? She swept the needles off the gray boards and rested her forehead atop her crossed forearms, recalling how she had once sworn never to become as uptight with her own son as she felt her mother had been with her. Katie recollected gathering from passages in Elise's NOTEBOOKS that her French grandmother had been quite the disciplinarian with Elisabeth Piagère, and Katie had recognized that Elisabeth Lowrie had been something of a disciplinarian with her. But had her own version of discipline with her own child now been so severe that she had driven him away, perhaps forever?

Katie hopped up, whistled for Baby Blue, and strode back across the clearing, thinking she must have mistaken the date or time of day when she and Pieter had agreed to meet. Should she just park closer to the stalls and toss the used food cans into the back of her truck anyway? She would be held blameless, but to proceed without him seemed too brazen. She dangled her legs from the lowered tailgate, splitting and spitting sunflower seed hulls at the dog who sat on her haunches, quizzically staring back.

Having already accepted his gifts and donations, Katie wondered if she ought to terminate further relations with the man. He wasn't her employer, father, or husband. His appeal as a lover had not occurred to her more than once. Should she drive off now without taking the supplies, without leaving any explanation, without responding to his complex overtures ever again? Yet she was somehow repeatedly drawn to him, and one question nagged her: why had Pieter and Ellen Tuelling never raised children of their own—at least none the Lowries knew about? Bringing up the subject would certainly be taboo in Elise Lowrie's code of behavior and perhaps prove offensive to Pieter in his Old World ways, but the question remained: had they had children, and something gone amiss? Perhaps Ellen couldn't bear children, or else Pieter couldn't produce the living seed. Or maybe the war-torn Tuellings had chosen not to bring children into a world which had provided sufficient evidence of man's barbaric inhumanity to man. Her mother was probably right. For Katie to probe the subject aloud would be worse than bad form; it could prove hurtful to a man whose sunny goodwill and outward bonhomie—marbled throughout with dark streaks of melancholia—were worth protecting. But exactly what was her attraction to Pieter Tuelling? Was she in some way already in too deep with the man? Everywhere Katie went in her mind, she brushed up against the boundaries of her own comprehension.

She shifted her position sideways to get out of hot sunlight. Baby Blue came to all fours, expecting action, but Katie merely flicked another wad of wet, cracked sunflower shells at the dog's snout. Turning away from the tasteless, desalted hulls, Blue went down and rested her head on her forelegs, closing her eyes. Why was Katie even bothering to worry about her relationship with the childless widower? Was their connection so complicated as to stop her from learning more from him about the nursery world, especially when they would start exploring whatever yet-to-be specified destinations he had in mind? The drawn-out and undetermined timetable of the plant salvage project was another matter, for it would mean they would spend more time together than ever. What would she be getting herself into if she committed to pursuing that plant relocation operation?

She heard then spotted his badly maintained sedan coming down the lane, one headlight beam flickering on and off, as if to signal that she ought not to move. Landing on her heels, Katie waited, adjusting the visor of her cap against the sunlight. Of course! He's like a father or an older brother to me. I just have to be careful now not to call him Dad or Jody in some stupid way.

*

"The doctor says: 'No more cookies, no more cigars. Drink less beer.' *Ach*, he's right, sure, he's right. But I can't decide what to stop first, so I keep up all three for now." He puckered his lips, dipped another butter cookie into his instant coffee and scarfed it down. "One these days—when *de dokter's* not looking—I'm going to serve you a real *koffie verkeerd*: half real coffee, half real milk, half real sugar."

"That makes three halves, Pieter, but it sounds good to me. Hey, remind me to give you some veggies that are out in the truck. Onions, radishes, asparagus. We've had enough asparagus till the fall."

"Thank you ... is kind ... *ach*, Katie!" he grumbled, shoving his leather driving cap off his forehead. "I pretty much gave up on that monkey business about living forever ... after Nico died ... then Drika. But onions, radishes, those I like. Asparagus too—with lots of butter and salt! Say, did you leave me a rake and a shovel in the barn out there?"

"I sure did. More than one."

"I got to get those darn camellia blossoms off the ground and out from where they're stuck up in the branches too. I don't spray for that sonagun petal blight and it's getting pretty bad, pretty bad. You see, Missus Katie? I stopped spraying after Nico died. Did I ever tell you that?"

"I don't think you did."

"*Jaja. Ex-Inspecteur* Tuelling may be one of the good guys after all, Missus Katie!"

"I know he is!" she concurred and they both laughed.

"No joking you now. When Drika got so that little park was all where she wanted to be...."

"You told me that part."

"Tell you the truth, Katie. I got so sick of going into greenhouses and smelling all those organophosphates. Getting out of the truck at some nice little family tree farm and smelling the Lindane a hundred yards away! Named after a Dutch chemist too—Van der Linden, the rascal. And my brother, he put everything on so heavy up here, oh boy! 'Pro-phy-lac-tic-ally,' as they say ... as I used to say. But when Drika was up here during her last couple months ... *nee nee*, no more poisons after that."

"You're really are a good man, Pieter."

"A good man who got to start picking up that mess of rotten flowers out there one these days. There's sure a lot of them too!"

"Why not pay some kid on summer vacation to do it for you? I bet some kids would like to make five or ten bucks. Couldn't you have them rake it all over the bank at the edge of the lawn, or would that still leave the spores too close?"

"So, you know about spores, eh?" He smiled. "Oh, Katie, look what I got to show you!" He pulled a folded piece of lined paper from his shirt pocket and passed it to her. "I dug that up back at the house." Columns of numbers and letters were penciled in cramped hand-writing on both sides. "That's a list of rhododendrons and azaleas, see? Can you make anything out? *Ach*, my writing was always so small. You want this magnifier?"

"It looks like a lot of dates and codes."

"The date when he got the plant and the date when he stuck it in the ground out there."

"And the letters?"

"That's what I got to do next, Missus Katie."

"What's that?"

"I got to one by one match what he put on that darn paper there and what we got on the tags on those plants out there. And there's another piece of paper like that with a list of the camellias too: japonicas, retic-ulatas, sasanquas, chrysantha—all like that. And Gordonia...."

"All like dot, huh? I don't know what you're talking about. You know this paper is going to fall apart pretty soon. You want me to Xerox it so you'll have something you can work with?"

"*Nee nee nee*," he protested, retaking possession of the sheet. "I do that, Missus Katie. Is Pieter Tuelling's job not yours."

She smiled at his boyish pout. It was hard to imagine that this man was once accustomed to reading the fine print on the toxicity warnings of the chemical substances he prescribed, the use of which he was responsible to monitor. "You know, my mom and I have been thinking that the whole thing might just work out."

"Me too, I think so too. The whole thing might just work out," he echoed, popping another cookie into his mouth and using two blunt fingertips to brush any crumbs from his moustache. "But I got to start making those cuttings of those bushes so we can transplant in the fall. When the rain comes, we stand back and watch them grow in the new ground and next spring? Strong, healthy specimens. Better roots, that way."

"Well, I don't know about moving on anything that fast, at least not at my end. I'm pretty swamped."

He didn't seem to have heard her and appeared momentarily distracted. She was sitting in silence, sipping her tepid instant coffee, when he rose and stood at attention, as if he had determined the time was right for action. "I got something else to show you."

"What something else?"

"Stay here. I'll get it from the car, be right back," he concluded, all but prancing out the door on his curiously light feet.

She was puzzling over the list of words she couldn't pronounce and plants she couldn't picture when he barged back into the cabin, carrying a folded piece of corrugated cardboard clamped closed with wooden clothespins on three sides. "Okay ... okay...." he muttered, tucking the homemade portfolio under his left arm and using his right hand to swipe crumbs and ashes from the tabletop onto the floor. "Look at this here, *ja*, you look at this."

She pulled her chair alongside his as he lifted the tissue paper from the first of several dozen unbound 9" × 12" watercolor boards.

"May I...?" she asked, before taking the top piece into her hands.

"O, *jaja*, you got to do that. You got to look closely, Missus Katie, to see what my Drika could do."

She turned the watercolor sketch of a California poppy to different angles in the natural light and then held it at closer range. "This is beautiful."

"*Jaja* ... is Drika...."

As she looked at the first few illustrations, Katie sensed that, however amateurish the artwork, the images showed a thorough knowledge of the species pictured and communicated an unalloyed delight in the visible features of the plants. Cliffport's native daughter grasped the place of these artifacts in the widower's devotion to his deceased wife: his sharing expressed his trust in Katie and honored the memory of Ellen Hendrika de Boers. She thumbed through three dozen boards without removing any, realizing there were no fully rendered landscapes or garden settings; the sketches focused on blossoms and leaves or entire plants, but with no attempt to present either a scientific portrait for an herbarium or a work of art for a gallery or museum. Whether a spray of berry-laden toyon, a clump of sword ferns, or a Sabine pine portrayed by its needles and a leafy shoot bearing mature cones—each sketch conveyed its own quiet focus; no botanical nomenclature was penciled in the lower right corners—only dates and common names.

"These are so cool," she said, leafing back through the lot. "They're all plants from California, right? Aren't there any from Holland?"

"*Nee nee*," Pieter stated. "She took up drawing when we moved here. She taught herself—oh, she took some art classes, sure, at the night school and all like that but...." The proud, heart-broken man fell silent and lit a cigarillo. "Now you listen, Katie. There are more of these, but I want you to show Elisabeth these first. If she wants to see more ... if you want to see more, then I show you more, sure."

"Don't you want to present these to my mom yourself?"

He closed his eyelids completely and spoke: "Take these with you, Missus Katie, please."

"But what if something happens to them? I don't know...."

"You borrow them, Katie." He had yet to reopen his eyes. "Show your mother for me what my Drika could do, please."

Katie watched him stick two thick forefingers behind his glasses and pretend to be picking something from the corners of his eyes.

"I sure will. She'd love to see them. Thank you for the trust, Pieter."

He opened his moist, blue, glistening eyes. "You got that from me, Missus Katie. Sure enough, you got trust and all like that coming from me."

After she had realigned the layered boards inside the cardboard carrier, she caught him sitting with his eyes reclosed, an unlit cigarillo in his hand. "Pieter...?"

He popped his lids wide open. "I got something more to show you too, Katie Lowrie. I don't know why but...." His words trailed off as he dropped his cigar in the ashtray and leaned sideways, taking his wallet from his back pocket and extracting a black-and-white photograph showing a white adult male standing in front of a country wall. The man wore unhemmed trousers and some sort of rural, rustic overcoat. A wide-brimmed dark hat sat atop his head and handfuls of hair hung long to either side of his round face—hair as white, soft, and thick as Pieter Tuelling's.

"Oh my god, Pieter! Is this your father?"

"*Nee nee,*" he replied, unlacing his intertwined fingers. "That there's my wife's father. That's Adriaan de Boers. This here is my father," he said, taking out another picture. "Hans Tuelling, before the War."

A man in his thirties or forties stood in front of a city building. He held a black fedora at one side and a leather attaché case at the other. His dark hair was creamed and combed. He wore wire-rimmed glasses and a loose, long-sleeve shirt with two flapped breast pockets and long buttonless lapels tapering to sharp points. Although his pants rode high above his waistline, the bottom of his broad, patterned necktie—held back by a chain—still stopped short of reaching the belt holding up the creased, cuffed trousers. His heavily lidded eyes looked back at the camera; the lower, clean-shaven jaw cradled no hint of a smile.

"So, this is your father, and this is your father-in-law, right? The one you lost in the World War Two, you told me."

"*Nee nee,* my friend."

"No? Didn't you tell me he died during World War Two?"

"He died but we didn't lose him. He was murdered."

"Oh ... shit ... right, I—"

"... is okay," he stated matter-of-factly, replacing the two photographs in his wallet.

He toyed with his cigarillo before lighting it, waving the wooden match until the flame went out. "He was murdered by Nazis in 1943. I been to that railway station in Bois-le-Duc where he was the stationmaster, Adriaan de Boers. I been on that platform where they forced him onto that train what was transporting Jews and resisters to that Kamp Vught. Not every Dutch Jew went to Westerbork then on to die in Sachsenhaussen, you know? Maybe one hundred thousand did, *ja*, one hundred thousand, but not everyone. There was that *Arbeit-seinsatz*, that forced labor system in Germany. But in 1943 they had that prison Kamp Vught in Southern Nederlands too ... a place to lose Dutch people in."

"Oh, Pieter, I'm so sorry. I—"

"... no, Katie, is okay, is okay. I understand, eh? It's just I have to tell you: I been to that place. His name wasn't on the list of the dead in Sachsenhaussen, so I went down into the North Brabant, eh? In South Nederlands, the countryside. After Klauss—my father's father—after Klauss died I went looking for what happened to my wife's father, the father of Ellen Hendrika de Boers. I found out. Then I stood in the rain one day on the platform of that station where Adriaan de Boers refused to let any more those poor people be put on that death train."

"You must have felt like the loneliest guy in the world."

"And how did he feel?"

"Oh my god. So, you don't know exactly where he was ... killed."

"*Alleen God weet het.*• En route to Kamp Vught? Later in that camp? Only God knows that. Adriaan de Boers. Lost."

He rose and stood at the counter with his back turned. She checked to be certain that the three clothespins were securely clamped in place along the borders of the cardboard folio.

"Well, I guess I'll let you head back to Cliffport," he said softly, his back still turned. "I got all that darn raking to do."

"But not today, you don't," she countered quietly. "Not all of it."

"You're right. Maybe not all of it today, eh?"

"And before too long," she said, rising to her feet, the portfolio under one arm, "you have to start taking me to those nurseries you've been talking about."

"*O ja! Das is waar*, that's true," he responded, turning around to face her. "We got to start making those pilgrimages, sure enough."

• *Only God knows (Dutch)*

Outside, she lodged the folder out of harm's way inside the cab before allowing Baby Blue Eye to jump in. "Hey, the vegetables!" she declared, retrieving the brown grocery bag from the footwell on the passenger side.

"So, you got a CARE package for the Old Man on the Mountain?" They smiled and, at the moment she transferred the weight of the bag into his arms, he winked. "Any cookies in here?"

"I can make you cookies sometime, Pieter, if you want," she responded, patting his forearm. "I make shortbread too but it's not as good as my mom's."

He blushed, looked away, then seemed to remember something. "Did I say I'm sorry for being late today, Missus Katie?"

"Sure, you did, Mister Tuelling. But I figured you for a stoned-out hippie the first time I laid eyes on you. And did I thank you for all these nursery cans?"

"You did, you did, sure. More than once."

"Okay!" she declaimed, breaking away. "Thanks for everything."

"Tot ziens!"

"What?" she called out over the engine noise.

"See you real soon!"

You got that right, Inspecteur T. she mumbled to herself then raised her voice: "Now don't forget there are those raspberries in your fridge!" Executing a wide U-turn in the unobstructed clearing, she waved and headed out the lane.

Where the non-maintained spur road's surface teed into the neglected, chewed-up pavement of Soquel Gulch Road, Katie eased the pickup into a sunny patch and killed the engine. Sunlight shone through the bullet exit holes in the backside of a leaning NO THOR-OUGHFARE street sign. A rusted, yellow, metal PRIVATE PROPERY sign—likewise riddled with shell holes—hung askew on barbed wire running along the base of a roadside wall of crumbling chert. A loud gang of acorn woodpeckers swooped out of the oaks on one side of the intersection and into the oaks on the other.

She leaned her head back and sighed, lowering the baseball cap's visor over her eyes, again asking herself if she wouldn't be making a mistake by committing to take on his plant collection. The prospect of letting Pieter Tuelling lead her on "pilgrimages" to numerous nurseries still intrigued her, but that plan didn't entail the longer-term dedication to the larger, multiphase project he had in mind. She had not pledged her word or signed a contract yet, but she had also not said no. Still, Katie thought, it would do no harm to have Ross over to the place, if and when he came back from commercial fishing; she could solicit his estimate for the work of converting the old orchard into an outdoor conservatory and at the same time grill him for information about the whereabouts and doings of her wayward son. Before or after Ross's visit, she could also invite one of the Avila family for a quote on the same work, if only to keep Ross Stewart honest. [2]

Could Katie share her concerns with her mother without divulging all her quandaries about Pieter T.? She pictured Elise seated in one of her favorite chairs, reading or daydreaming with her granny glasses dangling from one hand: the falling face and throat wattles; the age spots on her arms, the back of her hands, her temples, and her forehead; the mass of white hair coiled by hand and wrapped atop her head—Katie decided to telephone Suzanne instead. There would be no need to fill Suzanne Crogan in on absolutely everything, for no one had known Kaitlin Liliane Lowrie longer than her "aunt" had, and the woman would also know what to keep secret from Elizabeth too.

Katie turned on the ignition, put the truck in gear, and resolved to phone Cloverdale the next time she found Elise asleep or out of earshot. Steering through the strobic play of light and shadow created by the overarching oaks and bays, she imagined Aunt Suzanne's response: "You take care of yourself first, Katie. You have Elise to worry about, and your plants and the animals. If Donald ever shows up, you'll have him on your hands again too. However lovable your old fuddy-duddy Dutchman may be, you have plenty to take care of before turning his passion into your priority."

Aunt Suzanne, like Mother Elise, could be practical to a fault and would never unconditionally approve of her acting under any spell Pieter Tuelling cast on her adopted niece.

———

She sanded smooth a rectangular piece of plywood so her bedridden mother could prop herself up and review the two plant portfolios at the same time, spectacles lodged on the bridge of her nose. Elise took up a practice of setting like kinds of plants side by side, comparing and contrasting the variant common names and, sotto voce, reciting the botanical titles, savoring the syllables like a schoolmaster revisiting Latin. Even without considering the pressed specimens and the brittle seed packets, Mary McLoughlin's seventy-year-old compendium of colored pencil drawings was the more exactly local flora, with scientific binomial names, renditions of various parts of the plants on a magnified scale, and handwritten notes about her observations in the field and the dates each drawing was done. Ellen 'Drika' Tuelling's watercolor sketches had been executed en plein air, featured statewide species as well as those distributed inside the North Coast range, and didn't pretend to document anything but an obvious affection for the plants observed. Katie was relieved that handling the illustrations by two sensitive amateurs seemed not to agitate her mother into reminiscing too often or at too great length. Instead, the two portfolios seemed to soothe her, permitting her entry into a field of fondness and profound, calmative appreciation; growing older herself, Katie was less inclined to mock her mother's nostalgia for all that may never have happened.

When Katie phoned Suzanne on the sly, her aunt proved predictably concerned about Elise's daughter's puzzlement over Pieter Tuelling's motivations, yet nothing she said dissuaded Katie from continuing her horticultural pursuits with the man. As regards the transplanting project, Suzanne encouraged her niece to ask herself, and to keep asking herself, who needs whom most: the calf that wants to suckle or the cow that wants to nurse? As long as the benefits were mutual and Katie kept an eye out for any serious imbalance in the relationship, there might be nothing at risk. Katie closed the conversation by requesting that Aunt Suzanne not bring their call up to Elise.

Katie pursued Ross Stewart's whereabouts, leaving three messages with three different individuals answering the phone at number she had for him. Two weeks went by without news, so she drove up to Fern, putting out word that she was looking for one of Ben Lomond Mountain's well-known native sons. She spoke to the owner of the General Store and several familiar citizens, who could not or would not tell her more about his situation. Katie tacked a card on the bulletin board at the Community Center then went to the counter inside Fern's brand-new US Post Office and convinced Mr. Jeffrey's successor to let her slip a notice under the locked glass wall cabinet in the lobby.

One fogbound August morning, Ross showed up in Cliffport and gave her a fixed price—payable in cash—for cutting down the orchard trees, splitting and stacking the wood to size for their cooking stove and fireplace, and burning the slash in a bonfire on site. He also gave her a ballpark estimate for the stump removal, the construction of lath roofing supported by posts, and the irrigation installation, but they agreed that a firm quote for that subsequent work would best be addressed after the first phase of the project was complete. The incorrigible mountain man still wore his shoulder-length hair unbrushed and his ragged horseshoe moustache untrimmed, still chewed tobacco, and still dressed in unkempt lumberjack attire reeking of wood smoke and marijuana. Katie thought twice about inviting him into the house to say hello to Mrs. Lowrie, but when they did step inside, they found her deep asleep in the club chair, a trail of yarn leading to a ball of wool that had rolled out of her lap and onto the hearth.

Katie accompanied Ross down to his jeep, the two of them shooting the breeze about how fast Fern was changing: the new post office; the new playground at the school; the modern vehicle repair facility replacing the old mechanic's garage. Ross reported on renovations in progress at the aged Mountain Dogwood Motor Inn a mile above the village, the council members' approval of a new subdivision already laid out at Fern Flat, and the rumor that a 7–Eleven store might be coming to town.

"What the hell's happening around here, Ross? Is it all because of Monteflores?"

"You got that right, Lowrie." He squirted a dark stain upon the gravel. "The Vignettes at Monteflores, that's it in a fuckin' word." He said the trailer park, where he sometimes hung his hat, was "fit to bust" with all the out-of-area tradesmen staying on for the year-round construction jobs. But if she really wanted to catch up with the lowdown about developments on Cummings' old property, she ought to forget what she read in the Santa Cruz Sentinel or the weekly Mountain Lookout or even in the alternative Smoke Signal: she should start hanging around behind the Fern Saloon in the parking lot, which had become BBQ headquarters every afternoon when the Gath Construction crews and sub-contractors got off work. The sheriff deputy cruising that stretch of Grade Road, known as Main Street where it passed through Fern, had taken to scrutinizing the other side of the road, ignoring the grilled meat food fair and improvised beer and whiskey fests lasting until dark on weekdays and later than that on weekends. Even the local constable always seemed to have better things to do then to stop for a look around.

"Fern has a town cop now?"

"Remember Chad Smiley at Regional? He's Fern's part-time police officer now. Pretty scary prospect, if you ask me, giving that clown a gun. But he spends most of his time hanging out with the security guards at Monteflores. I mean, come on, that's basically who he works for, right?"

Old-time locals rarely joined the BBQ crowd, Ross reported, and he had never spotted a lady there, unless you could call certain middle-aged gals—some of whom had already secured their reputations back when Ross and Katie were attending high school—"ladies."

"Get that shit-eating grin off your face, Stewart." She hitched up her jeans and crossed her arms. "And what do those idiots in Fern say about me?"

"Ah shee-it! They don't say nothin' 'bout you. Those boys got bigger fish to fry than you, Missus Kate-Lyn Low-reeeeee."

They both shook their heads, agreeing that Fern had become nothing more than the nearest service center for Gath Construction and its dependents as well as a convenient stop-off for the first wave of well-to-do new homeowners moving into so called Vignettes One. They wondered together if all the little hamlets on the North County Coast might evolve into fancy mountain and coastal resort towns one day.

Katie held him longer under the oak, trying to squeeze information from him about her son, but his response was of no use: he shared nothing new about the boy's behavior following the months when Donald and Ross had hung out around the harbor at Pilar Point or the half year when they had banded together in Fort Bragg, hiring on for commercial fishing out of Noyo Harbor. Ross claimed he simply had no news to share since 'Don' had taken off in his truck for the Pacific Northwest after crabbing season ended.

The man drove off without giving her any reliable phone number at which he could be reached.

*

A Japanese-American potted-plant grower was going out of business in Watsonville; Pieter called Cliffport, Katie fetched him at an intersection on Freedom Boulevard, and that day she came away with a truck bed full of used, brittle, yellowed, corrugated 4' × 8' fiberglass panels acquired at bargain prices. She stockpiled the panels for future use as roofing material on various works in progress at Redwood Coast Nursery. Pieter phoned her on another occasion: an antiquated one-gallon-can production line at a metal manufacturing plant in Salinas was being dismantled. Ever since injected, molded plastic containers had been introduced, the old standby nursery cans—tapered metal containers coated with green, rust-resistant paint—were no longer a profitable enterprise; he convinced her to buy a trailer load of the cans at half-price and to swing by the Leonard Coates Nursery in San Jose to round out their trip.

After Labor Day, they regularly teamed up for excursions in her Ford F-250: Katie at the wheel, Baby Blue Eye at the passenger window, and Pieter Tuelling—accommodating the dog on the bench seat—sitting a comfortable distance from the driver. While making their raids for supplies and materials, the well-liked former ag agent introduced Katie to everyone as a provisioner of excellent ornamentals, and she was welcomed warmly by owners and staff. Pieter helped her scout out potential garden centers and landscape supply yards in the Santa Cruz area which she might use as suitable dropsites for her sold plant orders. His network of friends and acquaintances extended beyond Santa Cruz County to include the greater Monterey and San Francisco Bay Areas; they visited citrus growers in Mission San Jose, gladiola growers in Fremont, and cut flower growers up and down the coastline. As their daytrips took them farther and farther from home, the couple traded control of the radio knob. Pieter preferred classical music, when available; Katie played the dial, leaving it wherever the tunes struck her fancy; they both enjoyed jolts of authentic country music sounds. The first time they were confined in the cab together on a extralong day out on the road, Pieter asked her permission to smoke; she thought fast enough to pull the ashtray out of the dashboard before he did and, in a deft movement of her fingertips, hid the roach clip in her retracted hand.

"Everybody in San Benito County calls you 'Pete'," she remarked. "What's with that?"

"Oh, I'm just plain 'Pete' to them, see? That's country people for you, Katie, that's all. They don't have sophisticated hypocrites down there like we got in Santa Cruz."

She let out a hoot that startled Baby Blue. "But they do have hypocrites all the same?"

"*Jaja*, they got plenty those, sure enough. Just not so pretentious about it."

There was no color on display the day Pieter introduced her to a Portuguese dahlia grower in San Leandro, but the beefy, older Azorean Islander greeted them gladly and immediately presented each with a 10-lb. sack of his homegrown fava beans—for kitchen cooking or sowing out as a winter cover crop in the vegetable garden. "Don't panic, they're organic!" he yelled, slapping 'Pete' on the back then turning directly to the stranger. "I grow the beans. I pick the beans. No spray!" He chortled, almost pushing his surprise visitors down the steps into a basement, where he uncovered a vat and ladled out wine—homemade from his backyard grapes—into three dirty tumblers. "No spray!" he shouted as they clinked glasses and drank. He cut wedges off a round of cheese and sliced bread from a loaf, tossing surplus morsels of each to the cats at their feet and ladling out more wine.

Where the boundaries of Santa Cruz, Santa Clara, San Benito, and Monterey Counties converge, one mean-spirited loner presented the sole ugly countenance she ran up against during their travels. Pieter, navigating the farm roads by memory, happened upon the rutted dirt route running along yet another irrigation ditch separating row crops as far as she could see. On the other side of a riparian corridor packed thick with wild cane, a warren of rundown greenhouses sank in a field of shredded black plastic rippling in the wind wherever it wasn't weighted down or smothered by weeds. A farmer reluctantly emerged from an immovable Airstream trailer, and Pieter went to great lengths to overcome the questionable reception from the obviously isolate man with bushy black eyebrows, untrimmed gray hair, and a snarl on his grizzly, unshaven face. Katie was using the squalid portable when she overheard the old timer quizzing her guide: "What you got there, Pete? Bob Dylan's twin sister?" She didn't hear her guardian's response and kept quiet for the duration of the visit, her right eye twitching by the time she tore out of there, leaving behind them a high arching spray of dust thrown up by her fast-moving truck.

More than once, puttering about in some out-of-the-way nursery, Pieter's eyes popped open. "Do you see what I see?" he would say, pointing out a variety of Shasta daisy or a specie fuchsia she had never seen before. She followed her tutor's cues and grabbed a sufficient quantity of such plants, sometimes wondering if she was paying too much for undersized, out-of-bloom material in crumbling metal cans, plants that seemed to her of dubious value even as propagation material. Another time, her own enthusiasm carried her away when, for the first time, she identified the *Passiflora jamesonii* engulfing a six-foot high cyclone fence and swallowing a nearby abandoned garden shed in a little nursery. When she bought half a dozen bedraggled passion flower plants on her own initiative, Pieter shot her a puzzled look to which she let out a long-drawn-out *"Schooooon!"* in her best pseudo-basso.

On their trips to the University Botanical Garden in Strawberry Canyon and the Native Plant Garden in Tilden Park, Pieter seemed to relish his role as her teacher. During a full day exploring Strybing Arboretum in San Francisco, they were picnicking like tourists when Katie asked if he would escort her to Carmel Highlands in order to meet Lester Rowntree; he declined, explaining that if that woman were still living there, she would be in her nineties. "She's not riding burros into the Sierras anymore. Besides, I never knew her personally, Katie. We better leave her alone." Nor was he inclined to accompany her to the nearby farm and garden at UCSC. "I heard that Alan Chadwick flew away, by the way. But you go up there, *jaja*. Go if you like. *Ach*, Katie! I always heard he was a flighty sonagun, quoting Shakespeare, singing opera, all like that. Maybe he was too biodynamic for me, eh?"

They called on a carnation grower in Hayward and listened to him complain about imports from Latin countries: the competition could raise cut flower stems in Central and South America and jet them into the LA and San Francisco markets, where they still sold cheaper than any California wholesale grower could afford to do. They dropped by Domoto's Nursery. "Let's see if Toichi Domato's still at it. He's forgotten more about the California nursery business than you and I will ever know, Missus Katie." The nursery was open, but the master wasn't about.

Before the Thanksgiving season shut down their adventuring, they made a long-distance trip to Santa Rosa where, to her mentor's surprise, Luther Burbank's widow was still residing: the house and grounds remained off limits. Pieter thought that a visit to the famous horticulturist's former fifteen-acre farm in the Gold Ridge area of Sebastopol might be inspiring but was discouraged to find the property deteriorated, its status as a hot spot of agronomic experimentation fallen into some ambiguous limbo. With daylight to spare, they took a detour to the coast in an attempt to salvage their Sonoma County outing; there he lamented that they couldn't venture north beyond the Russian River, for that was where California rosebays grew like weeds and the true rhododendron country began. Plus, he knew a famous collector of variant forms of the tender, fragrant Maddenii series up the coast and had close friends in the business even farther north in Fort Bragg. After stopping for gas in Jenner, they turned southward, heading inland at Bodega Bay and loping through rolling dairy lands until connecting with the so called Gravenstein Highway outside of Petaluma, where Pieter fell silent, rubbing his chin while gazing at the gnarly branches of unpruned trees. *"Dat is het!"* he blurted out.

"What is what?"

"That's what these apple orchards remind me of! The ink and pencil drawings in Drika's Van Gogh book." He fell silent again, staring out the window while—without lighting it up—he rolled a black cigarillo between his finger and thumb.

Throughout their fall excursions, he had soft-pedaled the rhododendron and camellia relocation project. Yet on this trip home he made her promise that, come the first weekend in May 1974, she would accompany him to the annual Rhododendron Show in Fort Bragg, when they could see how Ernest and Betsy Schoefer's "Flowerland to the Sea" garden center was coming along. Katie was taken aback by his presumptuous attitude and wondered about the logistics of any overnight outing with the man. He had never before elaborated on their excursions so far in advance, but now he was all but demanding that she put the Oakland Museum's annual April Wildflower Show on her calendar, and they had better attend the Oakland Spring Garden Show, which was moving to the Dunsmuir House, or so he had heard. She said nothing while wondering if the usually down-to-earth plantsman wasn't taking her participation for granted, forgetting that one way or another, spring was always the busiest season for someone having to survive in the nursery trade. She worked away at her sunflower seeds, conjecturing that they had reached some unspecified limitation inherent in their relationship, a barrier that she as a single woman and he as a single man were bound to meet. Now that the first phase of her crash course in applied horticulture was coming to its end, was he anxious to hold on to guarantees that her companionship would be on tap? She had noticed that at least some of the people receiving them had looked askance at their ambiguous partnership. The pair seemed so different: she was lean, supple, younger if not young, and quiet; he was older, large, his stiff movements mitigated by a surprisingly light step and his hearty hello. Was she his sister, niece, or daughter? She looked like none. His new wife or girlfriend? On first appearance, people seemed not to know how to pigeonhole the stranger named Katie or her ties to their familiar friend.

During the remainder of their return trip from Sonoma, he stayed silent, smoking, brooding. Katie again wondered why, in all their forays, the widower always chose to avoid having her pick him up at his residence in Corralitos. Was he ashamed of a humble abode or still too shaken in the wake of his wife's death to allow another woman on the grounds? Even when it would have made far more sense for her to swing by his home address, Pieter made other arrangements, insisting on parking his car in Cliffport or being collected and deposited at some public landmark, where he would leave his Dart parked for the day. Toward the end of this day's drive, it came as no surprise when he all but begged her to stop at Duarte's Tavern in Pescadero before making the last leg of their journey to retrieve his dented, dirty sedan at One Grade Road. Over her beer and his gin, he announced that the change of season marked by daylight savings, as well as the retail nursery trade's general preoccupation with holiday sales, precluded any more expeditions in the near future. Nevertheless, he thought she should see one more place in Marin County and, after that, they could call it quits for the calendar year.

Chapter 7: The Education of a Nurserywoman

*

Their field trips ended on a dissonant chord on the seaward side of the San Andreas Fault in the Olema Valley. When Katie parked the truck at Hilde Richter's remote stone-and-wood house on a foggy ridge populated by bishop pines, she couldn't tell where the nursery and garden ended and the wildland began. Pieter had cautioned his charge about the maven's notorious opinionating, warning Katie that the aged proprietor—cut from German not British cloth—was renowned as a fierce proponent of using only California native plants in the garden. Hilde might try to make Cliffport's last native daughter sign in blood a pledge to convert the fledging Redwood Coast Nursery into a source of strictly California natives—that is, natives or nothing at all, which made little sense to the mild-mannered Dutchman.

Hilde Richter wasn't on site but Dora—a long-term employee and resident devotee—was standing in for the Germanic dragoness. Ever the diplomat, Pieter expressed the purpose of their visit—in brief, the further education of a nurserywoman—and asked permission to show Katie about; although years since his one and only other visit, he felt capable of escorting his pupil through the plants and plantings—unless Dora herself had time, of course. The woman dropped her bucket and hoe, knocked back the hood of her sweatshirt—revealing jagged, short-clipped hair—and turned her back on the man, baring yellowish fangs to launch an interrogation of the younger woman. Was Katie in the business of releasing non-native plants into the environment? Was Katie dedicating her enterprise to growing and disseminating California native plants—or not? Waving woven, fingerless-gloved hands, Dora went on a rant about protecting the purity of localized species against the contamination of foreign gene pools and the "holocaust" of invasive, exotic weeds dating from the arrival of non-Indians and culminating in the toxic factory farming of lettuce in Salinas and industrialized tomatoes in the Central Valley. Behind Dora's back, Pieter sent hand signals, indicating that Katie need not respond to the woman's rabid provocations; given his winking, blinking, and shrugging of shoulders, Katie sensed there was no use getting into a spat

215

with the woman, who wasn't that many years older than herself. In any case, Dora waited for no answer; done with her diatribe, she threw the cowl back up over her head, picked up her bucket and her weeding hoe, and—goat-like—clambered up the nearest incline through a colony of Yerba Santa.

Pieter made quick work touring the nursery grounds while pointing out the deep-rooted starting trays and the choice selections of native Ericaceae—California rosebays, western azaleas, manzanitas, huckleberries, madrones, western Labrador tea—all fully grown out in the ground with matching smaller plants for sale in unmarked, non-priced, homemade redwood boxes. Upon hearing grumbling coming from some coyote bush upslope, he motioned that they had best make their getaway before another assault.

Twenty minutes later, Pieter asked his driver to turn into the town of Bolinas for something to eat and drink before returning to Santa Cruz; she presumed they would be calling on one of his favorite saloons, but he seemed happy enough to sit outside a bohemian coffee-house with pastries and hot espressos.

"*Ach*, that crazy woman! I'm so sorry, Missus Katie, you didn't meet Hilde."

"It's not your fault. I just hope I never get like her."

"You? You'll never get like that one. She was probably so before she took up California natives. If it's not native plants, it's something else with such people and maybe even worse. *Nee nee*, you'll never get like that one. You got too many good things going on in your life."

"I do?"

"*Jaja*, you do. A person like that back there … she reminds me of the *Hitler-Jugend*, that German Worker Youth movement, eh? Natives, natives, natives or nothing—she thinks like that sonagun Hilde, but she got no charm, no charm. What the heck that Dora thinks Hilde Richter is, a California native?"

"Our adorable Dora didn't strike me as very native herself. Doesn't she have an accent or something?"

"*Jaja! Dat is het,* Katie Lowrie, that's it! Austrian, I think. *Ach,* nothing so zealous like a nonnative immigrant, eh?"

"She went bananas when I didn't start jumping up and down about what she was saying."

"*Jaja.* I know the breed. In the Nederlands too, I know it. Hilde? I can listen to old Fraülein Richter. She got culture, horticulture, humor. A hothead like that one there...? *Ach!* There's another good German Worker for you, Katie."

*

Katie recounted to her mother their disagreeable experience in Marin County but omitted mention of their stop at Duarte's Tavern over the county line, as she always omitted mentioning their end-of-the-day stops at watering holes with which the Dutchman seemed familiar. With no more expeditions on the books, Elise wondered aloud if Katie "ought not" to invite Pieter Tuelling to their table on one of the holidays. Elisabeth Lowrie had been known to gather in strays on Thanksgiving and Christmas Days before, whether Ross Stewart, a widow or widower from the defunct potter's guild, or one of DD's band members or surfing buddies, who happened to have found himself estranged from his natal household and was happy to eat the Lowries' food before hanging with Don out in the barn. But come Thanksgiving, the Lowrie women ended up making the drive to Cloverdale in order to feast and relax with Mike and Suzanne—the absence of Donald Duncan both salient and worrisome. Before mid-December, while mother and daughter did manage to decorate a small fir Katie cut from the woods, and Elise made her famous shortbread, the dilemma about hosting the widowed bachelor for Christmas supper was resolved by extraordinarily severe weather: an eight-day run of historically low temperatures forced Katie to dedicate every day-lit hour to salvaging nursery stock. The unprecedented cold snap devastated agriculture throughout Central California and proved fatal to her tender, fall-planted stock set outdoors at the Redwood Coast Nursery.

During shortened days, Katie redoubled her efforts to replace lost crops with new cuttings, but most of the mother plants in cans—if they had survived at all—were in no condition to provide suitable slips. When the Lowries attended the defunct Pottery Guild's annual Holiday gathering at Georgellen's, their hostess apprehended their situation and insisted that Elise and Kaitlin return to join her family on Christmas Day. By New Year's Day, Katie had not even gotten around to picking the fruit off the persimmon tree, so the jays, waxwings, and winter flocks of robins and crows pecked away, indicating just which pieces would have been the best candidates for ripening inside the house.

Contacting Pieter Tuelling after New Years also failed: the man never answered the phone. Elsie came up with her own explanation of his disappearance: the extreme weather had probably forced the veteran out of retirement in order to provide freelance consultation, pro bono; he must be traveling throughout Central California offering comfort and expertise to a wide array of nursery folk in distress. Katie didn't tell her mother how worried she was that, on the contrary, the man—ever moody beneath his jovial mien—might simply be incommunicado, drowning in his Yuletide cups.

Chapter 8

DD's Flight

Donald Duncan Lowrie spent his earnings from work aboard the CRAB MAGNET on motels, meals, beer, cigarettes, grass, and the aging pickup. By the end of June 1973, he was selling fireworks in Yreka then went over the state line to pump gas in Grants Pass. Drifting farther north, he hired on at a greenhouse range in the hills east of Salem, slept in his truck, and punched clock at 5:30 AM six days a week, pulling a reinforced leather sleeve up the length of his left arm and spending mornings cutting long-stemmed red roses—tight in the bud—and depositing them in pails at the ends of the raised beds. The buckets were periodically hauled to the cold shed where, after a 10:00–10:30 AM lunch break, he donned a leather apron and worked beside a dozen silent men and women wearing finger-free gloves to de-thorn, grade, and sort the budded stems before binding them, twelve to a bundle, in rubber bands. The paper-wrapped dozens were then stuffed into cartons loaded into the company reefer for mid-afternoon delivery to Portland Airport and daily shipments from there to flower markets throughout the United States. At the end of July, snatching his third weekly paycheck from the envelope tucked into his timeclock slot, Donald walked off the job.

In August, he was picking pears in the Hood River Valley and in September, apples across the Columbia River in Washington State. Looking after a Halloween pumpkin patch netted him food and gas money, but by Thanksgiving he was broke again, cutting holly in the foothills of the Western Cascades. Prickle-proof gloves protected his hands from the berry-laden branches, but the long johns underneath his blue jeans and the flannel shirt beneath his down jacket didn't shut out the wind. On a day of freezing rain, after an hour spent slipping up and down the rungs of an aluminum orchard ladder, he declared "FUCK THIS SHIT" to no one in particular, dropped his burlap bag, left the sheers and gloves with the foreman, and slogged over the frozen runnels between tree rows, his torn jeans and shredded jacket sliced by horizontal sleet. That night, on a quiet road far from any border checkpoint, he crossed over into Canada's Okanogan Valley and drove westward, following a lead about seasonal laborers needed in a small fishing port on the coast of British Columbia.

*

Donald stepped through the whitewashed bollards and hiked the concrete causeway leading out to Bounty Harbor's breakwater and working wharf, pausing to join an old-timer watching a trio of boys Don's age working their way through a stack of thick black mats spread on the seawall's shingles. Two of them braced the heels of their hip boots on a mat's grommeted edge while the third hit it with a jet of water from a black hose, driving slime from the dentate rubber surface. Once the topside was drenched, the pair grabbed the mat at its corners and hoisted it high enough for the third to bend his knees, creep partway underneath, and blast away at the underside with the liquid silver point. Donald asked the man if the canneries were hiring; he mumbled something, bummed a cigarette, and pointed to the block of linked Quonset huts lined up along the planked wooden pier.

Donald walked into the first corrugated hut. Backs turned, a dozen women were positioned at a noisy conveyor belt passing along the far wall of the room and disappearing up a shaft. They wore bandanas and wool caps, blue neoprene gloves, and slick white aprons over coats and sweaters. Their shoes were buckled into rubber boots. Woolen leggings covered the teenaged girls' denim jean cuffs and disappeared under the older women's long, thick, knitted skirts. He approached the line. Sheathing her blade in one of the hardened-leather pouches housing an array of knives belted around her waist, the closest worker disengaged herself from the line, her gloves and stained apron glittering.

"I'm looking for work."

"EH?"

"I'm looking for work. WORK!"

She gestured toward a man squatting underneath the conveyor belt where it angled up toward the shaft, transporting salmon fillets into another section of the plant. Donald nodded thanks and she resumed her place in line.

"EXCUSE ME!" Donald shouted. Wrenches in hand, the man backed out and stood up, slivers of shaved ice falling from his lap. "I'm looking for work."

The square-jawed, middle-aged mechanic looked him up and down. "Looking for work, eh?"

"Yeah. Are there any jobs?"

The man jerked his arm outward, sending more ice chips flying from the inside of his elbow as he pointed toward the far end of the adjacent hangar. Donald nodded thanks, and the man crawled back under the machinery's parade of headless, tailless, finless, fish flesh pummeled by a battery of shower heads flattening the gutted bodies against the belt.

In the connecting chamber, dwarfed by stockpiled pallets, a girl clutching metal stencils and a can of spray paint shouted at a boy in foul weather gear leaning toward her from the seat of his forklift; their shared breathing was visible about their heads; their speech, unintelligible. When the boy saw Donald, he bolted upright, deposited an ice-packed crate on the cement, threw his vehicle into reverse, spun a U-turn, and raced out a runway, his fist bouncing on the horn's button. Donald crossed the slippery floor and knocked before entering a framed door opening into a low-ceilinged, insulated room with pictures of fishing vessels posted on the wall and an assortment of plastic chairs in disarray around a wooden desk. A middle-aged man—intercepted in the act of leaving the room by a second door—broke his pace.

"Can I do something for you?"

He had well-combed, wavy, blond hair and wore corduroy trousers and a crisp white windbreaker with a maritime insignia on the breast.

"I heard there might be work here."

The man eyed the petitioner then took pains to study his wristwatch. "Are you sure?" he remarked, glancing down at some envelopes in his hands. "Here?"

"I need a job."

The man reset the yachting cap on his head. "You're an American, aren't you?"

"Yeah."

"Dodging the Draft, eh?"

"Not really."

"Do you have Canadian work papers then?"

Donald breathed deeply and shifted his weight. "I don't. But I've worked in places like this before."

"Oh, have you?"

"I was on a crabber for six months. I'm taking a look around BC now."

"I see," the man said and reseated his cap. "Where are you from in the States then?"

"California."

"You're here legally but you don't have working papers, is that it?" The man's hand went to the doorknob. "I'm sorry but I have an appointment. There is no work for you here and I'd be surprised if anyone else on the waterfront hires you on. In the day, yes, we took anyone willing to do this work but it's not the same now with Vietnam, eh? I don't know about the other Provinces, but I don't think you'll have much luck anywhere near the border in BC. Can't you make more money in California, son? A strong young guy like you willing to work hard? You can do better in the States than we pay up here, I think. Why not look around the Puget Sound? Take the ferry to Anacortes and look around there. Sockeyes are coming in early everywhere, not just Canada, eh?" He turned the knob and opened the door. "You can come out this way if you like. It's cold in there," he remarked, glancing toward the neighboring hall.

"That's okay," Don responded, turning and retracing his steps through the hangar.

As he walked behind the working line, two giggling girls his age whirled about, each flapping salmon at him until the partially sliced heads flew off and they were wagging two decapitated bodies, their own rose-chilled cheeks closing their eyes as they fell against each other in screes of laughter. Their supervisor barked, and the two girls turned back to the moving belt.

*

Outside Eugene, Donald cleaned dried weed in exchange for three grocery sacks of trash, repackaged the leaves and shakes, and spent a day selling nickel and dime baggies on the university campus. With his earnings, he had gas money to make it south to California, where he checked in at a residential motel of dubious legality in Smith River. Twenty minutes down the highway in Crescent City, he started picking up odd jobs around the harbor, trying to secure a place on any vessel in any fleet. Crabbers tying up at all hours of day and night made use of the quiet kid, tipping him pocket change on the spot for errands run and favors performed, but expenses—even in Smith River—ate up his quarters and dollar bills and, still hungry, he sometimes joined fellow drifters around the kerosene heater in a lean-to where bottles and joints were passed. During the lull between Christmas and New Year's, the harbormaster's assistant told him in no uncertain terms to stay off the dock: a new Fish & Game regulator was coming on duty as of January 2nd, 1974. Donald realized he couldn't wait it out in the northwesternmost corner of California for the spring planting season to start in Mendocino County.

*

Headed for Crescent City before midnight, he saw the strings of red and green lightbulbs and pulled off the highway, curious how locals celebrated New Year's Eve at the Washed Ashore Bar & Grill—and whether or not the roadhouse would serve him beer. He parked in the muddy lot, got out, stomped his boots, tucked in his shirt, hitched up his dungarees, combed his hair, and entered the building, where the live, amplified country-rock band drowned out whatever the people inside were yelling at one another. He climbed onto an empty padded stool where the L-shaped bar turned back to meet the wall.

Bleached blonde hair pulled up off her neck, dressed in a soft red sweater and a white apron over a black leather skirt—the hem hitting her thighs above the knee—the woman working behind the counter moved with ease despite wearing mid-calf, high-heel boots. He studied her large, cushiony breasts and wide, tightly wrapped hips. She had given up preparing individual drinks and was instead lifting bottles from the well and setting them down amidst the clutter of car keys, cigarette packs, Bic lighters, coins, and ladies' purses belonging to the drunken crowd clinging to the bar. Ashtrays weighted down dollar bills; peanut shells overflowed a tin trough running the counter's length. Whether the night was a boom or a bust for whoever owned the place, no one present at the Washed Ashore seemed to care—least of all Donald Duncan.

"Better see some ID," she said, facing him across the bar. Up close, he noticed she had a beauty spot to one side of the frosty pink gloss on her thin lips, and brown eyes—lashes coated in mascara, lids lined in reddish brown. When she bent to reach into a bottom cupboard, he saw the roots of darker hair growing from her scalp.

She stood up and with both hands tugged down on the sweater's bottom edge, the better to advertise her bust. "Getting hot in here," she declared, smiling at his mesmerized stare and using two long, painted fingernails to undo half of the dozen pearl-size, ruby-pink buttons at the throat of her fuzzy polyester knit. He gawked. "No ID?" She tossed a glance back at her tanked clientele helping themselves to the bottles abandoned on the littered countertop. "Show it to me, if you got one," she concluded, winking and turning away.

A waitress went behind the bar, deposited her round metallic tray on the back counter, then sat at the far end to drink with the bar huggers as the bandleader quickened the pace and the din rose. Donald couldn't take his gaze off the woman; when he did manage to look away, it was toward the curvaceous shapes of colorful liqueur bottles backlit on a glass shelf running across the mirror behind the bar. The next time she moved his way, he had his wallet out and his driver's license ready.

"So, you do have ID," she said, grinning as she took his card. "Five-eight, one hundred-forty-five pounds...." she read aloud. "Brown hair, brown eyes...." She paused, put the points of her boots together, and went up on the balls of her feet, leaning forward and scanning as much of him as she could see from where she stood—her considerable cleavage revealed. "You look about right. But let's see something...." she mused aloud, eyeing the license closer before passing it back to him from the tips of two cherry red fingernails. "Guess we better make it Coca-Cola, huh?"

He smirked then watched her reach for a bottle of Captain Morgan's Spiced White Rum from which she poured a dollop into a dark blue highball glass before turning sideways and sipping her drink while the transfixed teen took in her profile. "Okay. So, how about that Coke?" he asked when she turned her face toward him, pointer fingers dabbing at each corner of her parted lips. "Just like yours," he added. She winked again and produced a matching blue glass, scooped in some ice cubes, poured in some rum, gripped the nearest bar gun, and brought bright brown soda bubbling up to the rim. Dispensing with any coaster, napkin, or lime wedge, she set the glass down in front of him. "Too late in the year for formalities," she said, clinking his glass in a toast, throwing back her head, and exposing her bare white throat while she drank.

He took a swallow and reached for his wallet.

"Ah, forget it, kid," she said, tucking hair behind her ears; the gold-plated ear hoops dangled free as she shook her head at the sight of the sloppy-drunk crowd. "Night like this, first one's on me." She stood opposite him and lit up a long, slim, filtered cigarette; he gulped down the entire contents of the glass. "That was fast!" she stated, reclaiming his glass and mixing him another while he lit a cigarette before she could see his quaking hand. Noticing how much rum she was pouring into his glass, he straightened his spine and braced himself.

She again waved off his wallet and stood in clear view, smoking her thin cigarette, drinking, watching the tiny dance floor where partners seemed to be pairing off for the countdown to midnight. "On the house, I said...." she said without looking at him. She held one boot forward to the other, rotating it on its pointed heel and rocking it sideways to the drumbeat, then she switched the position of her feet. He was following her backside's sway, mentally undressing her, unzipping the leather skirt, lifting the sweater over her head—then he saw the wedding ring. He crushed his cigarette and pressed the bottoms of his boots down hard against the foot rail. *So, she's married and I'm underage. And drivin' a piece a' shit pickup no woman like her would ever ride in.* When she served him his third drink, he grabbed the glass with so much force ice cubes spilled out as he guzzled it down. *Now I'll never find out what's she wearing against her skin.*

The rest of band stopped playing during the drummer's crescendo solo. Premature cries of "Happy New Year!" filled the room. Jammed up against one another on the dance floor, inebriated couples performed one last shuffling between partners, as if the coming year's happiness would be determined by whoever was in their arms when the clock struck twelve. The house lights went out. Fluorescent tubes along the base of the bar mirror flickered and the disco ball reflected red EXIT signs. She was pressing against him. He froze. She placed her hands on the top of his thighs, squeezed, and moved in, her face coming closer. At first contact, her lips were hard and dry, then her mouth opened, their jaws widened, their teeth locked in place as their bites aligned and her tongue plunged as deeply as possible down his throat—the lights came back on. She drew away. He saw the beauty mark between her left cheek and her upper lip move as she smiled, winked, and used a fingernail to touch up the two corners of her mouth. One chorus of Auld Lang Syne deteriorated into hoots and hollers as she sashayed away, removing her apron and disappearing behind a curtain at the far end of the bar. He dropped off the barstool and started after her but realized her husband might be back there; they might even own the place. Dizzy, shaking, he didn't dare follow and staggered out into the drizzle with the first wave of departing revelers.

When he woke in the cab in the middle of the night, half-a-dozen cars were still parked helter-skelter in the lot, but no lights were on inside or outside the building. He nosed the pickup onto the shoulder of 101 and looked in both directions, momentarily confused about whether to turn right or left in order to get back to his crummy motel, where he could go back to sleep and try not to think about whatever had happened or would happen next. He knew there was no way to find out more about her without coming back to the roadhouse. He turned right. *Or maybe ask around Smith River*, he thought, gunning the engine. *And you don't even know her name.*

*

Donald made it back to the Washed Ashore around 3:00 PM on New Year's Day, tromping up the wooden steps and shoving the warped door open to discover that stepladders were up, toolboxes open, a table saw zinging, loose wires dangling everywhere; three men—all at least twice his age—had turned the bar & grill into a construction zone. "PLACE IS CLOSED!" one shouted above the noise.

Hair beneath a bandana, wearing a loose-fitting, yellow chenille sweater, she popped up from behind the far of end of the bar, a green can of cleanser in one blue latex glove hand and a wire brush in the other. They sighted each other along the line of the countertop.

"Said we're closed, sonny," the man said. "Now go on, get outta here."

227

Donald gritted his teeth, clenched his jaws, and left.

Ten minutes later, driving the straightaway to Crescent City, he noticed a Maverick closing in then tailgating even though the flat, empty highway offered ample opportunity for it to pass. He looked in his rearview mirror, deliberately slowing down in order to force the driver to pass. Its headlights went on and off, but the Maverick didn't pass. He threw his right shoulder back and twisted in his seat to look out the back window. Her hair brushed out like loose curtains to either side of her face, the bartender smiled and, both wrists draped over the steering wheel at twelve o'clock, wiggled her fingernails. He slowed to 40 MPH—twenty-five miles below the limit. Still, she didn't pass but used one hand then the other to comb her hair back behind her ears so that the two earring hoops swung free. As soon as the highway divided, he drifted into the passing lane and shifted down, bringing the pickup to 30 MPH. She maintained her speed so that, as his truck dropped back, the two vehicles came parallel, traveling below twenty-five. He looked back and forth between the roadway ahead and the woman driving the faded brown two-door sedan. Her lips slightly parted, the tip of her tongue swept back and forth between the ridges of her upper and lower front teeth. He tooted his horn, but her eyes never turned his way until Don spotted a turnout sign and held down his horn; then she did turn her face and saw him pointing at a paved stretch of wide shoulder just ahead. She winked and put on her signal. He let his truck fall back so that she was first to pull off, coasting the long-hooded fastback to a stop. He turned off his ignition and got out; she turned off her ignition but stay seated, rolling down her window as he approached.

"Is there something wrong, officer?"

He blushed at the sight of the bright brown eyes and fresh pink lip-gloss shining back at him. "You were following pretty close there ... ma'am."

"You bet I was ... Donny Boy." She smiled and left her jaw slack, the tip of her curling tongue pressing up against the bottom edges of her upper front teeth. "Still am." In the overcast daylight—without the barroom darkness or the obscure views of her head framed by his truck's rearview mirrors—he could see the maturity of her facial features: even without heavy makeup, her skin showed few wrinkles and no flabby skin. She unsnapped the buttons of her parka, revealing the scallop-shaped opening of the low-cut yellow sweater. "Aren't you going to arrest me and put me in jail, sir?" Her right hand to her throat, the filed, painted fingertips drumming on her collar-bones, she left her palm and her forearm resting on the contoured shelf of her bulging breasts.

Puzzling out the meaning of her words, Donald shifted his weight, refreshed his stance, looking up and down the deserted highway. "Okay then ... ma'am." He stuck his hands into his back pockets and flapped his straightened arms. "So, let's see your driver's license this time."

"Yes, sir." She rummaged through her floppy bag, passed him her license, her fingertips contacting his palm for so long he wondered if he was feeling the rhythm of her pulse or just his own heartbeat racing fast. She finally curled the fingernails, lightly clawing while retracting her hand. While he read over the license—WILSON, SANDRA, 176 Lily Lane Myrtle CA 95538 SEX F HAIR BRN EYES BRN HGT 5'05" WGT 120 LBS—she extracted one of the thin, filter-tip cigarettes from her bag and lit up. "Why, you're turning red as a beet, officer," she said, exhaling smoke the other way. "Is there something wrong?"

In the color picture, her brunette hair was trimmed short on the sides and up the back, and the bangs furled down over the forehead. Her reddened lips, slightly parted, drew his eyes back to the pink lips on the face whose mouth met him less than half-a-foot away, waist-high.

He passed back her license, and she placed her lit cigarette between his trembling fingers.

"I knew you weren't a real blonde, you know," he said, drawing on the cigarette.

"I'm not? Oh, no girl puts her real stuff on those things. One hundred twenty pounds? I wish! Anyway, I've been called a sandy blonde. A dirty one a couple of times...."

"Makes no difference to me," he stammered. "I mean ... either way ... you look...." Donald wanted to bury those smiling lips in his lap while messing up the hair on that head—sandy blonde, dirty blonde, or just plain dirty.

"How do I look ... Donny?"

As he gaped, she gestured for him to pass back the cigarette. "Hold on a sec'," he said, releasing the cigarette but leaving his hand extended. "Let me see that license again. Date of birth: 1949. Shit! You're a whole lot older than me, you know."

"I know I am, hon'. I checked that out last night, 'member?"

"Sure, I remember...." He passed her back the card and stuck his fists into his front pockets, his eyes grazing over the two mounds pressing the fluffy yellow fabric. "That's why ... but...."

"But what?" She dragged her cigarette down to its filter then let it drop to the ground. "You going to stand there eyeballing my assets all day or you going to follow me for a change?"

"Hey, wait a minute. It's *Missus* Sandra Wilson, right?"

"Sandy, to my friends."

"But ... is Wilson your married name or what?"

"I'm not married ... anymore."

"Then what about that fuckin' wedding ring you had on last night?"

"Oh, you noticed that? Good eye! That ring's right here in my purse, Donny. But I only wear that sucker when I'm working. Helps keep the greasy bear paws off."

"You mean ... there is no husband...?"

"I got rid of the Mister and kept the ring ... and the last name."

"So, is that where you still live, at the address on that license?"

"What if it is?" She blurted out, laughing. "Donny, I sure as hell am not taking you where I live. Are you kidding? I've got to go on living around here, at least for the time being. I have a better idea. There's a place up the road in Fort Dick ... vacation cottages for rent, right? Fort *Dick*, right? Unless you're busy this afternoon...."

He guffawed. "Busy?" He looked her all over and adjusted his hands to make way for the swelling in his pants. "Listen, I've got to tell you something. Truth is, I haven't got money for any vacation cottage. And I already paid for another night at this place in Smith River."

"That dump? Are you kidding me? I'm not going to that place and you're not coming to my house. Come on, hon'. We're going to rent a cottage a nice little old man runs about a mile from here. That is, unless you're busy...."

"I just told you I don't have any money, damnit!"

"Oh, for god's sake, I'll pay, okay? Nobody ever paid me for it before, but I'll pay for you." She raised her left forearm and shook the bracket's charms to ride freely over the cuff of her sweater's left sleeve. "Think I deserve a day or two off after last night, don't you? Let the boss fire me. I can't stand another night in that dive anyway. Same old drunks, night after night. The regulars know that place better than their own living rooms. Let 'em serve their own booze, know what I mean?" Her left shoulder lifted, compressing her breasts as she tilted rightward, adjusting the rearview mirror to check on her face. "You comin' or not, hon'?" She put her hand on the ignition key. "Cuz if you aren't, I can keep myself busy somewhere else this afternoon ... Donny Boy."

As soon as he had jumped back into the Fleetside and fired it up, she pulled forward then crossed an undefined strip of paving that cut right onto a frontage road. He followed, his gaze fixed on the back of her head, catching fragments of her face in her side rearview mirror. When the Maverick's turn signal came on, he spotted the wooden sign with its faded painted arrow and pulled into a neglected court-yard behind a row of redwood trees hiding the Northcoast Vacation Cottages in Fort Dick from nearby Highway 101.

*

When they separated the next afternoon, they agreed to re-meet at 5:00 PM at the diner still operating out of a defunct truck stop halfway between Smith River and Crescent City. Donald fetched his duffel bag from his motel while Sandy went home to feed her cat, shower, shampoo, blow dry her hair, change into fresh clothes, and pack an overnight case with toiletries, makeup kit, and undergarments. On her way out of her house, she collected the tip money she had been saving in a shoe box in her closet then locked the door.

*

"Come on, Sandy, let's go."

"Can't you keep Fort Dick in your pants for five more minutes?" She had put rhinestone barrettes in her hair, brushed rouge on her cheeks, and wore a pink, V-neck sweater with silver, tinsel-threaded icicles cascading over the ledge of her hefty bosoms. She bit the tip of her tongue as she gathered the sweater sleeves up to her elbows and smiled, straightening the bracelet's trinkets. "You just hold on till I'm finished eating. I can tell I'm going to need my strength tonight." She picked up her knife and fork, putting on a display of great gentility and restraint until they both cracked up laughing. "So, I guess you don't really mind if a girl can get a little ... overexcited sometimes, huh?"

"Not if you keep putting out the way you did yesterday, last night, and this morning," he replied, twisting sideway and throwing his legs up on the seat of the booth before lighting one of his cigarettes.

"God, Donny Boy! Been a long time since I had any lovin' like yours. You just don't know. I forgot what it's like to be in bed with a young stud, gettin' his beautiful pecker up over and over and over again."

He grinned and blew smoke rings.

"Want my toast?"

"Sure." He swept it off her plate.

"One of these little jams?"

"Nah. Hey, you want to know something funny? Anybody else called me 'Donny Boy' I'd make 'em shut up. Coming out of your mouth, I like it. Sounds like 'honey.'"

The waitress came down the aisle, topping off coffee mugs.

"That makes it easy then. When I say 'Donny' you hear 'honey.' When I say 'honey' you hear 'Donny.'"

"Works for me," he said, "now let's go! I can't stand sitting here looking at you all dolled up like that."

"Sure you can," she replied, pulling out a cigarette and lighting up off his. "That's what it's for."

"I mean—"

"I know what you mean ... honey."

He pushed their plates aside and leaned forward, whispering: "What exactly did you mean last night by 'any port in a storm'?"

"I said that?" she replied, dabbing at the corners of her mouth with a scrap of paper napkin.

"You sure as hell did! Don't say you didn't either."

"When?"

"When you were falling asleep."

"Well, I fell asleep and got woke up by a big boner more than once now, didn't I?"

They smiled, drank coffee, smoked.

"So? What'd you mean by it?"

"Guess I meant what I said. All positions, any position. Any port in a storm. Want to try?" She left her lips parted, using the nail on the pointer finger of her free hand to click against the front of her upper teeth and lowering her eyelids as she considered his mouth. "Anyway, we can give it a whirl if you'll be gentle when I ask you to. Boy, are you ever a hunk!"

He crushed out his cigarette. "Don't do this to me, babe!"

"Do what?" she replied, pulling on her cigarette.

"You're going to see this side of the table rise up to the ceiling if you don't hurry up."

"It's a pretty big table, Donny."

"It's a pretty big riser," he retorted. "Now come on. Race you back to that fuckin' cottage."

"Oh, okay," she said, chuckling while she left a ten-dollar bill under the ashtray. "Guess I'll get dessert some other time. I can see I've still got a few tricks to teach you, buckaroo-roo."

"Bitchin'!"

They caravanned to the Northcoast Vacation Cottages, where they were still the only guests, and she paid for a second night's stay.

*

On Wednesday morning, after a long hot shower, Sandy used the bedspread to perform one of several stripteases she put on for him while he lay awake in the queen bed. Striking poses throughout the room, she demonstrated the many ways she could arrange the green cloth. Sometimes she would simply walk with it wrapped under her armpits, so that the bedspread draping her bosoms responded to the lifting and lowering of her arms as she towel-dried her hair with white terry cloth. Other times, she would sit in the armchair, arch her back, and rest a hairbrush on the shelf of her jutting bust while using her fingers to detangle her wet hair. Or she would tie the bedspread behind her neck while winding a bath towel into a turban atop her head. Alternately, the spread tucked in around her hips, she would stand in front of the TV set and fake a belly dance, using a second towel as a veil over her upper torso then as a tent above her head. Or, half-dressed, quietly doing her nails, flipping through a magazine, touching up her lipstick, she would simply let the bedspread drop altogether. He was helpless. If she wasn't asleep or on a run to Burger King and the liquor store, he had no choice but to pay attention.

*

After his shower on Thursday morning, she sat him down and combed his hair this way and that.

"Ah, stop playing with me like I'm a toy," he protested.

"But I never had a handsome toy boy like you before.... Okay, now go look in the mirror. You look like Marlon Brando in that Roman movie."

"Or Napoleon!" he called out from the bathroom and they laughed.

"You're not short enough for Napoleon!" she called back.

He stood in the doorway and watched her stretching out on the bed. "And you look like a poster I once had of Jayne Mansfield."

She giggled and changed her pose.

"No, really!" he insisted.

"Oh, come on, Donny. Jayne Mansfield? I think you need a little fresh air."

"I'm not kidding. With your bod'?"

He lay down beside her and they shared her cigarette.

"My daddy once said, 'That Sandy'd fuck anything with pants on.'"

"Your father said that?"

"Not to me, to my mom. I overheard him say it to her. I guess I was a little too advanced for my age but nobody else seemed to mind. And I learned early ..." she said, sticking a fingertip into his knotted bath towel and working it loose, "I like it best when a man has his pants all the way off ... like you do ... now. Come on, Julius Cesar. Turn around and I'll scratch your back."

"And ... what else?"

"I'll get around to that.... Turn over now and lie still."

*

On their fifth day in the cottage, after she had paid another visit to her house and stopped in at the drug store, she found him waiting in their usual booth where they met for their daily hot-cooked meal.

"Don't you like what I have on?" she asked, sliding her bottom into the opposite bench.

"I sure do!" he replied, looking over the zipper cuffs on her pegged white jeans and the light blue turtleneck that made her breasts look bigger and rounder than ever.

"This is about the one place we can go where you're not messing me up."

She got out a cigarette and searched for a light. "Here you go," he said, extending his Bic.

She lit up and pinched the filter of her own cigarette between her teeth while gathering her sleeves, straightening out the bracelet's charms, and leaning both bare elbows on the paper placemat. "You were unreal earlier today. I mean, I haven't had anything like that in a long time, boy. Maybe never."

"That's what you said."

"Guess I never have been with a strong young man who could take instruction as good as you do."

"Well, for sure I never had any female teaching me like you do."

Their waitress came by with coffee and two menus. "Crab salad's fresh today," she said, moving on without looking at either one of them or waiting for a response.

Donald stuck out his tongue at her backside, pushed the menus aside, and leaned forward. "How come you aren't married?"

"What? Now wait. Don't you get serious on me, hon'. Not now, okay? I know you're just a fast trip in and out of town. Let's leave it at that and enjoy the ride."

"But why'd you kiss me like that in the first place that night at the bar?"

"Guess I saw one good lookin' buckaroo just waiting for the right cowgirl to take the lead. Was I right, or what?"

"When I thought about it later, when I woke up outside in my truck, I thought, I don't care if she's married. I don't care if I get shot at or taken out to sea and dropped in the ocean. I do not care. I'm goin' back to fuckin' find her. You're so bitchin', Sandy. Way you're lookin' at me right now? I still don't care if you're really married or how old you are—"

"... old? Did you just say *old*?"

"Oh, you know, older than me, older than I am. The way you jumped me on New Year's Eve.... I must've reminded you of some-body, huh?"

"Come on, honey, lay off it now. Let's go with that crab salad, 'kay?"

"Fuckin' crab!"

"You're not even lookin' at the menu."

"Too busy lookin' at you. And the less you have on, the longer I'll look too."

"If you can keep your hands to yourself, you mean." She unfolded her menu and left it propped up between them. "We better be careful, good lookin'. Don't let's turn this into one of those handsome devil leaves poor country girl with broken heart and swollen belly songs. You better start bein' careful who you pass your genes on to too."

"You think I'm thinking about passing on my genes? You said you're taking the pill, right? Shit, I see you in that blue sweater and those white pants, Sandy? All I'm thinking about is getting those jeans down below your knees."

"Whoa now, cowboy! You better have something to eat then I'm taking us to town and see about getting you out of those old dungarees into some nice butt-huggin' jeans yourself. A nicer new shirt too."

"You mean after we go back to the cottage?"

"No, I don't. I mean before we go back to the cottage."

"Shit!"

"Shush now and be ready to order something when the bitch comes back."

*

The sixth morning, Sandy announced that they would be overnighting at Eureka's famous Humboldt House. She told him she wanted to blow the last of her play money on one big night out, then she would have to find out if she still had a job at the Washed Ashore or find something else to do farther up the coast in Brookings or Gold Beach, Oregon. Before returning to her place to feed the cat and get dressed for the occasion, she settled up with the proprietor of the Northcoast Vacation Cottages and received permission to leave the Ford pickup parked on the premises for another twenty-four hours. While she was away, Donald shaved, showered, and changed into the Wrangler jeans and yoked cowboy shirt she had picked out for him at the Western Wear & Saddle Shop. Waiting for her return, he flipped on the TV and didn't hear the Maverick sputtering into the courtyard but caught a glimpse through the curtain of her dodging rain with a black handbag over her head. He hopped to, opening the door just as she landed two black ankle boots on the square concrete pad beneath the metal awning.

"WOW!" he exclaimed, sticking his thumbs behind his new belt buckle, sizing her up.

She had cinched her hair back and made up her face. She wore a black leather jacket with padded shoulders, narrow black slacks, and rivet-studded boots with two-inch heels.

"Well?" she asked, swiping water beads off her handbag. "Can't I come in?"

He stepped back to let her pass. She tossed her bag onto the chair and modeled her outfit for him, unsnapping the jacket and holding it open to reveal a white, crewneck mohair sweater. He had not seen her wear pearl stud earrings—imitation or real—before now. "You really like?" she said, tilting her head to one side and leaving it that way.

"I've got another change in the car I'm saving for tonight. It's a little too skimpy for the drive down."

"Oh man! I will never get tired of your tricks, babe."

"I decided to let out all the stops, you know? The Humboldt House? Come on, it's the classiest place on this whole sorry stretch of coast." She gathered the jacket in front and turned around, twisting her neck as if she were alone, inspecting her backside in a full-length mirror. "Okay with you?"

"Are you kidding me? You could be a model in a magazine."

"Which magazine? Okay, hon', got everything? We're putting our stuff in your truck and checking out of this hole. No! Don't you look at me that way, Donny ... not now I said! Humboldt House, here we come!

"I don't know if I can wait till we get to that place...."

"Just for once now, the answer is NO, Mister Studly. Come on, you're driving. It'll keep your hands occupied."

*

The wet, windy, winding drive south out of Crescent City began with a roadblock where an emergency crew of highway workers scrambled to cut a lane-wide passage through the trunk of a downed redwood.

"This could take a while," she said, producing a rolled joint from her handbag.

"What? Where the hell'd that come from?"

"I was saving it for later tonight but what the hell."

"You had weed back at your house all this time? You been holding out on me, Sandy!"

She laughed. "I just ran across this in my party purse at the house. Here you go...."

Leaving the windows closed, they shared the burning joint while watching men in yellow slickers using yellow equipment to push segments of the fallen tree out of the way. She burst out coughing and laughing. *"Holding out on you...?* I wouldn't say I've been holding out much of anything on you, honey pie."

He slid his right hand between her thighs and pressed in against her crotch. "Any port in a storm. Isn't that how it goes?"

"Careful now. One of these guys might be my big brother."

"Are you for real?"

"It could happen. If Rick's still working for Caltrans, it could. He used to."

After three hours, they reached Eureka where the landmark Humboldt House occupied a rise in the manmade terrain between the Marina and Old Downtown. While she went inside to handle registration, he sat in the car, sucked one more hit from the roach and, when it stopped smoking, swallowed it.

The Tudor Revival complex reminded him of Victorians gussied up for tourists in Capitola and Pacific Grove, or one grand mansion on West Cliff Drive in Santa Cruz, so hidden from view you could only see it from a boat offshore or while straddling a surfboard outside the breaking waves. Sandy waved from the carriage porch and waited there so they could enter the foyer arm-in-arm. The bellhop—about Donald's age—knew better than to offer the lady's escort any help with the overnight case he carried by his side.

In their suite, they downed the complimentary split of sparkling wine and spent the next couple of hours romping about the sturdy furniture and underneath the lace canopy of the double bed. After a nap, tired of waiting for her to get ready, Donald dressed and went downstairs to look over the carpentry work of the original redwood ceilings and walls, and to check out the painted and photographic portraits of presidents, foreign royalty, and Hollywood celebrities—fabled guests whose visits had graced the establishment since it opened in 1922. When she did appear on one side of the double staircase, he was semi-reclined on a round velvet sofa and, watching her descend, couldn't move except to blink. She was wearing a short black cocktail dress and fishnet stockings. She had done her hair up differently, with some curlicues dangling. When her spiked heels hit the hardwood floor, she paused, re-secured the chain of her beaded clutch purse on one slightly hitched shoulder, and turned three-hundred and sixty degrees. A shiver went up the back of his neck and heat flushed his face when he saw the openwork diamond pattern running from the heels of her shoes up the seam of her stockings and slipping beneath her skirt. She glanced left and right to see if any staff or guests had witnessed her going through her paces then, giggling, she trotted over. He sat frozen.

"Come on," she whispered, "get up." Shifting her hips to one side, she raised an arm to tuck some wisps of hair behind an ear; leaning the other way, she tilted her head sideways so that a long, beaded earring hung midair. "So, you like...?"

"I like, I like, but...." He rose to his feet. "It's like you're too sexy, babe. I'm worried some rich creep'll breeze in here and invite you for the weekend on his yacht or a ride in his airplane. Then it's bye-bye, Donny Boy, bye-bye."

"Oh, let 'em googly-eye me. Don't worry, hon'. Those guys have their high-class hookers way ahead in any line I could cut into." She lowered her voice. "Besides, you're the one I'm showin' a good time, right? Now come on, act older." She slipped her bare arm through his and steered him toward the lounge. "Let's try and get you a drink."

The barroom waiter was sorry to report that the bartender had looked at Donald's license and nixed the possibility of serving him alcohol, so he sat with a Coke while she snuck him long sips from three margarita cocktails she ordered back-to-back before they relocated in the restaurant for the early prix fixe meal and two bottles of wine.

*

Back in the lounge after supper, the same waiter received a five-dollar tip to convince the bartender on night shift to serve them spicy hot chocolates laced with Kahlua. They sat on a leather sofa, sipping their drinks and staring at logs flaming on andirons while rain hammered the picture windows to either side of the grandiose riverstone fire-place. Walking unsteadily back to their room, Sandy took her time stripping down to a hot pink triangle bikini top and matching bottom while Donald jerked off in the armchair—his pants at his ankles—and passed out that way. He woke later to find himself lying naked along-side her underneath the plush down comforter in bed and nudged her once—no response. He rose, slaked his thirst with tap water, got back in bed, and put his hand on her bare shoulder—she didn't stir. He positioned his pelvis up against her buttocks and rocked her hips; she moaned—"I just can't anymore, hon'. I'm sore."—and they both fell back asleep.

In the morning, she rose, showered, and changed back into her traveling clothes—leather jacket, pegged pants, riveted boots—before waking him up. "Check out time, sleepyhead. Come on, get up."

Over breakfast at Denny's, he asked her how much the hotel bill had come to.

"Enough to wipe me out for now."

"Jesus, Sandy. I can't figure out where you get that much money working at that honky-tonk."

"Ever heard of alimony?"

"Yeah?"

"Well, then...? Alimony covers my mortgage and food, but it doesn't pay for car repairs or vet bills. Shit jobs like that one pick up my bar tab and keep this little pony running in new clothes, know what I mean? But they don't keep me in play money forever."

After she had paid the bill, they stay seated at the counter, smoking and working on the coffee that one waitress or another kept pouring into their cups. "Do you really know about alimony, Donny? Your folks divorced?"

"I never met my dad. My mom never got married."

"Oh, hon', that's the shits. Your mom never got married at all?"

"No."

"So, she raised you all by herself? You got brothers, sisters?"

"No, just me. Yeah, she raised me, her and my gran'ma, I guess you could say."

"Yeah, well, sometimes that's the way it goes."

He grinned to himself and started swiveling his stool.

"What are you grinning about now?"

"I was just remembering how I used to use that as my pickup line."

"What are you talkin' about?"

"Sometimes I'd get girls feelin' extra sorry for me, so they'd show a little more ... action, sooner, you know? They wanted to comfort poor little Donny, you know?"

She shook her head and chuckled. "You guys really are bastards, aren't you?"

"What I am anyway," he said. "Born that way, I guess."

She snuffed out her cigarette, tousled his hair, grabbed her handbag from the neighboring stool, and spun off the seat. "Come on, Junior. You've got some drivin' to do."

*

North of Klamath River, the Maverick was brought to a halt near the head of a line of traffic backed up behind a mudslide that had brought out the Highway Patrol, a fleet of Forest Service vehicles, and several dozen men with miscellaneous decals on multicolored hardhats and a variety of company logos on their slicks. During the first lull in the rainfall, Donald got out to ask the STOP sign holder how much longer before the pilot truck would be guiding them through. "Might be a while," the grizzled veteran highway worker said. "Been here since dawn," he added, "fuckin' mud puddin'." Too jazzed on coffee to sit still in the car, Donald poked about the barricades then hopped over a log to stand behind a roadside tree, whizzing down the steep bank.

"You ladies gonna have to have to start lining up at that one blue box pretty soon," he said, returning to the car. "See it up there?"

"I see it. No thanks. I can hold out."

For the first time, he noticed that she had not made up her eyes, colored her cheeks, or touched up her lipstick since leaving the hotel. He went around and got back in the driver's seat. She was using two fingernail tips to worry the mole between her left cheek and her lip. "What's the matter with you anyway, you cold or something?" He turned the engine back on to generate some heat, but she pointed out the gas gauge needle indicating almost empty. He killed the engine but left the ignition switched on, scanning the radio static and pausing at the only station with halfway decent reception; she warned him about the older battery under the sedan's blotchy, oxidized hood; he turned off the key. "You have to pee bad? Is that why you're so bent out of shape?" She didn't react. "Or is it just cuz you're sore down there and all? Don't be sore at me about that! You asked me for it. You fuckin' begged me for it, remember?"

While looking straight ahead, she didn't say a word, so he turned away, drawing squiggles on the fogged-up glass. When he heard the clicking sound, he spotted the diamond wedding ring she was tapping against the window where she held her right hand cocked back over her right shoulder.

"Why'd you put that on?"

She kept at it: slow, steady, sure.

"What's that supposed to mean, Sandy? You tellin' me to keep my mitts off, is that it?"

"Like I tried to tell you, hon'," she spoke, continuing to tap the glass. "I'm sorry but the party's over."

"What's going on? Why are you so pissed off all of a sudden?"

"From now on—"

"... from now on what?" He seized her pack of cigarettes from the dash, tore off a filter tip, found a miniature redwood matchbox labelled Humboldt House, and lit up. She kept on tapping. "You probably really are married so now you're dumping me, right? Why don't you just drop me in the fuckin' mud right here and go on home to hubby without me?"

She stopped tapping. "I'm not married." She lit up one of her cigarettes. "I haven't lied to you about one thing, hon'." She swiped at the foggy windshield. "Not once all week."

"You're not married?"

"That's right."

"You're not married but you're wearing a diamond wedding ring!"

"I'm not married, Donny, but I do have a steady beau."

"A steady beau, huh? You have a steady boyfriend—so now you tell me!"

"What difference would it have made? There was no need to tell you till just now."

"So, is he and his friends going to beat the shit out of me when we get to Crescent City?"

"Oh, he's out of town, don't worry. Works as a lineman for PG&E. His repair crew has to go chasing all over the countryside during winter storms, just like these poor guys do."

"So that's how come you had money to waste on little Donny Boy. Sandy's got herself a sugar daddy, right?"

"Oh, come on, smarten up. He's not my sugar daddy and you are dead wrong: I don't consider any dough I spent on you this week wasted, not at all." She threw her head back and neighed. "It's been a fuckin' blast, baby! And you know what? It's over now, okay? That's all. It's over."

"Why's it over? Is Mister PG&E back in town?"

"Not that anybody's told me. But it's time for me to get back to work. I've gotta make back my nickel, right? And you have to ... move on." She saw his face fixed in a scowl. "Let's quit while we're ahead, okay? You know as well as I do...." She paused, cracking her side window one quarter of an inch and dumping her cigarette outside. "Well, maybe you don't know but I'm going to tell you." She started using the sharp end of the pointer finger's nail on her right hand to scrape behind the fingernails of her left.

"Oh, Jesus! Here we go again! Mother knows best. What are you going to tell me?"

"First time I get my period—which might be in the works, by the bye; first time I come down with a bladder infection or the flu—which might also be on the way.... Or say I permanently close my downstairs backdoor to you...? You'll wail like a baby and be out of here in no time. 'Course maybe you'd have to smack me good before you left Del Norte County. That'd be the manly way to go."

"I'd never hit you, Sandy. Okay? Never. Jesus."

"They all say that," she stated. "Now just let's stop it, hon'. You're a great kid—"

"... KID!"

"... and it's been a blast and a half but it's time to get real."

"Your boyfriend'd sure as shit hit you if he found out you've been screwing your brains out with me. He'd hit you and beat the shit out of me too."

"Probably would if he found out. That is, if you're still hanging around, right? But you're not going to be hanging around and he's not going to find out. Look at those poor saps out there."

"What poor saps?"

"Those guys," she said, smearing her hand across the inside of the windshield. "Sloshing around in all that mud."

"Yeah? So what?"

"My boyfriend could be out there right now—"

"... along with your big brother, right?"

"And my husband, my ex, that is. He used to work oil rigs in Alaska."

"I worked hard like that on a crab boat and other places."

"Yeah? My daddy worked the oil fields outside Bakersfield. Get it?"

"Get what?"

"I know these guys. Like I know you, Donny. I balled you. I'm not sayin' I'd ball them, just that I know where they're coming from. They're like family. I know what they're thinkin' about right now too, workin' like that in the freezing rain."

"That's not freezing rain. I've worked in freezing rain."

"I'm not sayin' you haven't, hon'. Bet you have."

A volley of car horns grew incrementally louder, reached a peak, and petered out. Wind-blown redwood needles and other leaf litter started sticking to the windshield, creating a dirty, liquefied curtain sealing them off inside the sedan. "Give me your hand."

"What?"

"Just give me your hand." She reached over and yanked his wrist. "Come on. Fuckin' give it to me, would you?"

"What for?"

"You'll find out."

He stopped resisting and let her guide his right hand into her lap. She lifted the leather jacket and the mohair sweater, which was no longer so white or downy as before, unbuttoned the top of her pants, and placed his hand below her belly. "Jeez your hand's friggin' cold!"

"What's this about? Thought you said I'm sore, hands off, it's over. You're weird, Sandy. You cockteasing me now?"

"Shush. Just relax your hand, would you? See if you feel some-thing where I put your fingers. Come on, cool it ...."

"What the...?"

"Do you feel a line there?"

"Where?"

"Right there. Feel it?"

"The top of your undies?"

"No. Just press a little—not that hard, I'll pee in my pants!"

"What? All I feel is the top of your panties and, you know, your hair...."

"You don't feel a narrow bead running about six inches across ... right ... there. You feel it now?" She slid his fingertips back and forth along a thin, horizontal, slightly raised seam of hardened flesh. "You feel it now, right?"

"Yeah, I guess so."

"Okay." She withdrew his hand, buttoned her pants, and stuck her hands into her jacket pockets. "That's a scar."

"What scar?"

"From a C-section."

"A what?"

"A cesarean—"

"... oh, okay, I know what that is."

"I had a baby when I was fifteen, Donny. There's a boy like you somewhere out in this mean old world who's my son. Not far from your age, too."

"Why do you have to tell me this shit right now?"

CHP and Caltrans personnel were realigning barricades to make it possible for the first caravan of traffic to navigate through the rocks and branches in the mounded mud; a pickup truck with flashing yellow lights prepared to guide them. But before they got the signal to move ahead, she had time to tell him how she had gotten pregnant at age fourteen, run away, come back home, delivered a baby boy in a private clinic in Vancouver BC, and how the baby was immediately spirited away for adoption; how she had woken from the surgery without ever having seen the newborn child.

Donald focused on the taillights of the car ahead until the highway opened up and they were traveling at the limit, but before the tight, narrow turns south of Crescent City they again had to wait for road-work; he turned off the engine to save on gas. The windows fogged up. There was no music, no heater, no joint, no bottle; they had run out of cigarettes and argument.

At the first filling station on the edge of town, Sandy purchased two dollars' worth of gasoline and used the restroom, then they drove through MacDonald's and sat in the parking lot, eating out of paper bags. He could think of nothing more to say except to ask her to buy him a six-pack and some Marlboros before they drove to the North-coast Vacation Cottages to part ways.

As they entered the courtyard enshrouded by trees, she said something about how she hoped he could get over this fling, get women like her out of his system, meet a decent lady—not so old, not so used—one who might make him a good wife. She said it had not worked out so well for her, but he still stood a chance—who knew? Maybe the dice would roll his way.

"Don't cry on me, now," he said. "You'll forget about me before those fuckin' bald tires of yours hit 101."

"Oh no, Donny. You don't get it yet. I'll always remember you, and I will cry sometimes too."

She fetched her odds and ends from his truck, and they stood looking at each other until there was no longer any reason to be standing in the rain with nothing left to say. She leaned forward and—without letting her breasts brush up against him—pecked her lips on his cheek before getting into the Maverick and driving away.

Donald drove north to see if he could get his old room back in Smith River. There was no one in the residential unit doubling as an office, and the door to his room was swollen shut but unlocked, so he shouldered his way inside, kept the lights low, and drank his beer. He guessed there was nowhere else in California where someone could stay for $3.50 a night—no tax—or even pay nothing at all. [1]

Chapter 9

Hired Hands

Katie discovered a padlock installed on the cabin door but no signs of other activity by the owner or anyone else. The park's dogwoods and maples were leafing out; a pittance of blossom showed on some camellia specimens languishing in the special collection. She stuck a note in the U-shaped lock:

> *Pieter T. You never answer your phone! Dropped by to see how you are. What is your mailing address in Corralitos? Please call me sometime. 875-2441 KT. Feb 8.*

A letter postmarked Boston, arrived in Cliffport the next day:

> *5/2/73 Dear Katie, Tomorrow I travel to England where my sister Anneke is sick with the cancer. They are certain it is the end for her. Her husband wrote that she wants me there now. I can be more use over there maybe than I am here. Can you visit Nico's perhaps to make sure nobody breaks into the cabin or camps on property? If you cannot get away do not worry over it. The key to lock on door is under that flat black rock where the dwarf specie Tulipa saxatile should be blooming now. I let you know when I come back. Please transmit my best regards and New Year greetings to Mrs. Lowrie. Your friend sincerely, Pieter Tuelling*

Gardening tools rattling in the bed, a brown, dinged, compact Toyota pickup with Colorado plates came to a stop under the oak at One Grade Road. Short, stout, strong, a young woman got out and squatted down to pet Baby Blue Eye, calming the dog even before Katie had stepped from the kiosk. Straightening her knees, the visitor came up out of a crouch, introduced herself as Letty, extended her right hand and, with her left, flipped ringlets of black hair off her forehead; Katie saw no trace of makeup tinting a broad, light brown face rouged only from working outdoors.

Hailing from Boulder, Leticia Morales de Novato said that, unless some job came along someday soon, she would be heading back to Colorado. She reported that earlier that morning a big landscape company's injunction against making purchases at the Redwood Coast Nursery had piqued her curiosity, so she had driven up the coastal highway to check out the forbidden address. Katie gestured that Letty could sit with her on the kiosk stoop; the chunky Latina tossed her car keys through the Toyota's open window—where Katie saw feathers, driftwood, redwood cones, seashells, and bulbous kelp glued to the narrow dash—and they settled down, hip to hip, on the redwood round.

After gardening in and around Santa Cruz for almost a year, Letty was trying to sink some roots in California, but prospects for steady paying work kept falling through; an hour earlier, before even clocking in for her first day at Buena Vista Landscape in La Selva Beach, she had walked away from the company's headquarters. She recounted how she had been issued a uniform, a nametag, and a pair of used pruning shears worse-off than the pair in her own leather holster, and the office manager had informed her that she had been assigned to a maintenance crew at the Monteflores development near Fern in North County, where Buena Vista had the contract to tend the ornamental lawns and plantings throughout the common areas. Katie listened closely, surmising that the prohibition against conducting business with RCN was yet another measure designed to punish the Lowries for not rolling over to Sea-to-Summit's demands. Over and above routine maintenance, Letty had learned, the company charged the property's management firm time & materials for projects as they arose: tree care, irrigation repair, "change-outs" of the flowerbeds bordering the main entrance gate and in "color spots" throughout the grounds. When she inquired about the possibility of performing side jobs for individual residents afterhours, the woman indoctrinating her summoned Letty's supervisor over the radio; José Santos came in from the yard and sat her down in the employee locker room to explain the delicate situation in Spanish.

It turned out that Monteflores' residents do indeed ask gardeners to design, install, and maintain features of their spacious forecourts and rear patios, and it was permissible for individual Buena Vista employees to accept such solicitations for out-of-contract services, but not to conduct such business under the auspices of Buena Vista or Coastal Property Management. Still, Señor Santos made clear, the supervisor was to be notified as soon as any member of the landscape crew was so engaged, and twenty-five percent of any fees paid to the gardener—including tips—were to be promptly turned over to the site manager. If any employee were found to be less than forthright about disclosing their financial arrangements with private homeowners, there would be *una reducción de la fuerza de trabajo** or, more precisely, the employee would be laid off—*indefinidamente*. Señor Santos had then added that the purchase of plant materials from the nursery located at One Grade Road was in all cases *prohibido*. Letty reported that when he had finished talking, she stood up, left the nametag and shears on top of the folded work clothes, and walked off. "I've seen the Mafia operate before," the young woman concluded her account, "and not just on TV."

"But what will you do now?"

"*Quién sabe?*" the twenty-year-old Chicana replied, shrugging and mugging. "My parents would like me to come home, right?"

"I bet they would."

• *a reduction of the work force (Sp)*

"I could go back to work on Uncle Manny's mow-and-blow crew, but I've been there, done that ... you know? I just like it out here in California, you know? And I really love Santa Cruz."

Katie offered to show the unsolicited visitor around and led the way uphill; at the first turn of the main path, they paused.

"What's your name?"

"Katie Lowrie ... Katie."

"Call me Letty, okay?"

"Okay, Letty."

"Katie, don't you love it here? I do ... *muchingo!* We don't have the ocean and the beach back in the Rockies! It's always too cold for me in winter back home, even with all this seal blubber!" she quipped, clapping both sides of her solid torso with two open palms. Katie detected no blush on the smiling girl's baby cheeks. "Maybe you need somebody to work for you, no?"

"Oh, so you can see that already, huh? Let me think about it," Katie muttered. "Come on."

Katie knew full well that with almost 15,000 square feet of growing grounds under glass, plastic, and shade cloth, and almost an acre in vegetables and herbs, of course she needed someone to work with her; her eighteen-year-old son's assistance would be nice but had so far proven unattainable. "I'm falling behind, for sure. Maybe if I had a good worker ... but just for a week or two...?"

"I know someone who is available," Letty stated, raising her chin to display full, rosy lips spreading wide over pristine white teeth. "A good *trabajadora* too, this someone...." She wiggled her natural black eyebrows up and down.

Katie laughed and they moved on until, seated side by side on the bench outside the glasshouse's rear door, they silently watched the morning sunlight moving over the shade structures across the way in a wide band gradually illuminating the meadow. Letty welcomed the sunflower seeds poured into her hands as Katie asked her what she had meant about seeing the Mafia operate before. Splitting hulls, nibbling seeds, Letty recounted how as the youngest child of an extended family of hardworking people, she had been educated early on about the business practices of one management firm riding herd over the shopping center complexes and condominiums throughout Boulder. Besides her uncle, her older brothers, her brothers-in-law, most of their friends and acquaintances were independent professionals who uniformly steered clear of all requests-for-proposals or bid announcements associated with Advanced Sentinel Properties which, over the years, had set up a slew of hollow shell companies. In response to their consistently low bids, these shell companies were awarded the contracts involving electrical work, plumbing, painting, fence repair, and roof replacement at the largest projects. Once the work was performed—typically by a revolving cast of out-of-area tradesmen driving blank-door vehicles—Advanced Sentinel Properties quietly recovered a percentage of fees paid.

"Sounds like institutionalized favoritism to me," Katie commented.

"The Mafia, you mean," Letty retorted, lifting her right hand into the air, orienting it leftward and rightward—the middle finger extended. "How about one hundred percent of this, wherever you are, *pinche basura!*" •

Katie laughed and doled out more seeds from her pack.

"Is that Monteflores place up that road?"

"Four or five miles."

"So, you're their closest nursery. Who else is growing plants around here?"

"Nobody, until you get up to Pescadero or down into Santa Cruz."

"That's so stupid. You could be their main source for the plants that do well up here, but I guess that would mess up whatever scams they're running down with their suppliers."

"I'm sort of amazed they even bothered to make a company policy about not shopping here. Flower purchases are nothing compared to those other expenses you mentioned. Flower costs are chicken scratch. But they really do hate me and my mom."

"Weird ... how come?"

• *fucking trash! (Sp)*

"It's a long story. Maybe I'll tell you sometime. Letty, haven't people back in Boulder got a clue what's going on with that monkey business?"

"Not much," Letty countered. "How about here in California? Do people have a clue out here? I don't think so. The directors on those homeowner boards and the shopping center owners back in Boulder get kickbacks too. I was taught to stay out of it. I tell you: my people don't need to stoop to that crap. We may act a little too proud sometimes, sure, but we're not *peones*. The Morales have been in Colorado longer than any of those *pinche* property managers at Advanced Sentinel."

"So, you and your relatives have connected the dots, even if nobody else has."

"If anybody else has, they're afraid to blow the whistle. Nobody wants to hear about it. 'Tell me a lie, please.' Isn't that the motto people live by after they get a little piece of the action? *"Por favor,* tell me a lie.'"

Hired on for a week, Letty thanked the owner-operator of the RCN for offering her double the minimum wage for agricultural workers.

"I wish it could be more. Now come on and I'll show you some real scratching chickens then I better get to work." Katie took the bright young woman through the barnyard and into the garden below the house, where hundreds of overgrown borage, calendula, and nasturtium—volunteer seedlings from plants that had melted down in December when the mercury went below twenty-five degrees—needed culling.

"Let me start on these, Katie. You just tell me what to leave alone. I can start weeding down here right away."

Three weeks later, Letty was still working in Cliffport six days a week and enjoying lunches at the Lowrie table. A shameless big eater, often speaking with one cheek full while shoveling yet another fork- or spoonful into her mouth, Letty started lingering on into the evenings, cranking out hot Mexican American suppers with spices and flavors familiar to a Morales from Colorado but new and fascinating to Katie—and frightening to Elise. After a month, she was making plant deliveries in the Ford F-250—Baby Blue Eye riding shotgun, the sheepdog's nostrils splayed by rushing wind. After six weeks, she moved her belongings into DD's former quarters in the barn, where Katie had long ago torn down the glossy porno-shots of mature naked women, burning them along with his dartboard-damaged posters of bikini-clad surfer girls with ripening suntans slinking against longboards stuck upright in the sand.

Letty proved to be productive, resourceful, and tireless in airing her open-minded curiosity. Did Katie think the phases of the moon influenced plant growth? Were native plants superior and what was "a native" anyway—was she one? What about someone starting a business creating gardens especially for birds and bees, or bats and moths? Did "organic" always mean "safe?" As long as her temporary employee didn't experiment on every idea that came into her head and out her mouth, Katie relished the lively company. And, despite her uninhibited manner, the longhaired, *zoftig* Chicana was always respectful and courteous toward the eldest Lowrie who, although used to her own daughter's *brusquerie*, was initially dismayed by their freewheeling, outspoken guest worker. Katie had to remind her mother that Letty was twenty and her exuberance was both natural and refreshing.

*

When a friend took Elise on a rare evening out, Letty lugged her milk crate full of albums into the main house, where she and Katie drank beer and championed their favorite music. Katie noticed Letty's stocking feet tapped and her fingers snapped to the rock-n-roll-like numbers in Alan Stivell's concert pieces, but when the suspended time signatures of the Breton's more ethereal, ceremonial Celtic tunes implied settings of sea mist and craggy heights, the girl lost patience and put on the Stones. Katie tried out a recording of the Carter Family then of Hazel Dickens dueting with Alice Gerrard or Ginny Hawkins; Letty moaned at strains of Appalachian harmonies and countered with Linda Ronstadt and Bonnie Raitt. Katie gave up trying to win her over to any old-time mountain music but played selected tracks from Joan Baez' first albums; the Coloradan found the old British ballads boring and the singer's renditions of Spanish-language ballads too highbrow. Instead, she played Katie her new Emmylou Harris record. Witnessing the Alabama-born singer's country voice and her naturally photogenic beauty on the album's cover, Katie was reminded why she herself had never become a singing star.

Katie never attempted imposing any of her longtime favorites upon the youngster, for she knew that the sounds of hardcore Scottish balladeer Jeannie Roberson, folksinger Jean Redpath, or American music maker Jean Ritchie were tastes—natural or acquired—which could not be forced upon anyone, least of all someone as independently minded as Leticia Morales who, if not running from a troubled past, was simply plowing so fast through her own firsthand experience that she followed few guideposts left by others and left behind no path markers of her own. Although Señorita Morales could muster little affection for any aspect of Celtic musical culture, Katie hoped the younger woman might be taken by the alternately slow and fast pulses of Scottish fiddle music recorded in homes along Cape Breton's Cabot Trail, and Letty did start to pump her feet and slap her blocky thighs to the energetic jigs and reels, finally jumping up and performing a playful step dance resembling a barn floor stomp accentuated by her hoots and hollers. Before long, however, Letty was usurping the record player again, turning up the volume of a Tex-Mex ensemble of accordions, guitars, string bass, and drums. Up on her feet, waltzing around the room with her eyes closed—a bottle of cerveza raised in the air at the end of one arm and an imaginary partner enwrapped in the other—she sang along with stylized polkas.

Joni Mitchell's *Blue* was the one album they could both listen to without interruption. When Elisabeth Lowrie returned, she found the twenty-year-old seated cross-legged on the floor, studying the printed lyrics—lines of verse her thirty-seven-year-old daughter knew so well she could silently sing them without moving her lips.

*

Letty was drawn to the community hanging out around UCSC's farm and garden project. Saturday afternoons, with her employer's permission, she took off from work to attend informal workshops there in cider making, heirloom seed preservation, solar fruit drying; Saturday nights she went to impromptu keggers off campus and, by her own brazen account, didn't shy off from rolling in the hay with some self-styled New Age urban farmers, many of them refugees from wealthy families in cities and suburbs back East.

One Sunday after brunch, once Elise had retired for her nap, the women were lingering out on the deck, enjoying the clear, warm, springtime weather, when Letty produced a torpedo-shaped joint. Katie accepted a couple of passes but held off when she realized it was unusually powerful stuff. And she couldn't take her eyes off the slippery cord of a thin leather necklace and its Puka shell almost hidden between the girl's boisterous bosoms. Her young female companion wore a white cotton, V-neck, short-sleeve tee-shirt; and cut-off jeans compressed her pudgy thighs. Letty snuffed out the joint, tossed off her baseball cap, shook the glistening locks of her black, ringleted hair, and turned her eyes–dilated black pools surrounded by copper rings–upon Katie. Katie's attention was galvanized. She caught herself imagining embracing Leticia, taking hold of the plump curves, burying her face between the succulent breasts, peeling off the stuffed jeans and exploring whatever warm, black, wiry wetlands squished between her legs–when the young girl averted her eyes. Katie rose from her seat, claiming to have forgotten something in the glasshouse. Letty pocketed the roach, said she was headed for Nude Beach, and they parted for the day.

Later that night, Katie woke when she heard the barn door being slid open and closed. She rolled onto her front to still her breathing and, clinging to her pillow, admitted to herself that she was confused. She pictured the farmworkers in the Brussels sprout fields up and down the North Coast, staring down from bluffs onto students and surfers and other free spirits populating the sands, frolicking naked or almost naked in the coves' breaking waves. Like those fieldworkers, she wasn't one of the bathers, and she knew her love life had become a forsaken affair: fantasizing sex with the Latina or anyone else was as frustrating as licking a sealed clear glass jar containing morsels of waxy honeycomb suspended within viscous amber—inaccessible.

*

Vilho, the Finnish metalworker who had fabricated her pickup's custom shell, no longer worked at Fern's upgraded garage, but Katie got directions to his home address and eased the truck across a sway-backed wooden bridge one fourth-mile outside town, cruising to the end of a once-paved lane and ringing the bell at a simple ranch house with new aluminum siding. The man recognized her as soon as he opened the door; she asked if he could look at some damage done to the shell when her worker had miscalculated the height and weight of a low-hanging limb, crushing the top seam along the roof's right side. The retiree slipped out of his house shoes and into his boots, leaving them unlaced as he went outside to assess the situation. All he could do, he said, would be to hammer the crumpled aluminum from inside out. She asked when; he said then, or as soon as he finished serving lunch to his infirm wife. Katie didn't ask how much it would cost; she knew him to be the sort of old-time immigrant who might leave the amount of payment up to her or else not even charge her for the favor.

She left him the key and strolled back out the country lane under a spring shower of big leaf maple seeds winging their way to the ground and red alders releasing their frass with the breeze. Crossing the bridge over the creek, she hiked back toward Fern center to see if Ross Stewart was still residing at the trailer park off Main Street. The hostess there reported that he had collected his things weeks prior but left no forwarding address; to the best of her knowledge, he had moved in with some relative in a hamlet on the north side of Ben Lomond Mountain. Katie didn't recognize the place name—New Faith—but she thanked the forthright woman and walked down Fern's new sidewalks to consult the topo map pasted on the post office wall. When she reclaimed her truck, she forced fifteen dollars into the man's arthritic hand; he kept the ten-dollar bill but refused the fiver, and she was soon veering off Grade Road, leaving Fern's new street signs and streetlamps behind in order to follow a circuitous route she hoped was the right way to New Faith.

Ascending to ridgetops, dropping into canyon bottoms, steering through closed forests and open meadows on county roadways far from officialdom and out of repair, she finally saw an antiquated wooden sign with barely legible lettering—New Faith Lane—and turned in. Large dogs immediately menaced the rotating front tires; glad Baby Blue Eye had stayed behind with Letty, Katie rolled up her window and coasted past a dozen one- and two-story structures spaced widely apart among a woodlot of limbed firs. The neighborhood looked inhabited: older and newer model vehicles were parked beneath metal canopy carports also serving as storage spaces for machinery and shelter for firewood. Several genuine log cabins were surrounded by the accretion of artifacts of an older way of life, when settlers and sons of settlers logged for a living, fished mountain streams, and hunted deer and trapped small animals all year round, while the women made babies, raised children, did the cooking, the laundry and the cleaning, all the while attempting to sustain some trappings of their ancestral cultures from the Old Country or back East. All her life, Katie had run across such vestigial, isolated communities tucked into the creases and folds of the Santa Cruz Mountains but, after passing these homes at the mouth of the New Faith Lane, she entered a zone of less certain definition.

Someone had plowed through an expansive thicket of tall wild roses to scrape out a primitive corridor sloping downward before opening upon an abandoned, treeless pasture in no man's land. A variety of vans and sedans were parked here and there. An unattended bonfire smoldered. A barrel fire smoked. She recalled photographs of encampments from the Civil War. A hairy, shirtless man in pajama bottoms and bare feet emerged from a broken-down horse trailer, where he had apparently taken up living quarters, and stared at her long pickup truck's passage through the settlement. Partly painted faces appeared at the partly painted windows of a blue school bus, its roof decked out with banners and flags. With babes in arms, a trio of topless women in drawstring pants issued from a stand of wild fennel and stood gawking at the Ford's slow movement over the surface of the dusty road. Farther out in the field, steps had been chopped into a giant stump's flaring base with a tipi erected on top. Most of the poles and posts belonging to a former horse corral had been dismantled but, in the center of its circular clearing, a two- or three-year-old boy dressed in nothing but his soiled skin spun in place, taking no notice of the traveling truck. Just as the temporary encampment in the sunken clearing fell out of view, the way was blocked by a chain suspended between two posts sunk in newly poured cement.

Unable to make a U-turn, Katie was preparing to back out in reverse when she noticed that the coyote bush opened onto some different sort of destination just ahead. Barred from driving, she locked the truck, stepped over the chain, and picked up a branch to ward off a hostile barnyard goose promptly ambushing her. Charging, backing off, charging again, the animal barked and snapped its serrated beak. She swiped at its neck—now extended, now retracted—and the goose only withdrew once she started pelting it with the sharpest, heaviest rocks on hand.

On the far side of a graveled circle, a premanufactured home sat between two deodar cedars seventy feet in height. Beyond the solo residence, the cables from a pair of dead-end power poles, anchored by multiple guy wires, terminated in a box mounted on a concrete pad—the end of the line. A dozen bisected truck tires—once painted white and planted to annuals—lay on their sides, creating an informal border between the cul-de-sac and the groundcover of fallen needles blanketing the lawn, the home, the steel garage, and the shed. From the concrete stoop at the front door, she was able to see the top of her own parked truck and part of the squatters' colony beyond the vegetation. Although no vehicles were parked at the head of the walkway and no one answered the doorbell, there were signs of current habitation: muddy tire tracks suggested that the residents of the doublewide trailer home—perhaps including Ross Stewart—enjoyed ingress and egress by a long, macadamized driveway, not via New Faith Lane. She peeked through the portholes of the detached garage's triple doors; in addition to a one-ton Dodge pickup, she identified a walk-behind Ditch Witch trencher, a compact Bobcat excavator with a bucket and an angle blade, and a stack of augers big enough to dig a well or sink a utility pole. Katie returned to the stoop, freed a Jehovah Wetness booklet from the grip of the storm door's handle, tore off a page, and wrote a note in some blank space:

TO ROSS STEWART I heard you're back.
Call or come by Cliffport to do the orchard job.
KT. 875-2441.

Armed with two fistfuls of sharp rocks, she made her way back to the truck and drove out past the encamped caravansary, removing herself from the neighborhood without incident.

———

Ross let his Irish Setters out the jeep's rear flap and hopped up onto the front hood, rolling a cigarette while watching Baby Blue Eye and his dogs reacquaint themselves and waiting for Katie to show up.

"Hi, Ross."

"Hey."

"You finally made it."

"I did, didn't I?"

"You got my note. So you are living up there. But why didn't you bring your tools? I want you to cut down the orchard like we talked about, right?"

"Hold on, Lowrie."

"What's wrong?"

He tried to salvage the flimsy, unlit cigarette by pressing it on the fender but flicked the mangled makings to the ground.

"What's the matter? I'm saying you're hired. Don't you want to do it?"

"First I want to know how you found out I'm living up in New Faith."

"Looks more like New Despair to me, at least that community next door does." Katie hiked up her jeans, crossed her arms, and tilted her head sideways. "The lady at the Fern trailer park told me, that's how."

"She did, huh?"

"I asked her. Is something wrong with that?"

"Nuthin', I guess," he said, dropping down and stomping his heels to force the pant cuffs to drop over the tops of his steel-toe boots. "So long as it's just you. But I guess I better tell that nosey bitch to keep her yap shut. I don't want everybody in the whole world knowing where I'm at."

"Why's that, Ross Stewart?" Katie tossed back her head and smiled. "You a fulltime outlaw now? I didn't see your picture in the post office."

"Oh, for Christ's sake, Lowrie! Don't mess with my mind."

"What? Are you running a still back up in there like the good ol' days?" She snorted and laughed. "Or maybe you and your friends in the meadow are tending a few big old weed patches in suburban New Faith, is that it?"

"What else do you know nuthin' about, Lowrie? Those fuckin' freaks aren't friends a' mine. Know what? You're pissing me off again. I got half a mind to take off and let some other damned fool tear down your fuckin' trees. Why don't you call your wetbacks in Half Moon Bay to do it for you, or did you try that already?"

"You don't know what you're talking about, you racist son of a bitch!" She shook her head and dropped her arms by her sides. "Oh, come on, let's cool it, Ross. What are we arguing for? I didn't call anybody else. Now do you want the job or not?"

"Yeah, I want it. I need the bucks. Looks like I'll never get paid for that last week catchin' crabs."

"Listen, I'm not screwing with you, Ross. I tracked you down because I'm ready and able to pay for the job, whenever you want to start."

"And 'cuz you want to pick my brains about Donald the Duck, you forgot to say...."

Katie stuck her hands in her back pockets, stepping closer to square off opposite the man far taller and bigger than she. "Do you know something about DD I don't know?"

"Damn I'm good! I knew that's why you wanted to see me."

"Well, do you? He was fishing with you, wasn't he? You must know more than me because by now I don't know where he is or what he's doing. Well, tell me, Ross. Where is he? What's he doing?"

"You get me a big cup of hot coffee with real cream and sugar, goddamnit, I'll tell you what I know."

"Tell me now. What is it? Is there bad news?"

"Oh, come on, he's okay, all right? Yeah, he joined the crabbin' crew the start of February, I guess it was. End of January, I don't know. But the whole season went fubar."

"What happened?"

"Said I'll tell you, Lowrie, didn't I?" Ross wagged his shaggy head of hair, sniggered, stuck a pinch of chew into his cheek, and raked his horseshoe moustache with yellow-stained fingertips. "Now what about that crank?"

"Okay, asshole, come on. I'll make you a whole pot of fresh coffee, how about that? But then you better tell me what you know."

"It ain't much, I swear, Katie."

"And if you don't...."

"Ohhhhh!" Ross guffawed, shuddered, and held his empty hands out upside-down—trembling. "I'm so scared of you. Everybody's sooooo fuckin' scared of Katelyn fuckin' Lowrie!"

She laughed at his playacting—and at herself—then preceded him toward the deck, but halfway up the stairs she turned and rested a palm on his vest, forcing him to look her in the eyes. "Are you in trouble with the law, Ross?"

He brushed her hand off, packed the wad of chew deeper in his cheek, and grinned. "No, I ain't *in trouble with the law*. God, you're such a sucker, Katie. I'm not in trouble, okay? I even caught up with some chicken-shit fix-it tickets, how about that? I'm a big boy, okay? Just fuckin' moved into a house of my own, didn't I?"

"You really own that prefab?"

"And the garage and everything in it. Hell yeah I own it, and half-an-acre parcel too. I never knew my Aunt Louise gave a shit about my welfare but in the end she just gave me the place."

"Sounds kind of familiar...."

"Huh?"

"Nothing, go on."

"Course I did help her out quite a bit after ol' Lloyd bought the farm, but nobody can say I did that to get their place. Swear to God, it still blows my mind. A house, a working garage, a goddamn Dodge Ram that'll haul ass over hill and dale. All I've got left to do is sign some fuckin' papers in Santa Cruz then start payin' the 'lectricty bill and property taxes. I'm sittin' pretty, Katie." His bullet of brown spit splattered the ground. "How about that?"

"Wow. You made it, Ross. You going to get a phone line connected anytime soon?"

"What phone line? Hanovers never had one. They didn't need to hear from people on the telephone and I don't either. Whoever needs me bad enough can find me. You did, right?"

"Maybe.... Anyway, good for you, Ross. You deserve it although don't ask me why right now. Sit down out here and I'll get your coffee, Mister Ross Stewart of New Faith Lane, New Faith, California."

"Better just make that New Faith period. I've got my own drive in separate from the one the regular residents use and those crazy-ass hippies in that gypsy camp." He spat over the railing. "Hey, what's that down there?"

"That's a soil shredder. That's as far as it made it up the hill, so far. It's heavy."

"Where you want it put, up top?"

"I want it at the planting area the other side the glasshouse."

"Hell, I'll drag that sucker up there," he said, "if you'll throw in some of your chocolate brownies or cookies or something like that along with that coffee."

"You will? Sure! I'll give you a whole bag of cookies to take home."

"You got it," he said and tromped back down the stairs to tackle the job.

*

"I see where your greenhouse's holdin' up pretty good. Is somebody movin' around in there?"

"Yup," Katie responded, settling a tray on the stump. "I've got some steady help for a change."

"Not one of those Avilas, or is it?"

"No, it's not. Knock it off, Ross. I have finally hired some excellent help, as a matter of fact. There's your coffee and cookies so tell me what you know about DD. My mom's heart's going to break if she doesn't hear something soon, hopefully something good."

"Speaking of your mother ... is it okay if...?

"Go ahead. Smoke yourself all the way to your grave, Mister Stewart, but tell me about DD before you get there."

"Whoa, you're gettin' mean in your old age, rowdy Lowrie." Ross rolled a cigarette on the broad arm of the wooden deck chair while Katie perched her coffee mug on her knees and leaned forward, waiting for his words. "I really don't know much, Katie. But first, you tell me how you knew I even got back early from fishin'?"

"I didn't know. I just had some time on my hands up in Fern so I dropped by the trailer park. You're usually gone till June, that's true. Just a lucky guess, I guess. So why are you back?"

"There were a few ... complications."

"Involving DD?"

"Katie, nobody fuckin' calls him DD anymore except you. You know that, right? It's Don or Donald not DD. Jesus!"

"Well, I happen to be his mother and I'll call him DD if I want to. Now what *complications*?"

"Shit started comin' down after a long run out, when our brilliant skipper for some dumbass reason decided to anchor in Trinidad Harbor instead of taking the haul right back to Fort Bragg like usual. Well, those bigshot maritime authorities in Trinidad don't know ye

265

ol' CRAB MAGNET like they do or pretend to down in Noyo Harbor. So they wouldn't let our stopover pass without boarding her for an inspection."

"An inspection for what?"

"Everything, turned out. Those boys even radioed the Coast Guard for help. It's like they were looking for opium from China, swear t' God. It took them so long, we got permission to go on land. One fat guy in this big ol' Hawaiian shirt and blue jeans and freakin' flip flops came out with the water taxi, sayin' he'd join us goin' ashore."

"Join who, you and DD?"

"And another guy named Jake who was on the crew. So, we get off at this little public pier where's there's a piece a' sand and a bait shop and one seafood restaurant. Good enough for us. We're enjoyin' a few brewskis, ordering our food, and that guy—I forget what he said his name was.... That fuckin' guy had a moustache makes mine look Mickey Mouse."

"So, what about him?"

"So, he claims he operates whale watching tours on weekends, right? So what's he doin' ridin' around Trinidad Harbor in a water taxi—"

"... Ross, are you going to get to the point or not?"

"Point is, he was one fuckin' lyin' sack a' shit. Tellin' us how he had been a chummer then a deckhand then worked his way up to get his license and bought his own seagoing vessel."

"How do you know he was lying?"

"We found out, that's how. So, whatshisname—let's just him the Hawaiian Eye—he keeps feeding us his chum and asking us what else we caught beside crab and all, like what else do we have on board—wink wink. Hinting how maybe there was some way he could help us offload our 'stuff' in a little cove he knew nearby, after the cops got off the boat—wink wink."

"What are you winking for? What was he talking about?"

"Contraband, Katie: dope. The Hawaiian Eye was a fuckin' lawman. A narc posing as a whale tour operator so he could work the three-mile limit offshore. While dumbass passengers scope the horizon for whales, he scopes for smugglers, get it? Then radios in suspect vessels, I guess. Pretty good cover for a cop, I must admit. Shit, they're all kinds of moonlit coves and forgotten landings up and down that coastline—"

"... Ross! What about DD?"

"Oh, yeah. So the man with the handlebars goes to make a phone call and this stranger at the next table tips us off: the guy's a narc—bingo!"

"So, were you carrying anything illegal on that boat?"

"No, nuthin', that's just it. But Donald the Duck split the scene even before Mister Waikiki Beach came back from his 'phone call'—probably went on the radio to the boat, I don't know. That upset the man, too, Don taking off like that, but what could he do? We weren't under arrest or anything. The captain had to stay onboard but we could get off, with a secret agent escort, I understood later. That fat federale said how he hated to see good food go to waste and oh what the hell, so he scarfs down everything on Don's plate and orders up another pitcher of beer. 'Put it on my tab,' he tells the waitress. Told us he'd be happy to pay our fare back out to the CRAB MAGNET too. Mister Big Shot. There's your federal tax dollars at work, Lowrie."

"But where'd DD go?"

"Do you by any chance know where Highway 101 runs right by that little town of Trinidad? I mean right by it.'

"Yeah ... I mean no but just go on. So?"

"Couple hours later I was completely free to go and I caught up with Don standing on the ramp onto southbound 101. The Coast Guard and the harbormaster's men had inspected that rusty tub and turns out everything about the CRAB MAGNET was out of compliance except for the catch cloggin' up the hold. No opium, no dope, no Canadian cigarettes, no booze, but man—the registration papers, the skipper's license and permits, the logbook—they were all just wrong. Out of date, expired, pages missing—what a clusterfuck."

"Nice talk...."

"What?" Ross shifted his weight, sipped his coffee, and looked overhead to follow a flurry of band-tail pigeons passing high.

"Ross, why'd DD run away?"

"He didn't run away, Katie. He just thought faster than me and Jake and split before they declared they were impounding the CRAB MAGNET and before maybe arresting us—for fuckin' nuthin'."

"They impounded it?"

"They did. Confiscated our catch too. Turns out they can do that, fuckin' feds. Lookin' like Don and Jake and me'll never get paid for almost a whole week's work out on the water."

"So, where'd DD go? I keep asking you."

"I just told you. When I caught up with him he was stickin' out his thumb. Told me he had better things to do down in Mendocino. Since nobody was ever going to pick me up hitchhiking on the side of any fuckin' highway, I waited for the daily Greyhound headed down the coast. Stopped off in Fort Bragg, checked the mail, grabbed my stuff, and came back to the Santa Cruz Mountains where I am right now, murder capital of the world."

"But where'd he go?"

"Don't know."

"Where'd he say he was going? Where in Mendocino?"

"I don't know. Inland. I told you, I don't know and that's the truth. I know he had connections with people in Willits, all around there. Don went his way and I went mine, back to the murder capital."

"Shit!"

"But that's what they're callin' it, Katie."

"Yeah, I know. I don't mean that."

"Say Santa Cruz to anybody and they'll say, 'Santa Cruz, the murder capital of the world.' I'm glad they caught that one maniac's been killin' people left and right and doing the weirdest shit with their dead bodies. Rape, mutilation, all the rest. I hope that guy burns in hell."

"Ross, stop it."

"I do. Never thought I'd be rootin' for the pigs. Turns out there's at least two crazed killers out there, Jesus! First thing I did when I moved in the doublewide was re-key the locks."

"Oh, Ross, I'll be right back."

Katie returned with more cookies, plied him with more coffee and, instead of sitting down, started pacing the deck, finally resting her palms on the railing and looking out over the hillside. Fingers hooked into her belt loops, she stood swiveling in place so that her jeans came up higher on her torso. "But what's he been doing all this time? What did he do when he wasn't fishing last year?"

"Bummed around the Pacific Northwest, I guess. I don't mean he was a bum. I mean odd jobbin'. Tryin' t'stay alive, you know?"

"Does he have a girlfriend? Has he ever told you he had a girl-friend?"

"Oh, Katie...."

"Girlfriends then, okay? Come on, Ross."

"I guess he's shacked up with one or two ladies along the way. He didn't say much about it."

"*Shacked up*, huh? Were they sluts?"

"Jesus, Lowrie! Your mother know you talk like that? I have no idea, okay?"

"Where is he now, Ross? I mean, I believe what you're saying, but where do you think he might be."

"I was just thinkin' how that PO box in Fort Bragg is paid for up till the First of July. You might try writin' to him there."

"Does he check it?"

"Could be. Used to. You could try."

She turned and bowed her head. "We haven't heard from him since Christmas. It's almost two years since he's been home. Two years, Ross, and he only just turned eighteen a couple months ago."

"I know it."

"It's not like he's away at summer camp. This is serious."

"Could be worse. He could be in jail, Katie, or in the army. They're not shippin' guys over to 'Nam anymore but they're still shippin' 'em back, dead and fucked up."

"My mom's best friend just lost her nephew over there. Farm kid named Duane from up around Willits, as a matter of fact. As soon as he graduated from Davis he won the lottery and lost his life."

"Shit, that's bad luck."

"But I seriously doubt DD has even registered for the Selective Service."

"You're probably right there. Hey, I can ask around. Down in Santa Cruz Harbor, up in Princeton."

"Yes, please. Would you do that, Ross?"

"Somebody might know what happen to the good ol' CRAB MAGNET. Maybe the feds hauled it out to sea, shot holes in it, and sunk the fucker. Maybe the Hawaiian Eye is using it for his own midnight drug runs, who knows? I'll ask around, Katie. Everybody knew Donald the Duck and they liked him too, the salty pup."

"And I'll write to that PO Box 179."

"Damn, you're good. That's the number all right. I couldn't remember it a second ago."

"I remember it."

"Sounds like a plan. So.... You want me to cut down the little fruit trees, do you, except that one big pear? And tear down all the old lath too, right?"

"Just like we said. I suppose none of that lath's worth saving."

"I'll burn it along with other trash. Cut and split the firewood to your stove size. You'll show me where you want it stacked. How about I start next month, that okay?"

"Sure. How long do you think it'll take?"

"Don't know. Week at the very most. They'll be lots a' noise, you know? Your ma....?"

"She'll be okay. She's pretty hard of hearing now and you never know when she'll fall asleep. Just do what you have to do."

"I'll do her right."

"I know you will. That's why I called you...."

They exchanged nods of mutual affection or at least familiarity and sat silently within ear shot of the pounding surf. In the twenty years since graduating from high school together, each had settled on a certain measure of the other that allowed for tolerance; further intimacy was not in the equation.

"Well, guess I'll let ya' go. Now where the hell's those dumbshit dogs a' mine?" He raked his moustache out of the way and used two fingers to produce a shrill whistle.

"Before you go, Ross, tell me what's going on at the end of New Faith Lane?"

"You mean those hippies?"

Three panting dogs showed up on the bank above the deck.

"I've seen hippie camps and shantytowns in the mountains ever since I was a kid but that setup's about as gross as I can remember. Who are they, Ross? It sure doesn't look like any New Holy City to me."

"I don't know who they are. I figure they're a bunch a' acidheads from the City trippin' out down here while the sun shines. They'll clear out soon's the rains come."

"They're not trespassing?"

"Not on my place they ain't. I don't care what they do so long as they stay on the other side of that chain I put up. That ain't no shantytown, Katie. That's just a place for them to camp their vans at for free." He turned in his chair. "Where'd those dogs go to now, damnit?"

"What do your redneck neighbors in New Faith think about the situation? Those people livin' up there for a generation or two or three. Don't they want to run them out or sick the sheriff on them?"

"None of those old timers are callin' any sheriff. They'll just load their guns if there's theft or somethin'. There's squatters like that all over the mountains, like you just said. One good rainstorm, a hard frost, they'll knock down their wigwams and move on south, I figure. They're not comin' onto my property, I can tell you that fur shure. Nobody's runnin' 'round half-naked around my place. Hell, if you'd come in on my driveway, you'd never even seen those freaks. Far as I can tell, they don't shoot guns or arrows and they don't ask to use my bathroom. I don't know their names and they don't know mine. I say let 'em be."

"But what if they have a big Deadhead gathering? What if there's a wildfire or they start asking to use your fridge or run electricity from your house? Will you still be full of Peace and Love then?"

"I'll give 'em an old Whole Earth catalogue and tell 'em to go shoppin' up in Berkeley—how about that? Oh, don't sweat it, would you? They're too screwed up to get anything together. Anymore they probably don't know what an emergency is. Five-point-five earthquake? Nine-point-five? What earthquake? They're hardcore stoners, Katie. Acidheads."

"Hardcore goners, you mean. Does that crazy goose belong to them?"

"I don't know who that bugger belongs to, tell you the truth. Been up there a while. I know Lloyd and Louise Hanover didn't keep geese. She had lap dogs and he had hunters. Sure is belligerent, isn't he? But he's better than a guard dog at scarin' off any strangers snoopin' around."

"Won't some big dogs get at a feral goose running wild like that?"

"I know my dumb Setters won't," Ross answered, pausing to whistle in his dogs. "That big ol' Graylag would probably whoop Little Red's ass if they had a confrontation. I really don't know who would come out on top. Motherfucker can be mean. I notice you still don't have any geese here on your place. Plenty of hens and roosters and those guinea fowl. And that spaced-out Billy goat still down there in the field but no geese. Probably smart. They can be a real pain in the ass." He yawned and raised both arms in a stretch above his head. "You hear where Monteflores got the green light for Phase Two?"

"No, I didn't. They haven't finished Phase One yet, have they?"

"Doesn't matter," he replied, rising to his feet. "Since Prop Twenty got passed, they're afraid they might be slowed down or have to do things different now. Ol' Cummings is quicker and slicker than green spring grass passin' out one of his prize bull's ass. Or I guess it's his kid now, Cummings Junior, runnin' the show. When it comes to gettin' the good people of Fern to annex another piece of his land, so they can extend city services further out.... Junior's good at that."

The Irish Setters showed up and their master ordered them down to the jeep; Baby Blue Eye went tumbling after.

"What a travesty," Katie continued as they headed down the stairs. "I read that by population Fern is now something like the third smallest incorporated city in all of California."

"Japs own that town now. YO-MIZO-fuckin'-SATA or whatever it is. People a' Fern don't seem to care. They're goin' to keep cavin' int' every demand comes out of Cummings Junior's mouth. Whatever," Ross declared, stuffing a wad of tobacco into his mouth. "I don't shive a git."

"You really don't care or you're just sayin' that?" Katie inquired, watching the man's dogs settling in the back of the jeep while Ross zipped the rear flap closed. "I can't believe you don't care at all, Ross."

"Yeah? What the hell can people like you and me do about it? Get this: pushin' back against Prop Twenty, that developer outfit ... what're they called...?"

"Sea-to-Summit?"

"That's them. So, they put a full-page ad in the Mountain Lookout rag."

"... I didn't see that. What for?"

"Like an open letter to the public and to the City of Fern.... How'd it go? Wait, I think I still have it." He fetched a copy from his jeep. "Read this shit."

Katie adjusted her eyes and read aloud: "The applicant respectfully requests that the City of Fern as the ultimate beneficiary of this project shall take full responsibility to obtain and pay all the fees for obtaining the state permits to satisfy the new environmental regulations—"

"...blah blah blah," Ross interrupted. "And Fern city council went for it, Katie. Can you believe that shit? Editorial in the Sentinel came out and called it a cabal or something. What exactly's a 'cabal' anyway?"

"Don't ask me. I didn't know you read newspapers, Ross Stewart. It's bad news you're reporting but I'm proud of you."

"You won't be so proud of me if I ever have to ask for a job at Monteflores. They're about the only bunch does any real hiring this side of the hill."

"I doubt that'll happen. Say, wait a minute. I've got some of the first strawberries set aside in the fridge. You'll eat 'em if I give 'em to you, won't you?"

"Bet your ass I will, you Whole Earth Mama!"

Upon her return, his jeep was idling, and he was ready to roll. "You're all right, Lowrie," he said, "no matter what people say." Securing the plastic bag of berries on the passenger seat next to the cookies sandwiched between a pair of paper plates, he put the jeep in gear. "Say hi to your ma for me."

"I will. Thanks, Ross."

"Early next month."

"See you."

He flashed her the peace sign and made his way onto the raised roadway running between the nutgrass in one ditch and the horsetail in the other.

*

With her employer's encouragement, after weeks of negotiating the tipsy portable toilet leaning into the overgrown coyote bushes and dragging a garden hose to shower behind the barn, Letty graduated to using the bathroom in the main house. When some small mammal littered behind the rotten planks stored deep in the barn, Katie insisted the Coloradan sleep in the house, and they arranged her son's childhood room to accommodate the young woman. First up most mornings, Letty fed the dog, made coffee, and fixed herself breakfast before opening up the glasshouse in hopes that a new flush of dahlia cuttings would be available for snipping and slipping into planting trays, where their baby leaves and stems could be pushed for faster growth with heating mats below, grow lights above, and timely doses of mild liquid fertilizer.

"When your son comes home I'll go back outside," Letty volunteered.

"You'd have to figure that out with him. He didn't want to sleep under the same roof with us old ladies for years."

Adventurous, self-educating Santa Cruz garden designers were learning that the Redwood Coast Nursery was where to procure hardy and reliant varieties of trendy perennials for use in their artisanal, gourmet gardens being installed and maintained from Half Moon Bay to Carmel. Katie and Letty raced to pump out the always popular coral-colored passion flower, and the RCN became the regional source for a lemon-scented jasmine from the Azores which, while tender to a frost, was a welcome relief from the overused pink jasmine and white potato vines or the common yellow winter jasmine which Caltrans plastered all over its highway sound walls.

After the spring rush, when Letty had proven invaluable, Katie gave her a raise and, once the nursery ran out of the season's first round of fuchsias and ivy geraniums, they readied the glasshouse for another batch, pre-sold to commercial accounts. Otherwise, Letty spent her days rotating between workbenches in various inside-outside structures on the hillside or hunkered down at the dirt pile, shifting plants into larger containers. Whenever urgent matters like watering or making deliveries let up, Letty yielded the machete with gusto and her shearing blades with flair, increasing the inventory of acanthus and saxifrage, or she would break open wooden half-barrels bursting at their seams with overgrown callas, naked ladies, torch aloes, and red-hot pokers. When Katie determined that they had sold all the herbaceous perennials she could afford to release without depleting her stock plants, she set the survivors aside so that, as time permitted, her helper could use a dull blade or a spade to whack away at the root clumps, dividing the plants into yet smaller pieces. With little guidance from her employer, the young woman seemed to relish using sand, perlite, vermiculite, and soil to concoct various recipes meant for growing plants with differing demands. If the sun shone and multiple extension cords let her play the radio stations of her choice, Letty seemed happiest when left alone to work.

Although their flowering displays regularly stunned tourists and reminded locals of floral treasures native and naturalized along their own coastal strip, Katie accepted that she could no longer, with impunity, scavenge plants from Cliffport's bluffs and gullies. She might have been able to get away with further raids upon the cattail pond at the bottom of Lower Steep Creek, but she no longer felt right about yanking plants from the little freshwater wetland the redwing blackbirds, song sparrows, marsh wrens, and western pond turtles made their year-round home. However, prying offsets from older plants, cutting stems or roots, diving clumps, Letty had plenty of material to work with and showed a knack for propagation; a high percentage of her handiwork struck. She also knew just when to open or close the glasshouse vents, when to give the trays an extra shower of mist, and when to sit still a bit longer than customary, listening to the elder Lowrie ramble or reminisce after supper or lunch. The Redwood Coast Nursery's proprietor realized she was finally free to take a vacation from Cliffport—or at least to spend a few nights away.

Ross used his chain saws to fell, limb, and buck the dead trees and employed his gas-powered log splitter for the firewood he stacked in one long, neat, chest-high pile, while building pyramidal mounds of the thinner branches for kindling. The first time he had noticed Elise in her house robe out on the deck—watching the orchard go down—he killed the engine and approached the house but stopped short when she waved him off, gesturing for him to go on with his work; the next time he turned around, she was gone, and for the rest of the time he worked there, he never saw her outside again.

The first day Katie called Ross inside for soup and bread, she regretted witnessing how sorely the man was taken aback by Leticia Morales' presence. The girl came in to lunch without ceremony, washing her hands at the kitchen sink, making herself at home between the kitchen and the dining table. When Katie introduced them, they only nodded at each other and, without speaking a word, Ross finished his soup, took his plate to the sink, and went back outside, thereafter carrying a brown bag lunch and a steel Stanley thermos full of hot coffee to Cliffport, shying away from the main house altogether.

During the second week, he brought in a ten-horsepower stump grinder with carbide steel blades and wrestled the equipment up the slope. Katie paid a visit to see how the grinder worked, and he again apologized if the noise upset her mother. "Thirty years ago, we'd have these things dynamited out in an hour. Twenty years ago, we'd a' burned 'em out but not no more. The 'environment'—Jesus! You want to call this off and leave the stumps in the ground? I could drill some holes, pour in some poison, and let 'em rot down the middle."

"No way, Ross. I plan to be putting plants in this ground. No poison."

"Okay then, boss lady. I'll be shoveling out lots of sawdust. Want me to throw it around or burn it too? On an environmentally approved 'burn day' a' course!"

"Don't you dare burn it. Save it. I'll use it for compost. Just pile it over there."

"Fur shure, Missus Lowrie." He grinned and gave her a mock salute. "That's what I'll do."

———

Katie had done as Pieter had bid, revisiting Soquel in March and in April and, opening the cabin, she found the scat of rodents paying house calls, if not yet committed to setting up homes. Walking the grounds, looking for other signs of disturbance, she was waylaid by the beauty in Hendrika Tuelling's private park. The pink and white drooping flower clusters of a ten-foot tall lily-of-the-valley; the coral rose of the semi-double flowers on one vigorous, upright camellia; the show of pure white flowers covering a waist-high rhododendron with fuzzy green leaves—she dropped to her knees on the pine needles and squirrel-whittled cones, wanting to pitch a tent and spend the night right there in order to wake to the scents of the place and to its sounds. During her first visit, she sauntered into the half-shell enclosure with its collection of plants wasting away. Few signs of green life showed under the bark or beneath her thumbnail when she scratched the defoliated bushes. Standing on the rim of the rough lawn, Katie looked out to the mountains and resolved to bring a sandwich—maybe even her guitar—on her next visit. The seclusion would be a perfect setting to test out her playing and her singing voice, or at least restringing the Martin after almost two years without using either instrument.

In the Davenport Store, she picked out a postcard with a panoramic view: beyond close-up clumps of blooming naked lady lilies, some unnamed coastal headland jutted out into the Pacific Ocean in the background:

> *Dear Pieter. Rodents getting into cabin. Park*
> *blooming like crazy—so beautiful! I have a*
> *helper at RCN this spring—staying small but profitable*
> *as per your advice, Inspector T! Hope you are well. Best, KT*

The clerk threw on some stamps and they both expressed hope that the message would reach him in a timely manner. Within two weeks, she received a thin aerogramme:

> *12/4/73 Wolcot Knoll. Dear Katie. I thank you for your kind-*
> *ness in writing. I remain at Anneke's home while she rests*
> *in Hospice House. It is not a happy situation for anyone*
> *but best we can do. I am not certain when I return to USA.*
> *Before rats move in to stay please spread some poison bait.*
> *You can pick it up at Mel's Feed Store (Aptos) where I am*
> *sure they will put it on my account or if not I pay you back.*
> *If plants are dry please water when you are there—good*
> *to keep the pump primed too. The floriculture of England*
> *is wonderful consolation for me during this terrible time.*
> *I take the children of my nieces and nephews to public*

*gardens once a week with some success. One of their fathers
said I am a welcome "avuncular" addition to family. Alone
I visited the airbase where I met Hendrika during WWII
before she became my wife. Why does life have to be so bitter
and so sweet too? Knowing you are there to read this eases
my mind and gives me courage.
I thank you very much for everything. En amité, bien à
vous,* Pieter T.*

When Katie revisited Soquel, she did not bring her guitar, but she
did carry a moisture meter and brought along a pad of lined writing
paper and a ballpoint pen. After she had baited for rats and field mice
along the wallboards, underneath the kitchen sink, and in the foul
toilet closet, she locked up the cabin and checked on the scraggly individual plants in the special collection. Three-fourths were dead and
the soil in the root zones of the other fourth seemed moist enough;
they would need something other than water if they were to survive.
Although the empty holes in the old orchard's terraces in Cliffport
were ready to receive the special planting mix and transplanted specimens, Katie sensed that the grandiose project that Pieter Tuelling
had proposed might in fact never happen. Back in the little park, the
fragrance from one loose, open, rangy rhododendron with funnel-
shaped white petals tinged with pink overpowered her self-control;
she flopped down cross-legged—crying, laughing, praying to she knew
not what or whom.

Under the pine, the picnic table's bowed and buckled planks
sported irregular patches of lichen—green, yellow, and rusty orange.
Katie positioned herself there with paper and pen, turning her back to
the distracting forest-clad ridges receding into haze.

---

* *In friendship, best to you (Fr.)*

May 8th

Dear Donald,

I have been writing this letter to you in my head
ever since I found out from Ross how crabbing season
ended. Can you come home now for a visit with your
grandmother? It has been half a year since you sent her
a card but you are never forgotten in her thoughts and
prayers. She wants to see you—so do I. We want to know
you are OK.

Mom's knee/back surgery is on hold while the
doctors watch for any further symptoms of angina and
arrhythmia. Dr. Healy says if her heart condition stabi-
lizes she can have an operation this fall. She's tapering
off some of her medications but starting others so
honestly I'm not that hopeful.

I know the pressure you felt coming from me and
how badly you needed to put distance between us. But
please send your grandmother a note. It would do more
good for her than any medication or operation. She does
not know I'm writing to you now on her behalf (as well
as mine).

After the brutal freeze last December most plants
recovered and I've made progress in the veggie garden
too. Things are different in the nursery since I hired a
steady helper who gets along with everyone and carries
more than her own weight. She enjoys her free time in
"good times" Santa Cruz too. Baby Blue Eye is starting
to slow down and mope around. The vet says she's missing
Mother Merle and getting older too.

Please try to read this letter more than once. I'm
going to send it and cross my fingers you check for
your mail in Ft. Bragg. The main thing is you believe
me when I tell you that your grandmother can't bear to
imagine never seeing you again.

I pray this finds you well and I send it for the two
of us here, with all the love in our hearts, your mother.

Chapter 10

Friends of the Family

"He said to remind you, you still have some planting mix to pick up. Who is that guy? He said he's 'a friend of the family.'"

"Is that what he said? *A friend of the family*?"

"Was he once your ag agent or something?"

"Yeah, he was my ag agent, I guess. But he's gotten to be much more than that to Mom and me. He is a friend of this family now."

"Is that his place you go to in Soquel when he's away?"

"Yup."

"To take care of his nursery?"

"There's no nursery. I just check to make sure everything's okay. There's a big garden, like a little private park where I liked to hang out."

"Is he rich?"

"No ... no, I don't think Pieter Tuelling is rich. It's not a fancy place, Letty, but it's primo."

"He was driving a brand new Chevy pickup—"

"... he was?"

"... with a deluxe camper on top. Looked new to me. It still had dealer plates. I'd like to have a rig like that the next time I go traveling—no, boss, don't sweat it. I'm not thinking about leaving anytime soon."

"Don't scare me like that. You better not be thinking of leaving. Did he go over to the house?"

"He brought your mother some presents, I think."

"I better go see what's going on. You okay for now? I'll help you with—"

"... I already did those."

"Oh, Letty! Don't you dare start thinking about moving on."

"Katie?"

"Yeah?"

"Can I see that guy's private park sometime?"

"For sure. I'll need your help hauling a big pile of soil out of there. But let me go see what my mom has to say."

Sitting with Elise, flipping through Pieter's house gift—*Een Nederlandische Herbarium-Florilegium*, a coffee table book of botanical art with images copied from early woodcut herbals and painted illustrations, the annotations in Dutch, English, German, Spanish, and French—Katie sampled the bite-size milk chocolate windmills he had left and listened to her mother's account of his surprise visit. Elise remained confused about the Dutchman's current living situation. After having stayed on in England following the death of his sister, he had been back in California for several weeks, residing in some cabin on a ridge. Or was he living out of his new camper while preparing to take off on a road trip? In any case, her mother relayed his clear message: Katie was to visit as soon as possible when—mornings until noon—Pieter could be found puttering about the premises before taking care of business elsewhere in South County.

*

When the man appeared at the cabin's screen door, Katie was still taking in the bright, blue Chevrolet Cheyenne Special C/30 pickup with dual-rear wheels and a detachable camper on top.

"Why, it's Katie Lowrie, here so soon!"

"I was told to get here 'as soon as possible.' Pieter Tuelling, how are you?"

They almost embraced but she held back, and his two paws settled on enveloping her extended right hand. "No Baby Blue dog today?" he asked, pumping her arm.

"Blue's taken a fancy to Letty. You met Letty, right? Blue hangs around with her now."

"*Jaja*, I met your helper. That one there's a keeper, Katie. I can see that in a blink of the eye."

"But there's no trash in your cab yet?" Katie remarked, eying the interior.

"It's still early," Pieter replied, "give me time. *Ach*, Missus Katie Lowrie, my favorite California native human being! Come into the house, come in."

A dozen of Drika's watercolors were tacked on the walls of the front room. Two raw pine bookcases were stuffed with books. An leather steamer trunk and a wooden storage chest sat open in the second room.

"Now you sit down there and I make us coffee. *De koffie verkeerd, eh?*" •

"Sure, thanks."

He hastily refilled his clear glass mug with water from a crazed ceramic pitcher with painted wildflowers fading on its side. "*Ach!* I forgot how good this spring water here at Nico's is. I get you a glass too." He took a second stein from the open-faced cupboard. "Then I got to serve you the real coffee!"

She surveyed the cutout handles of the wooden serving tray sitting in the center of the blue-and-white gingham cloth draping the table. Within its raised sides, the tray held a lidded sugar bowl, a covered butter dish, a napkin holder stacked with folded linen, and a set of milk glass salt-and-pepper shakers painted by hand in blue, a Dutch girl depicted on the salt and a Dutch boy on the pepper.

"Did you bring these things back from England?"

"*Nee nee*, those were in Corralitos."

"This place is looking good, Pieter. You are too."

• *Upsidedown coffee, yes? (Dutch)*

"I feel good. *Jaja*, I feel ... much better now. And you, Katie, you look more ... relaxed. Your face, Katie...."

"If you mean my crazy eye's not crossing, you're right, not lately anyway. Not since Letty moved in. But are you living here now full-time? My mom couldn't figure out from what you said...."

"*Jaja*, more or less, I'm living here now. That place of mine in Corralitos.... I came back, I took one look, I said, 'Piet, this monkey business isn't for you.' Mold everywhere. Termite damage. Junk inside and out. I never want to see that place again, Katie. Not to rent, not to lease, nothing. So, I sell, as is."

"You already have it sold since you've been back?"

"*Nee*, I will sell it. *Ach!* I let that place go to hell, Katie. So, I took out of there what I want to keep here, and I pay the Mexican men to clean it out. Haul it away, use it, sell it, I don't care. The realtor man, he says at least to give that house one coat of paint. Okay, so, let them paint it too. I can't deal with that house. Too many memories, eh? They're loading up my bed, my chair ... *armoire* ... *escritoire*—all like that, what I need to live like a lord right here, ha! They bring it all, maybe today while you're here, I don't know." He paused. "*Jaja*, Pieter's living at Nico's from now on, sure enough."

"For good?"

"I think so, Katie, I think so. Fix it up a little. Get me a new sink and a new toilet in that water closet in there. Replace the windows maybe before next wintertime, eh? I think so ... I think so. Here we go. Be careful now, is hot. You're going to like this, I hope. You help yourself to sugar, just don't do like me," he said, chuckling while shoveling two rounded tablespoonsful into his mug.

They sat to the sweetened coffee and an open box of imported *koekjes*. He thanked her for taking care of the place during his time abroad then confessed that he had disabused himself of any illusions about salvaging Pieter's decimated collection of rhododendrons and camellias by moving the skeletons to Cliffport. Yes, he reported having seen where she had prepared the terraces of the former orchard site, and he expressed his deep regret for the extra work he had caused her;

he promised to compensate her for all expenses incurred. Tapping on her knee, blinking twice, he rose with a grin and retrieved a book wrapped in paper tissue, setting it down on her woven placemat. "I took this to Cliffport yesterday but ... you see ... I wanted to put it into your hands myself ... like this." He slid her the gift and lifted his dangling, horn-rimmed glasses to his eyes to watch her reaction.

Katie leafed through the first pages of a pictorial guide to the great gardens of the British Isles, a hardbound book filled with historical images, contemporary color photographs, diagrams of the garden designs, maps, driving directions, cross-indexes, and plant lists galore. "Oh, Pieter, this is fantastic!"

"You go perhaps to England one day, Katie. Who knows?"

She left the book open in her lap and looked at the crooked, yellowed teeth revealed below the thin white moustache. "You were so sweet to think of this for me and that beautiful art book for my mom."

"*Nee*, is not enough...." he responded, averting his blue eyes and passing his left hand's swollen fingers across the top of his disheveled white hair. "Not enough...."

Katie rewrapped the book within the tissue paper and set it at the far end of the table. "How have you been, Pieter? What's been going on with you ... inside?"

"*Ach!* Is a story with a long tail."

"Tell me. I've got time. Letty's working for me now, remember?"

Even after Anneke's memorial services, Pieter had lingered at Wolcott Knoll until he no longer felt needed, gradually planning then finally pretending to travel in the Netherlands before returning to the United States. In fact, he had gone to London and stayed there, submersed in an extended gin bender before waking to the nightmare that his life had become and would remain if he didn't change. That was when he gave up drinking, he said.

Katie scanned the dishware on the open cupboard shelf and the kitchen counter: no suggestion of alcoholic beverages anywhere.

Pieter shared his master plan. Once the Corralitos property went into escrow, he was going to spend an undetermined length of time living out of the new camper on an unimproved piece of property along the Mattole River between the localities of Mattole and Honeydew. The land was owned by his fellow expatriates, Roger and Martine van Waes; Roger was his longtime steelhead- and salmon-fishing buddy and still worked as a Santa Barbara County ag agent. In the absence of the husband and wife, Pieter would try turning over stones, spending his days and nights alone with the plants and animals in remote Humboldt County; there would be no real angling this time of year but lots of time for walking in woods quiet enough to hear himself think for a change. He had big fat biographies of Van Humboldt, Darwin, and John Muir he wanted to read. "Maybe I can give up these too, eh?" he said, reaching for a tin marked "Panter Mignon" and extracting a thin, four-inch, tan-wrapped cigarillo before lighting up. He needed, he concluded, to figure out what to do with the rest of his life.

She watched his cheeks, ears, and nose flush rose as he smoked in silence, perhaps regretful of having exposed himself so nakedly. Eyes downcast, lids so lowered they might as well be closed, Pieter shot her a pleading glance, winced, then began to flesh out the horror of his London binge during which he had been overcome by the fact that he now had no wife, no brothers or sisters, no parents or grandparents; his only surviving relatives were the nieces and nephews in England and some distant cousins in the Netherlands; and, of course, he had no children of his own. He fell silent again, puffing on his cigarillo, then briskly scrubbed one palm across his face as if washing and drying it with a cloth. He wasn't asking for pity, he added, pity he did not deserve. But how ashamed he was that, since Nico's death, his recourse had been to drown his doubts in alcohol, a dependence only worsening after Drika passed away. And for the first time, he confirmed Katie's suspicion that he had prevented her from ever visiting his Corralitos address because he had been too embarrassed by the condition in which he had been living since his wife's death. Sober since his flight back to America, he had overheard a home inspector describing to his realtor the squalid state of the unmaintained ranch house and known that its neglected, pathetic condition only reflected his own.

"But how are you, Missus Katie? How is Elisabeth, really now? She told me nothing, not to worry me. But you tell me, I listen. Your nursery looks so good, so good." [1]

Katie emphasized how Leticia Morales' presence had lightened her workload. After the historical December freeze, spring sales had been brisk and her fall crops—including the perennials which Pieter had helped introduce into her inventory—were coming along nicely. Letty's residence was also providing a measure of relief in the household where, whatever else Elise might have told him, her mother's health was not good: the knee and or back surgeries she so badly needed were indefinitely postponed due to her weakening heart, and her sight and hearing were not as sharp as before, nor was her power of recollection so keen. Also, Donald Duncan remained incommunicado—which grieved Elisabeth—and Katie had heard nothing back after her last attempt to reach him by mail.

*

"I knew you had it in you, but I didn't know you had this much," Katie commented, as they re-circled the Cheyenne.

"How much it cost, do you mean?"

"Not that. How much truck you'd end up getting, I meant, and with a complete camper too. That's not a shell, that's a house on wheels."

"*Jaja.* When I got back to Corralitos, that Dart didn't start after sitting there since February, eh? So, I said okay I get another battery and keep that leaking car alive. But what do I need that monkey business for? The same as when I looked at the house, eh? *Que basura!*" They both laughed at his Spanish. "I pay for this monster here the day the house sells. Listen to me, Katie. I was a whore for the chemical companies for years and now the county pays me a pretty nice pension. I got no mortgage on this place here and soon I have *mas dólares* from selling that *hacienda poquito* in Corralitos. In a few more years? Social security—"

"... and more *dineros.*"

"*Si, señora, mas dineros!* Is like the water in your redwood tank. It goes down then comes up then goes down then comes up. My checking account goes from zero to zero every month and still I got plenty money coming in. Is lucky when you live in America...."

Lucky lager beer.... Katie heard the old advertising jingle in her head but, given her interlocutor's fragile situation vis-à-vis *las bebidas alcohólicas*, she refrained from voicing it aloud.

Crossing the yard, Pieter waved toward a dented, hollow copper weathervane shaped like a sitting duck but lying sideway on the ground near where the barn's sliding door still hung askew from the broken top rail. He planned to have the weathervane from Corralitos stuck up on the roof—"just for ducks, eh?" Pieter again expressed his gratitude for her having raked off the garden plant debris, deep-watered the shrubbery, and baited and re-baited the rattraps in the cabin and the springhouse; rounding the soil mound he said hoped she would still accept the special planting mix as a token of his appreciation. Katie paused to size up the load and wondered if, in lieu of hitching her low-sided nursery hauler and making multiple trips with the Ford, she could enlist Ross's help. With all the equipment he had sitting idle up in New Faith, he might manage to transport the whole pile to Cliffport with ease. In any event, using the Bobcat's front loader would make more sense than loading and unloading so many cubic yards by the shovelful.

They ambled onto the unkempt lawn where, out of flower, the fulsome forms of the grown-out shrubbery and trees still entranced her. With Pieter Tuelling, she could openly share her love for the plants, even while he lamented having missed the optimal timing for properly pruning and grooming them that spring. While Katie pointed out which bushes had—to the best of her recollection—charmed her most when coming into and going out of bloom, he deftly pinched off shoot tips with the broken thumbnails of his stout fingers, snapping off the sprigs and twigs he found ungainly and deadheading spent trusses with a quick push of his fat thumb against the bases of old flower clusters. Near the springhouse, a new wheelbarrow loaded with one-inch garden hoses still tied in twine suggested that the proprietor did indeed intend taking better care of Drika's park.

As they settled down on the wobbly bench, he announced that he would be purchasing a new picnic table set when he returned from Humboldt County, if not before. Katie volunteered to tend to the park when he went away on his retreat. He faintly protested; she insisted. "I love it here, Pieter. It's not work for me. It's more like a place of worship. I want an excuse to keep coming back here."

The breeze licked at tufts of his soft white hair. He blinked his eyes and bowed his head. "I hope you don't need any excuse, Missus Katie. You come to Drika's park any time you want. Sure enough, this is the place for people like you and me."

She rose and drifted off, pausing between the massive lily-of-the-valley and a sinuous strawberry tree. Still within his sight, she raised her arm and pointed at a camellia.

"'Shiro Chan!'" he cried out, as if on cue.

She pointed at another.

"'Gullio Nuccio!'" he called, coughing.

She turned in place, pointing again.

"'Kramer's Supreme!'" he shouted, clearing his throat. "That's 'Kramer's Supreme,' Katie!"

She buckled over laughing then one more time stabbed her arm in the direction of another camellia.

"'C.M. Wilson!'" he exclaimed, rising to his feet, one hand holding down his hair. "A variegated form of 'C.M. Wilson!' That's the best sport ever off the 'Elegans'!"

She clapped and performed a pirouette, unable to resist giving him a bear hug the moment he came within reach and, the moment she did, releasing him again and stepping back. "You're so smart and I'm so dumb. How can you stand it?"

"Don't talk nonsense." He looked beyond her. "Did you enjoy those there when they came into blossom?" he asked, raising his eyebrows and gazing toward a bank of medium-green, satiny foliage located between the level ground and redwoods upslope.

"Oh my God, when those were in bloom? It was like the ground was on fire. Orange and red and yellow. They're Western azaleas, right?"

"Those are the deciduous Exbury hybrids."

"Unbelievable...." she muttered, letting out a sigh.

They rested back at the mossy table. Warm air ruffled the foliage of the shrubs and trees. The redwood steeples purred.

"I'm going to write down those names, Katie. Then I get you those plants what you love."

"What'd you say?"

"*Jaja*. We never made it to the Rhodie Show in Fort Bragg this spring but maybe you can get up there by yourself while I'm away, eh? You pick up those plants for Cliffport."

"I don't follow you."

"*Ja*, you can do that, Katie. Where do you think these came from in the first place, eh? There's a place near Fort Bragg called Rhododendron Acres. My friends grow all these plants there, sure enough."

"Oh, I'd love to put those plants in our yard but I can't afford it. I have to sell plants to make a living, not buy them."

"*Nee nee*, you can do both. I buy them for you."

"What?"

"I pay for them, see? I write down the names and you take that list to Jack and Peggy. They take good care of you, sure. Any size you want: one-gallon, two-gallon, five-gallon, seven-gallon. I pay."

"How do you know they have all these plants available?"

"How do I know? Rhododendron Acres on Rhododendron Acres Lane in Fort Bragg?" He took a soiled handkerchief from his back pocket and blew his nose. "How do I know?" His put on his glasses. His narrowed eyes browsed around the grounds as he quietly recited more names: "'Anah Kruschke', 'Anna Rose Whitney', 'Pink Pearl', 'Mi Amor'. All what you pointed at, they got them twice as big as these, three times as big—they grow giants up there. And that straggly 'Fragrantissimum', and that other one there, 'Fosterianum'. You need plenty room sideways for those loosey-goosies. But you picked some good performers too: 'Lemon Mist', 'Snow Lady', 'The Honorable Jean Marie de Montague'—"

"... the who? Oh, Pieter. How can they have each and every one of these? When was the last time you were there?"

"Katie, you listen to your county agent now. A place like Rhododendron Acres does not change. You know how I know that? Jack van Winden's father was a bulb grower in the old country like my Oom Karl, *jaja*. It's almost like Jack and me, like we grew up together. Nothing changes with the polder people, Katie. Jack and Peggy not growing these plants at the end of Rhododendron Acres Lane? *Als de koeien op het ijs dansen.*" •

"What?"

"How you say ... 'When pigs fly...?' *Jaja, dat is het.* When pigs fly," he reiterated, patting his palm on the tabletop and chuckling before his face changed. "Last I heard from Peggy, old Jack doesn't get out of his easy chair much anymore—that sonagun em-phy-sem-a." He let his glasses drop back onto his chest and rubbed his eyes with his fists. "Peggy van Winden, what a wonderful woman that Peggy is, and what a worker horse! Oh, she take real good care of you, I promise you that. You can never go wrong with Peggy and Jack's plants growing in your terrace garden."

"You mean the old orchard?"

"*Jaja*, that is what I mean. And why not? Is an idea anyway."

"They'll do okay there?"

"O, *ja*, they'll do very okay there. You got good water, good light, good planting mix—why not? *Ach*, Missus Lowrie. You can fool me on anything but these kinds of plants, eh? Those ones you picked are all good old plants, Katie, the favorites. You got good taste and common sense to go with those ten darn good green thumbs of yours. If Jack and Peggy don't have those in cans then ... well, then they just don't exist, they never existed, they never will exist. But they do exist, look," he declared, gesturing with an open hand toward their surroundings. "I call Peggy and let her know you're coming. This how I repay you for

---

• *When cows dance on ice. (Dutch)*

... everything. We just forget about those sick and dying sonsaguns over there," he concluded, glancing toward the redwood hedge. "*Dat is nietig en ongeldig.*"

"And now what does that mean?"

"How you say ... in English ... 'null and void'?"

"I guess. Wow!" she said, blowing air out her open mouth. "What a trip! You'll show me where to plant what and...?"

"*En...?*"

"I mean, I guess I'll be sinking them in the holes already there. But can't we go up to Fort Bragg together to see your friends?"

He fidgeted with a splinter lifting away from the weathered tabletop. For a moment, he seemed to Katie like a man habituated to celebrating—or mourning—with a drink in his hand or at his lips. "Maybe ... maybe.... But just for now, you go ahead, Katie. First I got to soak my head in a cold river, eh, then dry it in the sun." He tapped his skull with a fat, curved finger. "Let's see what's left in here."

"Do you realize how generous you're being? How much will all the plants on my wish list cost you?"

"Forget all that, I told you: prostitution pays. What do you think? Maybe this dumb old immigrant will find some gold nuggets in that Mattole River too."

"What do you mean by saying 'prostitution pays' and 'being a whore'? A man has to make a living. You had to make a living like anybody else. I bet you helped lots of nursery people make the best decisions possible."

"I could have done more, Katie. I could have been different ... but...." His words trailed off as he shook his lowered head. "Okay then," he blurted out, pushing off from the unstable table while rising to his feet. "I write down the names of those plants for Cliffport's new ornamental terrace garden. And let's not forget the 'Saffron Queen'. I don't know why it's not here in Drika's park, but it belongs in your display garden. I show you how much room you need for the big ones, sure enough. And how to sink the root balls in those holes—but we got to sink them high, for drainage...."

"If you say so. I'll be putting you to work, 'Pete'."

"I work hard for you, Missus Katie, if I can, if I can."

"Sure, you can. I don't know exactly when I'll get up to Fort Bragg but I will, for sure."

"Before I forget, I give you the number of my new PO mailbox in Soquel. I write it down back in the house."

"You never do answer when I shout at you from Cliffport. A PO Box is a much better way to go."

"And when I come back, I get a telephone too."

"Yes, a telephone! So, you won't be living like a hermit after all."

"A hermit? Better not. Maybe that's not so good for people ... like me, eh?"

While strolling back to the cabin, Katie noticed a sore on the man's forearm when he rolled up his sleeve. "Wait a second, Pieter, what's that?"

"What's what?"

"That on your arm. Did you burn yourself ... or...?"

"Oh, is a mark of some kind. The reward of growing old, eh? I've had it for a while now."

"Wait, show that to me." She stood in his path and made him stop so she could look closer at the asymmetrical patch of brown, black, and blue the size of a silver dollar. "That doesn't look good, Mister Tuelling. Have you had anybody look at it? A doctor I mean."

"You're not the first person who said so, but I been so busy, Katie," he said, rolling down his sleeve.

"So?"

"After Mattole...."

"Pieter. Before."

He muttered something and preceded her back to the cabin.

*

Where the non-maintained lane teed into the non-maintained road, Katie rolled through the STOP sign then idled in the shade, listening until odds and ends ceased banging about in the back of her truck. She glanced down at the jacket illustration on the guidebook to famous British gardens in the British Isles, thinking she would have a hard-enough time getting to Fort Bragg, let alone ever managing any visit to England, Ireland, Scotland, or Wales. But if Pieter Tuelling could finish drying out in Humboldt County, she thought, and if he could stay on the wagon; if he could stop being so hard on himself; if he could make the cabin truly habitable; if he took care of that worrisome sore on his left forearm—then there was less likelihood she would wind up having to take care of the man in his old age, as she had taken care of Jan McLoughlin in her ill old age, as she was now taking care of Elisabeth Adélaide Lowrie in hers too.

———

"He was just here again."

"Who was?"

"That man, Tooley—"

"... Pieter Tuelling was just here?"

"You just missed him."

"Oh, for God's sake! How about he just missed me? Why can't some people learn to use the telephone? So, what'd he say?"

"Here." Letty passed her a scrap of paper with driving directions to Rhododendron Acres in Fort Bragg:

"I sent Peggy the list. You're expected and welcome. Good luck, P.T."

"See what I mean? No phone number for Fort Bragg! Anything else?"

Lifting a wad of moist burlap off some wet newsprint, Letty uncovered a bundle of leafy stems of varying lengths and diameters. "He said to recut these ends, dip them in number two hormone powder, and stick them in some deep tray with peat and sand, or peat and perlite. Then put the trays on bottom heat under mist."

"These are camellias ... from his collection...." Katie murmured, examining several cuttings.

"He said he's going on some fishing trip, so if you could water his garden once later this month and once every two weeks until he gets back. Some contractors will be putting in windows and a new bathroom, so he doesn't want to be around, I guess. I think that's what he meant. He said you'd understand."

"So, he's really doing it," Katie mused aloud, rewrapping the stems, wiping her hands on a paper towel, and taking the packet of sunflower seeds from her breast pocket. "Good for Pieter Tuelling. Anything else?"

"Oh yeah. Before he left he showed me a bandage on his arm."

"What bandage?"

"It's some pre-cancer or—"

"... cancer!" Katie exclaimed, letting her bottom drop onto a high stool. "Oh my God...."

"No, wait, he said it was not cancer, only 'seed cancer' or something like that and not to worry. They caught it in time to scrape if off."

"*Seed cancer...?*" Katie repeated.

"So ... Katie?"

"What?"

"Do you want me to plant those," she asked, nodding at the cuttings cradled in the soaked newspaper, "or what?"

"Oh, yes, plant them, for sure. Do just what he said. Those should all strike."

She sat in silence, brooding, nibbling seeds, holding each husk between a finger and thumb and cracking it with her inwardly tilted upper front teeth.

"Katie...?"

"Yeah?"

"He said not to worry, he's taking care of himself. I think he meant about his skin. Oh, I almost forgot. He said don't wait for him to get back to pick up the planting mix. So ... can I go there with you?"

"Letty, I know you want to see the place, okay? You'll have to go with me unless I can get Ross to haul that pile over here for me—cheap. Maybe I'll put you on deep-watering the park. That can take a couple hours."

"Cool."

"Did Pieter go over to the house?"

"No, I don't think so. He just poked around a little outside then drove off in that big blue machine."

"How'd he look?"

"What do you mean?"

"I mean, was he clean shaven, wearing decent clothes? Or did he look like he just rolled out of bed? You know, Letty: how'd the fat old fart look?"

"Looked fine to me, for a fat old fart. He's pretty light on his feet for such a big guy. Have you ever noticed that?"

"I have. He is, isn't he?"

"Does he have the hots for you or your mom or what?"

Katie lowered her eyebrows and trained her eyes on the younger woman, pocketing her pack of sunflower seeds and alighting from her perch.

"Just no, Letty."

"Just 'a friend of the family...?'"

"Sometimes I feel like he is family, know what I mean?"

————

Responding to Katie's second postcard, Ross showed up one day around lunchtime and they discussed the soil hauling project over quesadillas and bowls of Letty's chili. He dismissed the possibility of renting a dump truck capable of transporting twenty-five yards of soil in one fell swoop: the unstable roadbed of the Lowries' narrow driveway would never support such a vehicle's axle width let alone its gross weight, and if they dumped the mix at the gate, it would block the mouth of the drive and spill onto Grade Road. They might freight it to Cliffport in their pickups, offloading it under the oak before toting it up to the terraces in bags or wheelbarrows; but that would take many roundtrips and leave a heap in the turnaround, only postponing the deposit of the material uphill.

While the man mulled it over, hugging his mug of homemade Mexican coffee brewed by Letty in one of Elise's earthen clay pots, Ross listened to Katie's summary of Monteflores' latest harassment [2] before roundly cussing the "capitalist pigs," then he hit upon a scheme while rolling a cigarette on the chair's arm: he would load the Bobcat and a scoop attachment into the five-by-twelve-foot bed of Lloyd's heavy duty, double-axle, high-sided utility trailer and drive it to Soquel. After filling the trailer with as much soil as it would hold—the Dodge could pull any amount with ease—he would drive to Cliffport, where they could hand-shovel the payload to the bottom of the same pathway he had used while dismantling the orchard. He would return to Soquel however many times it took to move the mound; Ross guess-timated no more than three roundtrips would be required. Of course, he concluded—fishing the orange peel out of his ceramic mug and tossing it over the railing—he would have to go back for the Bobcat at the end, but it could be done in a day if he had help with the shovel work on the Cliffport drops—two days, if Katie wanted him to ferry the mix uphill and leave piles alongside the planting holes; the ground had held up under his stump grinder and would probably support the Bobcat too.

Katie asked how much it would cost; Ross stirred his coffee with a stick of cinnamon which he then also chucked over the railing—Letty swore at him in Spanish—and started rolling another cigarette while paying attention to some rooster freaking out in the yard.

"Hey, Ross, I'm asking you how much."

He pocketed his tobacco pouch and clawed at his horseshoe moustache.

"Ah shit, Lowrie. You know I ain't no good at this part. I don't know how much to ask you for."

"Well, say something. You know I'm not asking anybody else for a quote so just tell me your price, damnit."

Ross sealed his cigarette paper with one lick, lit a wooden match with his thumbnail, fired up his smoke, and snapped his fingers to draw Baby Blue Eye closer in. Avoiding their gazes, he rubbed his hand against the grain of the dog's nape and squinted, as if he were looking for fleas.

"*Madra mierda. Cuánto cuesta, Señor Ross?*" •

He scowled at her and turned toward Katie. "How about one-hundred-twenty-five plus one tank a' gas? That includes getting that dirt up to the orchard."

"What do you think, Letty? Sound good?"

"What? Is this one your fucking partner now?"

"Sounds fair to me, Katie."

"Then it's a deal, Ross."

"It's going to be one long day, ladies. One long two days. Dawn to dusk day one, fur shure."

"Then I'm throwing in lunch, supper, and breakfast, if you get here early enough," Katie said.

"Oh, I'll get here early all right."

"So, I'll finally get to see that place!" Letty exclaimed. "And—"

"... hey, Katie," Ross interrupted her, "you gotta ride with me the first time so I know where it's at. I have no clue where some 'unmarked lane at the top of Soquel Gulch Road' is."

"I'll show you. When can you do it, Ross?"

"Oh, I don't know," Ross parried, patting Baby Blue Eye's rump and chugging down the coffee. "Things are pretty busy right now." He looked from one to the other then grinned, his brown-stained buck-teeth showing below the uneven grate of his untrimmed moustache. "How about tomorrow morning?"

"You got it," Katie declared.

"This'll be cool," Letty chimed in.

"Oh yeah?" Ross countered, turning on her. "They'll be some serious shovel work involved. You sure you can handle a shovel, girl?" he said, leaving his head tilted toward Letty and batting his eyelashes. "Señorita, I mean."

• *Holy shit. How much will it cost, Mister Ross? (Sp)*

"Fuck you, Ross," she replied before they all burst out laughing and the dog barked twice.

"Hey, Lowrie. Your ma got any moonshine in that fridge in there?"

*

Ross ended up making four roundtrips between Cliffport and Soquel. On the first, Katie asked him for news about her son; he had none. On the second, she stayed home to prepare lunch for the work party, and Letty got her chance to see Pieter's cabin from the outside and explore the grounds. Riding shotgun in the cab, she also quizzed Ross about her employer's son: why was he never in touch? Why was he so hard to track down? What was the deal between the boy and his mother, anyway?

"Shit on a stick, now you're grilling me too. Did Katie put you up to this?"

"No, she didn't put me up to anything. I'm just curious. Sometimes his grandmother ... you know, Missus Lowrie...?"

"I guess I know Missus Lowrie, girl. Like ever since I was in fuckin' kindergarten at Mountain School with your boss, I've known Missus Lowrie."

"So, how was I supposed to know that? That old lady is sure a sweetheart," Letty reflected aloud.

Ross shot her a glance. "You got that right. That is one nice person. Put up with my bullshit all these years, I know that much. But I told Katie something and I'll tell you too: I don't know where that kid is, okay? Last time I saw him was hitchhiking out of Trinidad on 101."

"Where's that?"

"Up north. I hope he's okay. Fuck-a-duck, that Donald Duncan Lowrie's like a little kid brother to me. Just seems like he doesn't want us knowin' where he is right now."

"I guess. Sometimes Missus Lowrie gets talking to me and she sort of forgets herself, telling me how worried to death she is about that grandson of hers. I hope my people don't worry like that about me. My grandmother's gone, but at least I call my mother from time to time to put her mind at ease."

During the first delivery, Ross barely managed to negotiate the entrance through the driveway gate posts. "Next the fuckin' fathers and mothers of Fern Metropolis will petition to have the fuckin' name changed from Grade Road to Monteflores Grade Road," he said to Katie riding shotgun. On the second trip, he encountered difficulties keeping the trailer's wheels from slipping over the edges of the causeway-like lane, shouting out to Katie greeting them from the stoop of the welcoming hut under the oak: "I'll fuckin' kill those bastards someday!"

"How about 'The Western Gateway to Monteflores'?" Katie yelled back. "That's what they really want to call this place."

"Assholes!" Ross cried out, wrestling his rig around the turnabout after Letty jumped out.

"You sure you felt safe riding with that maniac?" Katie asked her, lowering her voice.

"Why, 'cuz he's a redneck?"

"He can get a little rowdy sometimes."

"Oh, come on, are you kidding? The guy's a softy. I've got cousins back home who'd make Ross ... what's his last name again?"

"Stewart."

"They'd make Señor Stewart turn red as a chili pepper. Yeah, I felt safe with him. You better ask him if he felt safe with me—no Boulder Colorado Morales take shit."

"I know they don't, Letty, at least you don't. So, if you want to ride back with him again...."

"But I still have to whitewash that glass. The part that got washed off by the sprinkler, remember? Let me get that done then maybe I'll go for a ride on the last trip."

*

Headed north out of Santa Cruz with the Bobcat in tow on their final trip, Ross stopped at Zee's Liquors on Mission Street to pick up a six-pack—or two. Letty held out a ten-dollar bill. "Get a bottle of gold tequila too, okay?"

"How the hell old are you, girl? Ain't you turned twenty-one yet?"

She glowered at him. He spread his lips, bared his brown-stained teeth, and snatched the bill from her hand. She let out a yelp; Baby Blue Eye yapped. "And make one of those six-packs Coors!" she called out to his back.

Upon reaching old Cliffport Town, Ross pulled into the turnout and killed the ignition before each of them popped open a can of beer.

"There's an awful lot a' weed grown in that part of the state where Don's at."

Letty stared ahead; Ross ruminated.

"Ah, gimme that," he blurted out, slipping the bottle of tequila right out of the brown bag between her thighs before she had a chance to stop him. "Just one hit, okay?" He broke the seal, twisted it open, took a swallow, and then passed it back to her without the cap. "Oh yeah! Guess that's why they call it tequila!"

Ross rolled a cigarette and lit up. They sat still, sipping their Coors and taking turns petting the dog, who remained sitting straight up between them, as if watching for whales.

"Wouldn't surprise me he's involved in some of that weed growing too," he said, "but don't you go blabbin' any of this to Katie or Missus Lowrie."

"I won't."

"You hear me? Cuz if you do ... oh fuckin' gimme that back!"

Ross ultimately chased down four slugs of tequila with three cans of beer; Letty took one sip from the bottle and limited herself to the one beer.

"Okay!" he declared, turning the key and flipping her the screw cap. "We don't tell Katie nothin' about this either. Right, Baby Blue?" he added, jamming the last two cans of Coors into the glove compartment. "Thanks for the hits, Letty, now let's go eat!"

"Next time I make us some *café de olla*, it'll put some of this in it, for sure," she said, recapping the tequila.

"Fur shure, Colorado?" he echoed, tossing back his head and howling as he took hold of the steering wheel and used both lanes of empty Highway One to make his wide U-turn.

In their absence, Katie had made a run to Davenport Store and brought back an extra-large pizza and a six-pack of Lucky Lager. Ross plopped his own six-pack of Budweiser on the table and they sat to eat and drink, agreeing that Ross would be leaving his front loader overnight and returning in the morning to transport the bulky mix up to the terraces by the scoopful. "You ladies'll be directing me where to leave little piles and you can use your shovels to spread it out, dainty-like."

On day two, over the last beers, Katie shared her vision of the garden terraces to be planted with the plants she would be fetching from Fort Bragg; the mere mention of Mendocino County alarmed all three, and all three avoided the subject of Donald's whereabouts. While the young people moved out onto the deck, Elise shuffled about in the kitchen, from time to time standing on the pantry's threshold, seemingly skittish about joining them. Katie reassured her that the project had transpired without a glitch, but there would be more noise for a while up behind the house. Ross rose and offered Missus Lowrie her seat, but Elise declined, and Letty escorted her back to her room. On her way back outside, Letty stopped in her room for the tequila and brought it outside along with three ceramic eggcups. They held a toast to the successful relocation of the planting mix and lounged on the deck until Katie paid Ross in cash; he loaded up the last of his tools and cruised down the driveway before dark.

*

LETTY: Would it be okay if I took somebody with me and we spent the night at that Peter's place? Outside, I mean. He's a friend of mine from UC.

KATIE: Sure, I guess. Do you need a tent? I can see if—

LETTY: ... no, that's okay. We have sleeping bags. He has stuff. Don't look at me that way, Katie. I don't know if he's a real boyfriend but he's sure nice to be with and all.

KATIE: What can I say? No campfires though, okay?

LETTY: Oh thanks, Katie, you are so cool!

Katie watched her employee go back to work and seemed to remember a time when all she imagined she needed was a sleeping bag, a boy, a bottle of wine, and a bonfire on the beach.

*

> Dear mom,
> I got your letter. I come to town for laundry supplies and food but I can't get home before thanksgiving, when I see you I'll tell you why. Can you bring grandma to Willits? I'll be at this Redwood Co-op Cafe on the main drag right near Safeway on noon Weds August 29 even if you don't show up.
> Don

Chapter 11

The Redwood Co-op Café

Katie phoned to accept her aunt and uncle's standing invitation, asked them about approximate driving times between Cloverdale, Willits, and Fort Bragg, and waited until the eve of her departure to sit on the edge of her mother's bed and announce that she was combining an overnight stay at Suzanne and Mike's with a nursery expedition to Fort Bragg. Elise resumed her crochet needlework, expressing her satisfaction that her daughter felt welcome at the Crogan's and assuring her that she would manage just fine alone. Katie relocated to the tan-hide rocker.

"Is there something else, dear?" Elise asked, glancing over her spectacles as she yanked more yarn from her bag.

"Not much."

Given the foggy evening chill, her mother had her legs tucked under a navy down comforter and wore a gray-blue shawl. Katie studied the face framed by fairytale-long white hair cascading down the shawl and decided not to mention the rendezvous with DD, instead describing some of the plants that Pieter Tuelling was buying them for their new terrace garden. Elise repeated some of the names, murmuring their sounds, then her stitching resumed. Katie let her rocking come to a stop. "Mom, I've got to tell you something."

"What is it?"

"When I was arranging DD's room, for Letty to sleep in—"

"... wait now, what is it?" she interrupted her, pushing the glasses higher on the bridge of her nose and stilling her hands. "What is it you say you're about to do?"

"That was months ago, Mom, when Letty started sleeping in DD's room."

"Oh, that, yes, that's working out just fine, dear, isn't it? I've grown quite fond of Leticia, you know."

"That's good but this is about Jody, Mom."

"Jody?" Elise removed her glasses and set her crochet needles aside. "What about Jody?"

"I ran across the box where you were keeping his boots. It's empty. Jody's boots aren't there. The box is empty, Mom."

"I know that, Kaitlin."

"You do? So where are they?"

"Donald has them, dear. It's all right. Donald asked permission to take Jody's boots when he left ... how long ago was that?" Elise sighed. "Far, far too long...."

"You're saying you let DD take Jody's boots?" Katie pushed the floor to start the rocker back in motion. "You never told me that."

"Well, he was wearing them for a while, remember? You hadn't put them on for years, had you? He had my permission, Kaitlin. He knew to ask permission of me, not you."

"Why are you saying that?" Katie braked the rocker. "Why do you talk to me like that?"

"I thought that might be what's bothering you. Oh, Kaitlin, don't be silly. I had no money to give him at the start of his big adventure out at sea. But he wanted Jody's boots so I let him have them. Was that so very wrong of me? If it was, I am truly sorry."

"I don't know. How come you never told me about it before?"

"I'm sorry if I've hurt your feelings, dear. The Good Lord knows I don't mean for that to happen, ever."

"No, I know." Katie kicked off the braid rug, quickening the creaking chair's rhythm. "I was just wondering where the boots went, is all."

"Well, now you know, dear," Elise said, reseating her glasses, lifting her needles yet turning her face to look out the darkened windowpane. "Jody was your only brother, Kaitlin. I realize that. But he was also my only son."

Katie studied her mother—an arrangement in whites, blues, and grays—and absorbed the abiding sorrow in her voice. As Elise returned to her needlework, Katie again recognized that her son and his grandmother had always trafficked in a black market of unconditional love which remained out of her jurisdiction. *If a mother's love is blind in one eye, a grandmother's blind in both. But without her love, where would DD be right now? Where is he right now? Maybe she always knows where he goes but pretends not to.* Katie released her breath, pushing down on the rug and up out of the chair. "Goodnight, Mom. I'm going to get an early start in the morning. I'll come say goodbye if you're awake."

Elise lowered her needles and smiled. "Oh yes, please, do that. Now if I can manage to finish this scarf tonight, you will take it to Suzanne for me, won't you?"

"Of course I will."

"But then again, she does always did like a bit more color in her clothing. Your Aunt Suzanne's a 'colorful' person if you know what I mean."

"I'm sure she'll like it, Mom. Goodnight now."

Katie bent forward to kiss her mother's forehead; Elise lifted her eyes.

"You aren't leaving me here all alone for long, are you, Katie?"

"No, Mom. Letty will be here, remember?"

"Oh yes, that's right. Leticia. What was I thinking?"

It seemed to Katie a long time since the pupils of those eyes had been clear hazel, and now they were cloudy gray. "I'll never leave you all alone, Mom. Never." Katie left the door ajar as she exited the room.

In addition to taking care of the nursery for thirty-six hours, Letty's duties would extend to keeping an eye on Mrs. Lowrie, tending to the chickens, and watching to see that Bamboo Billy didn't end up strangling himself on the high wire or otherwise tangling himself up in his cable; no need to mention feeding, watering, and letting Baby Blue Eye out to pee, for the girl and the dog had become inseparable.

———

Mike Crogan's bowling tournament in Santa Rosa allowed the two women to stretch their conversation from the moment Katie arrived mid-afternoon until Mike got home around 9:00 PM. Suzanne couldn't disguise her growing impatience with Donald Duncan Lowrie, citing how that she had changed his baby diapers, as she had on occasion changed Katie's too. What was the boy doing in Mendocino County that was so all-fired important he couldn't visit his ailing grandmother at home? Why couldn't he make the trek to Cliffport? Who did he think he was to expect her to travel all the way to visit him? Katie argued that making the trip to Willits without Elise would at least prevent her mother from being exposed to any bitter new truths that Katie might learn. Suzanne blessed her adoptive niece's wish to protect Elise, and she lamented that eighteen-year-old boys could be so callow, so vain, so self-centered, and just too damn cocky. She protested that the youth was exploiting the loving Lowrie ladies' goodwill. As Katie detailed her mother's frailties, Suzanne pledged to make the trip to Cliffport—soon—insisting that it need not be deemed a mercy mission: Elisabeth Lowrie was her closest, dearest friend. Katie had never thought of Suzanne Crogan—daughter of an extended family from Italian North Beach—as frail in any way, yet in the course of their candid dialogue she learned why Suzanne and Mike had never raised children: two miscarriages and a stillbirth had extinguished their hopes, and 'Ellie' had been Suzanne's chief confidante and consoler through all three experiences.

———

The Redwood Co-op Café's unfinished wooden walls displayed poster portraits of Chief Joseph, Muddy Waters, and the Maharishi. The wagon wheel chandeliers held multicolored bulbs and empty sockets.

Dripping from the ledge of an upright piano's top board, homemade candles had melted into hardened pools of wax covering parts of the keyboard. Katie didn't see her son among the young people milling around the counter waiting to order or among those hanging around the self-service station waiting for their completed orders to be called out, and she didn't spot him seated at any of the wooden spool tables either, so she checked the long hall to the bathroom, its air dense with patchouli incense, its walls overlaid with posters from San Francisco's golden age of Sixties' psychedelic rock: no DD.

She settled on a scratched, lacquered schoolroom chair in an alcove where the house cat lay coiled asleep between a rubber plant's leaning stalks and the cobwebbed tendrils of a hanging pothos. A corkboard beside her was littered with push-pinned announcements of past and future events in Willits, Hopland, Ukiah, Laytonville, and Cache Creek, as well as requests for rides to Ashland and to Eugene, to Berkeley and even to Santa Cruz, Big Sur, and LA. On the opposite wall, frameless oiled portraits of Brian Jones, Jimi Hendrix, Janis Joplin, and Jim Morrison were dated 1969, 1969, 1970, and 1971, respectively. The bench built into the bay window had been converted into an altar where the Crazy Horse album was covered by crystal amulets, beads, guitar picks, ticket stubs, and roach clips. A photograph of a shaggy-haired guitarist was propped between a tall burning votive candle and a pinched-necked ceramic vase with dry statice and dusty strawflowers. The flowers looked dead and they were; so was the musician, Danny Whitten: the obituary's headline was dated November 18, 1972.

"Hey, Mom, sorry I'm late." She turned toward a sturdily built young man with a sun-reddened complexion and scratches on his face. He was wearing shoulder length hair, a Baja sweatshirt, and a Bowie knife sheathed on his tooled leather belt. "What time is it anyway?"

"DD—I mean Donald!" She stood up. "It doesn't matter. I haven't been here long."

He let her hug his broad shoulders and took a step backward, flashing a closed-jaw smile.

"Let me look at you. You've gotten so ... strong!"

"Mom, cool it," he whispered, drawing a hand across his forehead to clear away the unbrushed brown hair and sending his eyes left and right without turning his head. "Let's order some food, okay?"

Donald led the way, obviously familiar with staff behind the counter and people helping themselves to glasses of water and flat-ware of miscellaneous origins.

"So, I guess Gran'ma couldn't make it," he said flatly, lighting up a Camel cigarette after they sat down at one of the tables partially draped by a faded, striped serape.

Katie explained how uncomfortable if not painful such an expe-dition would have been for her, as well as stressful to her health, and elaborated on his grandmother's diminishing capacities: the compro-mised mobility; the minor heart attacks counter-indicating surgery on her knee or back; ever more medications making her groggy, dizzy, and constipated. Mental slippage affected some portion of her communi-cations every day.

"Are you saying she's like getting senile or something?" he asked, turning his fork over and over without looking at her directly.

"I don't know what to call it. She can be with it one second then the next she just spaces out. She still washes herself and gets up a plate of leftovers in the kitchen to eat back in her room. Sometimes she goes out on the deck. But we have to practically force her to sit at supper—"

"... *we*?"

"Oh, I thought I wrote you how someone's working for me now. Letty's her name."

He flashed the same set smile—lips spread, cheeks bulging, exposed teeth clamped shut.

"Your grandmother puts a sash around her robe, steps into some clogs, and calls that getting dressed. Sometimes she goes for days like that, the days she does leave her bedroom. And she's lost weight. Well, she eats like a bird. And you know how big-boned she is."

"What does that mean, *big-boned*?"

"You know. Naturally large-framed. She could always carry some weight. Maybe too much at times." To illustrate, Katie placed her palms alongside her hips and slowly drew them outward, doubling her girth. "Only now she's losing too much too fast."

Sensing her right eye about to act up, Katie closed both lids, fearful she might spill tears at any second if her son did not warm up. A pregnant girl with long, braided, blonde hair sporting a daisy behind each ear served Katie a wooden bowl of salad, a wooden bowl of lentil soup, and a wooden spoon.

"Guess you didn't hear us call, Don" she said, smoothing out the pleats on the front of her one-piece, full-length, paisley print dress. "I'll be back with your omelet, and your dressing...." she trailed off, looking at Katie.

"This is my mom."

She giggled. "Hi, Don's mom."

"This is Amber."

"Hello, Amber."

"Be right back."

Katie examined both sides of the wooden soupspoon and spoke in a whisper: "It takes her so long to get anything done."

"What? She can't help it if the café gets super busy at lunchtime."

"No, I mean your grandmother, not Amber. I wonder how old that girl is...."

"How would I know? That's not my pumpkin seed growin' inside her. Go ahead and start eating, Mom."

"No, I'll wait." She set the spoon down and spread the cloth napkin across her lap. "But about your grandmother. I want you to know what's going on. Yesterday I watched her from the kitchen sink. She was out on the deck. She'd move a little potted plant here...." Katie took up the spoon to demonstrate, "and look at it for a while. Then she'd move it there and study it again. This went on and on. I wondered if she even knew what she was doing. She may have but maybe not, and I do wish she'd stop feeding all the feral cats in Cliff-port. They come out of the woodwork as soon as she sits down out there. She tells me she doesn't feed them, but I've seen her, and I keep finding crusts of bread and little pieces of cheese in her pockets. She likes the company I guess. When she sits down, they come in from all directions. Do you remember when we finally captured that big one we called the Mother of Millions?"

"No."

"Sure, you do. Out in the barn when you were little. That spring I finally let you throw rocks at all the toms. You don't remember that?"

"No, I don't."

Amber brought a creamer full of yogurt dressing and Donald's platter of home fries, toast, and an omelet loaded with cheese, stuffed with sliced mushrooms, and smothered in the red-hot *salsa de casa*; he plunged into his meal with his head kept down. Katie sipped at her soup and picked at her salad. The one time he looked up and caught her watching, he flashed that fake smile for a count of one-two-three then dove back down. When he had wiped his plate clean, he lit a cigarette, using the porcelain as an ashtray. She was still working on her salad when he spoke up: "You leave Gran'ma by herself to come up here?"

"I can't leave her alone. Letty's with her. I can trust Letty with your grandmother. I spent last night at Suzanne's and Mike's. You should go see them sometime, Donald."

"Yeah. So, who is this Letty anyway?"

"Who is she? She's Leticia Morales Novato—"

"Oh, gimme a break."

"Donald, she's a wonderful young woman from Colorado. I thought somehow you knew about her but of course not. One day this February this young Latin gal drives up looking for the Redwood Coast Nursery, and she's been with me ever since. She and Mom get along really well now."

"She's not one of your charity cases, is she?"

"What do you mean by that?"

"You know, starving hippies from the farm and garden project you have workin' at the nursery sometimes."

"Letty is nobody's *charity case*. She's a great worker, as a matter of fact, and I pay her as much as I can afford to right now."

"How much?"

"Three-seventy-five an hour, cash."

"That's better than farm workers get."

"More than twice minimum wage. Plus room and board."

"That's a sweet deal—wait a minute. She's livin' in the house? That's weird."

"Why is that weird?"

"I don't know. It just sounds weird to me. How old is she?"

"Your age. Maybe a couple years older."

"It still sounds weird."

"It's not weird at all. It's working out for everybody."

"I'm still hungry," he declared, squashing his cigarette butt on the dirty plate, shoving off from the table, and bussing his dish to the wait station en route back to the front counter.

While he stood bantering with the short-order cook then flirting with the girl at the cash register, Katie studied her son from behind. His thick hair looked like he was keeping it trimmed—with sheep shears; his hooded sweatshirt looked like a burlap bag that could be burned in a bonfire for a collective high; the tight fit of his soiled Wrangler jeans emphasized the shape of his muscular buttocks and upper thighs. She imagined he had no problem getting his so called manly needs met by "shacking up" if only for a night or a weekend with some of the females who were also checking him out—she saw them with her own eyes: runaway teens dressed like gypsies; high school truants experimenting with excessive mascara and cigarettes; wan maidens less than twenty-years-old attired in pre-Raphaelite gauze; and hardened women dressed in cow gal, plainly prepared to get their needs met by any available prey such as this younger man.

She rose and helped herself to a cup of coffee from an aluminum percolator, leaving a quarter in a piggy bank with Nixon's face painted on. Reseated, she redirected her gaze to the unlit wick in the deep crater of a chunky candle melded to the varnished tabletop and aligned the bottom of her mug with one of the white rings that other hot mugs had left behind. She realized that DD had yet to ask a thing about her, had not inquired about Baby Blue Eye, and had not volunteered one word about where he was living, how he paid his way, or what held him back from visiting Cliffport. Instead, he remained closemouthed, periodically flashing that transparently phony smile. Then she spotted her son grabbing a bottle of Tabasco sauce on his way back to the table with side orders of hash browns and toast.

"Does Dylan have a new album out?" she asked.

"Probably."

"Isn't that him right now?"

He cocked his head, listening to the sound system. "No, that's Townes."

"Townes?"

"Townes Van Zandt. Sounds like Dylan, I guess. That's 'No Deal.'"

"Never heard of him."

He attacked his food.

"Been playing much guitar, Mom? Singing?"

"No. No, I haven't."

"Ever since Josie left, right? Wasn't that when you gave it up?"

"I suppose. Are you sure that's not some early Bob Dylan?"

"I'm sure."

"Interesting.... How about you? Are you playing?"

He shoved his empty plate away, shifted his weight, and shot her the obnoxious grin.

"Oh no! Don't tell me you sold the acoustic your grandmother gave you."

He stared her down.

"Oh God, DD! You sell the surfboard I bought you on your thirteenth birthday. You sell the great acoustic guitar your grandmother gave you on your fifteenth. What's next?"

"The Fleetside," he replied. "As soon as my bonus kicks in, I'm going to sell that piece a' shit and buy a real truck for a change. That's what's next, since you asked."

"Jody's boots!" The words burst from her mouth, and she scooted her chair closer as if to prevent him from getting away. "You haven't sold your Uncle Jody's boots or have you? Please, don't say you've sold those too."

"I haven't. I haven't sold them, okay? Quiet down. Don't freak these people out. We're mellow up here, Mom. You know? Mellow … like Santa Cruz?" He laughed, stuck his hands into the single pouch of his sweatshirt's front, pulled out another cigarette, and lit up with a wooden match. "I still have those boots. I just don't wear 'em, okay? I don't dress up much, know what I mean? I like never dress up, actually."

Katie snatched the smoking cigarette from between his fingers and stomped it out beneath her heel. He laughed, leaned farther back in his chair, and lit another out of her reach, tipping his head toward the loudspeakers. "This one's called 'High, Low and In Between'. You ought to listen to that one, Mom."

"Okay, DD, knock it off. You want a piece of pie or something? Donald! I asked you a question. You want dessert? This meal's on me."

"No, I'm good. But I better be going soon—"

"Hold on. You haven't even told me what you're doing?"

"What I'm doing?"

"Since fishing season ended with Ross."

He chuckled. "Good ol' Ross…."

"Now cut the crap and talk to me. Stop acting like you've got it together. I'm your mother, you know. You can't fool me all the time."

Donald leaned forward and set his elbows on the table. "I'm working fuckin' hard, is what I'm doing."

"I believe you. I can see your hands and those scratches on your cheek. But working doing what?"

"Ever heard of the Hoedads, Mom?"

"The who?"

"The Hoedads. It's a work co-op out of Eugene. They just opened up a branch in Ukiah."

"What kind of work co-op?"

"We plant trees. Doug firs. After the timber companies clearcut, we go in and replant seedlings on contract with the Forest Service. Crew I'm on works in the hills around Covelo, Redwood Valley, Potter Valley. All around there. Out in the boonies."

"Hoedogs?"

"Hoedads. It's the tool we use. A hoedad and a pair of water-proof boots is all you need. Not corkers and not like these," he said, displaying the pair of simple work boots he had on. "Good gloves too."

"What about that?" she asked, raising her eyebrows at his knife.

"Comes in handy sometimes."

"You mean that's what you do, plant trees all day long?"

"Longer. You'd be amazed where we can end up when the sun goes down. Blows my mind sometimes when ye ol' chow wagon and our tents doesn't get there until after dark—lazy fuckers."

"Donald. How can you make enough money to buy a new truck by planting trees in a co-op? Weyerhaeuser and Georgia-Pacific make money cutting trees down not by planting them."

"Duh. But as soon as I can figure out how the system works, I'm going to get in line for requisitions from the Feds or the timber companies of whoever awards the contracts. I'm going to have my own crew and it's not going to be any co-op either."

"Wow. That is quite a proposition, D—Donald. But is it that easy starting a business, running a business? You saw me barely scraping by. And working contracts with some government agency must be a bear. You'll have to have a legit business already all set up—"

"... I'll figure it out," he cut her off. "I know some guys who know how it all works. I don't want to be poor forever, you know." He scowled. "I grew up poor enough."

"You did not grow up poor."

"No? Except for the Mexican kids from the fieldworker families, I was the poorest kid at Regional High."

"Oh, Donald, don't say it like that. How do you think that makes me feel, to hear that bitterness in your voice?"

"I don't know how it makes you feel. I know how it makes me feel: like making some real money. And getting a real pickup. I'm only keeping the Fleetside running till I get paid this fall."

"What do you mean? You're not getting paid now?"

"We get paid a little, enough to get by. What do they call it ... per diem? Yeah, I guess that's the word. But there's a big bonus at the end of the season ... depending on how many trees you plant. Around the end of October, depending on the weather, when planting ends, they tally up the number of firs you planted then BINGO—if you're any good—*muchas* moola. And I'm good. I'm the lead guy on our crew and everybody knows it. I'm planting tons more trees than the rest of those stoned-out hippies."

"They pay you whether the trees live or die? That can't be."

"Ahh ... trust me, Mom. It can work."

"I can't believe it works like that. Say somebody cheats, buries all their seedlings and just claims they planted them?"

"Supervisors check out every hillside as soon as we get done."

"Supervisors, in a co-op?"

"Listen, don't sweat it. I'm expecting a big bonus and I deserve one."

"I'm sure you do. I'm just—"

"... you're just worrying all the time like Gran'ma, is what you're doin'. Let me handle this. Next time you see me I should be drivin' some nice new wheels, like you and Mike."

"When is the next time we'll see you?"

"Thanksgiving...? Yeah, by Thanksgiving I should have things wrapped up and a new 1975 pickup if they're in the lots by then."

"From planting seedlings? Donald, nobody ever bought a brand-new truck direct from a dealership by planting trees for half a year."

"What are you driving, Mom? Isn't that pretty Ford F-250 with the extended bed parked outside yours? The one with the shell Ross told me about? What's Uncle Mike driving these days? A fully loaded GMC 2500 Sierra Grande 4 × 4? Or has he got something bigger than that by now?"

"But, Donald, you're eighteen. That's the first new vehicle I've ever bought in my whole life. And Mike has to be prepared to go fight wildfires. Don't forget, he's been working forever at that fire extinguisher company or whatever it is." She thought about adding that the Crogans had never had children either and so saved on expenses but refrained.

He crossed his arms over his chest, tilting his head first to one side—holding it there—then tilting it to the other. "Well, I don't want to wait that long."

"You're impatient."

"You better believe it. I want a truck and a big mean old dog and one day I'm going to buy a place in the country too. Damn straight I am."

"What about a girl?"

"No problem."

"I mean a steady girl, Donald. A real girlfriend."

"Right," he replied, pushing his chair back from the table and standing up. "Think I will get a piece of pie. You want one, or a granola bar made in Santa Cruz?"

"Very funny, wise guy."

The way he carried himself strutting to the counter; what he said when he did speak his mind; the hostile smile he brandished toward her—Katie moaned, relieved that Elise wasn't present.

After he was re-seated, she watched him gobble down the pie. "Listen to me, Donald, please. Now really listen. I hope you know what you're doing with those Hoedads or whatever they're called. I don't want to see you get ripped off, honey."

"*Honey?*"

"Okay, Vinegar—is that better? I just hope you know what you're doing up here, is all."

"I know what I'm doing."

"It's your choice and—"

"... it is my choice," he interrupted her, "and it's a good one too." He wiped his chin with the crumpled cloth napkin and tossed it onto the table.

"Aren't you going to have to pay taxes on your earnings? Doesn't that co-op report what you get paid?"

"Taxes?" he scoffed. "I'm never paying taxes. Or getting insurance. I'm not going to play that game, Mom. Sorry, but I thought you figured that out about me by now. I'm staying under the radar. They'll never catch me."

"You'd be surprised. Since those mobsters from Monteflores have been putting pressure on the county, our property taxes have tripled in less than a year, and we have to pay."

"They tripled?"

"And Gath Construction has fenced us out of the millpond."

"Assholes!"

"And they put a lock on the driveway, which is falling apart, but they won't fix it or let me fix it. They say the title doesn't say they have to upgrade the easement to accommodate commercial vehicles. The right-of-way mandates that the serviant estate maintain the road in a manner conducive to reasonable use and supportive of vehicles of no more than 8,000 pounds gross vehicle weight rating. I had to re-read that a couple dozen times before I understood it. They keep playing piddly-ass legal games like that."

"Motherfuckin' lawyers."

"Oh, Donald. I don't want to see anything illegal catch up with you. Have you registered for the Draft yet?"

"I'm not registering for any Draft. Come on, Mom."

"I don't think the Selective Service is still sending anybody to Vietnam. I think they're just bringing people back now."

"Strung out or dead. No, Mom. No taxes, no insurance, no Draft. Got it?"

"And no more education either?"

"What for? I want a truck. I want a place in the country where I can do my thing and nobody'll bother me. I need money for that. I don't need a degree. I'm free, Mom."

"You want to be free. Now I think I made a mistake giving you the keys to the Fleetside when you turned sixteen. Maybe you weren't ready for a truck."

"You think that was a mistake? Right! Well, too late now."

"When you left home, when you were hanging around Pillar Harbor, I could've had your driver's license cancelled, you know. Do you know that? Up until you were eighteen."

"Well, I'm eighteen now so you can't." He clapped loudly, coughed loudly, and waved to whoever was watching before snickering as he spoke: "You think I wasn't always driving without a license anyway?"

"You're crazy. Don't you think you'll have time to make money later in life? How about coming home and getting your diploma before you make any serious mistakes? I'll find out how the high school equivalency thing works. You'd probably be able to go to Cabrillo without setting foot on the Regional High campus ever again."

"I can find out about that stuff myself. They've got libraries up here too. I do know how to read, you know." He leaned back in his chair and picked at his teeth with a wooden match.

"When was the last time you went to a dentist?"

"A dentist?" He snorted. "Probably the last time you took me to one."

He eyed the door; she knew she was about to lose him. "You smell like skunk, Donald Duncan."

"Yeah?" He snickered. "Skunk?"

"Weed. You've been smoking dope."

"It's probably this drug rug I borrowed from one of the stone heads on the crew," he said, lifting his arm to sniff the sleeve. "I should throw it in the laundromat for him, huh?"

"You should throw it in the trash," she retorted. "So, how often do you get into Willits?"

"Every couple of weeks and—"

"... no, I'm sorry. You smell like dope. It's not just your clothes. Did you smoke just before you came in here?"

No response.

"Do you smoke every day?"

He looked at the surrounding tables then settled his eyes on her. "Duh. Everybody does."

"How much?"

"Oh, cut it out, Mom. I'm not doing this with you anymore. It's over. I'm on my own."

"You're free. You're on your own. Okay. So, what shall I tell your grandmother?"

He grimaced and took a deep breath. "Is Gran'ma going to die?"

"What?"

"Is Gran'ma dying or something? Is that why you're here? Is that what you were tryin' to tell me before?"

"We're all dying, Donald."

"Come on, Mom, you know what I mean. I remember once you told me Jan was dying then she did die. Now you're like telling me Gran'ma is going to die. I'd like to kick God's ass someday."

"Oh, Donald."

"I would!"

"She's not dying right now, if that's what you mean."

He was eying the front door out. "Listen, I really gotta go now. The guys'll be waiting for me."

She knew she was losing him—perhaps forever. "I heard from Josie the other day."

"Yeah?"

"I guess Jeff is going to the University of Washington this fall, in Seattle. Or is it Reed College? I forget."

"Right."

"I can get you his address if you want to get in touch with him and—"

"... no. If that was supposed to happen it would've happened by now. We've drifted apart, like they say."

He got up. She asked him for a mailing address, but he said that after closing the PO Box in Fort Bragg he had not gotten around to opening another one anywhere else. She asked for his phone number; no telephone number. She asked for the contact information of his supervisor in Ukiah; he didn't have any contact information, and he repeated that he couldn't get down to Cliffport until around Thanks-giving—too many opportunities, too much at stake. He was smiling, turning, heading for the door; she followed him outside; he was walking down the sidewalk with cowboy waves of his arm and his back turned. Then he was gone.

Katie went back inside and sat down. Looking in her wallet, preparing to pay the bill with shaky hands, she ran across Pieter Tuelling's handwritten driving directions:

> *1 mile east of Ft. Bragg on Route 20.*
> *North on Bishop Pine Rd.*
> *½ mile to Rhod. Acres Lane—go to end.*

She couldn't see herself facing Pieter T.'s friends that afternoon or making the long drive home; the most she felt she could handle— the one action she could imagine managing—would be getting in the Ford and heading back south on 101 to Aunt Suzanne.

———

– It was awful. He didn't introduce me to anybody. It was like he was ashamed of me. Oh, no, there was Amber. Another eighteen-year-old looking like she's about to give birth behind the counter at any second.

– So, you're still "The Mom."

– I'm so glad my mom wasn't with me, Suzanne. I never want her to see him like that. He looks like someone I wouldn't even like if I met him on the street. If I saw him on the mall in Santa Cruz or walking on the beach, I'd think, "Whose kid is that anyway?" But he's mine, he's my kid. Oh, God, Suzanne, what have I done wrong?

– You haven't done anything wrong, darling.

– Then why does he hate me so much?

– I don't think he hates you. He's young. He's confused. He's probably seen James Dean in East of Eden and Marlon Brando in The Wild Ones. He thinks, oh, so that's the way to be a real man.

– He kept pushing me away, putting me down.

– Twenty years ago, I listened to your mother saying the same thing—about you.

– She did?

– When you went back East. *Mamma mia!* Ellie was sure you were abandoning them.

– She told you that?

– I think she did. Or maybe I just knew that's what she meant. She was terrified you were dumping DD on her and leaving them forever. And you know what? She would've raised that boy without you. That's Grandmother Elisabeth. How old were you then?

– When I went back East? Around twenty-one, twenty-two or something. It was like right around 1960, right? I was so self-centered.

– Okay, so 1960 ... 1902 ... that's fifty-eight. At fifty-eight years of age your mother would have raised another child by herself all over again if she'd had to. But you came back. You never abandoned them. And you're not self-centered anymore. How old were you when you had DD?

– Eighteen. Like Amber. I was so screwed up. I was just so stupid and selfish—like he is now.

– But you grew out of it, Katie. It's his turn to be eighteen now.

– But I'm afraid he'll turn out to be somebody I won't like at all.

– He's not done turning out, Katie. He's still half-baked.

– His ideas sure are. He claims he grew up in dire poverty, Suzanne. Poverty!

– Poverty?

– That what he said: "The poorest kid in school."

– Oh baloney! Doesn't he know there are all sorts of poverty and all sorts of wealth? Your mother is the richest person on earth I know in terms of life experience. The wisdom she has? You can't buy that. DD can't see that now but you can, right?

– Suzanne...?

– Yes?

– One day, if you ever read Mom's NOTEBOOKS, you'll see how right you are. How wise she really is even though she's losing it now....

– I never have read those. Her memoirs, right?

– Eight notebooks covering her life up till she met my father. The story of her early life and her people in Europe before that. My people, I guess I should say. I don't know. I think she'd let me show them to you. They were meant to be passed down to DD, but the way things are going now.... I don't know if I would ever entrust him with them.

– I'd love to borrow them sometime, but let's not trouble her mind over it right now.

– Of course. Her mind ... wow.

– Okay, my one and only dearly and thoroughly exhausted niece of mine. I'm going inside to draw some bathwater for you and then you're lying down. I believe in naps and I know you didn't get much sleep last night.

– Did I disturb you and Mike? Did you guys hear me going up and down? I'm sorry.

– I heard you. Mister Crogan? He'd sleep though a nine-point-nine earthquake, that guy.

– I better call home and tell Mom I'm not on the way. What should I tell her?

– You tell Ellie you're spending more time with Ma and Pa Kettle in their good old folks' home outside Cloverdale. She won't object to that, I hope.

– Oh, no. She'll be happy to hear that.

– If she remembers who we are.

– That's not funny.

— I know it's not, not from what you've been telling me. I'm going down there, Katie, next week if I can arrange for a sub at the farmers' market.

— She'll always remember who you are. When the time comes she forgets who you are, then it's time for ... I don't know what.

— Go on now, phone her. Oh, no. Okay. Here we go. Come on, cry. Cry, baby, cry. Come on, let it all out. Come here, come on. I've listened to your mother cry over her husband and her son and her daughter, and I can listen to you cry over them. Go ahead, that's right, that's right. Lowrie family tears are good for us all. Oh, Kaitlin, *cara bambina mia*.* It's all right ... it's going to be all right....

*

— Thank you, Suzanne.... I'm done.

— Then I'll go start your bath. You know where the phone is.

— Suzanne?

— Yes?

— You've got to read Mom's NOTEBOOKS.

— I want to. Someday I will.

*

While Katie slept, Suzanne phoned her husband so he wouldn't be surprised that their houseguest was back for another night, and when Mike came home from work, he found their visitor swinging on the tire suspended from the white oak and invited her to join him at the stable while he performed lightweight chores. She caught up with him where he was leaning on the corral fence, hand-feeding culled carrots to one of their two aging quarter horses.

"I made a phone call, Katie, after Suzanne told me you had met with Don. There's something you ought to know about, I think."

Katie had never thought of her curly-headed uncle as a jokey-jokey kind of man, but now his tone was downright grave. "What?"

---

* *my dear child (It)*

Mike shooed the one horse away and clucked the other to the railing for its turn.

"Don told you he's working with some Hoedads, right? Planting trees for the Forest Service?"

"Yeah?"

"Mendocino National Forest, right?"

"That's what he said."

Mike lifted the bucket over the rail and upended it, dumping some misshapen vegetables onto the ground. "I never heard of any tree planting outfit called that, so I gave a friend of mine a call. Sam works up in the Willamette Forest out of Salem. Caught him in the office too."

"So? What'd he say?"

"He knows about that outfit. Seems like it's getting to be a pretty serious operation in the Oregon Cascades and all, planting Doug fir up and down the mountainsides. Hard work."

"What are you getting at, Mike?"

"I'll get there, Katie, hold on. Now, did Don really say he couldn't get down to Cliffport until Thanksgiving which was after planting season ended?"

"Because that's when the bonuses get doled out, he said."

Mike wiped the dirt from his hands, looked up to the sky, down to the ground.

"What is it, Mike?"

"Honey. Sam told me that's when the tree-planting season begins up there. Those Hoedads start in around Thanksgiving and plant baby firs in the wintertime. They don't plant them when it's hot and dry like now. Those seedlings need cool weather and rain to survive."

"Hhn...."

"And he told me so far as he knows those Hoedads operate out of Eugene and only out of Eugene. Seems like I would've heard of them if they were in Mendo or Sonoma County, and I was right. At our monthly fire meetings, we catch up on all that sort of scuttlebutt."

"So, why do you think DD told me that?"

"Because he doesn't want you to know what he's really doing."

"So, what's he really doing?"

The man looked up to the hills behind the house and down to the ground and gave the pail a nudge with his foot before engaging her eyes. "He's growing pot, Katie. Or working for somebody growing pot. October, that's about when they harvest all their little patches out on public lands, BLM land, Forest Service land."

"Oh, shit. So he's deep into it. You know, I kind of thought so but...."

"I'm sorry to be the one to tell you but it's pretty obvious, right? That crop he's talking about isn't conifers and it's sure not wine grapes. It's marijuana. There's a rash of that crap being grown in remote locations through Mendocino County."

She slammed her right fist on top of the nearest fence post. "I just knew he was bullshitting me; I knew it. No taxes, no insurance, contracts with federal government agencies? I just hoped he hadn't thought it all out yet. So, every time he flashed me his phony smile, it was his way of saying 'I'm not telling you anything.' She made another fist and pounded on the post. "But why'd he have to lie to me, why?"

"Hey, don't do that! You'll get splinters or break my fence post."

"But why, Mike? I know he smokes dope. But he lied right to my face about what he's doing."

"It's pretty disrespectful, I know that. I ran into a little bit of that when he spent time with us."

"You guys never told me he lied to you."

"Oh, Katie. From what I see nowadays, a sixteen, seventeen-year-old's almost got to lie to get by, to do what he wants to do. It's like the teenager's Fifth Amendment or something. Anyway, they were white lies when he was staying with us. Lies of omission, let's say."

"Well, that was no lie of omission he laid on me. Hoe-dads, Hoe-moms, ho ho ho! I should've known. My son, the marijuana outlaw. Whoopee! You and I both know he's going to get busted sooner or later if he keeps it up."

"That's what I'm getting at. Maybe he doesn't want you to know, so if he does get in trouble, you won't somehow get in trouble too."

"What? You're supposed to turn your own kids in now?"

"Nixon's latest executive order includes that too, yeah. Crazy times."

"So, his lying is about protecting me? No. Maybe part of it is. But now what do I tell Mom? Now I have to lie to her—by omission. You just do not lie to my mother—you know that. At least I can't."

"I can understand that."

They heard Suzanne's supper bell.

"You want to come in and eat with us or wait out here a while? Suzanne knows all about what I just told you. Do what you like, Katie."

*

They got through the evening meal without bringing up the subject, but when they were clearing the table, Katie muttered something below her voice.

"What did you just say?" Suzanne asked.

"I said he'll end up like his father. The way DD's going now? He'll end up mistreating women and messed up with drugs and in trouble with the law. Growing, using, distributing—whatever."

"Katie, are you in touch with DD's father?" Suzanne asked. "We didn't know that."

"No, I'm not in touch. He called me a couple years ago for like the first time in fifteen years. Said he was turning over a new leaf and wanted to see DD."

Suzanne pulled her chair back out from the table and sat down. "And?"

"And I said no. I said hell no. It had to be hell no. DD seeing his father coming off probation or something? I couldn't for one second believe any good could come from that, like there was going to be some sappy happy Hollywood movie ending. You can't trust a druggie and Richard is a serious druggie."

"Is Don in touch with his father?" Mike asked.

"That I don't know. Oh, God, say it isn't so. I don't think so, but I've been fooled before. Hoedad and Hoe-son, God! No good can come of them meeting up now either."

"I think you're right there," Mike chimed in.

"I hate to say it, but I do too," Suzanne added.

"What should I do, you guys? How can I get DD back or hold on to a piece of him? I don't really like him anymore. I don't. I love him, he's my son, but I can't hack the idea of running across him stumbling around like some burnt out acidhead on Telegraph Avenue. Want do you think it would take to get him back before it's too late?"

"Time," Suzanne said.

"But how much time do I have to wait?" Katie said. "For how long?"

"And grace," Mike added.

"You mean, like good luck?"

"No, I mean like amazing grace, Katie. I've heard you sing that song. You know what it's all about."

*

Katie got off to an early start and had the Rhododendron Acres plants loaded by noon. Inside the house, she got one long look at Jack van Winden hooked up to an oxygen machine, asleep in his reclining chair. Over sandwiches in the kitchen, she answered—to the best of her ability—Peggy's questions concerning Pieter Tuelling's well-being then, with a bag of the Van Winden's early heirloom apples on the seat beside her, Katie started on the four-hour drive home, planning to double back onto Route 20 once she had taken a brief peak at the Pacific. A surge shuddered up her spine as she drove by the Flowerland to the Sea sign—there was no time to drop in, using Pieter T.'s name as her calling card—then one glimpse of the Mendocino coastline hooked her, and she kept driving drive south on Highway One, planning to head inland at the Navarro River's outlet and connect with Highway 101 for faster travel home. Yet with no choice but to pay close attention to the cliff-hugging road and compelling views of the omnipresent ocean, the twists and turns of the coastal route took her out of her personal story so effectively that she followed the coastline all the way to Jenner-by-the-Sea before driving east alongside the Russian River. In Sebastopol, still several hours out, she ate some tacos and phoned Cliffport; Letty said it might be best if Katie spoke to Mrs. Lowrie directly—her mother was confused—and she put Elise on the line. Katie allayed her mother's anxiety and reported—without mention of Donald Duncan—on her visit to Cloverdale and Fort Bragg. If she weren't home by 8:00 PM, she'd phone again, she promised; otherwise, all was well.

Chapter 12

The Death of a Family

After long absence, Pieter Tuelling showed up in Cliffport sporting a narrow, white, Vandyke beard matching his neatly trimmed moustache; Katie went straight to her mother's room to announce his surprise reappearance but returned reporting that Elise felt indisposed. Over coffee and cake outside on the deck, he described his Mattole River retreat during which he had read books for hours without end; explored and discovered native plants in habitat; found he could, with adaptations, live with ease out of his truck camper by periodically availing himself of amenities at a county campground a few miles away; and he had survived many moods without recourse to alcohol. On his drive home along Scenic Highway One, he overnighted with the Van Windens and learned of Katie's visit, then he relished half-a-day visiting with the Schoefers at their Flowerland to the Sea. But Pieter enthused most over his immediate opportunity to succeed the camp host at a state park on the Sonoma Coast.

During a spontaneous stopover at Salt Point, he had enjoyed instant camaraderie with the current host who was distraught because illnesses in his family were calling him home before his contract expired. The retired agricultural agent's career in regulation, his considerable physical size, and his display of genuine bonhomie all made Pieter Tuelling a suitable candidate to fill in for him, and together they persuaded the regional ranger to intervene with the camp hosting organization on Pieter's behalf. As a result, the Dutch-man's position as Salt Point State Park's official campground host was to be inaugurated with a waiver of the standard training and without the usual unspooling and spooling of lengths of red tape: Pieter was to show up ASAP, presenting a valid first-aid certificate upon his first day of service. Mid-November, the weather would change, the abalone season would end, and the campground would no longer require an authoritative presence on site.

Pieter offered to pay Katie if she would continue to take care of Drika's park and keep an eye on his cabin where brand new plumbing and windows had been installed. She replied that she didn't want money but would be grateful if, before he left for Salt Point, he would show her exactly where to place her newly acquired plants in the garden terraces. His eyes closed as he smiled widely, his front teeth revealing their crooked ways. The following day, when their honored visitor came back for his garden consultation, unexpectedly donating six two-gallon cans of "Mine-No-Yuki"—the *Camellia sasanqua* also known as "White Doves"—toward the cause, Elisabeth Lowrie took pains to make a brief showing, stationing herself in the red armchair drawn in close to the round table in the main room. Katie appreciated how promptly the gentleman apprehended the elder woman's fragile condition by modulating his voice and muting the inflections of his renewed joie de vivre.

They spent the afternoon on the terraces taking measurements, making sketches, and discussing the cultural requirements of the plants she had brought back from Fort Bragg. With Katie's permission, he proposed to make yet another contribution: a special collection of containerized hellebores was being passed on to him by a horticultural hobbyist being moved into a retirement home; he could also—for a song—secure for the new garden an outstanding assortment of coral bells from a South Bay breeder who was being forced to relocate out of the way of mass transit developments. Pieter suggested that the hellebores could be massed under the higher-branching bushes, and the coral bells might be used as groundcover and edging—if she liked—where the large, white, full-peony form of his willowy "White Doves" would make fine accents in a low hedge defining the entrance to the lowest terrace. When Letty and Baby Blue dropped by, they all agreed that the time was auspicious to experiment with a drip irrigation system, which the Coloradan had learned about from a pair of Israeli wayfarers passing through Santa Cruz during their post-military-service *wanderjahr* abroad.

Katie thanked Pieter for all the kindness; he thanked her for making it possible for him to enjoy his second childhood: making campfires in steel rings, fishing for surfperch and striped bass, gathering mushrooms in the bishop pine forest, and generally carrying on like a happy beach bum washed ashore on California's true 'North Coast.' He wrote down the zip code where he was having his mail forwarded to the general store in Timber Cove, shook her hand with a double blink of his bright blue eyes, and almost danced across the hillside to say goodbye to Letty. Finding her outside the glasshouse, he slipped her a twenty-dollar bill.

"What's this for?" she asked.

"I don't know what all arrangements you got going with 'the boss lady' but I value your help, sure, here and in Drika's park. *En ... en....*"

"And what?"

"And ... *ach*, take this too," he stammered, extending another twenty. "Somebody like you right now, right here...? Taking care of Missus Lowrie in a situation like this...? Go on, Leticia, take that now, take it. *Jaja*, that's yours for whatever *jongoren* • do with a little money these days." He pocketed his wallet and scurried downhill.

———

The public notice posted on the telephone pole at the bottom of Grade Road stated that the County of Santa Cruz had issued Gath Construction a permit to demolish the gas station, hotel, and store; the teardown of the condemned buildings was to take place between

• *youngsters (Dutch)*

the twentieth and thirty-first of September 1974. The proprietress at Redwood Coast Nursery reveled in the notion of one grand finale: the theft of plants that would otherwise end up buried in landfill.

While assessing what she could get away with, Katie debated informing her mother about the demolition, and when she did tell Elise the news, she withheld information about her plan to steal all promising plant material. The older Lowrie seemed to take the ghost town's dismantlement as a matter of course, even arguing that the last time she had been down on the Coast Road, that widened strip had seemed nothing but an eyesore and public hazard. It occurred to Katie that her mother's flat affect in response to such an event—momentous in the history of Cliffport—was yet another sign of her general decline.

Katie and Letty executed the raid in broad daylight, parking their vehicles in the whale watch turnout so that passers-by would not suspect that people were busy excavating root balls and taking cuttings from overgrown plants situated between and behind the derelict buildings on the inland side of Highway One. Wrecking the foliage but keeping the roots intact, Letty dug up a slew of hot-poker plants and sliced bare stems off a hundred blooming naked lady lilies, saving the best two dozen flowering spikes in a white plastic bucket to present to Mrs. Lowrie before wrestling the swollen, crowded bulbs out of the dry ground with a forked spade.

Katie took dozens of cuttings from the same stands of the same fuchsia bushes from which Mrs. Ida Mackenzie had once made her famous berry jelly and, after Letty went uphill, made one final tour of the doomed structures, lingering behind the old Pottery Works, where brambles engulfed the firing pit and coyote bush occupied the court. Peeking into all three caved-in buildings—their interiors ravaged by hitchhikers, hobos, and vandals over the decades—she knew not to enter for their rotten floorboards would give in below her boots. *Anyway what good would it do*, she thought, *to find some old penny nails dating back to the days of the Whaler's Inn? So what if you could bring Mom a pottery shard retrieved from the kiln? The NOTE-BOOKS preserved the record of Cliffport best, even if Mom's done digging up the past.*

Before heading home, she considered crossing the tracks to snatch some plants from land belonging to either the State of California or Southern Pacific Railway but, after contemplating the sunstruck bluff, she shied off, disinclined to disturb the integrated composition of no man's design: a handsome tapestry of Dudleya, buckwheat, seaside daisy, and sea thrift carpeting the cliff.

———

October 1974 Cliffport

Dear Donald,

Your postcard arrived yesterday. I wish I had good news about your grandmother but I don't. They say the best thing is facing the truth but at times like this I'm not sure. The doctors have concluded that an operation is out of the question. She isn't in more pain but the medications cloud her thinking. Surgery would only make her more miserable in what little time she has left. A visit from you now would mean more to her than I can write.

Her old friends take turns spelling me from attending to her basic needs and I don't know what I would do without Letty taking care of the nursery and the house.

I know how badly you needed to get away from pressures here but I hope you're not doing anything you'll regret. We all make mistakes—I have. We can only hope it turns out they are not irreversible.

You are never forgotten in her thoughts and prayers. Not a day goes by without her looking at a few things you made as a little boy she keeps by her bed. She wants to see you and we hold out hope you will spend the holidays here at home. We want to know you're all right. Please come to Cliffport for her sake—better not wait for Thanksgiving either.

Love, Mom

———

"Dear, would you help me put those books in order?"

"What order?"

"Why, alphabetical order, of course: A, B, C.... By author's last name, I suppose. Yes, last names are best."

"But why?"

"Why are last names best?"

"No. Why rearrange them at all? You know where to find whatever you're looking for. Or I can find it for you."

Elise lifted her eyeglasses off the bridge of her nose. "Well, that's the thing. I no longer do know where to find things. And to think I was a librarian's assistant once. Did you know that about your mother?"

"What? Yeah, sure, I knew it, Mom...."

"Let's start then. I can't read the spines from here," she said, replacing the glasses on her nose. "Just recite the titles one by one, please."

"I thought you just said you wanted to go by the author's last names."

"Oh, Kaitlin. Please do not make this more difficult than it needs to be. Now what's that first book to the left on the topmost shelf?"

"Buck."

"Buck what?

"That's the author's last name."

"Please read the author's full name then the title then the author's last name again."

"Ma-om, come on. There must be two hundred books here."

"That bottom shelf is composed entirely of Uncle John's collection of those silly Westerns he loved so much. Bowers with a B. But let us leave those right where they are. You see? We're already down to one hundred and seventy-five!"

"Pearl Buck. The Good Earth. Buck."

"Well then, that will come right after the A's. Set that one aside for now."

"Mom?"

"Yes?"

"This could take forever."

Elise pouted. "If you'd rather Leticia helped me...?"

"No no, I need her to keep working outside," Katie responded. "Okay, let's see how it goes. H.L. Davis. Honey in the Horn. Davis. Last name starts with D."

"Why of course it does: Davis. And what a popular novel that was in its day. I suppose not a soul has even heard of it nowadays."

The reordering of the bookcase—and Elise's running commentary—consumed the better part of three evenings until Elise started requesting that every other book be set aside for her future rereading, and Katie found ways to reshelve the titles without her mother's notice. On the fourth evening, overcome with fatigue, Elise asked if her daughter would kindly complete the alphabetical rearrangement on her own some other time and dozed off to sleep.

*

"There is a huge banquet hall with oh a great many guests, and the speakers are on a raised dais. That's what it's called, isn't it, dear, a dais? The master of ceremonies rises to propose a toast but this fellow at one of the tables stands up and shows everyone all the food still left on his plate. He begins to move toward these ornate iron bars separating the dining hall from a kind of public corridor or arcade, where a beggar woman is reaching out her hands. 'You don't want to do that,' the master of ceremonies says. 'You know where that will end.' And sure enough a second beggar comes to the separator."

"That's it? That's the whole dream?"

"Oh no. What happens next, everyone in the hall starts chanting: 'Life! Life! Life!' And they all rise and move to share leftovers with the many other beggars who come swarming to the bars with their arms extended."

"Is that it?"

"Isn't that enough? I mean, such an affirmation! 'Life! Life! Life!' Such an inspiration, Kaitlin."

"Nothing mysterious about that one."

"No, I suppose not. My birthday is coming up soon, isn't it? What greater affirmation could there be than that one?"

*

Elise asked her daughter to bring her the carton containing the Santa Cruz North Coast Potters Guild archives, then she had her tape the colorful group portraits from the Guild's ten annual Christmas cards around the border of the dresser mirror. On the bureau top, she had Katie arrange the five black-and-white framed images of Katie's grandmother in a crescent around Liliane Piagère's Communion Medal, DD's last postcard mailed from Fort Bragg—a seagull sitting solo on a harbor pier—and a clay animal figurine fashioned by her son or grandson as a child. Elise inspected these things during her expeditions to and from the bathroom and paused—supported by her aluminum walker or leaning on her daughter's arm—gazing at the display.

*

"Another revelation was delivered me, dear."

"Another what?"

"Another marvelous dream sent from angels on high."

"What was it this time, Mom?"

"There was a waterfall and ... oh, you won't think me perverse, will you?"

"Of course not, come on. Nobody's responsible for their dreams. Try me."

"But it wasn't about the waterfalls at all. It was about the rocks below the falls. They were formed from a combination of smooth stones and shapely naked women ... yes, completely and purely naked ... and such lovely, lovely women they were!"

"You mean there were women sitting on the rocks?"

"No, I don't. I mean they were the rocks. They were rocks and they were women at the same time. The smooth stone, their smooth skin, all integrated and absolutely brilliant in the sunlight."

"Wow. So, it was like sculpture."

"That's right, it was like sculpture, but these ... these ... these stones in the nude were just alive as alive can be. And those lovely creatures, they were turning their faces toward me, smiling. Can you imagine?"

"Sounds like your angels are tripping out again, Mom."

"Oh, what a blessing! The smoothness of the stones, the supple breasts, the thighs ... and all such sonsy women, all just so perfectly—"

'*...Sonsy?*"

"Sonsy, you know, plump, but all so very comely. And their smiles were of such good cheer."

"What a trip."

"What trip?"

"You know, a good trip, a great dream. You just keep dreaming, Mom. Everything's going to be all right."

"Oh ... thank you. Do you take it as a good sign too? Oh, Kaitlin Liliane Lowrie! Thank you so very, very much...."

"For what?"

"Why, for always being just who you are, that's what."

*

Elise asked to borrow back the eight NOTEBOOKS she had composed and bequeathed to Katie as an account of her first twenty-eight years of life and what she understood to be the meanings embedded in that story. Although fearful that her mother's revisiting her memoir might set off emotional storms the enfeebled woman seemed in no way ready to weather, Katie complied; she was relieved when, after merely twenty-four hours, Elise placed her hand atop the stack on the bedside tray and matter-of-factly stated, "I'm done."

*

"What's going on, Mom? You keep asking me to tidy up your things like you're going on a long trip or something."

"I'm not? What about the surgery?"

"Mom, there's not going to be any operation. Remember what Doctor Healy said? The doctors decided your heart isn't strong enough. And you're not traveling anywhere soon, right?

"I suppose not. I just thought it was time to start putting things in order with my birthday coming up. After all: October 13th."

"That was like a week ago, Mom. Anyway, I don't know what that's got to do with tidying up. Can't we just cool it with all the re-arrangements?"

———————

Katie finished her coffee and relocated the rocker closer to her mother's bed. "I have a question for you."

"What is it, Kaitlin?"

"Is there any more stuff related to the McLoughlins around here? Not Jan's stuff, but any McLoughlin family history stuff that I haven't seen?"

Elise released a big breath. "So, there is. Can I see it now?"

"Yes. Yes, you can. I'll show you what there is. But you'll have to assist me."

Katie helped her mother across the braided rug, where the woman took hold of both knobs of the dresser's middle drawer and pulled it out, rattling its passage free of impediments. From within some folded fabrics, she exposed a cardboard box once used to hold a ream of typewriter paper. Katie escorted her mother back to the edge of the bed, where they sat down side by side, and Elise lifted the lid, using trembling fingertips to free a photography album from a bed of cotton stuffing.

The word FAMILY was molded into the ornamental design of an embossed floral bouquet standing out in relief from the cover's green cloth. Elise opened it gingerly. Although the binding had entirely come away from the inside spine, the album's dozen gold-leafed, double-back pages were still stitch-bound. Katie suspected that the prints lodged within the recessed, window-like openings carved into thick cardboard paper stock predated the album preserving them. [1] Twenty minutes later, Elise nestled the album back into the cotton bedding, slipped on the lid, and folded her hands atop the box in her lap.

"So, Mom. Can I hold onto that for a little while?"

"Can you keep it in your room, do you mean?"

"I want to go through it again. I won't remember everything you just said or not much. I'll bring it back and ask you questions though. Just for a while, please."

Elise smiled and released one hand from the other, licking her fingertip before dabbing the inside corner of her daughter's twitching right eye, gently patting the flesh all around the socket as if her finger were a declawed kitten's paw. Katie lifted her lids and gazed into her mother's filmy eyes.

"Of course, you may keep it, Kaitlin. Please, here, take it now. I don't know why I hesitated this long to share it with you. There, it's all yours now. Ask me your questions but keep it. It's yours for good now, dear."

*

"Oh, Kaitlin, I'm glad you're here. Do you have a moment?"

Katie replaced her mother's half-empty teacup with a full mug and tidied up the bedside tabletop before settling down in the rocker. "For sure, Mom."

"It's my manna in the morning."

"What is? It's fresh tea."

"No. I mean another dream!"

"Oh, okay...."

"I do think they're messages from the Divine. Please don't think me crazy. Would you like to hear this one?"

"Sure."

"Oh, if only I can remember it all...."

"Just start and see what happens."

Elise closed her puffy, pink eyelids and folded her hands atop the comforter. "Uncle John is driving to some monastery—no, it's a retreat center in the mountains, something like the Quaker Center in Ben Lomond but not exactly. I'm sitting beside him on the buckboard."

"Okay."

"We're in a mountain meadow where a festive table is laid out with great big bowls of spaghetti and tomato sauce and those jugs

341

of wine wrapped in straw. A man who looks just like John sits down with us. 'Are you twin brothers?' I ask and they both grin at me. 'Just lookalikes,' the stranger says. Then we hear a collective gasp and see a sort of gymnast on a platform in a tree right next to this deep, deep ravine. It was so many miles deep; you just couldn't see to the bottom. And before we knew it, he leapt into the air performing somersaults and miraculously landing on another platform in another treetop. That went on for some while but suddenly he dove headlong into the ravine after executing some movements of great balletic beauty. Then the choreographed part ends and he goes into a freefall. I cover my eyes, it's very scary. I'm sure he will be obliterated at the bottom of the ravine. But out of nowhere a loosely flying formation of cranes—I think they were cranes—anyway, these big birds with long necks appear from out of nowhere and their wings form a cradle that catches him—"

"... ah!"

"That's exactly what everybody in the dream says: 'Ahhh!' And the birds carry the man to safety out of our view. Of course, my eyes had been covered by my hands the whole time, so I don't know how I saw all that, but I did. 'Did you see that too?' I ask another person. Then a debate ensues: Was it an optical illusion? Was it a trick? But I know the signs of a miracle when I see one and keep the truth to myself."

"Awake ... or asleep?"

"What's that? Oh, Kaitlin. I do feel so blessed to have lived long enough to receive these gifts ... these absolute proofs.... But would anyone other than you know at all what I'm talking about anymore?"

*

They paused underneath the arbor.

"Why, isn't this 'The Sweetheart Rose'?" Elise asked, shifting her weight between Katie on one side and Letty on the other.

"This is 'Cecile Brunner', Mom."

"Yes, dear, that's the one. 'The Sweetheart Rose', *'Mignon'*, *'Cécile Brünner'*—all one and the same. There always seem to be blossoms on

'The Sweetheart Rose.' But do you suppose this is the same plant that was growing over the outhouse when I first arrived here so many years ago? Could it be?"

"It could be from a cutting going back to that one. Haven't they all been descendants of that one? I've never brought any other 'Cecile Brunners' onto the place."

"Oh, I suppose, I suppose. I've lost all track of such things, Kaitlin, you know that."

They were leading her up to the terraces. Although she might not make it all the way, the two women—and Baby Blue Eye—were prepared to dedicate the Indian summer afternoon to the endeavor. Letty had stabilized some lawn chairs along the pathway in case Mrs. Lowrie needed to rest. Now, not half an hour into the ascent nor halfway to their destination, Katie sat her mother down for a third time and sent Letty back to fetch a broad-brimmed sunhat from the deck. Katie stood and Elise sat still in a silence defined by claps of surf against distant, unseen rocks. Katie could just barely make out the black spine of the Santa Lucia Range trailing off into misty white-water off Point Piños across the mouth of Monterey Bay.

"Can you see where there are still poppies blooming, Missus Lowrie?" Letty asked, breathless upon her return.

"Oh, don't be silly. There are always poppies in bloom some-where, Leticia."

"But you should've seen this this spring. There were so many vari-ations. I never knew there was more than one kind of California poppy before."

"Well, they may as well all be one kind to me, dear. The same goes for roses on a bush, grapes in a cluster, peas in a pod—my eyesight being what it is, they're all the same to me now." She lifted her chin farther from her neck and turned her face from side to side. "Are we almost there?"

"Almost," Katie murmured, indicating to Letty that they would undertake no more climbing. "But you can see the reworked terraces from here, Mom. See, where Ross took down the trees and—"

"... but not the pear...?"

"Oh no, Missus Lowrie," Letty chimed in. "The pear's still right there, see?"

The woman's face turned upward, trembling on her neck like a bird chick's skull wobbling from the bottom of its nest.

"And the old tractor," Letty said. "It's there, see? Over there—"

"... well, you don't have to yell, Leticia. I can see it ... I think I see it ... over there ... is that it?"

"I'm sorry."

"Oh, don't be silly, darling. I'm the one should apologize for raising my voice on you."

"Oh, no, it's okay, Missus Lowrie."

"Okay, you two. Let's go on back now," Katie suggested. "I can read you the names of the plants we put in, Mom, back in the house."

"Oh, yes, let us do that. That would be lovely, dear."

Katie and Letty turned toward the keening cheeeewv-cheeeewv-cheeeewv of a soaring red-shouldered hawk.

"Are you ready to get up now, Mom?"

"I was just wondering if DD will be back from fishing any time soon? Do either of you know?"

"Ahh, no ... no, we don't ... Mom," Katie said, shooting Letty a glance. "But I'll ask Ross about it the next time I see him."

"Won't it be nice when Donny lives at home again?"

"Of course, it will. He could live here—"

"... *should* live here, Leticia," Elise interrupted. "He *should* live here and work in the nursery alongside you and Katie. Isn't that so, Kaitlin?"

"That'd be so cool working with your grandson, Missus Lowrie."

"Right...." Katie grumbled.

"What's that?" Elise turned her face to address her daughter. "Oh, sometimes I think Neddy and I ought to have named you Muley instead of Kaitlin."

Letty widened her eyes and mimed a double take while Katie scrunched up her face.

"Why's that, Mom? Because of my ears?"

"No, Kaitlin. Because you can be so thoroughly stubborn."

Now Katie performed the double take and Letty wrinkled her nose, stifling a laugh.

"When we get back down," Elise declared, "I want you to sign something I've written up."

"What is it?" Katie asked.

"It's a pledge to swear on the Holy Bible that you will on no occasion or for any reason sell the trees or alter the cemetery in Chapel Grove."

"Gosh, Mom," Katie groaned, rolling her eyes toward Letty. "You don't have to worry about that. Nobody's messing with this place while I'm still alive—"

"... or after you're gone," Elise interrupted her, "after we're all gone. However, I still want you to sign it. Leticia can be our witness. You never know how times change and with them their demands. Or their opportunities. Now, please, the both of you, can't you help me up? I better go lie down."

Her two attendants exchanged downturned smiles then hoisted the woman to her feet.

"Would you like a glass of mint-and-honey lemonade, Missus Lowrie, when we get back to the house? It's your favorite, you know."

"I don't know. What is it? I've lost my appetite for it, whatever it is. Ask me later. This could take a while now, girls. But we may as well just go."

*

To Whom It May Concern
It may be that in some difficult time, pinned down
by Penury and yearning for Release, or nagged by
Want past Resolution's power, I may be tempted to sell
or lease the trees or timber rights or the land of Chapel Grove
for cash. It well may be, but I shall not.

Kaitlin Liliane Lowrie (October 31, 1974)

*

Elise asked her daughter to draw Edna St. Vincent Millay's poetry from the bookcase and read "Renascence" aloud. After Katie had sat on the bed's edge and opened to a bookmark labeled Flowers of the Holy Land marking the page, Elise held her face turned toward the window and lip-synched the opening lines. When Katie reached the end of the second stanza, her mother had fallen asleep, head flopped to one side, lower jaw slack. Katie arranged the pillows and blankets and turned out the bedside light before resettling in the leather rocker, where she read the rest of the poem to herself.

*

"Mom?"

She knew by the bleached skin and curled fingers of the upturned palms that her mother had died in the night, but she still put her thumbs on both cool wrists—no pulse.

"Mom?"

She pressed the back of one hand against the neck—nothing. She brought her lips to the side of her mother's head—"Ma-om?"—then put her ear to Elise's open lips—no breath. Katie rearranged the long white hair, repositioned the hands side by side then stepped away, collapsing into the leather rocker. The body on the bed reminded her of Bill McGrath's cadaver in the basement of the lodge and also how she been first to pull back the curtain of Jan McLoughlin's suicidal tableau. Rocking forward, she propelled herself to her feet and selected the Communion Medal from the mix on the dresser then slipped the filigree chain around her mother's neck, closed the clasp, slid the afghan off the headboard, took the Holy Bible from the table, and sat back down.

Dorothea McLoughlin's Holy Bible resembled a scrapbook. When opened, leaves from the Gospels—long ago detached from the book's binding—slipped partway out; Katie reinserted them. A Science of Mind pamphlet, its paper stock flowery with molds, fell to the floor; she left it there. On a different sheet of heavy paper was typed a poem by Pastor H.H. Adamson entitled "Kind Words." [2] A felt bookmarker's saw-toothed borders had melded into a deep crease between the pages of the 23rd Psalm; Katie didn't try to pry the child craft loose as she reflected that her brother's hand had wielded the pinking shears which created the zigzag edges of the green Christmas tree glued onto the red background. Music sheets torn from a Mountain School songbook came free. As she glossed over the rhymed verses, designed as aids to remembering the names of the twelve apostles [3], and hummed the "Palestine Song" [4] —again hearing its lyrics sung to the tune of "Oh Tannenbaum"—she wondered if the pages dated back to Donald Duncan's time in Sunday School or even further back to Jody's interlude there more than forty years ago.

When Letty came inside for her second breakfast, she tapped at Mrs. Lowrie's door; slightly ajar, it opened fully of its own accord. "I was—*Oh Dios mio!*" she cried out, crossing herself and rushing to kneel beside Katie's chair. "What shall we do?"

"I don't know, Letty. I'll call my Aunt Suzanne now, I guess."

When Katie returned to the bedroom, she discovered that a blossoming sprig of Pieter Tuelling's "White Doves" had been set between the rigidified hands, petals already shattering on the blue comforter.

Katie fell at the foot of her dead mother's bed and wept.

*

By noon Suzanne had arrived and taken charge, enlisting Letty in a campaign to spare Kaitlin from having to deal with the exigencies of a death at home. After sharing a good cry and ascertaining that her assumed niece was fit to be left alone, Suzanne encouraged Katie to go for a walk before any representatives of officialdom arrived. Avoiding sight of razed Cliffport Town, Katie took to the main trail: her route down Lower Steep Creek gulch landed her where the McLoughlin dairy had once gripped the sand, straddling the freshwater outlet to the beach; before the trail uphill reached the millpond, she veered off toward Lookout Rock, where the footpath passed through scrub oaks and overgrown chaparral then gave her a full view of the Pacific.

Guided by Elise's prior communications, Suzanne made the phone call to Dr. Healy, who immediately drove up from Santa Cruz and upon arrival pronounced his beloved patient dead: *angina pectoris syncope*, he wrote down as the probable cause. He notified the Sheriff-Coroner's office and then the crematorium, the latter according to handwritten instructions Elsie had entrusted with Suzanne on her best friend's last visit to Cliffport. Katie returned to the house in time to see the Lowrie's family physician's sedan driving out and to identify the coroner's specialized station wagon and a green-and-white patrol car from the Sheriff's Department still parked under the oak. After answering a modicum of questions from the sheriff and surrendering the pill jars containing all her mother's prescriptions, Katie signed a release-of-remains form. Two uniformed men wheeled the draped gurney onto the porch then carried it the rest of the way down to the turnaround. Suzanne stripped the bedding and told Letty to air the comforter on the clothesline but to burn the soiled sheets somewhere out of Katie's sight.

*

The number of people who showed up at the Fern Community Church of the Redwoods blew Katie's mind. She didn't recognize some of the North Coast citizenry who came out to honor its adoptive daughter and to show respect toward her survivors. No Mackenzies, McLoughlins, or McGraths were present, and the sheer presence of so many individuals—none of whom had any political purpose for being there on a drizzly November Saturday—allowed Katie at times to forget that Donald Duncan was still somewhere missing-in-action. Pieter Tuelling—finishing out the season at Salt Point State Park—remained uninformed.

Flanked by Suzanne and Letty in the front pew, Katie couldn't stop herself from being transported by the nondenominational minister's eulogy, his text framed by readings of the first two verses from Psalms 90 and 101. While he recited chapter and verse—looking directly at her—she neither believed nor disbelieved him, but she sensed he was a

conduit for a transpersonal love. Closing the ceremony, the choir solo-
ist's voice soared through "Amazing Grace." Katie forgot the renditions
by Joan Baez, Judy Collins, Aretha Franklin—or her own—and felt she
was witnessing a vocal force not dependent upon studied diaphragm
control, a breath seemingly beyond the capacity of normal human
lungs, notes shaped by an intelligence other than mere singing craft;
the lyrics fountaining out the woman's wide-opened throat seemed to
be rising up from somewhere below her feet, below the floor, below the
foundation of the church building—Katie knew there was nothing but
Earth below all that.

In the assembly hall after the service, spoken testimonials came
from members of the Guild; separate outpourings from Georgellen
Davies, Eleanor Gates, and Amy Yamashita almost wiped Katie out
but, supported by her two companions, she remained attentive in the
loose assembly. She was touched by the words of those who did speak
but moved beyond all reason by the sight of people like retired Post-
master Jeffery standing against the wall with his entire family dressed
in its Sunday best, and Vilho the Finn—wearing a large tie in some
foreign, antiquated bow—keeping silent company with the Morans,
father and son, past proprietors of Fern's Mechanical Garage. Katie
spotted Dr. Healy slipping out the rear door. Physicians don't show up
at funerals, she told herself, at least not for patients in their caseload,
yet the man must have been in the chapel throughout the proceedings.
An elder woman came forward and identified herself as the librarian
at North Coast Regional High School in the era when Katie was a hell-
raiser and Elisabeth Lowrie had volunteered to help; she expressed
her condolences in the simplest, plainest terms and withdrew.

As the informal gathering broke up, Katie's contingent was
crossing the parking lot when she heard a voice call out and back-
tracked to greet a feeble, shrunken woman wearing an oversized rain-
coat over pajamas or a hospital gown; she was escorted by a teenage
girl in a denim jacket worn over a print dress. When the girl introduced herself, she motioned that her great-aunt, Hazel Smith, could
no longer talk; Katie recognized the former star route mail carrier who

appeared to have suffered a stroke. Her palsied hand passed Katie a card; the great-niece expressed honest condolences for them both, then walked her gaunt relation toward a car.

Once Suzanne, Letty, and Katie were in Suzanne's VW van, Katie read the preprinted card aloud.

"Oh, that one," Letty said, staring out the window. "That's Saint Teresa's prayer. I know that one by heart."

Chapter 13

Ross let her inside his house which, at first glance, seemed kept up; she avoided looking closely into the kitchen or bathroom as they headed for the den, where she sat on the sofa's edge. He said he was sorry about her loss and explained he had been up the Coast, trying and failing to secure a gig in one of the fleets running out of Fort Bragg, Trinidad, or Crescent City; he'd only heard about her mother and the memorial service upon his return.

"Did you see DD up there, Ross?"

He turned down the volume on the TV and settled into Lloyd Hanover's easy chair, crossing his legs. The hole in the sole of one wool sock revealed a second sock of a different color underneath. "No."

"Are you sure you didn't see him in Fort Bragg, or Willits, someplace like that?" Katie asked. "I know you did, Ross."

"How do you know that?"

"You saw him, damnit!"

"Okay, okay, cool it. I saw the guy."

"You did?"

"I did."

"Where?" She cleared her throat and straightened her spine, throttling an impulse to jump up and shout at the man. "Up in some barn somewhere cleaning MJ? Come on, Ross, start talking. I know what he's into. I wrote him a letter before Mom died but I never heard back."

"Hey, Katie, I really was bummed when I heard about your ma." Ross re-crossed his legs. "Okay, can't lie to you, Lowrie. I saw the kid when he blew through here about three, four weeks ago, just when I was heading out."

"He blew through here? So, I guess he still doesn't know about his grandmother."

"Don't think so, Katie."

"Wow! DD blew through Santa Cruz without even stopping in Cliffport where his grandmother was deathly ill. I don't know if I can get my head around that one."

Ross started reaching for his cigarette rolling kit then stopped. "Jesus, Katie! The way you're lookin' at me! What do they say? 'If looks could kill...?'"

Katie shook her head, closed her eyes, and felt the muscles of her right eye squeezing tighter than the rest of her face. "He could've stopped by to see his grandmother, Ross. Why didn't you make him?"

"Did you say, *why didn't I make him*? Come on, Katie. I'm not a cop. And I didn't know your ma was going to die. He said he was planning on gettin' there."

"Well, he didn't and now it's too late. The one person in the world who loved him no matter what. Shame on him, shame." She collapsed back into the couch, swinging her boots onto a pile of newspapers loosely stacked on the coffee table. "So, where'd he go?"

"He asked me not to tell anyone."

"Oh, knock it off, Stewart. Where'd he say he was going?"

"Shit!" Ross took up his tobacco pouch and cigarette papers. "Said he was headed for Baja."

"Baja, California?"

"No, Lowrie: Baja, Alaska, whaddaya think? Now give me a break with the interrogation, okay?"

"No, not okay. I'm serious. Why Baja? You know, so tell me, goddamnitall."

"He said he wanted to take it easy for a while, someplace where it's warm and sunny. And he wanted to get in some surfin' down there or somethin'."

"Oh bullshit! He hasn't been surfing for five years."

"I'm just tellin' you what he told me. He said he wanted to see some surfin' buddies, okay?"

"Where are these quote surfin' buddies unquote?"

"I don't know. Ensenada? Shit. Now I'm snitchin' on him."

"You're not snitchin' on him. I'm his mother for God's sake. But what's this sudden interest in surfing?"

"I don't fuckin' know. That's what he said."

Taking her boots off the table, she accidently dragged the newspapers onto the floor.

"Fuck 'em."

"Ross. Don didn't go to Mexico to conduct business by any chance?"

"You figured out about his tea business, I guess."

"Everybody knows what's comin' down in Mendocino. You knew about it all along without ever even telling me."

"I didn't fuckin' know about it all along, Miss Lowrie, so don't bitch at me, goddamnitall. And I'm not lyin' to you now. I thought he might be getting into that shit whenever he went inland but you know him better than I do. Your kid does not exactly talk a lot, right? I didn't ask and he didn't tell. No business a' mine what somebody else's doin' so long as they stay out of my shit."

"Oh, give me a break with the profound philosophy, Ross. When did he say he was planning to visit home? When he got back from surfing?"

"I forget. If he told me, I forget. Honest. When he passed through Santa Cruz on his way north again, I guess. He did mean to see his grandma, for sure."

"But not me," she added, smirking. "If you see him, Ross, I mean before I do.... Well, I guess you might as well tell him right off about my mom." She leaned forward and scooped some newspapers up off the floor.

"Just leave 'em there."

"Listen, Ross, it's lookin' like Thanksgiving Day we're going to have a little gathering in Cliffport. Just family and friends. DD didn't make it to the memorial service in Fern, but he might want to be in Chapel Grove when we spread his grandmother's ashes in the cemetery there. You ought to be there too, Ross."

He brushed some clumps of hair out of his eyes, raising his eyebrows. "Think I might do that, Katie."

"My Aunt Suzanne's coming down from Cloverdale and Uncle Mike's collecting Josie at the airport. Remember my old best friend, Josie Wilton? She's flying down from Seattle. They'll all be staying at the house. I forget, did you ever meet them?"

"Who, your aunt and uncle? Maybe. I've got a good memory 'cept it's a little short."

"Probably from smokin' weed since about junior high."

"Very sharp, Lowrie. You get a fuckin' A for observation for that one."

"Suzanne's not really my aunt. She was like my mom's best friend ever. Letty should come up to the grove with us too. And you. I'd give anything to be able to let DD know about it. You only get to bury your people once."

"Tell me about it," he said, letting his eyes drift toward the ads coming on before the five-o'clock evening TV news.

"Baja...." She mused aloud, her eyes likewise turning toward the flickering images. "Is DD running from the law, Ross?"

"Not that I know of."

"Then what's he doing in Mexico? What if he does get into trouble down there, then what?"

"I told you what he told me and that's all I know. He'll be okay. You think they haven't seen the likes of him south of the border before? I don't think they'll bother with him unless he messes up."

"How can you sit there so fucking sure everything'll work out? You know how long since he's been home for Thanksgiving or anything else? Anyway, this Thanksgiving dinner'll be a simple potluck. There's not going to be any fancy sit-down supper. Nothing's going to be the same in that house ... not without my mom there."

"Potluck's cool by me."

"And you don't have to bring anything, you dork. They'll be plenty to eat and drink, for sure."

The broadcast opened with an announcement about the latest gas prices and potential rationing.

"Can you believe what those fuckin' A-rabs are doin' to us again?" he volunteered.

"I haven't been following it but I'm sure not going to be keeping the glasshouse warm this winter if that embargo starts again. Natural gas prices go up right along with gas prices at the pump. Hey, what was DD driving anyway, the old Fleetside? Or did he score his big pickup truck after the crop came in?"

"He was driving one of those compact numbers. Ford Courier, I think it was. Totally bare of ornaments. Stripped down to the essentials. Brand new but cheap out the gate, fur shure."

"A mini-pickup?" She scoffed. "That's not the mean machine my little boy wants to be seen in."

"Good thing he's drivin' that and not a monster like mine with another oil embargo on the horizon. It's startin' to cramp my style, know what I mean?"

"*Your style?* Oh, okay, Ross, listen, I'm going. It's getting late and I want to get out of here before it's too dark."

"Gettin' dark earlier every day."

She put the last newspapers on the table and rose. "You sure you told me everything you know?"

"Yeah, I did, now get the fuck out of the way of the TV, would ya'?"

"Help me out on this, Ross. If DD doesn't join us this time in Chapel Grove he'll be sorry for the rest of his life."

"Course I'll tell him if I see him. Then he'll know I snitched on him too."

"Oh, come on. We're not in Mountain School's old playground anymore, Ross. You see him, you tell him, then you tell me. At least have the guy call home."

"Fur shure."

"Of course, you don't have a phone he could use. It's not your *style*."

"You know us Ben Lomond Mountain hillbillies aren't good enough for modern telephones like you rich people on the coast."

More commercials came on, and he walked her to the front door, standing on the stoop in his stocking feet.

"Those your dogs I hear out back?"

"Ol' Lloyd built a nice dog run with some shelter for his hunters. I'm tryin' not to let my animals into the house. I'd like to keep the Hanover's home nice long as I can, know what I mean?"

"Good luck with that, Stewart."

"I don't want any uppity visitors comin' from Cliffport drivin' away thinkin' I'm some sorta dirty hippie." He chortled, turning up the collar of his thermal-lined flannel shirt.

Lights had come on inside the houses of the hamlet off New Faith Lane.

"Hey, those people over there are gone."

"They are, just like I told ya'. Evacuated when the first rain came. Month ago, this fire marshal arrives—jerk-off. You can see my chain's down now, right? Cal Fire told me I had to leave that passage open for emergency vehicles. Something about being an 'unrecorded loop road.' You can cut through there on your way out now, save yourself some time."

She told him how Monteflores had sent the fire marshal up to harass her about defending her property from wildfire, then they exchanged reports about the razing of Cliffport Town and rumors that the old Mackenzie Lodge was to be demolished soon too.

"So, are you coming to the ceremony for my mom?"

"Yeah, I am."

"Good. Just don't tell anyone else about our gathering in the cemetery. This is going to be a private affair."

"Fur shure. I'm sorry you lost her, Katie. I mean, she was one real human bein', all the way down to the ground."

"Well, you come to Chapel Grove and you tell her that, Ross. She'll be happy to hear you say that to her in her favorite place on earth."

"I will then. I most definitely will." He walked her toward the truck until his socks reached sharp gravel and he stopped short, bending over for a handful of small stones he started winging into the wild fennel across the lot. "I won't have to make a speech or nuthin', will I?"

"Oh, Ross! Just show up at the house before noon on Thanksgiving Day. We'll carpool up to the Cuesta Ridge Lane off Everson Road and walk in. Thanksgiving's when we always lay wreaths on the McLoughlin graves ... and my brother's. I guess that's one tradition I'll be keepin' up alone from now on unless DD gets a clue. I better go now."

"Git then. Road down's already too dark."

"See you next week and don't sweat it, Ross. It'll just be like family."

"I'll be there. Drive safe now."

Katie steered off the gravel, easing the jostling Ford over the eroded dirt surface cut through the wild roses, then gunning it across the last stretch of crumbling pavement where Scotch broom and bracken ferns were breaking through the cracks. With a will all its own, her right eye twitched, and an orange and brown sunset through the trees aggravated the challenge of navigating the first stretch of curving, shoulderless, unmarked road.

*

Nov. 12, 1974

Coastal Property Management

PO Box 666, San Jose, CA 95113

To Whom It May Concern:

My mother, Elisabeth A. Lowrie, died November 3rd. We want to hold a private gathering at the cemetery gravesites of the family and forebears.

I am writing to ask your permission to lead no more than 10 people onto your private property on Thanksgiving Day afternoon. Some of the older people can not attend if they have to hike the difficult path within the boundaries of my parcel but they could reach the cemetery by walking in from the Cuesta Ridge Lane.

We would park no more than 4 vehicles outside the gate to the reservoir and exit out Everson Road before 3PM.

Please grant this exception so that the people closest to the deceased can pay their respects in a private memorial ceremony in Chapel Grove.

Sincerely,

Kaitlin Lowrie

Kaitlin Lowrie

One Grade Rd. Cliffport CA 94597

PERMISSION DENIED

Coastal Property Mgmt.

Fr: *Tad Kingsley*

Date: 11/16/74

CC: *Gerald Bartelson, CPM*
Neil Blazer, S2S
Bob Rasmussen,
Monteflores Film.

When Katie phoned Suzanne to firm up the Thanksgiving weekend plans, she read the letter she had sent—and Coastal Property Management's response—and confessed that she was in no condition to contest CPM's authority by appealing to S2S, Monteflores, or any other representatives of YMS, if they could be found.

"They say corporations have the same rights as real people do," Suzanne said.

"Who says that?"

"That's the law of the land, kiddo. Been that way for a while. Only they left out the part requiring corporations to show a little heart sometimes, like real people do. What cold sons-of-bitches would deny a simple request like that? People who hide like that inside some corporation have lost their souls."

"It makes me mad but I can't fight back right now."

"We'll make it work, sweetie. It's just so ugly what money lets people get away with these days. I'm glad Elisabeth didn't hear me cursing a minute ago. I'd be going to Hell!"

"You aren't going to Hell. People with souls like yours don't go to Hell. Besides, Mom never sent anybody to Hell."

"Oh, I know, I know. And there were some dogs she should've shot dead in their tracks, probably a few men too. She would've been justified. But all she ever wanted, after your father deserted you guys—"

"... and that was after her father deserted her—"

"... *Ahimè!* • All Elise wanted was to put a cot outside and sleep under the stars. That's all she ever wanted to do. She came up to Cloverdale after your brother died and then again when your dad walked out a year later. She asked me each time if she could sleep outside under the stars. Poor Elisabeth."

"I didn't know that."

"Of course you didn't, Katie. Now listen. Have we covered everything? Mike's picking up your girlfriend and he has to get back to work on Monday, so well be arriving in separate vehicles. Besides, I might

---

• *Alas! (It)*

359

want to stay on longer or something. But are you sure you have enough room in the house for all of us?"

"How does this sound? You and Mike sleep in my room. Letty sleeps in DD's old room. I'll make my seed room—"

"... your what?"

"Where I dry herbs and keep my seeds, my seed room. I'll make that comfortable enough for Josie to sleep in there. If DD ever shows up...."

"Yes...?"

"Well, who knows? We'll make it work. I guess they'll always be room for him somewhere, right? I invited Ross. He's an old friend of the family. And I hope Pieter Tuelling will be coming.... you remember him?"

"I remember. The friend of the family."

"He is. But Ross and Pieter can both sleep at home. I sent two letters to Pieter, one where he's been camping up the Coast and the other to his PO Box in Soquel. I don't know if he'll get them. He missed the service in Fern, but he really dug my mom, you know?"

"I still can't get over that baloney about not letting us walk over their property. Okay, it's not a big deal, I know. We'll just give ourselves enough time to hike up from the house. I hope I can still make it."

"I'll make sure everybody who's invited makes it even if we do have to trespass."

"*Mamma mia!* Take it easy now. Are you eating, sleeping? Kaitlin?"

"Suzanne ... I miss her."

"Don't do that. Your voice sounds just like Ellie's."

"But I miss her so much."

"Oh, baby.... So do I, so do I."

*

Donald Duncan Lowrie appeared in Cliffport, visibly hungover after having spent Sunday night in New Faith, where he had been informed about his grandmother's death and the plans for Thanksgiving Day. From Ross, he had also learned that his mother was fully aware of his Mendocino National Forest capers, that Leticia Morales was enjoying honorary membership in the family household, that the razing of Cliffport Town had been accomplished, and that the former orchard had been converted into garden terraces with ornamental, flowering shrubs. Now he remained speechless while his mother filled him in on Elisabeth's final days and, after a brief reunion with Baby Blue Eye, he declared his intention to sleep in New Faith, grabbed some clothes off the closet rack in his occupied room, and said he would be back the next day.

Tuesday, her son's deceit about the Hoedads didn't seem worth further discussion when he checked in before taking off on foot to inspect the place he had once called home. He studied the clever construction of the welcoming hut under the oak and the upgraded irrigation system's assembly visible aboveground, but he avoided the vicinity of the glasshouse on this way to scout out the situation at the millpond and conditions in Chapel Grove. Two hours later, on his way off the premises, he described to his mother the sorry state of the path to the cemetery, where poison oak and brambles encroached upon the trail so aggressively he had at times to bushwhack his way through with his Bowie knife. The rotten, waterlogged fourteen steps up, over, and down the mammoth fallen trunk were slippery and unstable. Some of the gravesites were indiscernible beneath plant debris. Don unilaterally declared he would devote Wednesday to making the trail to Chapel Grove passable and preparing the cemetery clearing for the event. When he asked his mother for the keys and combinations to the new locks on the gates barring the fire road winding closer to the trailhead, she reminded him that those roads and gates all belonged to someone else now, and she recited the regulations put in place while he had been away. He put his fist through the pantry drywall before bounding outdoors and driving away.

When he did return Wednesday morning, she watched from the picture window as the eighteen-year-old hauled tools and supplies from the cul-de-sac to the landing at Jan's bench overlooking the upper meadow. Each time he passed near the glasshouse, she grew alarmed: if he ran into Letty, the two of them would embark on their first encounter—or confrontation—beyond her command. Out on the deck, she used the binoculars to glass his movements uphill and down as he hefted a large roll of metal matting on his back then carried a backpack and a soiled canvas tote he plopped onto the ground; a folding saw, a folding shovel, a short-handle pickax, and a rubber-headed mallet spilled out. From the pack, he removed a carpenter's belt with a framing hammer, a burlap sack tied with rope, and a battered steel thermos; from his work jacket, he pulled out a pack of cigarettes and—seated on the mossy slab of the primitive bench—he sipped coffee, smoked, and stroked Baby Blue. It became clear that his covert operation in the forests of Mendocino had taught her son the skills and work habits which she had never been able to instill. The next time she raised the binoculars, he had disappeared into the woods and the roll of metal mesh was missing from his staging area. Baby Blue was hobbling downhill, no doubt making her way back to wherever Letty was busy keeping the Redwood Coast Nursery in some semblance of working order. Katie stepped into the house through the pantry and took another look at the new hole in the old sheetrock.

Toward the end of the day, Don reported having weeded and raked the gravesites and set aside a pile of long, flat, young redwood sprays for anyone who might want to lay boughs upon a grave. He had unrolled the mat of metal meshing and pounded it into the steps carved into the fallen log, as well as driven spikes to secure posts spanned by new handrails leading up, over, and down both sides of the staircase. The debarked poles might not support a body's full weight but would offer something to hold onto; the metal grid embedded in the risers, nosing, and treads of the steps would provide better footing. Respectful of his hidden feelings—likely hidden even from himself—and appreciative of his productive work, as well as wary of crossing the willful young man, Katie didn't question any of Donald's actions until he retrieved a duffel bag from the cab of the Courier and brought it up to the deck where he had left his carpenter belt and nail bag. While setting the table for their supper, Katie watched him pull some newly sawn redwood burls from the carryall—and Jody's boots.

"Wait, DD!" she shouted out the kitchen window before bolting outside. "What are you doing?"

He lodged one boot upside down between his knees and held his Bowie knife in his hand.

"Stop! First tell me what you're planning to do."

He said he was going to slit open the soles, set a redwood burl inside each boot, and plant them where his Uncle Jody was buried within the extension of the picket fence enclosing the McLoughlin's family plot. She dropped into a chair, composing herself before wondering aloud about the wisdom of such a move. He claimed that since the boots rightly belonged to his dead uncle—no one else—and since he himself would never wear them again, using them to establish a pair of growing redwoods seemed like a good way to honor Jody Lowrie and his "gran'ma" at the same time. Katie realized she was of no mind to argue and, in any case, he proved unstoppable: before she could open her mouth, he had punctured the sole with the tip of his blade and proceeded to slash an asterisk into the leather. She knew it was no use challenging him or trying to engage him in further dialogue; he sliced the second boot's sole the same way. Folding back the flaps, he experimented with different nails, tacking the star-shaped cuts open so that the burls wouldn't be impeded from sending roots into the ground.

She despaired of relaying to him the legendary account of John McLoughlin standing in the clearing with his thumbs in his overalls' straps, staring up into the cathedral spires, telling Elise—or had it been Jan?—how those original redwoods should be preserved. But what if the trees did take, she asked him aloud. Even if only one sprout survived, it would shoot upward and outward, eventually blocking all sunlight from reaching the ground. She explained that its growth would ultimately fill in the only opening in the ancient forest, which was the reason the graves had been sited there in the first place. The folly of siting a pair of redwoods in the middle of the cemetery had not occurred to him. She suggested planting the boots to either side of the trailhead near Jan's bench instead, where they would become a natural expansion of the forest's edge and create an impressive, twinned gateway to Chapel Grove. He stared at the second upturned boot between his knees and said nothing. She understood that he was eighteen, undereducated, and uninformed, and she knew he still remained beyond the reach of the historical and prehistorical tendrils that gripped her imagination and upon which the perpetuation of Cliffport's life-and-death cycles now depended, more than ever—upon her. Donald sheathed his knife, said he would consider her suggestion overnight and plant the boots somewhere in the morning; he placed everything back inside the duffel bag and said goodbye, heading downhill. Rushing through the house on her way to the front porch, she stopped herself at the door and did not call him back for food. *All right then, if he's his own man now, if he's too proud to sit with his mother and eat Letty's chili verde, let him get up his own supper somewhere eating beans out of a can in New Faith.* She wondered if her son would ever again share his feelings and thoughts with her while sitting together at the round table or out on the deck or up on Jan's bench. Katie put more split wood into the stove on top of which sat the Dutch oven full of Letty's slow-cooked stew, simmering alongside a kettle of beans and a pot of rice; even if Donald Duncan didn't see fit to do so, soon enough others would gladly heat up tortillas and help themselves.

She laid and lit a fire on the andirons then lingered on the hearth, her hands resting on the madrone mantelpiece as she studied the three framed photographs of her mother, which she had positioned on the shelf among ceramic vases full of yellow-flowering Oregon grape, white-flowering manzanita, and early red Christmas berries, as well as a yard-long branch of knob cone pine with its light green needles and whorled clusters of attached, closed cones. The first picture, a Brownie Kodak print dated 1931, showed Elise standing outside the A-frame studio which her husband had had built for them after their honeymoon abroad and before their first child; she wears a linen smock, her hair—held in place with a potter's tool—piled on her head, her clay-spattered hands hanging by her side, her fair face smiling. Another snapshot showed her hair pulled back off her face and her canvas duck vest zipped closed over a hooded sweatshirt; she leans her weight on the top rail of a fence, sticks one hand in her jean pocket, and engages in conversation with someone outside the picture's frame; Dickens the Beagle lies on the ground, his snout resting across one of Elise's boot tops; two children to raise, a yard full of animals to care for, a Victory Garden to tend, and a moody, frustrated, alcoholic husband to contend with, 1944. The third photograph showed her mother in profile, sitting on a folding chair, reading glasses on while earnestly making notes in her capacity as recorder at a meeting of the Guild; she wears a cardigan over a plaid collared shirt; her wavy hair, held back by a barrette, shows some gray; even in sideview, her hips look wider and she bears more weight; Elisabeth Lowrie, working divorcee, living alone with a seventeen-year-old daughter running reckless and wild, 1953.

Katie went into her mother's bedroom, closed the door, and wrapped her hands around Elise's cork-stoppered cookie jar. Earlier in the month, Suzanne had hand-delivered Katie's notarized authorization for the release-of-cremains from the crematorium and received in return the black plastic box with its conveniently hinged top, but no one had been present when Katie had transferred the contents to the ceramic jar and discarded the handout on regulations concerning the dispersal and disposal of human ashes.

She lay down on her mother's bed, draping a bandana across her eyes to rest before guests arrived. Although Mike would be bringing Josie with him later, Aunt Suzanne could show up anytime. Katie worried how long it would be, if ever, before her aunt's invocation of "time" and her uncle's faith in "grace" would effectively bring her lost son back into the dwindled family fold.

*

Thanksgiving Day, the houseguests at One Grade Road fixed their own late, light breakfasts and loafed about until Pieter Tuelling arrived in his Cheyenne, delivering a bouquet of handpicked flowers and foliage, then Ross and Don showed up in the Dodge truck; without dropping by the house, DD headed straight uphill. By noon, Katie was guiding the procession above the glasshouse, skirting the upper meadow, and pausing at Jan's bench, where their presence provoked a severe scolding from Stellar jays. Given the raw evidence of Donald's planting project on either side of the trailhead—a pair of old cowboy boots, heels and soles sunk into disturbed soil, toes pointed toward Chapel Grove—Katie encouraged her son to explain the meaning of the gesture to the assembled family friends. He declined, so she summarized before re-shouldering the woven sling bag, leading the company in slow, silent, single file.

Surrounded by a dozen trees in Chapel Grove over two-hundred-and-twenty-five feet tall—at least three towering above two-hundred-and-sixty—the group formed a circle around the jar she placed in the clearing. Once the jays' squawking had faded away, Katie stepped forward: "Nobody's in charge, okay? If anybody wants to speak, speak. I have something to read I'll save for when we spread Mom's ashes. Then whoever wants to can take some of those boughs Donald piled up over there to lay on the McLoughlin graves—or Jody's.... That's what Mom taught us to do around Thanksgiving every year, to honor their memories. Now we're honoring hers. Suzanne?"

"I didn't want to be here doing this today, or ever, but I guess I'll begin with something Elise gave me the last time I saw her." She retrieved an envelope from her jacket's inside pocket and broke the seal. "She asked me to be sure to read this ... well, now. I wouldn't be able to do this if I didn't feel like I know you all. This is the first time we've met, Pieter, but I feel like we've known each other a while."

"*Jaja*, is so, Suzanne, sure enough."

"I never met you two guys before," Ross interjected. "But I've sure heard a lot about you."

"I've heard lots about you too, Ross—"

"... all good, fur shure," he said, grinning and shaking his mane.

"Anyway," Suzanne continued, "Ellie was my closest friend in the world, bar none."

"Why don't you tell them how you guys met," Katie proposed.

"Mike and I were talking about that on the way down. We met Elise when Mike and I were newlyweds in Santa Cruz. And we're pretty sure it was at an arts and craft fair at the grand opening of the Vet's Hall downtown that Mike had worked on. I was into making jewelry at the time and selling it about six months of the year in a shop in Capitola Village. What years were we living in Santa Cruz, Mike?"

"1930 to 1938."

"Then we must have met your mother—your grandmother, Donald—in 1931 or 1932, right in there."

"Just so everyone knows," Katie volunteered, "Suzanne carried my brother, Jody, out of the hospital when he was born in 1932. That's how long she's been part of the Lowrie family."

"Not exactly, Katie, but I was there when he was born in the house."

"Wasn't Jody born in Santa Cruz Hospital on Soquel Drive like me?"

"That's what your father wanted, but Elise knew a public health nurse trained in midwifery. So, with a doctor on call at the old Davenport Hospital built for the cement plant families, Ned let her have the baby at home. Jody was born at home. And I was carrying your brother around his very first day on earth. I held you in my arms the day after you were born, too, four years later."

"Wow ... see what I mean, everybody?"

"Anyway. Mike and I moved to Cloverdale in 1938 and we've been there ever since. But we stayed in touch with the one and only Cliffport Lowries all these years. She was the best friend I ever had or ever will have. She was a little older than me. Nobody ever had a better sister...."

Mike slipped some reading glasses out of his coat pocket and passed them to her.

"I guess that's my cue to shut up and read this. I'm starting to repeat myself. Can everybody see where Ellie wrote the word CREDO on the envelope? I haven't read this before, so it'll be the first time for all of us."

Donald crouched down onto his haunches. "What does Credo mean?"

"What someone believes." Suzanne replied. "Isn't that right, somebody?"

"*Jaja, das es het*, that's it," Pieter responded. "Credo: This what I believe."

"Wow. It's pretty long. Okay, so here goes:

To Whom It May Concern:
I would like to write a tribute to all the people who have made it possible for me to pass the last days of my life at home rather than in the hospital. Living is not an illness and dying is not a disease. Being able to release my grip on this life while staying in my own home has been a blessing beyond words. I hope that before the time comes to read this, I will have had the opportunity to thank every one of you from the bottom of my heart but that may not happen. You know who you are, and you are treasures to me.

What I want to declare is that since I was a child I have seen and felt God's Love working for me (as it works for all of us) and, in adulthood, I have felt Christ's death and resurrection, not as abstract beliefs but as concrete facts. For various reasons, I found it best not to put my Christianity on parade. I may have been mistaken in not doing so, but I felt no need to join a church. I even feared that any talk of dogma or doctrine might alienate members of my family and friends who mattered to me most. Instead of preaching or proselytizing, I dedicated myself to becoming an instrument through which God could work, and I have prayed constantly that I might be worthy of the task. If God feels

368

that I was worthy the suffering of the cross, I must accept his evaluation and judgment.

I believe that I was not wrong in my decision. When I have needed help, help was there: Family, friends, doctors, ministers, and, most of all, my books and a practice of prayer (however imperfect) have been my allies. When my heart was broken, I did not join social groups or church groups. Rather, the Holy Bible was my textbook, which led, sustained, nurtured, protected, and loved me in a way it is impossible to describe. I have read many other books too difficult for me to comprehend only to find one sentence in them that would lead me back to the Book and open the door to greater understanding.

Let me make it clear that I do not think myself unique. At times, life's twists and turns forced me into a state of misery which many have known; but that condition has allowed me to discover that I need God's mercy and forgiveness, as does anyone. I believe that God loves and seeks each one of us, and we are only saved when we find the courage to face our own weaknesses and shortcomings and those of others. Through my sometimes-painful experiences in the related experiments of marriage and parenting, with successes and failures, I have been led to the most meaningful revelation of my entire life: The Love of God and His redeeming act in the life, death, and resurrection of Jesus Christ. This faith has been the most dominant emotion of my adult life. How many times have I stepped out on air and found that rock beneath my feet!

During this difficult period, as the weakening of my heart prefigures the demise of my earthly existence, I know that I am now where I am by the grace of God. I have great faith for the future and in the Creator who works in each life for the good of all and the eventual coming of the Kingdom of God on earth.

*In closing, I strongly encourage whoever is hearing
these words to believe in yourself. Your commitment to
maintain a sense of personal integrity is the worthwhile and
Christian endeavor in this life. This I believe.
God's blessings on you and yours.*

Elisabeth Piagère Lowrie
September 21, 1973

Suzanne folded the pages, passed the glasses back to her husband, dried her eyes, and exhaled. "Don?"

He sprang to his feet as if from under water. "What?"

"Would you like to go next?"

He looked at their faces then down at the ground. He crossed, uncrossed, and re-crossed his arms. He shoved his fists into his back pockets and bent backward, arching toward the redwood tops whose innermost ring seemed to lean inward, framing the gray sky. Out of sight, a prop plane flew up or down the coastline.

"If I could say what I want to, that sky up there would crack wide open." The circumference of the circle shrank according to some shared, unspoken pulse. "But I don't know how. I didn't even under- stand everything Gran'ma wrote in that." Everyone moved still closer. "I just know those ashes in that jar are my gran'ma's." He caught his breath and, when he noticed that people had moved within arm's reach of one another, dropped back into a squat, crossing his arms over his knees. "I don't know what to say. You go, Ross." A flicker's persistent keew-keew-keew grew faint. "Or you, Mom." Donald sat all the way down on the ground and crossed his legs.

"I'll go at the end. Do you want to speak now, Ross? You don't have to. Nobody does."

"Yeah, okay, but I didn't write a speech or anything. Like Don said, it's hard to talk about. Know something, Katie? I guess I've never even been here before."

"Never?"

"Never have. But I can tell you right now I feel more at home here than in that pioneer cemetery the other side of the mountain where my people are buried. Weird, huh? Okay. Katie told me the other day that her ma would be listening, so I'll tell her what I told Katie: Missus Lowrie, you're the kind of people makes a Stewart proud to be from around here no matter what anybody says about us. That goes for you too, Katie. Now goddamnitall, that's all I'm goin' t'say." The women stepped back to their places after sharing a packet of tissues. "And thanks for invitin' me, Katie," Ross added, "to say goodbye to your ma like this. And your grandma, Don. She was always real kind to me."

A jetliner cruised invisibly high overhead.

"Now you go, Letty," DD said.

"Me? Why me?"

"Yeah, you. You've gotta say something too."

"That's not so, Donald," Katie stated.

Letty took one step closer to the jar and spread her boots wider than usual.

> *Nada te turbe,*
> *nada te espante*
> *todo se pasa,*
> *Dios no se muda,*
> *la paciencia*
> *todo lo alcanza,*
> *quien a Dios tiene*
> *nada le falta*
> *solo Dios basta.* [1]

"Now tell us what's it means," Ross said.

"Yeah," Donald chimed in. "Like translate it or something."

"That's the prayer card that lady gave you, Katie, in the church parking lot in Fern. That was my grandmother's favorite prayer. It's so weird but I feel like my Ita's here with us right now."

"Maybe she's calling you back home, Letty," Katie said. "Now everybody, listen. I'll put that card—in English—over the fireplace when we go back down to the house. Anything else, Letty?"

She shook her head no and took one step back.

"Josie?" Suzanne said.

"Wait a sec'. I've got to sit down for this."

"It's not wet on top of the needles," Donald said.

Josie lowered herself to the ground and kept her knees hugged together. "I've known Missus Lowrie all my life. See what I mean? I still call her Missus Lowrie as if I were a little kid. Katie and I went to Mountain School together and then high school. Ross knows, he was there."

"Yeah I was."

"When I look back I think we had a pretty good childhood growing up around here, and a lot of it was because of Missus Lowrie. Two brainless girls without a care in the world, right, Katie? Then your brother died, and that's when Katie came to live with my family for a year. Wasn't it a year?"

"About."

"It probably sounds self-centered to say this right now, but that was a huge turning point in my own life. I mean, up until then Missus Lowrie was just there like a second mom to me. I took her for granted. Then when she wasn't there—when she was recovering from Jody's death and all—I got to know you like the sister you will always be to me, Katie. That's when we learned how to play guitar, right? God, your mother put up with a lot of nonsense from us."

"She did."

"Remember how we used to take sleeping bags and sleep out on the porch and keep her awake all night long?"

"Sure, I remember."

"Coming back here for this ... give me a second, please." A band of Stellar jays squealed, pausing in the branches before passing out of the clearing. "Coming here I was thinking that Elisabeth Lowrie defined for me what it meant to be from here and live with dignity."

"Hey! That's what I was tryin' to say."

"Right, Ross, I got it, I got it. The way Missus Lowrie was in charge at the store and helped in the high school library and always gave away produce from her garden ... your garden now, Katydid. She took me on my first visit to an art museum in San Francisco. Remember that, Katie?"

"No, but I believe you. I'm sure she did."

"Then when Katie went back East, I got super close to Elise when her back was so bad and there was my son, Jeff, and you, DD—"

"It's Don now."

"Sorry, right: Don. So, I had you two monkeys on my hands. But she was so appreciative of anything I did for her. Before that I always felt welcome to sit at the Lowrie's table but after that I felt it was a privilege. Most of you probably know what I'm talking about, so I'll just finish by saying that Missus Lowrie was the kindest, most generous, forgiving person I've ever known. And nothing in what you read a minute ago really surprised me."

Branches stirred in the treetops as a breeze shushed through the grove.

"I might as well say something else. I'm glad I never saw her in the last year—there I go sounding selfish again—"

"... she did get pretty persnickety sometimes," Katie volunteered, "right, Letty?"

"But I mean, this way I can think of her before she got so sick. From now on every time I see a simple ceramic mug or a simple pot or a simple bowl—how did she used to say it, Katie? '... an honest piece of pottery...'?"

"Oh, boy, that's Ellie all right," Mike said, nodding his head, chuckling. "Honest pottery!"

"Right, Katie? '... honest....' Anyway, I'll know she's somewhere nearby." Josie released hold of her knees, crossed her legs, and addressed the center of the circle. "I miss you, Missus Lowrie. I'll always love you and be grateful for what you gave me for as long as I live."

People looked to one another to see who would recover and speak next.

"Why don't we all just sit down," Katie suggested, "whoever wants to." After a moment only Mike and Pieter were left standing. "Mike? Pieter? Do either of you want to say something before I go?"

"I'll pass," Mike responded. "Like Suzanne said, I don't want to be here doing this, you know what I mean? Talking about it just makes it worse, for me anyway. Your ma...." He went all the way down to the ground and shielded his brow.

"Pieter?"

"*Jaja*, is my turn, sure. I first want to thank the Lowrie family for everything. I wasn't going to say anything but after Letty, I got the courage now to recite something you all know."

"Why after me?" Letty asked.

"Because I'm going to repeat that sonagun Psalm Number 23—in Dutch. Sure, why not?"

"In Dutch?" Ross said.

"Psalm Number 23?" Donald Duncan blurted out. "I don't even know what that is."

"Sure you do," his mother corrected him. "The 23rd Psalm."

"Sorry, but no I don't."

"Well, listen and we can look it up later."

Pieter cleared his throat and rested his hands on his front, fingers incompletely interlaced. "Your grandmother ... your mother ... she knew her Bible, *oh ja*. So, she'll understand this one even in Dutch. It's the Lord's Prayer, eh?" His heavily lidded gaze settled on the jar as he recited the words then, with difficulty, went down to the ground while Kaitlin Lowrie rose to her feet.

"When I was going through Mom's things—she had everything arranged perfectly, of course—I mean, she was like one-hundred percent considerate of me as her executrix or whatever they like to call me down in Santa Cruz. Her papers were all in order, that part's been easy. But by mistake or on purpose, she left a diary in her bureau. I never even knew she kept a diary. Did you know that, Suzanne? No? Me neither. I never saw it in her dresser before and I've been in and out of there for years. So, I guess maybe she was hiding it, until the end."

She extracted a schoolchild's composition book from the woven bag.

"She only kept it for a little while, I guess, when she was finishing up her NOTEBOOKS … the story of her life … most of you know about that, right? Anyway, in her diary she wrote things she felt like didn't belong in her memoir. She even wrote that somewhere. Stuff she didn't want me to be reading back then, I guess. When you get down to it, I really don't know if she wanted me to read the diary now or not. Swear to God, I don't know if I shouldn't've just chucked it into the fireplace when I found it. But I didn't. I read it. Was that right? Was that wrong? I don't know. I guess deep down I think she really did want me to read it after she was gone. Or maybe she meant to burn it and just spaced out. Anyway, I'm going to read a few short excerpts now. It feels right, so…. Now some of things she says are what we've been talking about, but other things might not be so clear right away. Still, do me a favor and wait till we get back to the house before you ask any questions about what I read, okay? Just see where it lands, let it sink it. We can talk about it later." She took a deep breath and freshened her stance. "Okay, Mom, here goes. This one's dated February 17th. That'd be 1965. This is only part of it:

Yet who can really own a redwood tree? Who is truly in charge of sacred burial grounds? Jan McLoughlin? Big Creek Lumber? In moments such as this, I see—clearly, as the redwood spires shooting into the blue sky above the morning fog wreathing the trunks of those same trees—this truth: no one owns the trees, the fog, the sky. Meanwhile, the dead sleep in their graves and, for now, the giant redwoods stand.

A couple months later—May 20th—after Dorothea McLoughlin died—she wrote this:

I could not tell you what else I wanted to know. I wanted you to be at peace, to be beyond pain, to be rewarded in death for all your selfless kindness in life and undeserved suffering. You were the one in pain, you were the one nearing the end of your earthly life, yet you were the one concerning yourself with me! Was there anything else I wanted to know? Of course, I broke into tears—there was no help for it—and once my sobbing stopped, you made a state-ment that landed squarely in my lap and has stayed there ever since: "Try not to be angry with your father, Elisabeth. It was not his fault, you know. A man like that is to be pitied. People generally do the best they can, they really do.

The next one is a little longer. It's the very last entry, dated June 1st, 1965.

I have left Kaitlin the Eighth Notebook with a letter on her bedside table. I have done my best; they are all hers now. Liliane Piagère, Thomas Lowrie, Dorothea McLoughlin, Uncle John—with so much written about their dying, I discover my beloved daughter and grandchild are still very much alive for me! However, I am done with composing this memoir and weary of getting facts straight, then presenting my feelings about them—presentably! I simply would not have the fortitude to remain composed on the subject of Jody's death—so sudden, so early and unnecessary and unfair! Or Neddy's leaving. Kaitlin and I will have to air that old wound in conversation or else, dear diary, I shall address you alone.

Whether we will be thrown unceremoniously off this place or somehow allowed to stay, I shall always be able to close my eyes and see Aunt Thea standing on the back porch with one hand propping open the screen door. She faces a noontime breeze or an evening one. Her gray hair is coiled atop her head or let loose and held back from her face with her other hand.

To hold Dorothea's Holy Bible in one hand and Mother's in the other gives me a staying power otherwise beyond my

*capacity to invoke. Better to mediate in Chapel Grove—no
better place to pray than on that burying ground. If only
Mother or Dorothea were here now, to help me understand
the workings of the Lord!*

*

From the picture window, Katie watched her son and Uncle Mike
scrutinizing the older man's pickup; Josie was in the vegetable garden
collecting the salad makings; Suzanne was working in the kitchen; and
Letty was sitting at the fireplace, reading an American Standard Bible
that Katie had pulled from the bookcase in the hall. Having fetched a
1.5-liter bottle of Chianti from his truck and plopped it down on the
dining table, Ross was sitting out on the deck, rolling and smoking
cigarettes. Pieter Tuelling was also smoking while wandering alone in
the planted terrace garden. When the table was set and her spaghetti
almost ready, Suzanne called everyone to the table. Katie stood back
as Aunt Suzanne brought on bowls of steaming tomato sauce; at the
sight of the Chianti wrapped in its straw basket bottom, Katie realized
she was revisiting one of her mother's last dreams but whatever had
happened after the feast in the meadow in the dream—she couldn't
quite recall.

After the meal, people left the table, self-absorbed or pairing off
in quiet conversations while Letty made up batches of her Mexican
coffee. Katie and Josie settled in by the fire to restring and tune the
neglected household guitar; Mike and Pieter paced the enclosed
porch, speaking of forests and wildfires in the West. While Ross and
Suzanne seemed to be finding common cause out on the deck, where
he spiked both their mugs from his metal flask, Letty took Mike up to
the glasshouse to show him a problem with the heater, and Donald
tagged along. Whether due to her having adjusted the thermostat—
reducing the frequency and duration of its use—or some undetectable
draft, the pilot light wouldn't stay lit. Mike came back to the house
alone, telling his wife that he would be replacing the heater's thermo-
couple on Friday once stores opened again. Katie and Josie went for a
hike to Lookout Rock.

At first sign of dusk, Pieter left his new phone number with Katie and excused himself for his long drive home; he needed to get back to the cabin before night fell on the unpredictable roads above Soquel Gulch. Ross hailed Don and they left for New Faith, taking a round-about way home, turning south on the Coast Highway until it became Mission Street then, after snagging some items at Zee's Liquors, they drove down Route One to the turnoff for Route 9 leading up into the San Lorenzo Valley. Ross knew a connecting road out of Ben Lomond that would drop them close enough to New Faith to make the detour—for half a gallon of eggnog and a bottle of brandy—well worthwhile.

Friday, Josie borrowed Suzanne's VW bus to visit old friends in Santa Cruz and returned with a set of strings to replace the dead metal relics on Katie's Martin. Mike and Letty went to the plumbing store for supplies to repair the heating unit. At lunchtime, Donald showed up in his mini-pickup. Mike looked it over and promised the boy that, if he brought the accessories, Mike would help him install them on Saturday morning. Without a sturdier frontend, however, the older man didn't see how they could equip the compact truck with the beefy power winch Donald coveted. Mike told the two women he had made the kid a standing offer: Mike would work on the winch attachment in his home shop in Cloverdale if Donald ever showed up there clean.

Saturday morning, Mike and Donald went to work mounting a set of new mud terrain tires, wiring and affixing fog lights above the windshield, and attaching a roof rack with readymade clips to secure a fire extinguisher, a jerry can, and a short-handle shovel—all like those on Mike's truck only smaller. Katie and Suzanne joked with each other about "penis envy," and Suzanne elaborated on her husband's dilemma, for Mike Crogan knew exactly what was going on in the hills and forests of inland Mendocino County. He had been inspecting rural properties for Cal Fire for years, been fighting wildfires for years, and had twenty-three years of employment in at ABC Fire Equipment Company where, as one of its vice-presidents, he worked with departments involved in facility management, purchasing, product development, and public relations. The man could hardly afford to have his name bruited about within the fire protection district, or in Santa Rosa's Press Democrat, as an associate of a rogue marijuana grower operating on government land. Nor did he approve of outlaw businesses paying no fees or taxes so not contributing their fair share to the upkeep of public roads and schools. When the boy took his enhanced vehicle for a trial spin—and never returned—neither Mike nor the women had to wonder aloud about how Donald had earned the cash spent on the new tires, lamps, roof rack, and a Christmas tree air freshener hung from the rearview mirror.

Letty harvested enough Meyer lemons, pineapple guavas, and Hachiya persimmons to fill a shoebox traveling in Josie's luggage and a cardboard carton Mike would carry to Cloverdale after dropping Josie off at the airport for her night flight home. During their afternoon walks and talks, as Katie and Josie had caught up, it became apparent to both that adult life had dealt the two former girlfriends radically different hands. Josie's husband, Bob, was a postgraduate research assistant in electrical engineering at the University of Washington and anticipated joining the work force at Boeing as soon as the next round of hiring commenced. Her son, Jeff, remained undecided if he would spend all his undergraduate years at Reed College or transfer out when he found an academic focus. Josie's own volunteer work at Planned Parenthood was positioning her, she hoped, to land a steady job there once she started her new life as an empty nester.

Suzanne left Cliffport on Monday morning, insisting her niece spent Christmastime in Cloverdale. Katie remarked to herself how quiet it seemed with everyone gone and Letty working somewhere in the nursery. Baby Blue Eye seemed to sulk like so many of her predecessors who had lain on a rug in the pantry, growing older there.

*

Donald drops acid and wants Letty to trip out with him at Hidden Beach. Stalking her inside the glasshouse, he mouths words. Everything about her is round—bosoms, buttocks, face, but why does her skin keep changing colors? Her black ringlets form a halo around her head. Her brown eyes are round. He wonders why she keeps staring back at him. Her smooth cheeks are round. He follows her moves and pictures using the tip of his tongue to slide from the top of her head, down the middle of her face, in between her tits, around and around the dark brown aureoles, over her plump belly, inside her navel, between her legs, up her asshole, licking her all over her butt, up the trough between her shoulder blades, up the back of her neck, and back into her oily, glistening hair. "Maybe some other time. I better keep working." He hears someone coming and runs down the hill behind the house, abandoning his truck and racing through the stump field.

*

Katie returned early from her day trip to Salinas, surprised at finding Donald's Courier and Letty's Toyota still parked in the cul-de-sac. Entering the house, she prepared to pack the persimmons in the empty boot box, entered her son's old room without knocking and found him lying in bed there, smoking. His jeans and Letty's jeans, his underwear and Letty's underwear, his sweatshirt and Letty's sweatshirt—piled on the floor. She heard the shower running down the hall. Donald flashed his hostile smile, teeth bared. She backed out through the doorway, slamming it despite her intention just to bring it to a close.

When she got back from a long walk up Waddell Creek, neither pickup was under the oak. She found a note on the table:

Dear Katie.
I better go home for Xmas now.
The chickens are cooped up. Billy is in the barn.
I closed up the house in case you came back late.
I hope you can forgive me. I'm so ashamed.
I'll call or write you from COLO.
Un fuerte abrazo, •
Letty

• *A warm embrace (Sp)*

*

KT   Who do you think you are, screwing around with Letty like that? Paul Newman?

DD   Mom. I don't know about when you were my age, but you must've heard of free love?

KT   Oh, free love. You're all for that, right? Now don't try and tell me you're in love with her. You barely know her. You don't know her. Or do you screw every girl who's impressed by your bitchin' bod?

DD   Depends. Every sexy one. Every woman too.

KT   What's that supposed to mean?

DD   You know, when's a girl not a girl anymore...? Don't start pretending you're some innocent. You know what people say about you?

KT   What people? What do people say about me?

DD   People up in Fern. In Swanton and Davenport. People from around here.

KT   What do you they say? This better be good.

DD   People think you're a weirdo.

KT   So what? Let 'em. What do I care? What do you care what they think of me? Anyway, name one person around here who's not a weirdo. This whole North Coast is full of weirdos. The Santa Cruz Mountains ... North County ... Santa Cruz is lousy with weirdos. That's just bullshit.

DD   No, Mom, I mean it. People think you're really a weirdo. The goat lady. The scarecrow. The crackpot potter's daughter. I've heard shit like that since high school. Maybe that's why nobody'll ever give me a job around here.

KT   That's not why. Now you're really talking BS, DD.

DD   DON!

KT   You should've seen how many people turned up at your grand-mother's memorial service in Fern. All "weirdos" by your definition.

DD   That service was for Gran'ma not you.

KT   Wrong. It was for your grandmother and for me. People asked about you too.

DD   About me? What do they care?

KT   People were paying respects to us. You're still too young to get it.

DD   You want to know what Josie said about you?

KT   Josie? What did Josie say about me?

DD   It's too bad you never got remarried or something.

KT   She said that? You're making that up. Remarried? Her memory's slipping. Anyway, Jojo lucked out in the marriage department, I'll admit that.

DD   You know what else she said? She said she wishes she knew a way to get you laid.

KT   She did not.

DD   Did too.

KT   Josie wouldn't say that behind my back.

DD   She said it to my face.

KT   When did she say that?

DD   When we were down in the garden. She said, "I love your mom, but I wish we could find another way to get her laid."

KT   What the hell? Josie said that? What'd you say to her?

DD   "Don't look at me."

*

Katie started the tub water running and stripped off her clothes but, realizing she had neglected to stoke the fire, trotted down the hall to refuel the woodstove. A car's headlights swept Grade Road, then its taillights were swallowed in the obscurity farther up. With houselights off and no streetlamps, except for a purplish glow from the glasshouse, Cliffport was pitch black on a rainless, moonless night. The kindling caught, light flashed through the stove's open door, and she glimpsed the image of a naked stick figure reflected back to her from the picture window. "People probably do call you a scarecrow," she told the skeleton as the flareup died down and the fading image turned into a ghost. She latched the stove's door.

Bare feet numbing, she hugged her shoulders and hurried back to the drafty bathroom. The medicine cabinet's mirror was angled open such that she saw herself from the waist up: flat breasts, flat belly; turned sideways: flat back, flat butt. She tucked some hair behind her ears and stepped closer to gaze into the black-spotted glass. *Do the two inside teeth tilt in more or the outside ones stick out? At least they're still white, almost. But what lips would kiss those thin chapped lips?* She glared at the mask; her right eye twitched. *Distress written all over your face for all the weirdos in the world to see.* Katie adjusted the faucet and—without any urge to primp or mug—took another look in the glass. *The crackpot potter's daughter they say? At least I don't have a moustache or hairy cheeks like the bearded lady in a freak show. And my head's not cracked yet.* Without thinking why, she reached for the scissors and cut off the heavily dangling hair at the level of her ear lobes then stepped into the tub, closing the tap with the big toe of one foot and settling lower in the hot water and surveying herself. Her pelvis made her look to herself like a heron or a crane or an egret with foldable wings. Between hips and ribs, her waist neither bulged nor indented; crescent-shaped, her breasts were barely shadows and her nipples, small dark dots underwater. She sank, letting the water adsorb her hair, then surfaced. Floating lines—snippets of brown and gray—matched the color between her thighs and under her arms. Her forearms and upper arms were bare of hair and sinewy. She lengthened her legs: their muscles, sculpted by hard use, were as toned as her biceps. She wondered how those arms and legs had once upon a time taken on everything some men wanted to do to a woman's middle, and if they would ever wrap around another man's hips or head again.

As she passed the washcloth up, down, and around her limbs, back and forth across her chest, in between her legs, she wondered if some sexual stream inside her had run dry forever—or was she merely in the middle of an extended drought? *Maybe Josie was right; perhaps you need to "get laid." But Josie had no right to be so blunt behind my back in front of my son and he had no reason to be so cruel.*

Soaking, hoping her nervous eye wouldn't go haywire over Christmas with the Crogans, she remembered one winter when the Meyer lemon had lost its leaves yet, fertilized, had leafed out again in spring. The bare buckeye in the stump field always sent out new foliage—among the first green hands to applaud winter's end. And didn't the sycamores' dry leaves cling so long the trees looked dead before old growth was sloughed off by new? The persimmon usually held on to a few leathery brown leaves among its deflated, bird-pecked, ornamental fruit, draped like wet, empty gloves rotting out of reach, but, come spring, its branches always decked themselves out in new greenery. *And maybe my sex life will sprout again too,* she thought.

*

Katie   Where's DD?

Ross   I don't know. Guess he left for Baja.

Katie   When?

Ross   Yesterday...? Yeah, yesterday.

Katie   Did you know he cleared every last thing of his out of the house? Is he moving to Mexico now? What a joke! Or will he be coming back here to live with you?

Ross   Jesus, Lowrie, I'm not your kid's parole officer. You look fucked up. Are you loaded?

Katie   I'm not loaded but I am pissed off. Where's his stuff, Ross? Did he take it with him?

384

Ross   It's out in the garage.

Katie   Did he tell you what happened?

Ross.   Said you guys had a fight, is all.

Katie   He didn't tell you what else?

Ross   I don't know, what else?

Katie   He didn't boast about balling Letty? I wonder how long that's been going on. Maybe you know the answer to that one too.

Ross   Oh cut it out. He never told me anything like that. Leave me alone, would you?

Katie   Now she's gone too. She left for Colorado.

Ross   She comin' back?

Katie   How should I know? She said she'd call or write or something.

Ross   Bummer.

She collapses into the couch; he settles into his easy chair.

You want something to eat or drink or something?

Katie   No. Ross, I'm not going to repeat the things he said to me. What's happened to my own son? He hates me, I know he does.

Silence.

I'm so ashamed for him. Or of him. Or about him, I don't know anymore. I hope he's ashamed too, tell you the truth. I guess he's ashamed of me. Something's missing in that kid's makeup.

Ross rolls a cigarette and lights up.

Listen, Ross. I'm going to spend Christmas and New Year's up in Cloverdale. Maybe longer. I can't take it in that house right now.

Ross   I can dig that.

Katie   Do you have any idea how he's hurt my feelings? Before all this came down, I was planning to invite him up to Suzanne and Mike's too. Mike offered to help him trick out his little toy truck in his shop, but he'd have to show up clean.

Ross   Like straight?

Katie   Like not smoking dope. Not stinking like dope. Not carrying dope. Not dealing dope. Like that's going to happen sometime soon. God, Ross, he's only eighteen.

Ross   Exactly how old is that Letty anyway?

Katie   I don't know. Nineteen or twenty. Twenty, I think.

Ross   We did some crazy shit when we were eighteen, nineteen, twenty ... right?

Katie   Tell me about it, Stewart. But DD's digging himself into a really deep hole. Anyway, I came up here to ask you a favor.

Ross   What favor?

Katie   Would you take care of my place while I'm away?

Ross   Take care of it? For how long?

Katie   Are you going to be around between now and the middle of January? It'd be like a little side job, whatever else you're up to.

Ross   What else am I up to and where else would I be? What do you want me to do?

Katie   Visit Cliffport once a day, or twice I guess. Check around. I'll pay you, Ross. Let the chickens out in the morning and change their water. Keep an eye on that damned Billy goat. I've got him staked in the yard now and the barndoor propped open so he can get in and out. Throw him some brush to chew on. Throw some sticks and stones at him—no, don't do that unless he jumps you. I don't know. Throw him some chicken scratch from the barrel in the barn and check his water in the bathtub. Make sure nothing dead's floating around in there. Just make sure he's not doing any damage to himself or anything else. If the weather seems right, you can open up the glasshouse and the doors to the hoop houses. Then you have to come back and close everything up again before nightfall. But make sure you get any critters out of the greenhouse before you do. You can spend the day there if you want.

Ross   You expect me to water all those plants?

Katie   It's cold and wet. They'll be okay for a while.

Ross   What about the ones in the greenhouse?

Katie   No. I've got the bottom heat turned on low-low-low and the overhead misters off. I'm turning off the heater. What survives, survives. Maybe the Redwood Coast Nursery won't have a super-duper crop of new plants for sale this coming spring. I can't deal with that right now.

Ross   How about the dog? I could keep the Blue Baby up here. Might be easier that way.

Katie   She's coming with me. But you'll have to check inside the main house. Use some ammonia to douse the ants if they come out of the kitchen cracks. Leave lights on, you know, make it look like somebody's home. Collect the mail from the box at the gate and the Sentinel from the tube. Take that home with you if you want. Hell, you can stay overnight in the house, live there.

Ross   Where?

Katie   In my house. Sleep there, cook there. You know, live there.

Ross   No way, Lowrie. I'm not staying overnight anywhere. I got my own place to protect. You may not've heard but there's been a hella rash a' burglaries up his way. Something like five since Thanksgiving. Fuckin' meth heads.

Katie   Who?

Ross   Speed freaks livin' out of those crappy trailers left over in the canyon bottom. And they're not shopping for Christmas presents either, know what I mean? They're after money for dope or stuff they can turn into money for dope. Anyway, they're thieves. No, I gotta stick around here at night for the time being. I rigged up a wire to open the kennel and sick my dog on the fuckers from my bedroom if I hear anything suspicious.

Katie   Oh god, Ross. What if it's a raccoon or a cat or something? Or somebody else, like one of your neighbors.

Ross   That's their problem. I've got big signs posted. Most people can read nowadays—except meth heads.

Katie   So how about it? Can you get behind my idea, getting down to Cliffport twice a day? I'm telling you: I'll pay whatever's fair. It'll be like a double commute for you. And you can have all the vegetables you want out of the garden all next year. I haven't got any mouths to feed except mine from now on.

Ross   How about flowers?

Katie   You want flowers? You can have flowers from the cutting beds anytime, no problem.

Ross   Just bullshittin' you, Lowrie. A man can't eat flowers.

Katie   Ha-ha, very funny, macho man.

Silence.

Ross   When'd you say Letty's comin' back from Colorado?

Katie   If she's coming back. Not till spring, if she does. I just sent her a card with the number where I'll be in Cloverdale. Tell you the truth; I don't expect to hear from her for a while.

Ross   Okay. It's a deal. Long as I don't have to spend the night there or water any plants, I'll do 'er. But you gotta make a list of what I have to do and the number you'll be at, shit like that.

Katie   For sure. And I'll leave you the key. Here, might as well take these now.

Ross   Two keys, that's all?

Katie   That's to the pantry door and that's to the front door. That's all I need until Coastal Property Management starts locking the driveway on me or Monteflores' completely fences me in on all four sides. You want some money in advance?

Ross   No, no money. It's going to be a favor, like you said. With your ma and all ... and Donald the Duck actin' like such a jackass.... Hey, I know you're on a bad run right now, Lowrie. And you're goin' need all your money for gas if the price goes up.

Katie   Then I'll buy you a tank of gas when I get back.

Ross   No you won't, not with the monster double tanks I've got. Don't sweat it. I'm livin' like a king now.

Katie   So it's a deal?

Ross   Deal.

Katie   Ross, like I said, if some plants die, they die. Don't worry about it. If there's a freaky hot spell—and you know that can happen—I'll come back and save the nursery stock. Those plants are about all I've got left now....

She rises to leave.

Ross   When you want me to start?

Katie   What's today, Thursday or Friday?

Ross   Thursday, I think. Maybe it's Friday. I don't know.

Katie   So, Thursday, Friday, Saturday, Sunday.... That makes Monday Christmas Eve Day, right?

Ross   Don't ask me.

Katie   I need a couple more days to get ready. God, I gotta get out of there. A house without a Christmas tree? Let's say the day after the day after tomorrow.

Ross   Now how can I remember shit like that? You sure you're not loaded?

Katie   Sunday. Start Sunday. I'll leave a list on the table and anything else I think of. I sure wish you had a telephone, you bozo.

Ross   Us real mountain men are allergic to telephones. You know that.

They walk to front door and step outside.

Katie   You are kinda livin' like a caveman up here, Ross.

He grins and pounds his chest.

Ross   Me Tarzan!

She steps down from the stoop and walks backward toward her truck.

Katie   No thanks, brother. Me no Jane!

Ross   Fuckin' Katie Lowrie...

Katie   What?

Ross   Nuthin'. You have yourself a merry little Christmas, sis'.

Katie   Merry Christmas, Ross. Thanks a lot. See you next year if we both make it that long.

*

At the stables in Pescadero, she had her nursery trailer loaded with aged horse manure and her pickup shell filled to the roof with bales of clean straw to spread over the vegetable garden wherever the fava beans were not standing at least knee-high. Back home, in a rush to further action, she collected a wheelbarrow full of moss rocks and dumped them below the lowest terrace, lifting the largest to set in place—then she came to her senses and let the first rock drop: daylight was fading fast. *They'll be time to build stone walls. Plenty, since stones have replaced people in my life.*

Inside the house, she tore through her son's room, trashing whatever was still tacked to the walls or hanging in the closet, stripping the mattress of blankets and sheets and starting a bonfire in the yard. Restoring the seed room to its former status as her working office and horticultural library, she ran across Jan McLoughlin's Chinese box and sat down with it in front of the fireplace. Katie knew who must have locked the little chest—but what was sealed within? There was no one left alive to answer that question for her. She lay on her mother's bed and reflected upon how—neither kin nor next of kin, only the person nearest to next of kin—she had somehow become the sole guardian of the repository of the collective memorabilia of Mills and Mary-Helen Belcanto and of Jan McLoughlin's Cliffport clan. [2]

*

Pieter Tuelling's magnificent floral bouquet had been left wilting in Elise's amphora since Thanksgiving weekend. Saturday morning, Katie tossed the stalks and, by noon, was driving to the end of the unmarked lane at the top of Soquel Gulch Road—one last stop before vacating Cliffport—with Christmas gifts on the seat between her and Baby Blue. When Pieter saw her vehicle coming in, he finished driving another metal screw into the case of a retractable awning he was attaching along one side of the camper shell and tossed his drill in with the clutter in the front seat. Lifting his woolen flat cap, sweeping back his white hair, redonning the cap, he bowed slightly as she got out of her cab. "Missus Lowrie. Good! Come on quick, we go for a walk before it rains. I got to show you something special."

"Okay," she replied. "Want to come along, Baby Blue?" The Australian shepherd dog sat moping, undecided.

"*Ach*, come on, old gal," Pieter said, walking his thick fingertips back and forth along the dog's furry spine. "We got to keep the old bones moving now."

Blue reached the ground in several stages and sidled up to the man. "Let's go before those sonsaguns clouds drop wet rocks on our heads," Pieter said, leading the way across the clearing, around the garage and into Drika's park, where Katie couldn't help but slow down amid the generous displays of multicolored sasanquas.

"Yours will look like this one day, Katie. But come on, these are not what you got to see today."

The rough lawn terminated at an untended border of salal and huckleberry through which he forged an informal trail into a corridor of bay laurels. Katie called back to the dog resting at the picnic table.

"Wait there, Blue. We'll be right back."

Her guide's gait up the sloping terrain was nimble as ever, whether because he had lost some weight or not she couldn't tell—his blue jeans were always loose and baggy, especially in the seat—but he still stepped lively. After the wet dirt road crested, the view opened: at the far margin of a grassy patch grew the largest specimens of Ribes and Garrya she had ever seen. Fulsome in shape, perfectly in place, the crimson blossoms of the gooseberry and the greenish-yellowish catkins of the silktassel hung in full bloom. "It's like a fairytale."

"*Jaja*, is a fairytale, sure enough. *Das is het.* But who wrote this fairytale? That's what I want to know now. No man planted these beauties here, *nee nee.*"

Katie glanced at her companion; the pensive plantsman carried no shears and wore no loupe around his neck. "Thanks for showing me these, Pieter. I would never have known they were back here."

"Maybe who owns this land does not know that either. We're no longer on Nico's property ... or my property now, I should say, eh? So, I say 'shhh' and maybe peoples will leave them alone. *Ach*, can you hear that rain coming now? Let's go back. I make up some hot coffee."

"*Verkeerd?*"

"*Koffie verkeerd, jaja!*"

Nearing the cabin, she detoured to retrieve the carton from her truck and rejoined him in the renovated two-room house as hard rain hit the roof. "You're sure making it nice and cozy in here, *Inspecteur Tuelling.*"

"I think this chimney is maybe new since you were here, no? The old one, so full of crud," he commented, fiddling with the damper's shining, spiral handle located halfway up the pipe. "You going to feel the heat in one minute now, Missus Katie, in one minute. This stove is working real nice now."

"Oh, shoot! I forgot about Blue. Let me go put her in the truck."

"*Nee*, bring her in here, bring her in. Maybe my house mouse will smell a dog and run away but I doubt it, that sneaky little sonagun."

With the dog nestling by the wood stove, they settled down to coffee and cookies. Katie opened the carton's flaps and took out the ceramic vase. "I want you to have this, Pieter. I don't know exactly when, but Mom made it years ago."

His cheeks blushed as he blinked at the eighteen-inch tall piece of earthenware. "Is too much ... too much...." he muttered, massaging the outside corners of his eyes with his two pinkie fingers.

"It's yours now, Pieter. A couple days after Thanksgiving I was looking at your beautiful flowers in this and I realized the vase belongs to you now. Please, take it. Mom would want you to have it." She placed it squarely in the center of the table. "I was so grateful you were with us in Chapel Grove. I hope you know that."

"*Jaja, ik weet dat.* I know that, Katie. Was my honor to be there."

"Okay, and here's a small bag of lemons I think you can use."

"*Oh ja*, never too many lemons!"

"And half-a-dozen persimmons you have to let ripen ... but you know about that."

"*O ja*, the Hachiyas. But, Katie, I got nothing to give you back...."

"Don't be silly. Oh, there are these too, look," she said, extracting a half dozen of Drika's 9" × 12" watercolor boards from a protective cardboard sleeve. "I found these mixed in with the McLoughlin's wild-flower album when I was straightening up. Mom must have held on to these by mistake."

"That was no mistake, Katie. I can't take those back from you." He lifted his reading glasses to his face and smiled. "But let me see what Elisabeth appreciated so much she stole them from me like that." He held the vellum sheets tilted in the best light. "The elderberry, *jaja*. The Western azalea, why sure. The baby-blue-eyes—no, not you, you silly old girl," he said, his blue eyes widening and shooting out over the top of the horn-rims as he smiled upon the dog. "*Dat es een braaf meisje.* • And look, Katie, the silktassel what we just now saw, you see? And the coast dogwood ... what's this now? The coast trillium, *jaja.* You see?

"But they belong with the rest of your wife's pictures, up on the walls here, wherever you want to put them."

• *That's a good dog. (Dutch)*

"But doesn't something tell you Elisabeth liked these best of all? No no, they belong to the Lowrie house now. You keep those, please. So, you see? Now I got something to give to you for Christmas, eh?" He grinned so that his teeth showed—crooked and yellow as ever—between his neat moustache and trimmed white Vandyke.

"That is so good of you, Pieter. I'll frame them. Yeah, I'm going to get them framed. Maybe in a long panel mounted in one long frame."

"I know you will take good care of these. Here, you take these back with you. Frame them, hang them, like you say, in Cliffport."

"Thank you." She set the protected watercolors back inside the carton. "So, I have some news."

The man lit up a cigarillo and left it smoking between his thin lips while flattening the pudgy fingers of both hands on the tablecloth, as if he had felt tremors and were bracing for an earthquake.

"Letty went back to Colorado. Probably for good."

"Oh, I see...." he replied, relaxing his arms, removing the cigarillo, and tapping the ashtray.

"I got so used to her being in the nursery, in the house, everywhere. I was taking her much too much for granted, I guess. Anyway, she's gone. And my son's gone too. Not with her. Not that I know of at least. He's just gone."

"Ah-ha...."

"It's funny. 1975 was going to be the year we put Letty on the books."

"*... on the books...?*"

"On payroll, you know, make it official. Social security taxes, benefits. We both agreed it'd be better that way. And I was going to give her a nice raise this New Year's, not that I can really afford it. Anyway, she's gone now."

"Did she give you a reason, Katie?"

"She's been missing home, I knew that. She was planning to go back to Boulder for the holidays anyway. But then I happened to catch her and my boy messing around ... in bed. It was a shock."

"*Jaja....*"

"I think she thought she'd feel too uncomfortable around me after that. I know I would, tell you the truth. So, she split."

"*Jaja*, I understand. *She split.*"

"I don't know how my son impressed you on Thanksgiving Day, but about right now I've got to say I'm pretty disgusted with his whole sorry act. Forget I said that. It's not your problem."

"Is not your problem either."

"What do you mean? I think it is my problem. I meant, it's just not yours."

"All what I see, young people all over the world is in this open rebellion. It used to be in Berkeley, in Amsterdaam—you see the young people in Amsterdaam today? *O mijn God!* But what I mean is, this rebellion is all over the world now, Katie. Sex. Drugs. So little consideration for other people, older people. I don't like the lying politicians and their Watergate business, their Vietnam business—I don't like that one bit either. But there is something more now. So many *jongoren*, they got no respect for other people or for each other, looks like to me, eh? In London—*O mijn God!*—what impolite little boys and girls they become. I never saw that before in England, Katie, in England! So, please, understand. Is not just your son. Is mothers and sons, and fathers and sons, and daughters too. Some good will maybe come out of it, I don't know. Sometimes I think maybe Pieter and Drika Tuelling were lucky, not to have children." She watched him adjust his weight in the chair, place his cap on the table, re-cross his thick legs, and leave his gaze lingering on the wood stove. "Now isn't that a sad thing for a man to say?" The lit end of his neglected little cigar glowed red as he puffed it back to life, directing his eyes from the stove toward the sink, up to the cupboard, across the tabletop—she sensed he was still breaking his habit of ruminating with a drink in hand. "But, Katie, what about you? What you going to do, all alone in Cliffport now?"

"I don't know. Without my mother, without Letty, without my son—I don't know. I'm going to spend the holidays with Aunt Suzanne and Uncle Mike in—"

"... *das es goede!*" he interrupted. "That's good peoples there, *jaja. Das es goede.* I'm glad you got those peoples to go to now."

"And you, Pieter? What about you?"

"I wait for a phone call, that's all."

"A phone call?"

"*Jaja*, they tell me where to pass the winter—in some park, or some monument, or some historical preserve, all like that. Starting in January, eh?"

"I don't get it. Who tells you?"

"The Southwest Regional District. I filled out the forms and passed the tests. I even got a new first-aid card. So now I'm high up on the waiting list." He grinned. "I'm going to be a snow-bird for the US government, Katie, *jaja*. Maybe a camp host. Maybe a clerk at some visitor center or other. A docent maybe. Some place where the sun shines: Nevada, Utah, Arizona, New Mexico—even that sonagun Southern California desert perhaps if that's what they got for me. They always need people to fill in, see? Somebody gets sick, somebody does not show up after holidays, somebody drops out—"

"... there's a lot of that going on. Dropping out, I mean."

"That's why I'm putting that ... what you call *de zonnetent* ... awning...? That's it: that new awning on the camper. I think warm weather will be good for the aches in my bones—eh, Blue? *Dat es een braaf meisje.* But the doctor, he tells me to keep my skin out of the sun."

"Wow, I'm impressed. Good for you."

"I wish I had somebody to stay here but I just go. I lock this place up and hope for the best."

"I wish I could—"

"*Nee nee*, I don't ask that of you now. You come here anytime you want but you never *must* come. No. You got enough to take on now. *Ach*, it doesn't matter. Everything will be okay here. I just got so much to puzzle out ... *in het land van got*. In God's country, as you say."

Katie observed her friend lapse into reverie. His slender moustache was still maintained within definite borders and his goatee carefully tapered. The horizontal hairline cracks across his forehead dropped into a V-shaped furrow between which the wire threads of his white, wild, untrimmed eyebrows twisted this way and that. Even while open, his blue eyes showed no larger than pumpkin seeds, and she saw more fine-lined wrinkles radiating out below his lower eyelids. He started, woken by rain plashing the windowpanes, a muted music compared to the amplified splatter against the sides and roof of the glasshouse at One Grade Road.

"What were you just thinking, Pieter?"

His cheeks flushed rosy. "*Ach*, I almost forgot you were here, Katie." He extracted another cigarillo from the pack then let both pack and cigar drop, resting his hands on the tabletop, his fingers interlaced to the extent that he could fit them together.

"I tell you something now, Katie. You going away, me going away, all like that ... I better tell you now. When we were in those redwoods where your little cemetery is, I got a feeling again. When you read from Elisabeth's ... what did you call it?"

"Mom's diary?"

"*Jaja, haar dag boek*, her daybook, *das is het*. But what I mean is ... is hard to put into words, Dutch or English. But with Nicholas gone, Hendrika gone, Anneke gone—and your mother, of course, Missus Elisabeth. But what was it she wrote? If only her mother were there to help her understand the ways of the Lord...? Was that it?"

"You remember that? Amazing."

"What I say, when you read that it was a feeling I got like when we put my sister—*God zegene haar*•—into the ground. Before she died, Anneke asked me to arrange for a pastor from Scotland to conduct the service. I never been much of a real religious man. You know me, Katie. Ever since I grew up, I been a man of science, eh? The German von Humboldt, the Britisher Darwin, the great American Luther Burbank, all like that—they were my ministers. Science was my religion, sure. Now I don't know. That crazy sonagun John Muir, he's making me think. He's the one I got to puzzle out next. I always thought faith in

---

• *God bless her (Dutch)*

science was enough for any reasonable man. Then I heard that man from Scotland preach—"

"... you heard John Muir?"

"*Nee*, I'm not that old! I mean that sonagun pastor from Scotland. Of course, he had the great big long philosophical beard, not like this little thing here," he said, stroking the white pelt of his pointed goatee. "And of course he spoke in that funny accent they got. What do they call it?"

"A brogue?"

"*Jaja*, a brogue, *dat is het.*

"What did he say?"

"He spoke about what it is for a human being to be human—ha! How's my English, not bad, eh? Okay. I can't repeat exactly what he said but I been puzzling it out ever since then. Up on the Mattole River, at that Salt Point, wherever they send me next ... puzzling it all out."

"So, what did he say about being human?"

"It was about souls, Katie, souls! The three souls of a man. I can't believe I'm saying this. He said there's an innocent soul you grow out of, then a soul you grow into as an adult, so you got the power to help other people, to share with other people. But he said there's a third soul, a soul we keep forever. This is a soul never changes in time or in space, eh? He said it had the word 'eternity' attached to it. Now isn't that a curious thing to say? And just before we threw the dirt on her box, he looked at me, Katie, he looked right at me. And he said: 'Does everybody and their third soul understand what I'm saying now?' So, there it is. Wasn't that a strange way of speaking, looking right at me? 'Does everybody and their third soul understand what I'm saying now?' *Nee nee*, I got to keep puzzling this one out. Is maybe a fairytale too? Just a fairytale for weak sheep like me getting old."

*

That rainy night before leaving for Cloverdale, she packed a dozen persimmons in the empty boot box, bedding them down in straw, and tucked six others with newsprint into a paper bag. In the attic, she secured the saturated casement window with screw nails and tightened all the sashes downstairs. She turned off the hot water line to the dripping bathroom faucet and loaded perishables into a carton before turning the thermostat in the fridge down but not off, lest the six-pack she had bought for Ross go warm. Katie considered opening a stray bottle of Paul Masson Claret dragged out from the back of the cupboard, but she left it on the counter for Ross to discover and poured the vinegary contents from an old jug of Chianti down the drain: if Pieter Tuelling could discipline himself to decline dancing with the devil, she told herself, she could too.

*

Raining. Raining all over. Into ocean waves overlapping sand. Against rocks. On the roof of this house where Jody was born I never knew that before. You must've known I'd be lying in here one night listening to rain against your windowpane. Then the silence when the wind dies down. It wasn't raining the night you died alone in here, letting go, letting it all go. But tonight it's falling on and off and on Jody's grave dissolving into ground growing new grass out of old where DD dumped your ashes. The way your life ended right here in this bed with your Bibles beside you, my bed now. The same way Jan snuggled up to her last bottle. Did Death come to you like an old friend killing all pain? I wonder if Josie knows how jealous I was when she was talking about her special relationship with you because you always did want a stylish daughter who'd grow up to be a faculty wife, I know you did. Is it letting up or just the wind changes? How you ate up that Professor Jackson or Johnson or Jansen or whatever his name was, eavesdropping on us while I pretended I didn't notice you were so infatuated with that guy. And with Pieter oh my God the two of you. What a sad long time to live without a husband at home. Or in your bed. In my bed now. Raining gently now. Pitying rain. Laughing rain. What was Bob's brother's name again? That dirty dog, he must have told Jo or Bob about our week screwing around after they left for Seattle. 'I wish we could find another way to get her laid.' That still blows my mind like she was the one who set me up with whatshisname in the first place. I'd probably do it again if

399

he ever showed up again, or someone like him. Don't tell JoJo that or she'll pay for his ticket and he'll think he can come to Cliffport and screw me whenever he wants or move in here for good. How Jan showed up again during that winter storm threatening everything Mom lived for. Her Saint Thea and Saint John. I better bury that Chinese box when I get back and that album with all those pictures of those people I never knew. No. No, you don't burn those images. You leave those alone. But you bury Jan's box in Chapel Grove where her fantasy love life with that boy Mills belongs.

*

Before dawn, she confirmed that the stove and fireplace coals were cold and closed the damper and the flue. Leaving the front light on, she latched the porch screen, locked the front door, gripped her suitcase in one hand and her guitar in the other—the words to Jan McLoughlin's Castle Song folded into the case's accessory compartment along with picks and a second set of strings—and headed out the pantry door.

"Come on, Blue, get up now, get up. God help us, let's get the hell out of here for now."

Notes

CHAPTER 1

(1) The authorship of the Castle Song—found among the papers of Janet Muir MacRae (b. 1893, Superior WI; d. 1983, Shelton WA)—remains unknown to me.

> *The Castle walls, but without the halls,*
> *Where the chiefs of Mackenzie were born,*
> *Stand lonely there, in ruins bare*
> *In the light of the early morn.*
>
> *No warden call on Castle walls,*
> *No sound of joy or grief,*
> *No clansman shouts in wassail rout,*
> *No child, no wife, no chief.*
>
> *Where are the men of the green glen?*
> *I ask of the idle wind.*
> *Ah! Gone like the snow of a year ago*
> *And left but the wind behind.*
>
> *So I stood in the calm of a summer dawn*
> *On the rock of the western sea,*
> *While ghosts of the past came fleeting fast*
> *And crowded over me.*

For the relevance and significance of the Castle Song, see Volume II, Book Four, Chapter 7, pp.109-110.   (p.30)

(2) After the first dozen pages, the display of corner-mounted prints became disorganized, all handwritten captions disappeared, and the rest of the album resembled a neglected scrapbook. Items were pasted at odd angles. Homemade Christmas card frames in the shapes of stars and trees were missing pictures. Katie no longer had names for the women wearing full-length black dresses, holding babies in their arms, steadying toddlers, standing close by as four children sat bareback—two facing forward, two backward—in the swayback of a sorry barnyard nag. She couldn't identify the girls in white aprons waiting on men, the young women playing cards with young men at a table under a grape arbor, or the mustached men standing off by themselves, stiffened in their Sunday—or funeral—clothes.

The final photographs in the album's first section conveyed impressions of Cliffport in a more recent yet also bygone era. Could the boys balancing atop a haystack and gripping the reins of a horseless springboard wagon be Jan's brothers, Johnny and Glenn? A family picnicking in the upper meadow must be the McLoughlins before the effects of World War One and the Spanish Flu had decimated the family, yet there were only five people on the picnic blanket spread in the grass; Katie couldn't find a sign of young Jan in that pastoral portrait, unless hers was the shadow on the ground, lengthening from the camera toward the subjects. A man on an orchard ladder and another man on a tractor had stopped work, staring at the photographer. Dogs rested under the oak—younger and smaller then—while a group of men sat their horses, enjoying conversation. In the field below the house, a dozen school kids stood atop the largest stumps—three, six, even ten in a row, with arms outspread and fingers touching. A well-attired family gathered in the porte-cochere of the old Mackenzie Lodge—the man and woman must be Mr. and Mrs. John Mackenzie and the two girls their daughters, Laura and Rose-Marie. In the slanted angle and odd composition of an amateur shot, Katie couldn't make out the doings of some fifty people shown assembled for some ceremony in Chapel Grove. Had it been the same ambitious yet naïve photographer who pointed the lens up and down Coast Road, resulting in a wide, horizontal panorama of the western fronts of Cliff-port Town's original store, livery, and hotel—all buildings presenting a unified if unfocused roadside façade in elongated view? Turning oceanward, the camera blurrily gazed out from the whale watch past Sea Lion Rocks to the horizon—there were no fences or guard rails back then. (p.32)

(3) At an earlier date, during an extended dialogue between Katie and Jan, we learned the details of Jan's twin brother's suicide and how their mother, Dorothea McLoughlin, "... looked out the window and saw the men carrying a body in a bloody blanket tied at both ends. You know, on a pole slung between their shoulders, the way they'd bring in a deer.... She saw those men carrying his body the way they'd carry in a stag from the hunt, Katie, and that's the truth." Cf. Volume I, Book Two, Chapter 7, pp.169-73. (p.33)

(4) Katie finally turned to the accordion file, freed the elastic cord from around the cardboard carrier, and lifted its stiffened flap. Each of the four musty pockets contained manila envelopes with faded ink on the tabs:

    1. Harry Landmark Jr., Greek Isles, 1928
    2. Lloyd Griggs, MD, Wyoming, 1933
    3. Michael Doty, Lieu., Inside Passage/Alaska, 1937
    4. Charles Lambert, Architect, Venice, 1951

Recognizing the names of Mary-Helen Belcanto's successive husbands, Katie pinched the winged clasp of the first envelope, dated 1928, and broke open its gummed seal, dumping a loose bunch of prints and pamphlets under the desk lamp and bracing herself for the opening parade.

The formats ranged from a professional 5" × 8" size, to prints on heavier paper stock designed as postcards, to diminutive 2" × 3" snapshots slipped into transparent acetate sleeves of compact "album-ettes." Some prints gave the impression of having been excised from a cannibalized photographic album, for they still bore corner mounts and patches of black paper adhered to their backs. Whatever the format, the focus was upon Mr. and Mrs. Landmark—particularly upon Mary-Helen Landmark in all the glory of her first honeymoon in the Greek Isles.

Whether leaning on the groom's arm or standing off on her own, the woman was always wearing a different outfit and looking right back at the lens. Seated at the captain's table, lounging in a deck chair, standing at the rail on deck or in the bar—a cigarette in one hand and a drink in the other—she was the center of attention: Mary-Helen, astride a donkey led up switchback steps by a local guide, with espadrilles on her feet, a wide-brimmed straw hat on her head, sunglasses on her face, and a woven bag slung over the shoulder of her embroidered peasant blouse; Mary-Helen, dressed like Ava Gardner, playing Carmen on Pirate Night on board ship or in a tricorne with ribbon decorations at the Hat Party, head thrown back—a drink in one hand and a cigarette in the other—laughing; Mary-Helen, at sea or on land, with her husband or without, on docks and in dinghies, in the shade of Corinthian columns, under sun umbrellas in open-air tavernas—Katie leafed more quickly through the touristic clichés: Patmos, Delos, Kos, Piraeus; the Acropolis, the Parthenon, the Agora—the Cruise to Antiquity now served merely as a backdrop for impressions of the newlyweds, especially of the bride radiating her legendary allure. Katie didn't expect Jan McLoughlin to be featured: Jan would have been back home, managing the nascent Belcanto Company and providing a pied-à-terre for eight-year-old Mills, recently shipped off for his first semester at boarding school in Washington State.

This landfall cruise was no improvisational junket. A printed booklet remained in one piece within its spiral binding. On textured white paper with blue border designs, the program provided the overall itinerary, daily schedules, sample menus of the dining room's three main meals of the day, and a list of offerings at the vessel's several snack bars. Individual, perforated sheets described opportunities for optional shore excursions in addition to basic information about ports of call. A rusty staple attached a carbon copy of twelve common salutations transliterated into English from Greek and appeared to have been inserted as an afterthought. She stuffed everything back into the envelope and traded it for envelope—and husband—number two.

Several dozen loose prints had been stuffed inside a more substantial program guide. Katie spilled the photos across the desktop and studied the cowhide cover of the customized publication, its subject—FIESTA '33—literally branded into the front and a schematic Rod of Asclepius embossed on the back. The interior pages were bound together by a broad leather tie. A hand-drawn, fold-out map pasted inside the back cover indicated the prominent landmarks of the cattle range country where the ABarB Ranch was situated at an oxbow bend of the North Platte River whose slow, placid water wound through a portion of the basin with the Medicine Bow Mountains to the north. The list and affiliations of the *invitados* to the annual gathering of the American Asklepion Club's private gathering included heads of medical schools, directors of major metropolitan hospitals, a Wyoming State Senator, and two assistants to the Secretary of the U.S. Department of Health; the chairs of several governmental advisory committees were named as well as a smattering of representatives from private industry. The agenda promised a week far from home, where the leaders of North America's medical establishment could circle their wagons against the world-at-large in order to relax, party, and play. Daily doings and optional activates included fishing in the Platte's nearest tributary creeks, antelope hunting "...for early risers ..." and skeet and trap shooting; tennis, swimming, and golf on the dude ranch's irrigated nine holes. Another schematic map showed the horse riding trails, and an insert listed the rates for piloted tours conducted from the private airstrip. When she turned to the individual prints, Katie recognized that some photographer hired to document the week of fun and games had taken many pictures of club members posed in various small groups but relatively few shots of the newlywed couple alone. More informal pictures of the general company showed the physicians, surgeons, politicians, and businessmen accompanied by women; no children were present, and not every woman appeared to be a wife, at least not the wife of whichever man she was escorting that week at the ABarB.

Katie flicked her way through the photographic record of Jan's prized clotheshorse going through her gaits in the not-so-wild West of the landlocked resort; FIESTA '33 had given the re-married bride opportunities for clothes changes galore. The settings did vary but the theme remained the same in every frame: the physician's bride demonstrating her fabled feminine appeal while sitting in the front seat of a jeep wearing a safari hat, a pressed denim shirt, a bandana around her neck; in the saddle wearing dungarees, boots in the stirrups, a straw cowboy hat on her head, a bandana around her neck; surrounded by young male cooks hanging around the chuck wagon at a BBQ on the open range—a bottle of beer in one hand and a cigarette in the other—a ribbon-trimmed cowboy hat on her head and a Western shirt finished off with the obligatory bandana around her neck. The snapshots were all about Mary-Helen Griggs *nee* Belcanto smiling in the camera's direction. By the pool during a pause in festivities, one side of her swimming robe draped halfway open over the lounge chair's arm. At the cocktail mixer in the main lodge, decked out in a flouncy patchwork skirt and an embroidered cotton blouse with an O-neck collar and puffy three-quarter sleeves showing off her cuff bracelets and new silver-and-turquoise necklace. But had her partner willingly taken the picture of his new bride encircled by a herd of genuine buckaroos boasting rodeo belt buckles and wearing chaps, all of them grinning toward her from beneath the broad, broken brims of their felt hats? Was it her husband she was smiling at from inside another semi-circle of silver-haired gentleman crowding closer as she lifted her head and laughed, leaning back against the counter of the bar? Would Dr. Lloyd Griggs have wanted to create a record of such moments at FIESTA '33?

Opening the third envelope, Katie turned to the official "Inside Passage to the Alaskan Frontier" program guide. Its motifs had been appropriated, without attribution, from the Tlingit, Kwakiutl,

Haida, and other Amerindian cultures of the Pacific Northwest. The front cover bore generic illustrations of totem poles; the inside pages swam with half-tone drawings of sea mammals, native seagoing craft, leaping salmon, eagles in flight; a woodcut print left a bear's claw on the back cover. A brief history of the VIGILANCE distinguished it from the larger commercial steamers plowing through the Inland Passage. A former Coast Guard patrol boat, the small cruise vessel had been retrofitted, renamed the OFF DUTY, and recommissioned as a yacht for naval officers and their guests on pleasure excursions up and down North America's West Coast.

The desiccated rubber bands around photographic prints turned to dust at her touch. By now Katie expected mostly more of Mary-Helen, wearing a new last name, basking in a shower of approval from an all-male audience, young and old. She fanned the deck across the desktop. The developing dates had been printed on the borders, but the sequence didn't matter to Katie; she picked up pictures at random. In the elite ship's lounge or in the brisk open air, this class of vessel and the new scenery had obviously called for an entirely new wardrobe, one more suitable to the Arctic than to summertime Greece or Wyoming. Glaciers and fjords viewed from the deck rail; gift shops in coastal villages; an Eskimo with a harpoon posing beside the bow of a kayak hauled out on a pebbly shore—Katie thumbed through the anonymous snaps until landing upon what she had been fishing for: an image of Mary-Helen with a white gloved hand laid upon the gold-striped sleeve of her new husband, Lieutenant Michael Doty. The aging gold digger seemed to be playing it more conservatively this third time around, at least pretending to be on best behavior when in the company of her high-ranking military man and his peers. These pictures appeared to have been separated from an album of some sort, for bits of black paper also stuck to their backs. Had Mary-Helen dismantled each honeymoon album after the dissolution of each marriage? Or had Jan done it later, when the bottom fell out of her world at the time of Mary-Helen's betrayal and the demise of The Belcanto Company? Katie would never know; no one would ever know. She debated whether to bother with the fourth envelope. Would its gallery offer only more of the woman's vanity after vanity passing itself off as the epitome of glamour and success? What more was there to learn?

Tearing open the last envelope's flap, Katie copped to her own perverse delight, anticipating the point at which Jan McLoughlin's alter-ego would start to show her age, her capacities on the decline. Katie couldn't celebrate the self-centered woman's shameless displays as marriages and decades sailed by, but she could savor a taste of revenge against someone who had so destructively exploited Jan's adulation. But why had Jan let herself be exploited for so long? For the excitement by proxy, Katie answered her own question, and in exchange for the other woman's son.

The record of Venetian vacationing followed suit with the pictures in the other envelopes—none of Mills, none of Jan—but here there were fewer dedicated to Mary-Helen advertising her diminishing charms. Charles Lambert, the architect, struck her as yet another conquistador in his chosen field and another handsome catch for the divorcee— certainly as handsome as any Hollywood casting agent could wish for a leading man lolling about in an aesthete's semi-aquatic paradise. But husband number four—no simple retread—was obviously competition for the aging bride when it came to attracting attention. The suave San Franciscan wore his light blond hair longish, the sideburns framing a smoothly shaven face. His Italianate clothing must, as far as Katie knew, have been the very best that American dollars could buy. His white slacks and monogrammed jacket almost demanded a hand-kerchief puffing from the breast pocket or an ascot at the throat, and he was usually depicted sporting one or the other or both. The architect didn't merely conform to conventional norms of cosmopolitan fashion: he defined the classic form. With eyeglasses framed on his face or dangling from his fingers, he stared toward the camera, positioning his leather footwear at subtle angles. Projecting an unabashed image of the chic, whether inspecting a chapel's fresco or sipping a cocktail in a silk smoking jacket at some world-famous hotel bar, his air of entitlement seemed to envelope the figure alongside him: Mary-Helen Lambert *nee* Belcanto was growing heavy in her face, weighty on her feet, and stingy with her smile. The new husband's star appeal simply outshone that of his over-ripened wife's.

No one had bothered to annotate the borders or the backs of this last set of prints, but the names and places didn't matter to Katie, who wasn't expecting to be touring Italy anytime soon. She stuffed the pictures back in the envelope, shoved all the envelopes into the cardboard carrier, and stretched out on the bed while the last images flickered beneath her closed eyelids: Mr. and Mrs. Charles Lambert boarding a vaporetto with a crush of matching suitcases in tow; the unmistakably American couple—husband posed in profile—on a canal bridge; Mary-Helen alone, looking flummoxed amidst a swarm of plaza pigeons then enthralled while standing among a band of idling gondoliers.

Mary-Helen and Mills had been dead for more than a decade; Jan McLoughlin, for six months. Perhaps Mary-Helen had destroyed all wedding albums proper, but what about some photos from her Asian travels and the disastrous trans-Pacific flight with her son on the Pan-Am Clipper—where were those? Maybe it was Jan who had jettisoned those too painful reminders of Mary-Helen's failure as a mother and Jan's own failure, finally, to be happy living a vicarious life.

(p.42)

CHAPTER 2

(1) William McGrath was the last proprietor then final resident of the disused Monteflores Lodge; in 1920, he and Jan McLoughlin were wed but spent the entirety of their marriage living far apart. After his death in 1964, the legal widow inherited the lodge and the last one hundred acres remaining in the Mackenzies' once-extensive property encompassing Cliffport. (p.46)

(2) December 1970, the deed and title documentation was finally squared away in the Office of County Records, Hudson took the

back pay he deserved, and Katie inherited the $14,300 remaining in Jan McLoughlin's estate. When her mother confirmed that she was declining surgery for the foreseeable future, Katie realized she could finally get a new truck and would no longer have to hold her breath while turning the Fleetside's ignition key, bracing herself to see if the engine would turn over or cough a black exhaust cloud out the pipe and die. The Lowries started giving Donald a generous allowance, and the family enjoyed a festive exchange of Christmas gifts, inviting Suzanne and Mike and the Wiltons for the big holiday meal. Josie announced that she and Bob and their son, Jeffers, were relocating to Seattle in January. After the party, when her mother and her son were asleep in their rooms, the prospect of losing her best friend's company—and her son losing his—drove Katie into ruminations by the fire.

Winter weather always brought plant sales to a halt, and Katie usually spent her time perched on a stool at her propagation bench, listening to the rain and the radio while sticking starts in planting mix or writing out hundreds of plant tags by hand. During serious storms, she remained in the house. Except for leaving the three framed photographs displayed on the redwood shelf, she had stored the rest of Jan's memorabilia in the closet and converted the spare room into her office. There she handled business papers, piled her mail order catalogues, and sorted her seed packets, resolving to use a dry-erase board and a pair of hanging wall calendars to keep track of her 1971 and 1972 planting schedule.

In the evenings, face to face with flames on the andirons, counting her blessings, she let herself dream big, as Jan McLoughlin had once advised. No longer to mend the polyethylene flapping from the arched ribs of PVC pipes forming the hoop houses or to swing a mallet at the doors until her cussing brought their splintering frames into alignment. No more afternoons at the end of a hose, dragging lengths of it from plot to plot, wrestling with kinks, repairing leaky couplings, replacing dripping gaskets. And no longer to rely on the non-galvanized pipes whose rusted joints revealed themselves wherever eroded soil brought the main junctions into the light of day. Couldn't

Katie upgrade it all—no longer pressing the war-weary poly houses into further service, not repainting the rotten benches with water seal, and no more patching of the tattered shade cloth? The easement driveway in and out, the path surfaces up and down the hillside, the water mains, the makeshift greenhouse structures—with her mother foregoing surgery, Katie could now afford to upgrade them all.

(p.49)

(3) [VERBATIM A]

SIDECAR BAR & GRILL:
Hey, Chili. How come you never asked me about this scar? No chick'll ever hit on me now, not with this on my face.

Ay cabrón! Give me a break, Ricky.

Go ahead, señor. Take a closer look. Don't be chickenshit like everybody else till I catch 'em and they turn away. Like a piece of hot barbed wire burned right into my cheek, know what I mean?

That sure is ugly, man. Is it always going to look like that?

Like a fuckin' rattlesnake, you mean? My face went through the windshield, man. I was in that PG hospital for a week, head all wrapped up in bandages. I was so zonked out I didn't know what was going on. They asked me questions but what came outta my mouth was like uughh-balaaaaa. Broken ribs, bruises. This knee all crushed. Then I woke up and found out that besides the DUI the fuckin' DA was lodging charges for me carrying like three fuckin' joints they found in my Marlboro hard pack. Possession, first offense. I was lucky.

You call that lucky?

Look how long I went before getting busted? And what if I was carrying a little boo "for personal use," know what I'm sayin'? Did I luck out or what? But lying in that hospital bed, I started imagining what was underneath the bandages, you know what I mean? Then they took off the tape—whoa!

You're right, man. That's sure not gonna bring in no ladies.

411

*

I blew it. I had a good thing goin' and I fucked up, that's all. It still blows my mind I wasn't carrying a delivery inside that van. They found not one trace, Chili. Maybe they didn't even look for chalk. Hey, what to hear a good one, Chili burger?

I think I heard all the good ones by now. Twice.

You dumb shit, gimme me another beer. Chili, I mean it, you gotta listen to this one.

I got shit to do back here, Ricardo. Cual es tu pinche problema? •

I saw the weirdest thing this morning. This huge motherfucker was walkin' right down the middle of Alvarado Street. And he's like screamin' his fuckin' head off: "I'M GOING TO DROWN MYSELF! WHICH WAY TO THE BAY? I'M GOING TO DROWN MYSELF!"

Sounds like some very bad acid, man.

Big guy with his clothes all torn up. Looked like a Vietnam vet. I don't know why I'm sayin' that. Out of his fuckin' mind.

That loco's dead by now or behind bars.

They'd have to shoot him with horse tranquilizers. I mean, the dude was big and he was spreadin' traffic out, walkin' right down the middle of Alvarado screamin' at the top of his lungs. That shit's just not supposed to happen in ol' Monterey, right?

*

That happen to me once. They took my license away. So what? I got it back. There was this naco used to come in here. His DMV was so messed up he had to choose between drinking and driving, he got busted so many times.

So, what'd he do?

The man gave up his license, Ricky. Turned it in and never drove again. But he sure drank to make up for it.

How old are you, Chili?

• *What is your fucking problem? (Sp)*

I going to be sixty, dude. Sixty years old.

You got fifteen years on me.

Ol' Chili, he never thought he was going to live to see sixty years old.

COUNTY OFFICE OF SOCIAL SERVICES:

Have a seat. Running a little late this morning, Mister Debruen?

Hey, sorry. Guess I didn't read the bus schedule right. Next time I'll get it together.

It's eight-fifty. That leaves us ten minutes.

I'll be here eight-thirty next time, okay? A guy can be late once in a while, know what I mean? What, you want me to fill this out all over again?

You'll have to be clearer on that questionnaire. If we're to use our time together to help you figure out what it is you want to do for a living, and to help you do your utmost to pursue it.

Sure.

From what little I could make out there, it's obvious your work experience has been in the media: the technical aspects of audio and visual media. And you seem to have some experience in radio. Exactly what, isn't clear to me, with so many of those lines there left blank. And you failed to fill in the dates, or the reasons for your leaving. Please, spend some time completing this or just start over. Do you want a new form?

What if I can't remember the dates? Or why I left those gigs?

Take a stab at it. Now it's almost nine. Here. Please fill in this questionnaire one more time—legibly if you don't mind. There's a table and chair right over there.

I'll do my best.

You can leave it with the receptionist on your way out. Just tell her it's for Tom Fuller. And try to be on time next time.

Yes, sir.

We need the full thirty minutes.

I'll do my best.

THE SIDECAR BAR & GRILL:

I saw some chick in one of those new Thunderbirds this morning, Chili. With the heavy-duty grill and suicide doors? Man, that cunt's got it made, toolin' around the Peninsula in something like that. Power Flite Steering and Suspension. I once drove a brand-new T-bird.

Yeah? You? And when was that?

I did. I had to 'cuz my dad and his buddies once got so blasted up in the Catskills. We ended up in this tavern on the Hudson River on the way back to New York City. He kept feedin' me nickels to play Flyin' Home on the jukebox.

Flyin' Home?

You know, man. Benny Goodman.

Oh, Benny Goodman. Wasn't that dude in my uncle's mariachi band?

Right, your fuckin' uncle. So, my dad and his gang were so fucked up they took over this roadside joint and had me feed the jukebox nickels. Flyin' Home, Flyin' Home, Flyin' Home. Funny, huh? But I flew that T-bird all the way home to Brooklyn. I didn't even have my driver's license yet. Somebody should've given me an award for good driving. Now here I am in California and they take my license away. Yippee! Cali-fuckin-for-nie-aye! They take away your wheels, they take away your pride, man, know what I mean? I'd sure like to connect with some bitch drivin' a nice set of wheels around Monterey. Head down the coast to Big Sur and see if George Lloyd's still blowin' down there. Up the Russian River. Wouldn't that be the life? But no, I have to sit tight and take advantage of all the "career opportunities" the fuckin' coun-ty's got to offer me.

You got to stay out of prison's what you got to do.

Fuckin' lady in a T-bird!

I met this junkie once in county.

Yeah?

That lowlife belonged in Soledad. I don't know what he was doin' in Salinas.

So?

So, the dude claimed he bought his girlfriend a Thunderbird the color of her eyes, man.

What color were they?

Now how should I know that, Ricky?

That's crazy.

Everybody on junk's crazy. You know that.

*

What, you think I'm going to start peddlin' a bicycle down Del Monte Avenue like some loser on multiple DUI's?

So, what did you get busted for, homeboy? Jay walking?

One DUI plus possession. My first offense. Come on, give me another cigarette, man, I'm out. Up till now it was like a couple of speeders, red lights, shit like that.

Big deal.

I cleared those off my DMV every time. I've breezed through traffic school more than once. I should get a medal for the all the miles I've driven without any accidents. Are you kiddin'? I did traffic school in two different counties at the same time once, can you believe that? But this time I fucked up. It won't happen again. I'll get my license back. I'll get the Beast back on the road. And I'll get off this fuckin' Peninsula forever. I'm not pickin' up any more charges in Monterey County, know what I mean?

At least not stumbling back to that motel. Now go on, Ricardo, get outta here. I got to close the place and go home.

I thought that was my job.

You're good at closing down the bar, Ricky, that's true. You're the last one in here again tonight. Here, take the whole pack but go, vamos! See you tomorrow, vato.

What'd you just call me?

Go on now, man. Hey, can you walk?

*

That was a great gig while it lasted, delivering equipment to all those junior colleges and settin' it up. Then hangin' out till it was time to pack it up and take it back to MPC or somewhere else. I was goin' to movies on campus, checkin' out records from their little libraries, checkin' out coeds in their little short shorts.

Was you a student?

Me? I was an employee with benefits and whadayacallem, perks.

"Perks?"

Benefits. Like lots of free time hangin' out at the little radio stations just gettin' goin' on the campuses. A couple of those colleges have student centers with like lounges with music listening rooms, magazines, newspapers, can you dig that? After a while I knew where to pass the time of day inside a pair of headphones and get fuckin' paid for it. That was the best deal ever. Then I lost that job overnight. You can't blame them for firing me. Hell, I totaled their van, wrecked a lot of expensive equipment. I know I blew it. Then DMV takes away my license. Welcome to the fuckin' Monterey County bus system, bro'! Physical therapy for this knee. Drug court. Probation officer. Caseworker. A career counselor who is square as square one. I think they might make me see some county shrink before probation is up. Was that what my caseworker meant or something else?

You asking me?

Or did she mean I had to choose between career training, career counseling, or what'd she call it, "therapeutic counseling?" Therapeutic counseling. That's fucked up.

*

Here, you want this. Go ahead, it's free. Take that with you but don't light up in here. You better be glad the judge didn't put you on urine testing.

You wouldn't exactly pass with flying colors, you chulo.

But I'm not on probation, you are.

Fuck you, gimme that.

Aloha from the island of Hawaii, Ricky. A freebie from Chili Con Carne to you.

*

Hey, Chili, you see that Mustang Boss 351 prowlin' the streets? Now that's an automobile. Lucky sonovabitch. Hey, whaddaya say we find a little jazz on that radio? Let me step behind there for a sec'.

You ain't stepping behind anywhere and messin' with no dial. These people don't want to listen to no jodido jazz, man.

COUNTY OFFICE OF SOCIAL SERVICES:

Didn't whatshername, Brenda, my caseworker ... didn't she send that info to you yet? She said she was going to.

I found out this morning that Missus Hawkins sent it to the employment office by mistake. It'll wind up here before I see you again, don't worry. Now tell me more about your vocational training. You studied some broadcasting journalism, I saw that. Did you ever take any other vocational courses?

Getting a little late for that, doc.

Are you saying you've ruled out re-training?

I don't know. I took a couple classes at SF State once upon a time but that was a long time ago. To be honest with you, I had to prove I was in school fulltime—to stall the Draft Board. So, snoopin' around campus I happen onto this baby radio station. That turned me on, so I worked with the equipment then I was like the unofficial campus jazz DJ for a while. Till they found out I wasn't enrolled anymore. Then I got eighty-sexed I mean eighty-sixed. Then I did have to deal with the Selective Service for real. But listen, you remember what I said about that A-V gig, right? My best gig ever, for COCC.

COCC...?

The Consortium of Community Colleges. Shuttling audio-visual stuff between campuses. That lasted from ... see? I forget dates.

Please remind me how much longer before you get your driver's license back?

Ten months from now. One year total.

And you're still residing in the Anchor Motel in Marina?

It's on the main bus line and you can't beat the rates.

Because of their financial arrangement with the county, you mean?

Wait a sec'. The Anchor's in Seaside, isn't?

The address is listed as Marina, for some reason. Now we only have ten minutes left and I'd like to hear more about your position with the community colleges.

What about it?

Am I right in saying you held onto that longer than any other job in your life?

Yeah.

For about the last ten years, wasn't it?

Maybe, about. Anyway, that was definitely the longest I've ever held down a straight job.

What did you like best about that position?

What did I like best, besides the windshield time? I liked runnin' the sound on live performances.

Anything else?

Yeah. I liked recording the dance classes and performances. There was one dance instructor who asked me to help her students with play-backs on a monitor. Freeze frames, zoomin' in and out, fast forward, rewind.... Do you know what I'm talkin' about? That became my specialty: dance classes. Then I did like hundreds of interviews of jazz musicians. No wait, that was before the college gig.

You conducted hundreds of interviews, did you just say?

Well, maybe not hundreds but dozens. But that had nothin' to do with those junior colleges. That was on my own time over in Half Moon Bay.

THE SIDECAR BAR & GRILL:

Fuckin' Cliffport. You know where Davenport is up north of Santa Cruz?

Si, señor.

You know where Año Nuevo is?

Si, Señor Ricardo.

Well, my boy lives right in there between Davenport and Año Nuevo. With his mom and her mom. On their old ranch or farm or whatever it is. From the top of the ridge on that place you can see all the way to those pink ice plants at Lover's Point. And that Point Piños Lighthouse at night. You can hear the ocean from the house sometimes. It's like a ghost town on One.

Is that where there's that turnout for watching whales?

You got it, that's it, Chili, that's the place. How'd you know that?

I spent years ridin' the roads, Ricky. That's where your son lives?

Far as I know he does. Been living there all his life.

What's his name? Hey, Poncho, what's your son's name?

Don.

Ron?

Don I said. Donald or Don. I don't really know what he goes by, okay? Anyway, I've learned my lesson the hard way but they're not turnin' me into a criminal. You make one little mistake—

... and you get caught—

... and they basically try to turn you into a criminal. If only I still had that job workin' for the colleges. I'm not sayin' I can ever work for them again. I'm just sayin, I'd never risk a stunt like that again, rippin' off the equipment and cashin' in on it near the airport in South San Fran. I was in a bad way that time. That's what snow'll do to you. I swear I'll never get strung out on blow again, that's for fuckin' sure. Chili, I'll tell you what coke'll do to you.

To me? I already know what coke'll do to me. No va bueno.

Well, I'm tellin' you how it went down for me. I can't tell this to anybody else so you gotta listen. I told you about my college job, right?

More than once, you told me.

So, one day I go to work and report how the van got busted into. All the stuff that wasn't bolted down got ripped off. The tape-recording machines with COCC engraved into the case, the supplies.

COCC?

Consortium of Community Colleges. They signed my paycheck, okay? Cameras. Tripods. Everything missing, stolen. I filed a report with campus security then at the Gilroy police station. This happen over at Gavilan College. You know who pulled off that job?

You did.

How'd you know I was goin' to say that?

'Cuz that's what yola will do to you.

Damn, you're good, Chilidog.

And you're loco, ripping off your own set-up for dope money. Now look at you.

That's what I'm tryin' to fuckin' tell you, man. Coke made me do that, know what I mean? I even wrecked my own fuckin' 8-track cassette player that night. Tore it out of the dash.

So, it wouldn't look like an inside job. Everybody knows that trick, you gringo.

But it worked, I didn't get caught—

... that time.

Coke'll make you do crazy shit like that.

I seen worse.

Yeah?

How about los nacos selling their own sisters for sex? It's no good, man.

Yeah, that's pretty bad.

Always high and always short. Short on time. Short on dough. Hiding stuff, stealing stuff. That's no life. I been there, man. Is no good. Chili, he's too old for that shit.

You're right. I mean, I'm goin' to stay away from it when I get off probation. You're pushin' and you think you'll never start usin', right? You know what I mean? I'm weak, man. I'm weak when it comes to that shit and I'm weak when it comes to pussy. You tell me, Chili. What is that power they got down there?

You mean that jalapeno pepper between their legs?

I can't help myself. I always want to get at it. Just look at that stuff standin' over there.

That culona there?

Will you look at that big beautiful butt movin' those pants around. I can't stand that shit, man. I want to get inside. I want to get up inside her—

... keep it down, man. Wow. They got that head doctor lined up for you yet, Ricardo? You better talk to that guy not me. You been talkin' some crazy shit lately.

COUNTY OFFICE OF SOCIAL SERVICES:

So, Mister Debruen. In reviewing your file, it looks to me like you haven't followed up on the school district lead we discussed. You're required to check in at the employment office every two weeks, and my records show that you haven't been back since your initial registration. Unless there's information that hasn't reached my desk yet. Can you please tell me if you still have any questions about that basic requirement?

I've got a lot on my plate, doc. Physical therapy for my leg in PG twice a week. Meeting with Ramirez, my probation officer, in Salinas, once a month. Calling in to the caseworker every Monday morning before noon. It's a lot to keep up with, especially without wheels. You know what I'm sayin'?

And coming here every other week.

And comin' into Career Counseling every two weeks, that's right. It's a lot, man. That trip to Salinas is only once a month but do you have any idea how humiliating it is ridin' the bus from Monterey to Salinas and back with all those Mexicans on board? I mean, do I look like José Jiménez? My name is José Jiménez, you know what I mean? Wearin' this scar on my face, those people look at me like I'm some badass bandito. All just to punch the clock and meet a probation officer who looks like he'd like to punch me out and clean my clock.

But ... I don't....

That's okay, doc. Don't knock yourself out tryin' to understand everything I say. Just believe me: what I'm goin' through, it's a lot.

Yes ... well then ... when our time's up here today ... or how about right now? Yes, right now. Why don't you head over to the employment office right now? That job description sounded like it was right down your alley and you don't want to miss any opportunities....

THE SIDECAR BAR & GRILL:

I ever tell you about that broad I knew who liked to take it up her ass?

Keep it down, Ricky.

She asked for it, Chili. She loved it. Then there was this fag in the Greenwich Village building I lived in. Knocks on my door, treats me to a BJ then bends over and shows me his cornhole.

Madre mierda! You're talking too loud, man. You got to keep it down or Chili's goin' throw you out.

I'm not kiddin'. He could pack a rod too, know what I'm talkin' about?

*Ay, es bien pedo, wey.**

After the first inch or so's pure pussy.

Shut up now, Ricky. I'm gonna throw you out.

O come on, you know what I'm talkin' about, Chili. You've been in the can. But you can't do that to those little boys and girls all the time. Just some the time. They get sore down there, know what I'm sayin'? Gimme me another.

No more.

What was her name anyway?

Go on home, Ricky.

O Christ, Chili. Don't you be a prick too! *Una mas cerveza. Un trago de tequila.*

You want me to call Kenny?

Kenny?

• *Oh, he's really drunk. (Sp)*

You know Kenny, the cab driver. He'll take you back to your motel.

I thought maybe Kenny's one of those little boys.

Oh man, you're sick in the head. I'm calling Kenny.

I said no. I'll walk. 'Sonly a couple three blocks.

You know which way to turn once you get outside that door? I better call him, Ricardo.

I got a better idea. Call Ginny.

Ginny?

Yeah, call that one. You don't remember Ginny? That fatty barfly used t' hang out here.

That fucking roja cabeza? She is only trouble, man.

How come she never comes in here anymore, huh?

She's not welcome here no more.

Chili, come on, man. *Una maz cerveza. Por favor....*

No way, José. I'm your friend, Ricky, but I'm tellin' you to go home now, man.

Not you too, Chili. O fuck this place. Fuck the fuckin' Sidecar 'n Grill.

Cool it, Ricardo. Go on. Get out of here right now.   (p.74)

CHAPTER 3

(1) [VERBATIM B]

THE SIDECAR BAR & GRILL:

You never asked about my accident? Pass me the sugar. Or about before the accident.

But you going to tell me. Okay, one more of your bullshit stories but then I gotta make a run to the Safeway before I open up. I can't find the key to the cooler anywhere and I'm going to need some ice back here.

I was workin' the Monterey Jazz Festival.

Workin'? What, the slot car races in the parking lot?

Fuck you, Chili. This guy I met had me luggin' his equipment around. Hey, that meant tickets for the whole shebang.

Muy chignon!

So, I spotted this lady behind the bandstand on Saturday afternoon. I mean, you saw her and you just knew this is some sophisticated pussy. First thing I spotted was her ass. When she was bendin' over to straighten those little schoolgirl socks they wear in their little schoolgirl shoes. Then she's gettin' up on a barstool, like one of these.

That's cool.

Lifts one hip up then the other. What a bod. Wearin' this red tube top and white jeans and every move she made broadcasts like pure sex, you know what I'm sayin'? Latin lady, okay? Long thin legs, bracelets on her ankles. I wanted to lift her up and carry her around the stage on the end of my dick!

Ay carbon! I'm cuttin' you off you start talkin' shit like this when the people come in here later. I mean it, señor.

But isn't that what every cat thinks, you get an eyeful of stuff like that? I wanted to eat the whole enchilada right then and there. I told you before I can't resist females. So, listen to this, she shows up at this BBQ party, all these wolves drooling all over her. I thought, O man she's another cockteaser, you know what I mean? Just leave it alone, Richard. But the closer I got there was nothing stoppin' me, and I lit her cigarette. One look she let me know she was willin' to put out.

Sure she did....

No, really! I didn't have this face back then, man. I had the right moves. Patricia was her name. Only she said it like Pah-tree-shee-ah.

Pah-tree-shee-ah...?

That's right. Pah-tree-shee-ah. Brazilian chick.

Las chicas son mas lindas en Brazil, si como no? •

• *Chicks are prettier in Brazil, no? (Sp)*

425

Whatever. Gimme some more coffee. So, Pah-tree-shee-ah is decked out with all those feminine touches that just kill me. Big brown eyes outlined in black. Red lipstick, some soft hair over her upper lip.

The chick had a moustache?

No, she didn't have a moustache, stupid. It was just like some soft brown down. And she had one of her ears pierced with some kind of a cow clip.

What the hell is this lowlife talking about now?

Who you callin' a lowlife? Chili, listen to me. It was like those metal clips they put on cows. And she had these big beautiful white teeth and wore that deep red lipstick. So, she tells me about the party after the show that night. I couldn't believe it. Like was I the guy goin' to be peeling those white jeans off her that very night?

One of many, coco-head, one of many.

Yeah, well, I'm was one helpless motherfucker at that point. And that was what got me in so much trouble. She was basically hangin' out with these Brazilian musicians that afternoon. I don't know who owned her. But when she got up close she told that to me about the party. She had like brown bangs straight across her forehead. Her skin was smooth, Chili, smooth and white. Pale, white skin. Almost looked like skim milk, you know, tinted blue.

What oregano was you smoking that time, gringo?

She gave me the signal, I swear it. I'm not dreamin' this up. Rings on her fingers and bracelets. Thin gold chains around her neck. Those little chains around her ankles. Pah-tree-shee-ah. I can still see her.

So what happen, Don Juan? Hurry up, man. I gotta go to the Safeway and get back.

So I was on my way to that party. At least I thought I had the right address. But you know what? I was so fucked up by then I'll never know if it was the right address or not. I was totally blasted out of my mind.

Why do I have no trouble imagining that?

So that's what happened to Mister A-V man and the college's A-V van. That was the last I remember before I woke up in the hospital.

And you never saw sweet little Pah-tree-shee-ah with the cow clip and the moustache again.

A face to fuck, Chili, a face to fuck. Chicks are too much for me. Hit me with a smoke, I'm all out.

Here. But you gotta start buyin' your own, dude.

You know I'm crazy about chicks, Chili, right? Why don't you put in a good word for me with some of the broads comin' in here? Big ones, little ones, skinny ones, fat ones. I'm like open to anything feminine. I should get a Boy Scout badge for every time I control myself with a sexy broad. I think lots of dudes are like me but they won't admit it, know what I'm sayin'?

Could be, Ricardo, could be. You better come with me.

Young, old, pretty face, not so pretty face. I'm helpless when I see a woman. Say she's chunky, like your sister in the white cocktail dress in here last night.

You be careful now. I got sisters but that wasn't no sister of mine.

You start undressin' them in your head, don't you? You start wonderin' what it would be like, you know? Young little twats. Old elegant bitches. You name it, I'm game.

All of them?

Not all of them, you asshole. Not if they're too young or too old. I'm not a fuckin' pervert.

One guy used to come in here boastin' about older women he claimed he was ballin' in Carmel. Said it covered living expenses. "They don't tell, they don't swell, and they're grateful as hell." That was his saying.

And he knew what he was sayin'. Those rich bitches. Set me up, Chili.

What? Go slow, man, is too early. You're going to the Safeway with me, come on.

427

No, I mean, set me up with a chick. This scar fuckin' drives 'em away.

I thought maybe that's why you always sit down there in the dark at the end of the bar.

You'd hide down there too if you wore this on your face.

Hey, no offense, man.

Far back as I can remember, it always gets to the point with some chick where you get punished for stuff you don't do, for shit some broad thinks you do behind her back. You get punished whether you do it or not, so you do it anyway, what the hell? If you're gettin' punished for it anyway, why not enjoy it too? Just gimme one shot and a chaser then I'll go with you.

I said wait till we get back and I open the bar then you got to give Chili five dollars and fifty cents. You still owe the bar five-fifty, Ricky, from last night.

COUNTY OFFICE OF SOCIAL SERVICES:
Morning. Have a seat.

How about that? 8:30 sharp. I made it!
So, how are you today? Have you come up with any ideas about a job search since you were here last?

Oh man, you askin' me that first thing in the morning? I can't handle it. I don't know about you but it's still early for me.

Well, then ... how about we put your job search aside and you just tell me about some of your heroes, Mister Debruen.

My heroes? You mean like Dick Tracy?

No, of course not. Your heroes in the music business, I mean. Just off the top of your head.

I don't know. Do I have heroes in the music business? It's kinda late for kid's stuff, doc.

Please, don't call me "doc." I'm not a doctor. You know my name is

Thomas Fuller and you can call me Mister Fuller or Tom. Just not "doc" anymore.

That's cool. You call me Richard; I'll call you Tom.

It's a deal. So, what about your earliest heroes in the music business?

My earliest heroes in the music business? Lemme think. Right away I remember visiting my dad at one of his pads in the boroughs when I was a kid. Lying on my stomach listenin' to this old record player in the bottom of this console with this tiny TV screen. Remember those first little TV screens? I remember listening over and over to his swing big band records. That music made me feel like I was somewhere else, man.

Yes, but, Richard, that's not what I asked. I meant, think of some figures related to the employment side of the music business. You must have had—maybe you still have some models of what that would be like. Forget about any job search for now. Just fantasying.

I came up readin' music reviews by Nat Hentoff and Leonard Feather and those guys. When I got older I thought about writing liner notes for albums, but I never met anybody who was doin' that for a living, not a decent living.

Reminds me of the sound sheets business you've mentioned.

Right on ... Tom. I started out majoring in journalism, broadcast journalism, up at San Fran State. But I never finished that. That's history. Heroes on the business side of the music, huh? Yeah, I guess I can name a few but you've never heard of 'em.

Try me. For instance?

Orrin Keepnews? He could've retired after Riverside but he kept on. Oh this is crazy. You've never heard of him; he's never heard of me. What difference does it make?

So, teach me. Who else?

Rudy Van Gelder? Nesuhi Ertegun? Heard of them?

You're saying that these people were producers not musicians?

They've stood the greatest names in modern jazz. George Avakian.

So, I take it you could see yourself enjoying some similar role in the music industry.

Oh come on, Tom. I couldn't touch those cats. I was happy to get airtime as an unpaid DJ on that campus station so I could string together my programs for the radio. Different versions of the same standards, instrumentals then vocals, you know what I mean? Different renditions of the same tune played back to back. Different cuts on the same date. Alternate tracks when I could get my hands on enough vinyls or tapes. But that work was for free. I've never earned a dime in commercial broadcasting.

But maybe you could if you applied yourself. There seem to be many roles to play in the music business, besides being a broadcaster. I'm learning just by listening to you.

That's cool but like what, for me I mean? What are you drivin' at? If a guy's not a player, if you're not an owner. What, like a sleazy promo man? Like a slick operator in PR? Like a flunky gofer boy in a studio? I'm not a boy anymore. Look at me. I'm getting' old.

We're only exploring your options, Richard. From what you've said, if I've understood you correctly, you have always enjoyed sharing what's valuable to you with others. And—

... Tom, listen. I can get behind what you're saying right now but don't make me out to be one of those big shots. I missed the boat. It's obvious.

Richard, I'm trying to identify some practical possibilities for you. Working with what you know, with what you feel comfortable with. Something that might serve you as a marketable set of skills to secure a paying job—that's all I'm driving at.

I'm sure not gettin' any job with the COCC again. Or driving a delivery van or transporting equipment. I couldn't get a job stacking fucking library books for AMBAG or the MTC.

Please, don't swear. Now what do those abbreviations stand for?

You don't know what AMBAG is? Let me think a sec'. Just what does that stand for? Association of Monterey Bay Area Governments. There you go.

And the MTC?

That's a no-brainer: Metro Transit Commission. You know, like the nine counties surrounding the Bay Area?

I see.

Nobody in those agencies who takes a look at my record is goin' to be handin' any company vehicle keys over to this guy anytime soon.

I see. Well....

Did I tell you about building a recording studio?

No. No, I don't think you did. You built a recording studio?

I didn't say that 'cuz it never happened. But I thought about it. I was planning on it. It was when my kid was born and I was still livin' with his mom. Right across Monterey Bay up Highway One out of Santa Cruz. See, what it would've amounted to was her lettin' me convert the old barn on their place.

Oh ... I see.

I was ready to run power out there and create a soundproof room. I knew where I could pick up a used console and tinker with that. I knew how to control for hum without a lot of extra equipment I couldn't afford in the first place. Tom, there's nothing like dickerin' with faders while you're sittin' in a little room lit up by VU meters.

You're talking about recording live music, right? Perhaps producing albums?

That's right. Trackin' and mixin' and then takin' it someplace else for the masters. I could've got behind all that if it'd worked out. You know, with the lady and the kid.

Oh ... I see. Okay then, let's see. Do you think you would know how to operate in a contemporary recording studio today?

Good question, man. I've been in enough rinky-dink setups in my time. I think I could handle the real thing if it came along. Remember, I took that course in sound engineering up at SF State. Dubbing, layering, but that was like twenty years ago. Anyway, how can you follow a dream when love goes south on you and you have no dough? If only I'd made a connection with some guy like Norman Granz when I was younger. Ever heard of him?

Norman Granz?

You were talkin' about heroes at the top of the set, right? You'll see Norman Granz' name on the best jazz music that's out there, Tom. You know Bill Graham?

Of course I know Bill Graham or know of him. Bill Graham I've heard of.

Right. Well, Norman Graz has been something like the Bill Graham of jazz. People who see him as just another Jew in the entertainment business, they're ... how would you say it? They're messed up in the head. Racists. Hey, Tom. I used to put on a good little radio show. I even had a little fan club. There was a journalism major wrote up reviews of every in-depth series I ever did and got them printed in the student newspaper. Like my history of female jazz vocalists? The Black Queens of Song I called that one. Every singer got a two-hour airing. I showcased Carmen MacRae, Abby Lincoln, Nina Simone, who else? You know any of them?

I may have heard of—

... Ella and Lady Day and Sassy, they got their due. There's no denying the best of the best but hey, what about Betty Carter? Dinah Washington. You've heard of Dinah Washington, right?

Yes, I have.

I did another series I called The White Lizards. I don't know if these names'll mean anything to you: Gerry Mulligan? Stan Getz?

Yes—

... Chet Baker?

Yes, I've heard of Chet Baker.

All right, doc! Art Pepper? No? I tried not to do too much talkin' during those radio series, if you can imagine Mister Motor Mouth not talking too much! I did one on the evolution of the tenor sax, but I told it through the music, cut after cut played to show what was the progression of ideas and styles being passed on down the line. As much uninterrupted listening as possible, that was the idea. That guy with the newspaper column even suggested I could do a little more talking, more explanation, if you can dig that. I just wanted to pay tribute to Bean, Pres, Dexter Gordon, Sonny Rollins, Trane—heard of them? Lester Young? No? I did one I called The White Lady Singers of Jazz. "White and Light" is how the reviewer put it in his column but screw critics, if you know what I mean. He put that series down. I don't care. Julie London, Julie Christy, Anita O'Day. Rosemary Clooney, Peggy Lee. I forget if I fit Doris Day in there. Could she like really sing jazz? I don't think I ever went that far.

I do recognize several of those names.

Of course, you do, Tom, of course you do. That reviewer went off on some trip about black and white politics. Hey, if a guy like Norman Granz—a white guy, a Jew—hadn't done all he did to break down the color barrier, nobody'd be watchin' Louis Armstrong and Carol Channing singin' Hello Dolly on TV today. But you know, you just can't win with some people so you side with the music. You know how that ended? Some asshole—

... please don't swear in here, Richard.

Right. So, some friendly fellow called in to the university administration and informed them that I was broadcasting on the student radio without being enrolled as a student. Maybe it was the same guy. Black dude. What was it, a two-watt transmitter covering campus? Who cares? Anyway, that shut me down.

Richard, I may not know all those musicians you've named but regardless of my knowledge or ignorance, maybe we can find a way to tap unto your expertise. Let's find a way to channel your passion into a career that would allow you to express yourself. And to pay your way. How about that?

Well, I told you my ex-old lady couldn't wrap her head around having a recording studio on her place, right? If I had a little capital back then I could've set that up and kept interviewing musicians travelin' up and down the coast. Some older cats but mostly the young lions. Back then I even thought about my own recording label, how about that?

But how about right now and not back then? Do you think we can put our heads together today—well, our time is about up today—but let's set up a plan of action that might take you in the direction you want to go, moving forward. Give it some thought, Richard. Between you and me, I can see those job listings on that board at the employment office are not going to be much of a match for your capacities.

You got that right. Or that dumb binder they've got. So now you've got me thinkin' about workin' in the industry again. That's pretty good, Tom. But those people I just named are all players and I could never play. Hey, check this out. Remember those producers I was just talkin' about?

The ones you considered role models, people you could emulate?

No no....

Then I'm not sure what you're getting at, Richard. But I'm afraid we're running out of—

...just let me stretch out on this for a sec', would you? I've been thinkin' about two-record sets lately. You know those deluxe editions? The record industry knows how to put together those packages of greatest hits. Norman Granz has his Song Books. But what about compiling my radio series? Oh what the hell am I talkin' about? Nobody is goin' to lose bucks backin' me. What, Richard Debruen's special selections as a Christmas present at a record store near you? Come on. But can you copyright an idea, Tom? Do you know anything about that?

No, I'm sorry. I can't help you there and—

... a freak or two might still recognize me down in LA but I don't have connections anymore. Anywhere. It never seems to add up, you know what I mean? I'm always right back at the starting line. Look at me now—oh, there's your next guest. I know I know, I gotta give up the mic, I'm leaving. But look at my situation. Do I know what I'm going to do next? No. Do I know where to direct my passion or whatever you said earlier in the set? No, I don't know. I have no idea what'll happen to me next. But believe me, as the song says: "Everything happens to me."

Let's save that for next time, Richard. It's nine o'clock and there's someone scheduled to see me. We'll talk again next week and in the meantime—

I know I know. Go to the employment office.

Goodbye, Richard.

See you, Tom.

THE SIDECAR BAR & GRILL:

You see what's happenin' to my Giants up there, Chili?

Ever since the All-Star break.

The Say Hey Kid's in a slump.

I noticed that too, Ricky.

My whole fuckin' team's in a slump. Turn that crap off and turn on some jazz, you fuckin' greaser. There's nobody comin' in here. Shit, I'm glad I don't have any dollars, or I'd try to score a couple lines. I'm so fuckin' bored with this probation bullshit.

Vato, you ever know anybody donated blood for dope money?

Yeah, I've heard of that.

I did.

You did?

Yeah, that was me. I got strung out real bad. I was eating that gelatin shit to clean out my blood. But I messed up and they ran a test and I ended up doing what? Cleaning stalls in the San Benito County Fairgrounds horse stables. Mierda de caballo. Six-thirty to nine-thirty, six mornings a week, with some cowboy cop watching me carrying a gun. Chili's done with dope. You better stay away from it too, my man, you know what's good for you.*

Hey, Chili. You know when you see a good-lookin' chick with her mom some place. You know when they're both good lookin' and you don't know which one you'd fuck first. Know what I mean? What do you think?

I think you got pussy on the brain, Ricardo.

That's for sure.

I think you better talk to that shrink.

Did I ever tell you about when I was hangin' out at the warehouse in Emeryville? Home of the Fleshpot Film Company. No kiddin'. That was some crazy shit. Talk about people gettin' strung out. These cigarettes taste like shit today.

What you expect on top of that birdcage breath coming outta your mouth.

What bird cage, where?

Here. Eat some of these mints, coco head. No? Okay, Ricardo, you go for a walk or back to the motel now. Take a siesta, man. Brush your fucking teeth and get some sleep. Nobody's here except you and me. You want me to close up for a couple minutes and I drive you to your motel?

• *Horse shit (Sp)*

COUNTY OFFICE OF SOCIAL SERVICES:

Did you just see that? That's so cool.

See what?

How I sat down without using my hand to cushion my leg. It didn't even hurt. No wonder they signed me off at PT.

I'm glad to hear you're feeling more mobile. How's the job hunt going?

Can we like switch the record?

What do you mean?

Change the channel, you know. Change the subject.

But that's why we're here, Richard. Isn't that the channel we should stay on?

OK, I'll tell you my latest thinking. I was thinkin' about a possible gig.

Yes?

But I'd need some introductions. You know, references, so that wouldn't get far off the ground.

What is it? What kind of job do you have in mind?

What difference?

It might make a difference in how you approach it.

I haven't got anything very specific in mind yet. But I'm still thinkin' about lookin' for a straight job as a studio technician up in San Fran.

Well, I'm here to help you clarify just such thoughts. And adjust your job search accordingly. I'll be happy to look over any written materials you bring in here along the lines of a resume, for instance, or letters of inquiry. I'll be happy to practice a job interview with you, role-play situations you can expect to encounter. You have considerable talent, Richard, and loads of specialized experience. Frankly, I don't see that many cases sent ahead from Probation with your sort of imagination. I want to see you exercising your creative faculties at large.

You mean you want to see me get a job.

Yes, I do, that would be nice. We've been over job descriptions for—

Do we have to back announce everything every time I get here?

"Back announce?"

You know, go over what we talked about all over again.

I believe it helps us stay on track, Richard.

Yeah, I guess, if that's your bag.

And I did see where the physical therapist signed off on your last session. Which implies that you're fit to try out for many positions in the general work force. So, what are you waiting for?

Tell you the truth, doc? Once probation's over, I'd be happy just to have a little pad of my own somewhere and pick up disability for a while till I'm ready to—how's that go?—"reenter the work force." A little closet space with a transmitter and a hook-up so I'd be able to broadcast out of there on a couple of watts. No big deal. Non-commercial. No commercials. Maybe up around Half Moon Bay again, that'd be cool. You were askin' me for my fantasy, right? Okay, that's my fantasy. I've got enough vinyl LP's in storage. Like my Blue Note albums.

"Blue Note?"

You know, Blue Note Records. The blue note, Tom. The third, fifth, seventh note of the scale, flattened. Anyway, the Blue Note series—of which I probably have one of the most complete if not the complete set of every release from 1947 to 1979, you know what I'm talkin' about? And I've got a 78-mono recording of the Esquire Concert in '45 that's in mint condition. I wasn't there but by 1947, I was ... what was I? Like twenty-one years old and buying my own albums. I inherited my dad's old 78's and those are not garage sale items, in my opinion. I've got some of the original 12-inch 33⅓ rpm vinylite LP's that Columbia released, also in mint condition I might add. Also from my dad. I sure hope I don't ever end up livin' in some cold-water pad in the Tenderloin partin' out my collection to make rent. One Japanese joker appraised my Blue Note collection at two thousand dollars then offered me twenty-two hundred cash on the spot. At least over the phone that's what he said: "cash on the spot." I'm glad I wasn't hard up at the time. I didn't take it. That's ridiculous, man. I could piece that collection out and make five times that much, ten times. I don't know where he thought I was comin' from, you know what I'm sayin'? But I don't trade my albums like guitar players trade their bitches.

"Bitches?"

Their guitars. Buy 'em, sell 'em, trade 'em, like baseball cards. Did I tell you I had to get my ass over to SF State during the strike a couple years back to get my Miles Davis albums out of the studio there? I mean, just check out what happened to the Bank of America in Santa Barbara. They burned that mother to the ground. See? I was loaning my Miles Davis collection to this student DJ. Anyway, all my records play well. I do not tolerate nicks and scratches and greasy thumbprints on a single piece in my Prestige issues. Columbia's twelve-inch 78-rpm vinyl pressing of Coleman Hawkins? Mint condition. Yeah, I think I'd be happy doing a little jazz broadcasting every day. I know, rock and roll is here to stay but there are still some die-hard jazz freaks who would appreciate my programming.

THE SIDECAR BAR & GRILL:
Another part of that college gig was snatchin' up tickets to concerts at half-price. And I'll tell you something else.

You talk too much, man.

I told you about my girl dancers, right? They got used to me hangin' around. I got to be a pretty well-known dude around the college dance studios. Once word went out about my video playback thing, they all liked to see themselves on the monitor. So, I got to hangin' around those young ladies, you know. I mean, what was I? Fifteen, twenty years older than most of them, and they just got used to me in the dressing rooms, like I was some fuckin' harmless uncle or something.

They'd be half naked, changin' in and out of their leotards with me right there. Can you dig that? What man in his right mind wouldn't want that job? Always practicin' their moves and massagin' their buns, stretchin' their legs. I had some itchy fingers, Chili. There was maybe one or two butterfly boys in the batch but fuck that, I mean who cares? Hey, where is everybody tonight, Chili?

Maybe you scared them away after last night, Ricardo.

(p.92)

CHAPTER 4

(1) "Are you an only child, Katie?"

"My older brother died when I was eleven."

"That's the shits. When I was eleven I still had my older brother, Marco. Still do, sort of. And by the time I was a teenager, my father and his two brothers were in the grocery store business. Mario, my dad, his store was in Modesto; Uncle Martino's store was in Manteca; and Uncle Maximo ran the one in Merced. The 3M's in the 3M's. My uncles had lots of kids, but any family only has one firstborn son, right? So, who do you think was in line to inherent those three stores? The three oldest boys, of course. It didn't matter that I worked in the Modesto store since I was thirteen. Didn't matter that as soon as I could drive a car I was in charge of keeping all three of those joints stocked up with Nonna's spaghetti sauce. That was 3M's one and only private label product and instead of going to college after high school, I was pushing spaghetti sauce up and down Highway 99. Pretty soon after that I was in charge of making Nonna's sauce. In my family, the women get used to smelling like onions, garlic, basil, chives, oregano— and don't forget the stewed tomatoes! So, when the 3M's got ready to pass the business on to the next generation, they went to the next 3M's: my brother Marco and the other two—Matteo and Marcelo, right? The second 3M's decided to sell the Merced and Manteca properties. Fuck the grocery business, they said, this is about real estate. They kept the Modesto location, tore down the store, and built one big supermarket on the same site. So, here's where I made my biggest mistake. Somehow I got the idea I'd be on board when that flagship super store sailed out of port. During the construction, I was taking courses at this business college. I expected to head up a new, expanded line of 3M's private label products. I thought I would get deep into supplier relations, business-to-business stuff. So, when it opened up, I was called Head Merchandiser, and I was doing the window displays, which was a pretty big attraction at 3M's Modern Supermarket. I had the recipe and the connections and started supervising the making of the sauce instead of making it all myself. I knew how distribution works and all those merchandisers' pissing matches for shelf space. Hell, I knew more about end caps and presets and plan-o-grams than all three owners combined. And I was fired up about using the new twenty-foot truck to place our products in other grocery stores in Sacramento and Fresno and everywhere in between: Tracy, Lodi, Madeira, Turlock—anywhere we could deliver it direct. I figured we could eventually go up into the Foothills where so many people were living fulltime when they started moving out of the cities. Well, I was dreaming. Hey, I know you're still there, but I can't see your face in the dark. You want to hear the rest of this or not?"

"Sure."

"Well, while the three Salomone boys were scheming, little sister Angelita was dreaming. My merchandising budget got cut, and all I had left to do was handle the spaghetti sauce and dress the store's windows and help with the stupid weekly newspaper ad. I didn't mind doing the window displays. It was fun making those up, at first. You should've seen my windows at the grand opening. The Sunday Modesto Bee ran a feature article on my windows and a full-page picturing all six of them. At the front door I had this picnic scene with pictures of Grandpa and Nonna from the Old Country on this checkerboard cloth thrown over a crate. I put out a platter of pasta and vegetables—made out of plastic— and of course I had all the ingredients of Nonna's Spaghetti Sauce. Chucks of plastic cheese. Plastic grapes. A big glass jar of olive oil— that was real. And some jugs of Chianti—what do you think? Sounds pretty corny now but it was cute and all in a six by six by three foot space. But when the party was over I realized that was it, that was my job: stacking jars of sauce on the shelf and dressing windows, besides cutting out pictures of the port of Naples for the newspaper ads. See, I never paid attention when my brother and cousins and my dad and my uncles were drawing up the legal papers for the transfer of ownership. You can't say I was squeezed out because I was never let in in the first place. Pretty rotten treatment for somebody who'd kept at the business even when every girl I knew was getting married and starting a family of her own. Oh, I had a bright future in the big-time supermarket business, I thought. I only saw the light after the 3M's hired this supposedly 'independent management firm' to study the operation and make recommendations. So, these guys come in and study the books and survey the store. Then they start interviewing employees. Department heads, clerks, everybody—me too. Just gathering information, looking for input, right? 'Outside consultants'—my ass! Well, you already know about Angela Salomone's big mouth. So, when they got to me, I made my grievances known. I told them how my cousins and my brother, Marco, they treated the staff pretty poorly most the time. Not everybody was so happy about how things were going in their new Super Mercado—no. I told them it bothered me how they always squeezed loyal suppliers, threatening them with replacements they were stringing along with false promises at the same time. Always trying to get the best deal for 3M's. That's business, sure, but they were low about it. What do you think happened next? The so called 'outside business consulting firm' submitted its final report and the head of that 'outside business consulting firm' became the new head manager of 3M's."

"What?"

"It was an inside job. Their bean counter became the new 'controller.' I was so ashamed of my family acting that way. Whoever had spoken out during the 'confidential' interview process—like yours truly—we found ourselves without a job. No, that's not true. I still had my job if I wanted it: dressing windows and stocking shelves. It was an insult. I wouldn't talk to my brother. My cousins, Marcel and Mattie, they tried to sell me this line about how it made good business sense to push the burden of merchandising on the distributors and all. They cut me out. Same old story. I was a disposable woman ... or is it 'dispensable?' Anyway, I quit. Except for visiting Nonna in the nursing home, I walked away from the whole family. No more gatherings at the holidays—screw that. And before I left for the Peninsula, I rented a van and went in there one night with the key to my old storage room and took everything that wasn't nailed down. All the junk you can think of for window dressing. Tools, tapes, glue. Artificial flowers, dry flowers. Fishing line, fabric, mirrors, lights and banners, hats, balloons. And I set up shop on the Peninsula. 'We go to great panes.' That was the motto of the business I started on my own, Great Panes. I got the hell out of the Valley and rented a studio apartment in San Bruno and a little roll-up in Millbrae. 'We go to great panes,' spelled p-a-n-e-s. Yeah, great pains and you know where! So, it took me a couple of years to max out on my connections in the Italian grocery store world. You have any idea how many crazy wops there are in the produce and deli business in the Bay Area? Hey, are you still awake?"

"I'm awake."

"Katie, I was dressing and undressing the windows in all the high-end grocery stores: Petrini's, Lunardi's, Lucca's. Standalones like that Piedmont Grocery, the Deli Maggiore in Oakland. I trained one girl in each of those joints to work with me. Keep the displays dusted. Cover for me if I was sick or hung over, whatever. Father's Days I did a maritime theme. There was a bookcase with a model sailboat and an Atlas and a globe. Pennants, a life preserver, a beach with real sand and some of those glass and cork float nets. Don't forget the food and the booze! Salmon pâté, crackers, champagne, I forget. All kinds of plastic fish hanging in the air, that was easy. On Cinco de Mayo I used a Mexican blanket and a bullfight poster. Palm tree leaves and a sombrero—what else? Chips and salsa, Mexican beers, of course, tequila—that was a cinch. But after five years of that hustle I looked around and I was beat. I was exhausted. I lost my drive, just like that. That's when a friend of mine studying psychology helped me see I was killing myself trying to show my brother and my cousins I could make it without them when really that family feud—it didn't matter to me anymore. But in the meantime, I had picked up a few bad habits. So, I dropped all except a couple of big accounts and took a few courses at the community college. That's when real estate development caught my interest. And now look where I'm at! Back to being used by big boys selling real estate instead of tomato sauce. Big boys selling big golf courses that sell big houses. Big deal international so-and-so's! Now whenever I see a clever shop window I want to get back in there with my scotch tape and thumbtacks. Give me a platter of plastic lasagna and a loaf of plastic bread and get me the hell out of this unreal real estate development game!"

"How's that 3M store doing these days?"

"Okay, I guess. They farmed Nonna's sauce out to some canning company and food distributor who resold it right away. Last I heard that brand disappeared after the quality went downhill. I don't know. I see most everybody at the funerals and baptisms I do go to now, but I'm basically a black sheep. I hang out with some of the women. Of course, all their husbands act like a flock of pure white angels when I blow through town. Angels, my ass! They touch my assets once I'll blow all their covers wide open!"

(p.119)

CHAPTER 5

(1) Katie is referring to eight handwritten composition books making up the mother's "memoirs." In her cover letter composed January 7, 1965, Elizabeth Lowrie elaborates upon why she felt compelled to sequester herself in the attic during the Christmas storm of 1965 in order to produce a presentable account of the first twenty-eight years of her life: Katie's incommunicativeness and her infatuation with the temporarily resident landlady had convinced her mother that "... [composing the NOTEBOOKS] seems to be the only means at my disposal to create a reasonable record of events and to find out what I am really thinking and feeling, as well as my only hope of sharing what

I am thinking and feeling with you. You must admit that, once Jan McLoughlin moved in for the duration of the storm, you were hardly able to listen to your dear old mother for ten seconds at a time!" (cf. pp.185-187, "Chapter 8: A Winter Storm Passes," Book Two, Volume I). The texts of the NOTEBOOKS constitute eight of the fourteen chapters in Book Three of THE THREE NAKED LADIES OF CLIFFPORT (cf. Volume II). (p.142)

(2)

Date Jan. 28, 1972

Redwood Coast Nursery
One Grade Road
Cliffport CA 95017

RE: Notice of Violation(s) Zoning Ordinance (District A-2, BP2-4)

Dear Mrs. Kaitlin Lowrie:

As owner of record of the sole proprietorship operating under the fictitious business name of Redwood Coast Nursery located at the above-referenced address, you are hereby notified that a Category 4 (Other Violations) priority response has been assigned to a complaint submitted to our office on January 22, 1972.

As the Code Compliance Investigator conducting the investigation, I have confirmed that the advertising sign located at your business address is out of compliance with Santa Cruz County Zoning Regulations. A visual inspection of the sign installed on or near portions of your property dedicated to Redwood Coast Nursery business activities has identified its critical proximity to, and view from, Scenic Highway One.

I herewith cite the relevant sections from the County Zoning and Development Code:

[13.10-581] Visibility of sign within a designated scenic corridor shall be minimized by the use of appropriate size and location.

(1) Freestanding sign shall not exceed seven feet in height measuring from the finished grade at site of installation.

(2) Maximum total sign area* shall be 50 square feet.

Total sign area defined as area on one side of a sign with a well-defined border, which encloses the letters, symbols, graphics, and logo.

To resolve the violations, within 45 days (before or by April 1, 1972) the sign must be removed from view or altered to conform to items (1) and (2) in the paragraph above.

If you require further clarification concerning the nature of the violation(s) or request further information regarding your next step toward resolving the violation(s), please contact me by certified mail or address your questions to counter staff in the Office of County Planning.

Be advised that if you do not resolve the violation(s) within the prescribed time period, enforcement sanctions may be initiated, and the matter may be referred to an Administrative Hearing Officer for the imposition of civil penalties or reference to Superior Court. If the case is referred to the Superior Court, the County will request a court order allowing the recordation of the Notice of Violation on the property's title.

Joseph Brecker
Code Compliance Investigator
Telephone 408-333-6575 ext. 02

(p.149)

(3) Having decided, in consultation with her mother, that all funds left over from the inheritance should be expended on the nursery, Katie outfitted the glasshouse with heating mats for seedling trays and water wands screwed onto brand-new, tightly coiled hoses without leaks or kinks. She sited indoor/outdoor thermometers at various locations and worked with a mechanic from the Fern Garage to wire in the gas heater's thermostat and fire it up. The same man returned to position the horizontal flow fans and hang a battery of punched-hole convection tubes to distribute the heated air.

She surrendered the new Ford to the retired Finnish metal-worker in Fern to have him fabricate a high aluminum shell cover for the truck's extended-length bed so that containerized plants could be protected in transit. Stranded in Cliffport without a vehicle for almost four days, Katie settled down to her annual prespring tasks in the new glasshouse: fashioning bamboo stakes; assembling tripods for training upright fuchsias; dipping plant cuttings into rooting hormone powder. With and without the radio turned on, she spent hours placing semi-hard dahlia tips one by one into a mix of vermiculite and horticultural sand, slipping semi-soft fuchsia tips into perlite and sand, and sticking the springy stems of leafy ivy geraniums into perlite and sand amended with screened peat moss.

While resisting any reckoning with her short- or long-term solitude, she busied herself addressing the practical problems that arose in the new greenhouse, learning how to moderate its stuffy atmosphere by adjusting the hand-cranked vents along its gable roof and opening or closing the doors to augment or diminish cross currents of fresh air. She fine-tuned the dangling mist emitters and experimented with a drip line on some rowed-out cans. Struggling to transport planting mix from the tarped pile outside to the open bins beneath her indoor worktables, she constructed a wheelbarrow ramp to span the metal threshold of the sliding side door, then found out she had periodically to clear spilled soil from its clogged bottom track. The discharge from the gutters needed to be diffused, so Katie fit burlap bag extensions onto the ends of the downspouts such that the rainwater would fan out across the miniature deltas she created with gravel borrowed from the drive. But how to control the runoff sheeting across the wheelbarrow-wide paths zigzagging the hillside? She hit upon the idea of excavating 6"-deep × 6"-wide trenches where the worst erosion was taking place, jamming 2" × 4" stubs spanning the open channels lined with redwood bottoms and sidings. During the next serious rain, the surface water ran down the channels and percolated through the sandbags strategically placed alongside the paths.

Even though they wouldn't be releasable until summer or fall, Katie enjoyed the friendly company of the baby plants growing up all around her. With Baby Blue curled on a towel at her feet, she relished the uterine warmth of the heater's forced air and felt shivers up her spine and blood pulsing through her veins when rain squalls struck the glass roof and sloshed down the transparent, womblike walls. As she grew used to navigating the greenhouse—a pane glass galleon in which she was by turns captain, first mate, and galley slave shackled to the bench—she mulled over prospects for the coming season. She had a thousand square feet of new shade cloth draping empty, open-sided frames. Her miscellaneous one-gallon perennials would be sellable as is or ready for division and shifting into larger cans. The mother plants around the old lodge were out-of-bounds, but her purloined stock plants in seven- and fifteen-gallon containers were robust and would provide ample material for propagation.

(p.150)

Notes

(4)

COASTAL PROPERTY MANAGEMENT

February 21, 1972

ATTN: Kaitlin Lowrie
RE: Right-of-Way Violations at One Grade Road, Cliffport CA 94017

You and/or other persons acting in complicity with, for, or on your behalf, have been observed (Date of Incident: February 22-25, 1972) engaged in non-permitted activities upon the access easement drive (hereafter called "the roadway") of property owned by Yo-Mizo-Sata International Ltd.

You are hereby notified that you or any agent in your employ or under your direction are hereby barred from further activities other than ingress to and egress from your property upon said roadway. Find attached the detailed parcel map which clearly delineates the location of the relevant lot lines of the adjoining properties and the extent of the roadway boundaries.

The affirmative easement created by conveyance of deed entitles you, your immediate family members, and authorized guests use of the road for ingress to and egress from your parcel to the nearest public highway (Grade Road) but does not allow for proprietary management activities. You may therefore not perform maintenance duties or make alterations of any nature on the specified property under any circumstances.

Furthermore, you are hereby notified that if you or any agent in your employ or under your direction are found altering the property at issue after the date of April 1st, 1972, presence shall be deemed a trespass upon said property herein described and the owner, or duly authorized representatives shall take every measure permitted by law to prosecute such trespass, including physical apprehension and arrest by a police officer. Should you make use of the road for any purpose or in any manner other than passage to and from your parcel, the Sheriff's Office will be notified, and a criminal complaint lodged against you in Superior Court.

Yours,

Gerald Bartelson

Gerald Bartelson
Vice-President
CC: William Leitcher, Attorney and Counselor at Law

Enclosure: Parcel Map, being a subdivision of Parcel L-364, as filled on December 12, 1971 in Book of Maps at pages 177-8, Santa Cruz County Records and lying within Unincorporated County of Santa Cruz. No scale, consisting of one sheet.

COASTAL PROPERTY MANAGEMENT • PO BOX 666 • SAN JOSE, CA • 95113

(p.150)

CHAPTER 6

(1) [VERBATIM C]
COUNTY OFFICE OF SOCIAL SERVICES:

Maybe you're right, Richard, and maybe you're wrong. Maybe part right, part wrong. We can discuss it another time. Right now I need to know if you have or have not applied for that job. One job is all you need.

Come on. I'm like forty-five.

I know that. Don't you still have to buy food and pay rent?

What do you want from me? Who's going to hire a guy my age just comin' off rehab with this on this face? Tell me, who? Nobody is, that's who.

Especially if you never apply. Richard, I'm going to need more cooperation on this. You need to decide what to pursue and then pursue it.

I thought about writing for the sound industry magazines but that's out. I can't write. I mean, not like I used to.

Could you see running a music spot?

A club? Maybe, if I could be on the side of the players, you know what I mean? On the side of the players who are on the side of the music not just the owner's money. At least I'd feed the musicians, unlike most places. Pay them decent money, feed them. I'd like to support the kind of jazz that commercial radio can't, you know what I'm sayin'? A while back you asked for my fantasy. There it is. That's my problem: I still have ideals.

How about working for an agency, booking talent for nightclubs?

Club owners, station owners, label owners—I know that breed of cat. I know their jive talk.

Well? Could you see yourself as a talent scout then? Or as a musician's representative?

How about just one job as a technician in one studio? That'd be more like it. Booking studio time, managing album pressings. But the union has those jobs locked down, you know what I'm sayin'? I was thinkin' of goin' up to the City to get work as an audio-visual technician in some independent operation. A payin' job but for an independent producer. But it's not exactly a level playing field out there, you know what I mean? I mean, you apply for a job and they check out your experience then maybe call up a past employer or something. It's not looking too good for Richard Debruen. Then there's this.

Well, if it's any consolation, that scar looks far less intimidating every time I see you. Sometimes I don't even notice it. But I wonder—now I know this is a personal matter—but I wonder if you would ever consider cutting your hair.

Cutting my hair?

Yes, Richard, there's still a lot of resistance to such long hair on a man. You may find that hard to believe. I'm just suggesting that if you'd get a haircut.... I'm not criticizing your hairstyle, but the reality is, long hair on a man, even in a ponytail, it's not something a lot of employers welcome during an initial job interview. You must know what I mean.

I'm forty-five years old, doc. I think I can wear my hair however I want.

You can. You just might not be met with open arms by a potential employer, is all. What do you think? Makes sense? Richard, I'm asking you what you think. It does no good to scare people, especially when you're asking them for a job.

THE SIDECAR BAR & GRILL:

Day like today, I'd like to get over to Santa Cruz and check out some people I heard are applying for ten watts to do some experimental radio. Maybe they could use some help, know what I mean?

How the hell you gettin' over to Santa Cruz, swim?

I belong where the freaks are, not this side of Monterey Bay. That cocktail lounge music they call "jazz" on Cannery Row is tired stuff, Chili. Once I get off probation, I hope I never hear of Marina or Seaside or fuckin' Sand City ever again.

Easy, gringo. Sand City's my city now.

Hey, whaddaya think? My face lookin' better or what? It's not so bad as it was. Some of the stitch marks still show—like a run in some chick's stocking, know what I mean?

You know what they called Al Capone, don't you?

Don't fuck with my head, Chili. I'm flyin' outta this watering hole before too long too.

You jumpin' probation?

I don't know yet. I gotta get through some more sets with that career counselor then maybe get my collection of vinyl's out of storage and revive the Honda. I sure hope those album covers are holdin' up. You think they might be warped if it got too hot inside the storage unit?

It never gets hot around here.

I'll probably have nothin' but problems gettin' the Beast started, know what I mean? Maybe the salty air got into it, sittin' there idle so long. I'll have to go all through that fuckin' fuel system one of these days.

You know something, man? Your counselor was right, what he said. That scar isn't half as bad as when you first showed up but it still turns kind of a weird color sometimes.

I thought about maybe tellin' the ladies I got this over in 'Nam.

I know guys at Fort Ord cut your cojones off, you start lyin' about stuff like that.

Hey, I'm not that low. I only thought of it. I didn't do it.

Not yet. But it's too bad about that scar, Macaroni.

Whaddya callin' me Macaroni for?

You always bragging what a big assman you used to be, so I was thinking about Yankee Doddle Dandy. "Stuck a feather in his hat and with the girls be handy."

Yankee Doodle?

Hey, I may be half-black and half-Chicano but I'm all-American, Ricky baby.

You know what else I've been thinkin'? I'm thinkin' of selling the Beast as is, Chili. I need some moola. You know anybody wants a used Honda 350? I'd like to trade it in on that Blue Norton with a FOR SALE sign over on David Avenue.

I didn't see that one. I told you I don't get over that way.

Check it out. I don't know how much I'd owe the guy, but I'm sick of tinkerin' with that Honda. The Beast is on its last legs. It'd be good for somebody younger than me, just startin' out. I'd give it to my fuckin' son if I could get in touch with him, you know what I mean?

You got a job lined up?

That's what Tom Fuller the Brushman always asks me: "So how's it going with the job search?"

What do you tell him?

"Oh, it's goin', it's goin'." Something like that. He has my file; he knows how it's goin'. Goin' nowhere fast. I've gotta get rid of that guy somehow.

COUNTY OFFICE OF SOCIAL SERVICES:

I thought you might ... like ... get me a little better by now, Tom. But maybe you don't know what it's like to be in the situation I'm in. Have you ever had your license taken away? No, you haven't. Have you ever totaled a company vehicle? I doubt it. Have you ever been in trouble with the law? Probably not. And you want to help me find a job? You're just repeating yourself, you know? You said all that at the top of the set.

"The top of the set?"

You know, since the minute I came in here. But I'm tellin' you, until I get wheels I can't get ahead, know what I mean?

Regaining your maneuverability will make a difference. I recognize that. I acknowledge that you feel limited in your choices right now because of transportation challenges. But are you sure that getting back on a motorcycle as your sole means of transportation might not also limit your options?

A bike can go anywhere a car can go, only faster.

What about in bad weather, in winter?

There should be blue stars given out for riders like me, ridin' in winter without gettin' into accidents.

Uh-huh. So other than the transportation challenge, how is the job search going? Have you made those follow-up phone calls? No? Letters? No? Any of the things we've talked about? So, no. Have you taken the resume writing self-tutorial yet up on the third floor?

That room with all the typewriters upstairs? I'm workin' on getting' up there, doc. Did I tell you I made a phone call to the dance instructor at MPC?

No.

See? There's something you didn't know. Turns out she's goin' on a six-week tour with a dance company this fall. I saw the announcement in the Pink Section in The Chronicle. "The Adrienne Bloch Dance Company." They're goin' to tour the Pacific Coast States on some big arts grant. Performances, master classes. "The Adrienne Block Dance Company." I found out they already have a pianist and a percussionist, but they might need a technician, right? To travel with them on the road.

So, do you think there's work for you there?

I don't know. I'm just sayin'... could be, could be.... I'll be off proba-tion by then if I play my cards right. I left a message, offering to troubleshoot the sound system during their rehearsals in San Francisco. Told her I'm not askin' for any pay for that ... not until we hit the road when all I'll need is travel expenses and some pocket change, you know? That'd be one way to get back in the game. Hey, I'm not free but I'm cheap! That was just a little joke, doc.

*

How are your prospects with that traveling dance troupe shaping up?

That'd be late October. It's like the Big Time in the world of "The Dance" as they like to say.

What's so funny, Richard?

Just thinkin'. Most guys into "The Dance" are like this, you know what I'm sayin'? I sure wouldn't mind traveling with all those females though. And I wouldn't mind if other cats see me as a stud so long as nobody takes me for one of those faggots, know what I'm talkin' about? If I get that job.

What do you think your chances are?

It's a happening thing, doc. Did I tell you I saw their itinerary?

No.

They've started rehearsals up in San Fran. They'll be takin' off the middle of October.

And...?

That's just it. I haven't heard back from Adrienne. Or the Beck.

"The Beck?"

Rebecca. The dance teacher. She and I used to get along pretty well. We were a unit once, I guess you could say. She's one of the main dancers in the company. But I haven't heard back from either one of them.

I want to ask you a question, Richard. Why do you keep coming here?

Why? Because the Man sent me here and you know what? I'm goin' to keep comin' here as long as I have to, to get through probation. That's why.

And after all this time there's not one thing in your packet indicating that you have taken any real steps towards securing employment or begun retraining in a field leading to future employment.

But what about the dance tour? And I've been to that employment office twice since you wrote me up. I sign in, look over the announcements. That's what you said I'm supposed to be doing, right?

I believe I said that's the bare minimum. Just signing in and flipping through the binder doesn't mean you're headed anywhere. That's only a baby step. Come on, you know what I mean.

THE SIDECAR BAR & GRILL:

How long've I been here?

Oh man, how do I know that? You got here before those people over there came in, right? Three hours maybe?

No, I mean, how long've I been comin' into the Sidecar. Has it been a year yet?

What am I, your probation officer?

I don't stand a chance on the Peninsula. I mean, I stand out like one of those Most Wanted Men posters hangin' up in the PG Post Office. As soon as my probation's over, I'm headed over to Santa Cruz where the freaks hang out. This side of Monterey Bay's for squares and retired army farts. Or rich people.

These people in here today don't look too rich to me. And what about Chili, Ricardo? Do I look rich to you?

You know I'm not talkin' about you, Chilidog. Jesus Christ! And with all the rubberneckers swarmin' the Peninsula on weekends? You can't even find a bench to park your ass on from Cannery Row out to the lighthouse, you know what I mean? It's too crowded. Everybody wants their picture taken at Lover's Point. And the Beast has just not been cooperating. I cleaned out that fuel system, like we said.

No va?

It starts but it runs ragged, man.

Wait a minute. You been drivin' around without a license, Macaroni? Or'd you get it back?

Couple more months, *Chile sin carne*. Two more fuckin' months. Hey, some time I'm going to tell you how I met her.

Who?

Kate, the mother of my boy.

Okay, but not now. It's getting busy all of a sudden.

And you won't say anything when I tell you, you fuckin' chulo. You'll shut up and listen, okay?

Hey, I been workin' this counter long enough to be a shrink myself.

Well, I'm sure not lookin' forward to meetin' a shrink and it looks like I might have to. Some of the shit those shrinks run down just messes with peoples' heads. He'll probably start buggin' me about my kid. Sometimes I think I must be the unluckiest guy in California. I didn't even know what name my kid goes by. Don? Donny? Donald? No. DD. Fuckin' DD, she called him. I wonder who's fuckin' his mother now if anybody is. You hear what I just said?

Keep it down, man.

I have a right to see my boy, but the Bitch from Hell shut me down. If I went over there, you know, just showed up at her place anyway? She's not above shootin' me, I'm tellin' you.

Ai yai yai.

If I make a move, she'll probably put out a restraining order or what-ever to keep me away. Could she do that now that I've had my little skirmish with the law? Could she?

Do I look like a lawyer to you? Come on, man. I gotta go. There's more people in here than just you.

Chili, I'm askin' you. Could she do that?

You're not my only customer, Ricky. Cuál es tu pinche problema? •

COUNTY OFFICE OF SOCIAL SERVICES:

So, you made it in.

How late am I? Shit, Tom! I missed the early bus.

And what about two weeks ago?

Same thing. I missed the early bus and the second one. The jerk driver saw me, but he wouldn't stop.

The bus driver wouldn't stop? Come on now, Richard. Get serious.

No, sir! When I got up to the curb he pulled away. I waved and shouted and everything. He could've stopped; it wouldn't have cost him anything. No such luck. So, that's what happened last time.

And you're fifteen minutes late today. We have less than fifteen minutes. I thought we had an understanding about tardiness, not to mention not even showing up two weeks ago.

Is it such a big deal, doc? I mean, I've missed a couple of times, okay?

Don't call me "doc"—

... whoa! I meant "Tom."

No, don't bother to sit down. Did you hear me? I said, don't sit down. Richard, I've come to the conclusion that you think you can keep bluffing your way in here until the end of your year on probation. Missing an entire appointment? Rushing in here at eight-forty-five? It's not acceptable. You know I always have someone else scheduled for nine o'clock. I'm sorry but I'm going to have to write you up as absent again today.

But I made it, I'm here.

• *What's your fucking problem? (Sp)*

It's ten-to-nine. Your appointment is at eight-thirty.

Oh, go ahead. Get a hard-on about it. Write me up. Jesus! Ramirez always loves to have something to beat me up with.

I was hoping after all this time you might start showing some interest in taking advantage of the opportunity that these appointments have provided.

What opportunity is that? And what about the dance tour job? That's legit. I just haven't heard back from anyone yet. That's how I'm planning to pay my bills, you know what I mean? Once I get booted out of the Anchor Motel, there will be bills to pay.

Have you done anything more to pursue that job, Richard?

I just told you. I haven't heard back from them. Sir.

"Sir?" Are you trying to provoke me?

No. Sir.

Okay, we're done, that's it. We're all done here.

You mean I can go?

I mean this is your last appointment with me or anyone else in the Monterey County Department of Career Counseling.

What? What's that there, a fuckin' pink slip?

Don't swear in here, Richard.

I can't believe it. You're firin' me? What are you writing down there?

I'm using this form to sign off on the department's participation in your rehab program. This will travel with your file to your case-worker.

What the hell? You're kickin' me back to court!

I don't know what Missus Hawkins will do with this information.

What information?

I've written you up as absent for today and two weeks ago. And I've tallied up all your other significant tardiness.

But I'm right here.

Are you? Take a look at that clock on the wall. It's five minutes before nine o'clock.

Oh man! Won't this look great on my record! Hey, should I put this on my resume too?

What resume? I haven't seen any resume. We're done. It's just not working. You've racked up enough "couple mistakes" as you like to call them to satisfy any definition of non-compliance.

"Non-compliance." Ramirez will love this one!

Ramirez?

My probation officer.

I can't speak for your probation officer and I don't know how Missus Hawkins will proceed. I can't speak for them or the court. But I can speak for this department, and you're no longer in our program, starting today. Here. Take this with you.

Shit on a stick!

I said, don't swear in here, Mister Debruen.

What if I go to the employment office right now and two weeks from now I show up back here on time with a resume?

I'm afraid it's too late for that. I'm done listening to your empty promises and lame excuses. Maybe I shouldn't have been listening all along. Now there's someone waiting to see me. Or do I have to call Security?

Can't a guy get a second chance with you?

A second chance? Did it ever occur to you, all these months, did it ever once occur to you that I'm not the one on probation, that you are? When the judge granted you formal probation instead of jail time, he must've thought you could do better for yourself. Your case-worker must have thought you could get something out of meeting with me, or somebody like me. But have I managed to wrest one genuine commitment out of you? Have you shown me one scrap of evidence that you've applied for a job?

I told you I called The Beck a couple places. And I was about to contact her again later today.

Anyone can dial a phone number, Richard.

Yeah? You think it's so easy chasin' down work when I'm still recovering from everything that went down?

I'm afraid you'll have to continue your recovery somewhere else. Now there's someone else who's waiting to see me—

Right, yeah, nice! Throw me under the fuckin' bus!

I asked you not to speak like that in here. The county has a department of behavioral health and—

Behavioral health? What's that?

I'm not aware of all they have to offer but in a case such as yours, perhaps psychological counseling. You'll have to take that up with Missus Hawkins, I suppose. I've written down that you might benefit from therapeutic counseling more than you seem to have benefited from career counseling with me. In any event, I'm done with your— how did you put it once? "... going through the motions." If you won't let yourself be helped, if you won't let me or somebody like me help you—

... game over?

Game over. Psychological counseling is not something I do. It's out of my purview. When are you scheduled to see Missus Hawkins again?

Monday morning. I don't see her. I call her.

Well, I'm certain she'll have this at her desk before then.

Can I have a look at what you wrote in there?

No, you may not. I'm afraid this is a confidential communication. But it's essentially what I've just told you. Non-compliant. Non-productive. Candidate for services at Behavioral Health. I'm sorry.

Fuck!

Now I'm telling you for the last time: do not use that language in here. Okay, it's past nine. Goodbye, Mr. Debruen. Or do I have to pick up this phone...?

(p.179)

(2) A second lengthy appendage to Chapter 6 (Verbatim D) can be found under the NOVELS drop-down menu at peterboffey.com.

CHAPTER 7

(1) After having met the sensitive, well-mannered widower from the Netherlands, Elisabeth Lowrie had shown no concern about her daughter's welfare during his subsequent visits to Cliffport or Katie's own trips to Soquel; her seventy-year-old mother was capable of unguarded praise of the man, and Pieter T. had labeled her a "wonderful person" too. Born in 1902, Elise could still be a stickler on outward forms and displays of propriety that her daughter's generation dismissed as obsolete—mores and customs deemed superficial if not downright dishonest—and loyalty to certain persons and fealty to certain convictions ran deep in her mother's sensibility. Katie's grandmother, Liliane, occupied pride of place in the woman's private pantheon of the elect, where her "Aunt" Dorothea and her "Uncle" John were also enshrined, company augmented by Eleanor, Georgellen, and Amy, three members of the extinct North Coast's Pottery Guild with whom Elise remained steadfast friends. No male other than John McLoughlin had been included in her mother's herd of sacred cows until now when, after only one encounter, Pieter Tuelling seemed to have been inducted. (p.195)

(2) Baby Blue was dozing off when Katie snapped her head forward and slapped her hat down onto the dash. "Goddamnitall, Blue!" she cried out. The dog sat up, straightened her forelegs, and perked her ears, looking about for the cause of her mistress' distress. "Another

Dutchman is fucking up my head!" Katie reclaimed her cap, wadding her hair into a handful she shoved through the opening of the strap closure in back. Martin Wildeman had been a Dutch immigrant to California, yet she felt toward Pieter Tuelling none of the animus she still harbored against Wildeman, the sculptor from Holland who had denied Katie's mother her birthright as his legitimate child: Pieter Tuelling wasn't Katie's maternal grandfather. And she foresaw no possibility that her dealings with the retired widower would ever have negative impacts upon her future the likes of which her teenage enslavement to Richard Debruen—an American but of New York Dutch descent—had had, and still had, on her life. She also recalled how she had enabled Aidan Quinn-Kergorentin to take her on a serious bend in the spiral of her own existence as a dreamy young woman still acting out juvenile fantasies—no, a man didn't have to be Dutch to screw up her life. Still, just like Martin Wildeman and Richard Debruen, Pieter Tuelling was in fact Dutch—as if it were written that she fulfill some destiny with the Netherlanders.   (p.205)

CHAPTER 8

(1) A lengthy appendage to Chapter 8 enitled *DD's Dreamlife* can be found under the NOVELS dropdown menu at *peterboffey.com*.

(p.248)

CHAPTER 10

(1) She related how the developers were still hassling her to sell out. Their latest tactic had been to demand that the Santa Cruz County Fire Chief send out staff to determine if Cliffport's sole residential water system could supply sufficient flow and volume in the event of a fire. The man who took the measurements turned out to be one of Katie's peers from high school, and he confidentially shared that it had been Sea-to-Summit who had pressured the Office of the State's Fire Marshall to carry out an inspection. They both knew that with all the enhanced irrigation in her nursery operation and its network of

backup pumps and piping, the water supply exceeded all county and state requirements for an unincorporated rural locale. And they both knew that calling the property's fire-fighting capacity into question was simply another bogus power play by Monteflores' promoters. The fireman assured her that, after he submitted a glowing report, nothing more would come of it.

She continued her account of grievances against the developers. Midway through the County Tax Office's 1973-1974 fiscal year, the same neighbors had instigated another assault. Historically, the North Coast region's field assessor rotated through all the parcels in his assigned territory on a more-or-less regular circuit, eventually getting around to a cursory inspection of the Cliffport property on a three- or four-year cycle. Although the Lowries had already been charged a nominal uptick in their property bill for the 1972-1973 season, the receipt of a supplemental tax bill in January of 1974—calculations based on tripling the property's total assessed value—had taken them by surprise. Katie's inquiries confirmed the Lowries' suspicion that the irregularly executed special assessment was due to pressure applied by S2S, who had indeed inveigled county officials into making a prompt re-assessment of their parcel's increased real estate value occasioned by the construction of the glasshouse and other visible improvements, as well as the customary calculations of highest land value based on best possible use. The Tax Office had complied and the Lowries' tax burden was immediately adjusted to the higher rate. Elisabeth Lowrie bristled at the county's obeisance to the moneyed interests, yet her angered daughter was advised that the Lowries had no legal standing on which to challenge the exceptionally swift application of law. They paid the supplemental bill and knew that the significant tax rate hike would be included in their annual bills, beginning with the county's 1974-1975 fiscal year. Pieter commiserated: the intervention was yet another strike by the hostile, faceless, absentee corporate ownership.

(p.287)

(2)

COASTAL PROPERTY MANAGEMENT

March 8, 1973

Kaitlin Lowrie
One Grade Road
Cliffport CA 95017

RE: Gate Key

Dear Mrs. Kaitlin Lowrie:

Find enclosed two (2) copies key to padlock attached to chain on gate NE end driveway easement i.e. private roadway teeing into Grade Road at One Grade Road.

To date, Coastal Property Management has seen fit to leave the gate unlocked in order to facilitate your legitimate travel to and from your parcel as stipulated by conveyance of deed. Let this letter serve as notification that CPM, in consultation with the owner, is reconsidering that courtesy practice; as a consequence, you are hereby being provided with the key should our gate policy change at any future date.

Also, it has come to our attention that unauthorized use equivalent to non-compliance with easement restrictions appear to be recurring on land trails on the property surrounding and adjoining your parcel. Relevant clauses in the deed explicitly forbid passage on said trails by wheeled and/or motorized vehicles of any sort except in emergency exiting in the event of fire or other natural catastrophes. We take this opportunity to remind you that access to all so-called "fire roads" and "logging roads" was never intended to be, and shall not now be, included in the terms of the easement. The scope of the easements [i.e. Established and designated footpath customarily known as Lower Steep Creek Trail from Highway One to Millpond Reservoir and (unnamed) trail from so-called Chapel Grove Cemetery to so-called Lookout Rock] permits travel only on foot and/or horseback and only by you, members of your immediate family, and your authorized guests.

Should you or your authorized guests not adhere to these conditions, we will have no choice but to pursue any and all legal remedies available, including but not limited to fencing, gating, and installing locking mechanisms in order to enforce all strictures to which you are legally bound.

Your cooperation has been requested; we trust that you will practice a prudent use of the privileges and rights to which you are legally entitled.

Be advised that the keys being entrusted to you remain the property of CPM and are not to be duplicated. A $25.00 (twenty-five dollars) charge will be collected prior to supply of any replacement keys.

Sincerely,

John Wheelwright
Central Coast Regional Manager

Enclosures: 2 keys

CC: CPM, Head Office, Santa Monica

COASTAL PROPERTY MANAGEMENT • PO BOX 666 • SAN JOSE, CA • 95113

(p.297)

CHAPTER 12

(1) A faint ambrotype was centered on the album's first page: the portrait of a frail elder—a great-grandmother many times over—in a rocking chair, her shrunken features facing the camera, her clawed hands gripping the tail ends of the black shawl enshrouding her shoulders; she looked terrified. Double portraits of the McLoughlins' male and female stock followed, the married couples typically sitting in matching chairs or standing, or shown with one spouse seated, the other standing. The facial hairstyles of the men and the crochet lace collars of the women varied over time, but the hair lengths of the husbands changed more often than did the wives' tightly cinched heads of hair, parted—without exception—right down the middle. The likenesses were hand-tinted, glazed over by a brownish hue clouded with gray; the bearing of these ancestors from successive generations bespoke Presbyterian solemnity, fortitude, hard work, thrift—the last a virtue which Jan, their final descendant, had abhorred and ignored until the end of her life.

The ancestral McLoughlins were pictured while they still resided in the British Isles then in Eastern Canada. In carefully chosen, softly voiced words, Elise offered commentary as if members of the interrelated clans—the Macraes and Macleods and Mackenzies in Scotland; the Leos and Casses and Kellys in Ireland—were still residing in and about Cliffport, Davenport, Swanton, or somewhere along the six miles of Mackenzie's Toll Road ending in Fern. The family line had never been portrayed in oil paintings, which the mobile emigrants would have been hard put to conserve during their relocations and would not have been able to afford in the first place. No chronicler had written in the names or when and where the formal photography sessions had occurred. However, it was evident to Katie that her mother—the Cliffport McLoughlins' adopted daughter—had memorized whatever her "Aunt Thea" had relayed; Elise might as well have been reading captions, and her remarks betrayed no slippage of memory.

(p.340)

(2)   How many days might lose their gloom,
How many nights their sorrow,
If we should wait to criticize
Until a kindlier tomorrow.

A night aft changes hate to love;
a taunt left unspoken
may bring sympathy and cheer;
and keep a heart unbroken.

How many times we might be spared,
How many hours of sadness,
If men should only utter good,
and speak but cheer and gladness!

A word may break a lonely heart,
Or save a life that's broken,
Then let all evil words be stilled,
and only good be spoken.

Homer Howard Adamson (1870–1944) was the author's maternal great-grandfather. Born and raised in Lawrence County, Kentucky, he practicing his evangelical ministry primarily in Indiana, Tennessee, Ohio, and Michigan.   (p.347)

(3) TWELVE APOSTLES
These are the twelve Apostles names,
Peter and Andrew, John and James.
These four brothers fished by the sea,
When Jesus said to them, "Come follow me."
James the Less and Jude were called too,
Phillip and also Bartholomew,
Matthew and Thomas who doubted his word,
Simon and Judas who betrayed his Lord.
                                    (p.347)

(4) PALESTINE SONG

> First the line on coast we make;
> Merom next, a marshy lake;
> Then the Sea of Galilee,
> Exactly east of Carmel, see.
> The Jordan river flows thro' both
> To the Dead Sea on the south;
> And the Great Sea westward lies,
> Stretching far as sunset skies.
> Looking northward you may view
> Lebanon and Hermon, too;
> Carmel and Gilboagrim,
> Tabor, Ebal, Gerizim.
> Near Jerusalem we see
> Olivet and Calvary.
> Judæa's hills rise south and west
> Of lonely Nebo's low'ring crest.
> On Zion stands Jerusalem;
> Six miles south is Bethlehem;
> On Olives' slope is Bethany,
> Bethabara by Jordan see.
> Our Saviour drank at Sychar's well;
> Of boyhood days let Nazareth tell;
> At Cana water turned to wine
> Showed our Lord to be divine.
> Capernaum by Galilee,
> Near its twin Bethsaida see;
> Cæsarea Philippi
> At Hermon's base is seen to lie;
> Along the coast these three appear,

Gaza, Joppa, Cæsarea;
South to Bethel we may go,
To Hebron next and Jericho.
From heathen Tyre materials came
To build a temple to God's name;
The sorrowing widow's son at Nain
Jesus raised to life again.
See Dan, where Jordan's waters rise,
Beersheba nearer tropic skies;
North and south these cities stand,
And mark the length of Israel's land.

(p.347)

CHAPTER 13

(1) SAINT TERESA'S SIMPLE PRAYER

Let nothing disturb thee;
Let nothing dismay thee;
All things pass;
GOD never changes.
Patience attains
All that it strives for.
He who has GOD
Finds he lacks nothing:
God alone suffices.

Saint Teresa of Avila (1515-1582) was beatified in 1614 and canonized
in 1622.

(p.371)

(2) Using her penknife to pry open the hand-painted, black-and-gold lacquered lid, she discovered three transparent, plastic packets. She worked the melded flap from one and removed its mix of 4" × 2" and 5" × 3" black-and-white snapshots. Jan had used a fountain pen on the backs to note when and where and on what occasion each picture had been taken. Baby's first steps, the boy's first day of school, the little fellow's first flannel trousers. Mills, aged one, in diapers on the sand at Neptune Beach in Alameda, 1921; toddler Mills, 1922, aged two, dressed in a bulky one-piece jumper, a jumbo bow above his bangs; Mills on a tricycle, 1923; Mills, aged four, an oversized driver's cap on his head; Mills in a cowboy get-up for Halloween, 1925 ... as a pirate, 1926 ... and Mills Belcanto, aged 8, in the pressed wool trousers and belted jacket of a would-be military uniform—"First vacation home from Lancaster School for Boys, 1928."

The second packet yielded a crop of double portraits of Mills and his Aunt Jeanette, photographs that must have been taken by obliging strangers wherever the duo traveled. Mills with Jan at the base of the Lincoln Memorial; Mills and Jan atop the Empire State Building, in front of the New York Public Library, on the Boardwalk in Atlantic City, at a hotel entrance in Victoria BC, in the dining car on the train to Banff ... Mills and Jan ... Jan and Mills ... Mills and Jan.... Katie paused, lingering over the last image of Mills Belcanto and Jan McLoughlin, the twosome standing side by side but with no trace of a childish smile left on his face. He wore casual civilian clothes: a polo shirt, white bucks, a pair of slacks belted slightly above his waistline: "June 17, 1937—the day after Lieutenant and Mrs. Mary-Helen Doty's wedding on Treasure Island." By then Mary-Helen Belcanto's son was a head taller than the female guardian clinging to his arm, her head turned sideways, her eyes facing upward, her attention fixed upon the young man. Katie calculated that Jan would have been forty-seven; Mills, seventeen.

The third packet contained a handful of mutilated photographs cut into halves and thirds or simply torn to pieces by hand; any notes on the backs had been blackened out. Katie concluded that, perhaps in a fit of rage, perhaps in a drunken stupor, Jan must have used a heavy black marker to eliminate the written annotations then scissors to extirpate any images of Mills' mother, leaving only Mills and herself intact in the archival record.

Katie stuffed the packets back into the box, closed the lid, turned off the lamp, and stared across the room at the window's perspiring pane glass. Of course, there were no pictures of Mills in Cliffport, for by the time Mary-Helen had come into Jan's life, Jan had cut herself off from her family, leaving behind the cows, the eggs, the canning shed, "chicken kitchen." After that, she had organized her life around Mary-Helen, the Belcanto Cosmetics Company, and—most of all— around her surrogate son and substitute lover. Katie understood how, forty years later, after Mills had been murdered and the company laid to waste, Jan had ripped up those snapshots then sealed the Chinese box, incapable of ever inviting the extant images of his innocence— and her fantasy life, destroyed— back into her broken heart.

(p.391)

ACKNOWLEDGMENTS & RESOURCES: Volume III

I offer my heartfelt thanks to James Barrett, Barnes Boffey, Ophira Druch, David Gilpin, Daryl Henderson, David Johnson, and Eric Kiviat for reading parts of the manuscript and offering encouragement and companionable support. To David Johnson and Kari Samlaska, for the hospitality and house in which to retreat with the manuscript without distractions; to Darlene Belmonte & Steven Green, for helping define appropriate models for the fictive business entities; and to Brandy Kuhl, Director, Helen Crocker Russell Library of Horticulture (Strybing Arboretum, San Francisco Botanical Garden) for creative assistance with the rare book collection housed there—I thank you.

For the biographies and curricular vitas of several characters' backgrounds, I have drawn on numerous "bios" associated with articles in a variety of publications including those of the California Native Plant Society (especially the Santa Cruz & East Bay Chapters); the Friends of the Regional Parks Botanical Garden (East Bay Regional Parks District); Save the Redwoods; Sempervirens Fund; Save Mt. Diablo; Mt. Diablo Interpretive Association; Mt. Diablo Audubon Society; Klamath-Siskiyou Wild; Klamath Bird Observatory—all non-profit organizations deserving recognition and worthy of our support.

In the process of composing Book Five, I have knowingly and unknowingly swapped ideas with a host of published authors whom I have never met; whether living or dead, their influences have been so thorough as to become both consciously and subliminally indistinguishable from my own thinking. I can trace the following allusions in Book Five to the following specific sources; I must beg pardon from other authors from whom I have borrowed and/or stolen ideas without attribution here:

- p.4: "Good to the last drop": advertising slogan of Maxwell House Coffee.
- p.26: "Little Boxes": song written (1962) by Malvina Reynolds.
- Chapter 4 *passim*: The encounter between Katie and Angelita was indubitably written under the enduring influence of a scene realized by Alain Tanner & John Berger in their 1976 film *Jonas Who Will Be 21 in the Year 2000*, i.e. when the banker visits the "commune."
- Chapter 6 *passim*: Inspirational models for Drika's watercolor sketches and Mary McLoughlin's colored pencil drawings are plentiful. Two particular examples are the Ernest Clayton Collection *https://sfpl. org/index.php?pg=2000036401* and the art of Eugene O. Murman as featured in *Conifers of California* by Ronald M. Lanner (Cachuma Press, Los Olivos CA) 1999.
- p.171: Suzanne's question echoes this saying from the Talmud: "More than the calf wants to suckle / the cow wants to nurse." [*Yoter Mima Shehagel / Rotzeh Linok, Lehainik. Pesaschim*, 112a.]

- p.231: viz. *Pieris japonica*; Camellia japonica hybrid variety 'Gullio Nuccio'; Rhododendron hybrid variety 'Snow Lady'.
- p.232: i.e. Rhododendron hybrid variety 'Fragrantissimum.'
- p.288: The prosody of Elise's note spins off from the sestet of Sonnet XXX ("Love is not all....") in Edna St. Vincent Millay's cycle of sonnets entitled *Fatal Interview* (1931).
- p.332: viz. closing quatrain of *"My Grandmother's Love Letters"* (1920) by Hart Crane:

  > Yet I would lead my grandmother by the hand
  > Through much of what she would not understand;
  > And so I stumble. And the rain continues on the roof
  > With such a sound of gently pitying laughter.

- p.354: cf. Leporello's aria, Act I, *Don Giovanni*, libretto by Lorenzo da Ponte.
- p.365: "We go to great panes." Slogan snatched directly from the subhead of John McCloud's article "Checking Out Windows" in *East Bay Monthly* [Date/page/issue unknown by author].
- p.385: "The Twelve Apostles" [traditonal].
- p.385: "Palestine Song" from *hymnary.org/text/first_the_line_on_coast_we_make* .
- p.386: St. Teresa de Avila (1515-1582); text appearing in Chapter 12 and in NOTES to Chapter 12 is a translation taken from *www.catholiccompany.com/getfed/nada-te-turbe-teresa-avila-poem-5760* [posted Oct 15, 2015].

To the "deep background" texts cited in the Acknowledgements & Resources of Volumes I & II, I want to add these titles as influential upon Volume III:

- *Indian Herbology of North America* by Alma A. Hutchens (Merco, Ontario Canada) 1969.
- *Sunset Western Garden Guide* (Sunset Publishing, Menlo Park CA), miscellaneous editions.
- "Traversing Swanton Road" by Jim West *(http:/arboretum.ucsc.edu/pdfs/traversingswanton)*.
- *Two Among the Righteous Few: A Story of Courage in the Holocaust* by Marty Brounstein (Tate Publishing, Mustang OK) 2011.

About the Author

In *The Three Naked Ladies of Cliffport*, as well as in his first novel, *Two Half Brothers, or Separating Out* (2014), Peter Boffey has drawn upon his experiences while traveling—with brief residences—in France, Israel, and Morocco. Fifty years of living in Northern California and Oregon, with a career in applied horticulture—gardening, landscape design, nursery production, and the seed trade—have also informed his narratives.

When not out exploring the West, particularly throughout the Pacific States, with a focus on flora, fauna, geology, and cultural history, Peter—a grandfather—lives with his wife, Ophira, in the San Francisco Bay Area, often volunteering as a docent at the Ruth Bancroft Garden in Walnut Creek. For more of his writings—including poetry, translations, interviews, and essays—and to contact the author, visit **peterboffey.com**.

CPSIA information can be obtained
at www.ICGtesting.com
Printed in the USA
FSHW010013220621
82556FS